MW00743861

ABOUT THE AUTHOR

CAT SPARKS is fiction editor of *Cosmos Magazine*. From 2002–2008 she managed Agog! Press, an Australian independent press that produced ten anthologies of new speculative fiction. She's known for her award-winning editing, writing, graphic design and photography.

Cat was born and raised in Sydney. Her early adventures included winning a trip to Paris in a *Bulletin Magazine* photography competition; being appointed official photographer for two NSW Premiers and working as dig photographer on three archaeological expeditions to Jordan. She has worked as a media monitor and a graphic designer and is currently studying young adult post-disaster literature for a PhD through Curtin University.

In 2004 she was both a graduate of the inaugural Clarion South Writers' Workshop and a Writers of the Future prizewinner. She has edited five anthologies of speculative fiction and over sixty of her short stories have been published since the turn of the millennium.

Cat has received a total of seventeen Aurealis and Ditmar awards for writing, editing and art including the Peter McNamara Conveners Award 2004, for services to Australia's speculative fiction industry.

In 2012 an Australia Council emerging writers grant enabled her to travel to Key West, Florida, to take part in an exclusive workshop tutored by Margaret Atwood.

Her first novel, *Blue Lotus*, is finally nearing completion.

http://en.wikipedia.org/wiki/Catriona_Sparks
www.catsparks.net

THE BRIDE PRICE

THE BRIDE PRICE

THE BRIDE PRICE
CAT SPARKS

Ticonderoga
publications

For Rob, with love

The Bride Price by Cat Sparks
Published by Ticonderoga Publications
Copyright © 2013 Cat Sparks

Introduction copyright © 2013 Sean Williams
Afterword copyright © 2013 Cat Sparks
Cover illustration copyright © 2013 Cat Sparks

Typeset in Sabon and Bellerose Light

A Cataloging-in-Publications entry for this title is available from The National Library of Australia.

ISBN   978-1-921857-41-6 (limited hardcover)
        978-1-921857-42-3 (hardcover)
        978-1-921857-43-0 (tradepaperback)
        978-1-921857-44-7 (ebook)

Ticonderoga Publications
PO Box 29 Greenwood
Western Australia 6924

www.ticonderogapublications.com

10 9 8 7 6 5 4 3 2 1

ACKNOWLEDGEMENTS

Margaret Atwood, Damien Broderick, Terry Dowling, Brendan Duffy, Sarah Endacott, Russell B. Farr, Jason Fischer, Justin Healey, Robert Hood, Alisa Krasnostein, Amanda Pillar, Tracey Rolfe, Ekaterina Sedia, Ian Shadwell, Kaaron Warren, Sean Williams, my Clarion tutors and classmates and other writing group alumni: Thorby Avenue in its various incarnations, Infinitas and Bill & Di's unnamed lounge room gatherings.

CONTENTS

INTRODUCTION

SEAN WILLIAMS

The Bride Price collects twelve short stories and one novella by Cat Sparks. It's a superlative collection—feel free to skip this introduction and discover for yourself—but it begs the question, as all collections do: *Why?*

Not: *Why a collection by Cat Sparks?* That question is easily answered. Cat is as renowned for her writing as she is for her editing, publishing, and being an all-round mainstay of the Australian speculative fiction community. (She's also one of my favourite drinking buddies, as it happens—let's get that out there nice and early.) I'm frankly amazed it has taken this long, and very pleased the wait is over.

What I mean is: *Why these stories?* Cat's oeuvre includes sixty-odd published stories and ranges in content from the time gun operating below Hemingways in "Home by the Sea" to the suspicious *sentients* of "The Jarrah Run" so it's a valid question. What's in these thirteen stories that thirteen others couldn't have provided? Why not a completely different collection called *The Delicacy of Dragonflies*, which sounds about as literary as it's possible to be? Why not *Meltdown my Plutonium Heart*, for those with quirkier tastes?

This is the crisis faced by everyone who's ever anthologised or collected anyone's work, including their own. You can't put in everything. A collection needs to be as thoroughly alluring as a blue bottle-cap to a horny bowerbird. It needs to contain the best the author has to offer. It needs to *shine*.

At the same time, you don't want a stream of disconnected stories that lurches from one genre to another. You want a sense that the stories belong together. A collection isn't a novel, but you still want to feel that it's going somewhere, that it's trying to tell you something, that there's a unifying theme of some considerable heft.

In other words, you want a collection to have all the strengths of a novel but none of its weaknesses. The reader won't ever be bored by any of the settings, because their brilliance is glimpsed in passing. The reader has enough time to flirt with each character before sweeping onto the next, speed-dating style. The reader is constantly delighted and off-balance, like a new ballroom dancer in the arms of a master. The reader leaves wanting more.

The collection you hold in your hand perfectly meets these criteria. Each story opens onto the broad landscape of Cat's imagination, where you'll find surprisingly few tropes of speculative fiction: no vampires or giant robots, for instance, no conventional aliens or wizards. Cat delights in creating her own tropes, such as the petrous whales of "Beyond the Farthest Stone", the Tidefront of "The Alabaster Child", and the grisly honours of "Sammarynda Deep". Each story takes the reader deep into unfamiliar territory while remaining carefully grounded in things we know to be true—things that will always be true, whether we find them in post-apocalyptic wastelands or far-future fiefdoms. There are people we recognise and understand as people, and therefore there are dreamers, schemers, and those who stand in their way. The stories in *The Bride Price* remind us that to be human is to fantasise, but to achieve one's fantasy is often a very bad thing.

The most common fantasies in Cat's stories are of everyday things—lost love, safety, truth, etc—rendered unattainable by such barriers as distance, time, or law. Good speculative fiction relies on the clash between ordinary and extraordinary, and it's in the worlds Cat creates for each story that we find the latter. These worlds are often divided into regions pitched against each other, such as the above- and below-ground habitats of "The Sleeping and the Dead", or the very different haves and have-nots in "The

Bride Price" and "Seventeen". Breaching the gulf between times drives the crisis of "Arctica", as does a meeting between survivor cliques in "All the Love in the World." Crossing simple physical boundaries brings together people of vast cultural difference in "Scarp", and where difference exists there is always conflict.

Cat's characters are determined to escape their particular situations and resourceful in their methods, sprinting across a deadly freeway in "Hollywood Roadkill" or scavenging a spaceship graveyard in "Dead Low". However, in Cat's fiction as in real life, what seems simple at first becomes delightfully complicated in execution. Fate loves a twist ending, and so does Cat, but here "twist" doesn't come with the slightest feeling of being forced or contrived. Every ending achieves that rare delight of being unpredictable yet arising naturally out of what came before.

Finding the surprise in what seems to be familiar is the essence of writing good genre fiction. You'll think you know the worlds contained within these pages. But over and over again Cat reminds us that it takes more than just ideas to make speculative fiction a powerful medium for wonder: it's the people who inhabit the ideas, people who are fundamentally unpredictable. The spark (forgive the pun) that drives "A Lady of Adestan" is not simply the depiction of misogynistic cruelty in a world that isn't our own; it is the drive of one sister to be reunited with another and the lengths each will go to in order to make that happen. Similarly, the mysterious UFOs of "Street of the Dead" are not enough on their own to give the story its life; what keeps you reading is the plight of the every-family that's not entirely aware of the strife they're in, but knows it must flee, somewhere.

Cat deftly weaves you through known and unknown, familiar and unfamiliar. Her characters are trapped and desperate. They're literally dying to escape, even if *escape* means finding themselves somewhere much worse than where they started. You'll understand their yearning even if we don't always sympathise with it. In aiming for the unattainable, or attaining something they didn't realise they were aiming for, Cat's characters reveal themselves in the very best and the very worst possible lights.

The Bride Price is a collection united by themes of desire, transformation, and humanity. We might be nothing but a species of dumb fucks who never listen (to paraphrase the epic conclusion of this collection), but why should we listen when even the gods are liable to make a mess of things? All we can do is follow our heart, wherever it leads and whatever it costs us. That is the true bride price. We've all paid it, one way or another. To open this book is to peer into thirteen lives that, under the shades and spectacles of Cat's art, look remarkably like our own, as we rarely allow ourselves to be seen. And that, I think, is entirely and sufficiently *Why*.

SEAN WILLIAMS
ADELAIDE, APRIL 2013

A LADY OF ADESTAN

The prim maidservant did not smile or answer any of Dena's questions—she simply set out the teapot and delicate cups and left her alone, cup empty, in the parlour in silence.

Dena studied the pattern on the china, almost afraid to touch the cup lest she break it with her clumsy fingers. The walls of her sister's mansion were covered with paintings of houses and lakes, men on horseback and women in stiff, elaborate gowns.

The silence of this house unnerved her. How long would they keep her waiting? Dena knew so little about the city of Adestan and its inhabitants, even less about the family her sister, Nadira, had married into.

She sat and waited, her heart beating more rapidly as the minutes passed. Dena had last seen Nadira a year before, when the wedding carriage had come to take her to Adestan. She had thought she would never see her sister again, as was customary when girls from the plain married into wealthy city families. Yet here she was now, surrounded by opulence and luxury, having been issued a hand-delivered invitation as if she were a person of great importance.

The double-oak doors at the back of the parlour swung open. Three women swept through as if borne on a breath of wind. It was a moment before Dena recognised which was her sister. Surely the creature before her now was a queen, not her own flesh and blood! What had happened to little Nadira, the girl who'd played chasings around the pinebark trees? Skinny Nadira, in her plain cotton shift, splashing the younger children in the river? A hundred memories swirled and evaporated one by one as Lady Nadira, Mistress of Thorsten Mansion, stood before her, accompanied by a handmaid and a translator, who each took smaller steps behind.

Nadira's gown was like the gowns in the parlour paintings, only richer and finer than oil on canvas could depict. Deep burgundy, azure and charcoal. The Adestani seemed fond of sombre hues. The only brightness came from the jewels sewn on her bodice and the string of blood-red rubies around her neck.

Lady Nadira (for that was who she was now, not little sister, prettiest of them all) settled herself on the hard divan. Her translator sat in the chair immediately to her right. The handmaid went about the business of making tea, pouring it into the waiting cups the maid had already set out on the low table that separated the Adestani women from their guest.

Dena realised she was slouching. She immediately sat up straight and folded her hands in her lap, not knowing what else to do with them. She felt so clumsy and awkward in her sister's presence.

Nadira's hair was pulled back tightly from her face, fastened into slim braids with tiny clasps of gold. Each braid was woven through with gold thread so fine that Dena only noticed it when Nadira turned her head and the threads caught the light. The end of each braid was capped with golden beads and ringlets interspersed the braids.

When she met her sister's gaze, Dena feared she might burst into laughter, all the pomp and finery and foreignness forgotten, but Nadira did not laugh, and neither did Dena. They stared at each other until, prompted by the handmaid's offer of fresh tea, the conversation began.

Dena understood that grand ladies of Adestan were not supposed to speak. When Nadira had accepted master Etan's offer of marriage, an elegant lady from the Adestan court had presented herself at the family home accompanied by two handsome bodyguards. She had taught Nadira handsign, the language exclusive to high-ranking women in the city of noble stone. No one had noticed Dena spying on her sister's private lessons through the downstairs study window. No one had caught her practising the elegant gestures when the fine lady and her bodyguards had gone.

Nadira signed to the translator and the translator spoke to Dena.

"Welcome to Adestan, and to our home. My husband regrets he cannot be here to meet you, but he has been unavoidably detained by business on the estate. I trust your room is comfortable. Please let Housemistress Keony know if there is anything you require."

Dena shifted uncomfortably in her seat. How strange it was to hear Nadira's words spoken through the mouth of another. Her gaze fell to the rubies adorning her sister's neckline. "You're so beautiful. You always were, but now more than ever," she said.

Nadira nodded, acknowledging the compliment gracefully. She paused before signing again.

"Is our mother well? How are Angus and the ducks?"

Dena smiled and relaxed a little in her chair. "Scruffy old Angus misses you. You were always his favourite. But the ducks are as fat and as greedy as ever—I do not think they've even noticed you've gone."

Dena felt sure mention of the ducks would raise a smile, but Nadira remained as composed as ever. Her tea lay untouched on the table, as of course it must, Dena realised. Nadira needed her hands for talking. Dena began to babble, recalling every little detail from their street, hoping that if she spoke long enough Nadira would relax a little, or at least drink her tea. But the tea grew cold and eventually Dena ran out of gossip. Silence fell between them like a heavy curtain.

Then, translated, "Ardena, you must convey to our mother some joyous news. She will be a grandmother before year's end."

A baby! Dena glanced at Nadira's belly, noticing the swelling for the first time. How could she possibly not have seen it before? She had been entranced by the rubies and the fabrics, distracted by the welcome sight of her sister's face.

A look passed between the translator and the handmaid. A small thing, but Dena caught it. Something Nadira had said was not proper. But what could be improper about announcing the expectation of a child?

"Of course, we are exceptionally busy here. Our mother may not receive an invitation to visit until next year," said the translator.

Dena paused. Her sister's hands had been still this time. The translator had spoken for her. She glanced upwards and met her sister's eyes, but they betrayed nothing. No emotion whatsoever.

"Nadira, your tea is getting cold," said Dena.

The handmaid leaned forward quickly, picking up the cup and passing it to Nadira, who accepted it without gesture of thanks. She brought the delicate porcelain rim to her lips and sipped.

◇◇

After tea Dena was permitted to accompany her sister on a stroll around the rose garden and down to the gazebo beside the lake. They did not attempt conversation, despite the presence of the translator. Dena told more stories from the plain and her sister listened, her eyes on the bevy of black swans that sailed back and forth across the still water. Dena felt obliged to fill the silence with chatter, but all she really wanted to do was throw her arms around Nadira's neck and squeeze her until she returned to her old self.

When her chatter was exhausted, the three sat in silence. Dena hoped the translator might leave them alone so that they might talk freely, but she kept her place and they watched the swans glide until the shadows lengthened and it was time to return to the house.

They walked slowly. Grand ladies of Adestan did not rush, but it was Dena who set the pace this afternoon. Dena who did not want the visit to end.

The women came to a halt at the farthest end of the rose garden. Nadira signed farewell, wishing good health on her mother and her sister, promising to write as often as time permitted.

Dena grabbed her sister's hands suddenly, squeezing them in her own. "Are you truly happy here?" she asked. She could feel the translator stiffening beside her, clearly disturbed by such an undignified display.

Nadira smiled. A kindly smile and her eyes shone brightly, but Dena saw that it was the smile of a grand lady of Adestan, rather than her sister's smile.

How could so much have changed in a single year?

◇◇

Back in her room, Dena was served a sumptuous baked partridge on a silver platter. As delicious as her meal was, Dena understood full well that she was dining alone because the Adestani did not wish her to share their table. She had been permitted to see her sister and that was enough. Tomorrow the coachman would return her to the plain, back to her proper station in life amongst common folk. She would never return to this beautiful house.

More food had been provided for her than necessary, and she ate more of it than she ought, but she felt so awkward, so nervous and uncomfortable sitting alone in the pristine room. It was a relief when Housemistress Keony came in for her dishes.

"I tried to open the window but it seems to be stuck," said Dena.

"The window does not open," replied Keony as she filled her tray with Dena's dirty plates. "I see you have a keen appetite," she smirked.

Dena blushed, embarrassed. She tried to engage Keony in further conversation, but the housemistress' answers were short and sharp. In Adestan, speech was only for men—and the coarser kinds of women. Keony did not wish to advertise her own inelegance.

Sleep did not come easy to Dena that night. The bed was too large and the mattress far softer than she was used to. She twisted and turned, tossing aside the covers, while outside the wind shook the trees and rattled the windows.

She awoke to the clinking sounds of porcelain and cutlery. Dena lifted her head to see Keony setting out her breakfast tray, and not making any effort to be quiet about it.

"Regrettably, your departure from Adestan must be delayed."

Dena sat up and hugged the bedclothes tight to her chest. "Why is it so dark?"

"A frightful storm." Keony went to the window and pulled aside the curtain in a futile effort to let in more light. "Apparently the road has turned to mud. Whole sections have been washed away." She let the curtain drop. "You are to stay here until the road is once more passable by carriage."

"Oh," said Dena. She glanced around the room at all the now-familiar objects: the dresser, the pitcher and basin on a stand, the heavy oaken drawers where her few undergarments were stored, neatly folded. "May I see my sister again?" she asked suddenly, her face brightening at the thought.

"No," Keony replied, heading for the door.

Dena understood that she was not to be given a reason. "I think I shall go mad cooped up in this room," she added, more to herself than to the housemistress.

Keony paused at the door and turned her face to Dena. "Whoever said you must remain in here? The city square is only a few blocks from here. There are many shops suitable for a person such as yourself. I should not be hiding in here all day if I were you."

Keony and her smugness left the room. Dena threw back the eiderdown and touched her feet to the wooden floor. She ate her breakfast quickly before the last of the heat faded from it, dressed, then peered out the window into the grey and the gloom.

She was met downstairs at the side door by an older servant, who neither smiled nor spoke. She presented Dena with a heavy cloak.

"If you please, which way to the city square?" Dena asked. The woman gestured to the left. Dena thanked her and tried to catch her eye, but the woman had already turned away.

The rainfall was lighter than it appeared from indoors. She pulled up her hood and trod carefully on the slippery stones. The chill wind whipped at her face, invigorating her, driving away all lingering traces of slumber. She gulped icy lungsful of air deep down into her chest until it hurt. Anything to clear the stuffiness and oppression of that house!

Men and women hurried along the footpath with great industry, shielding themselves from the wet as best they could. Dena headed in the direction indicated by the servant, remembering to count the number of streets she crossed so she could find her way back. Flat stone walls soon gave way to small shops with sturdy awnings, their interiors warm and inviting as glimpsed through their front windows.

Dena paused at each one, enchanted by the exotic displays but was too timid to go inside. She had a little money, but did not wish to draw attention to herself. Her mother had made her promise to memorise every detail of her encounters, although all details were irrelevant now compared to the news of Nadira's baby.

As she gazed longingly at a row of tiny pearl-and-diamond earrings, a sudden blast of sleet buffeted her up against the glass. The rain had resumed its pummelling in earnest.

Dena was about to seek shelter inside the jewellery shop when she saw several people on the stretch of pavement ahead hurrying inside what was clearly an alehouse. Dena decided to join them. She would be far less conspicuous there than in a tiny shop where she could plainly not afford the wares.

Warmth and noise enveloped her as soon as she crossed the threshold. Dark shoulders swept her further into the interior's warmth as more people crowded in to escape the fierce wind and rain.

"Let's get that cloak off you," said a friendly voice. As the wet fabric was peeled from her back, Dena turned and was met by a smiling red-cheeked woman. "Get yourself over by the fire there, lass, or you'll catch yourself a nasty chill."

Dena joined the others warming their hands before a roaring hearth fire. They made room for her automatically, just as plain folks would have done back home. The surrounding noise soon fractured into individual snippets of conversation:

"An' bales were banked up row after row on the Port Daran docks with no way to shift 'em."

"He might've seen that landslide coming after last year's floods, eh."

"Better make mine a double this time, Linsy, I've three manors on my inventory before lunch."

The sound of chit-chat was almost more comforting than the fire after the oppressive silence of her sister's house. Dena had presumed the whole of Adestan to be soundless and austere, and she was relieved to have been wrong. Adestan was a city like any other, its regular folk the same as on the plain.

"What'll you be having, Miss?" asked the red-faced woman who was now serving behind the bar.

Unsure of what to ask for, Dena had been about to request tea when another spoke for her.

"I reckon she looks like she be needing the special tea today, Linsy—as will everyone else who finds their way through your door."

A man leaned on the bar, dressed in well-worn leather and black linen. A lean man, yet strong. She could see the curves of his muscles against the weave of his shirt. His posture was casual, as if he had ordered a thousand drinks in a thousand inns.

Linsy handed him two mugs of something hot and fragrant. He held them close and breathed in the aromatic steam. "To your health," he said to her, then left the bar, carrying his mugs across to a table to where sat another man.

"I think a half'll be doing you," said Linsy. She placed a smaller mug on the bar and smiled. Dena nodded and gave the woman a copper. She took the mug in both hands and sipped, blowing on the liquid to cool it.

It was indeed tea, but with a sting of rum in its tail. As Dena sipped, she glanced across the room at the dark-haired man in leather and black. He was deep in conversation with his companion. She wondered if he might glance back her way, but he didn't.

"You look a little lost, Miss," said Linsy.

"Oh, no," said Dena, "I'm visiting my sister. I was to return home today but apparently the road is unpassable."

Linsy smiled knowingly. "Your sister? Would she be a noblewoman, perhaps?"

Dena nodded, taking another sip of tea. "She is Mistress Nadira, wife of Master Etan. I am staying in their house, only it's . . . "

"Lonely?" Linsy nodded, understanding. "I can imagine it might be. Beautiful grounds on their estate, from what I've been told. I do believe I've seen your sister in her carriage. Yes, I think so—I can see the family resemblance."

"Oh, no," blushed Dena. "There's no resemblance at all, not hardly."

Linsy was called to serve another customer. Dena sipped her tea in silence, listening to the crackle of the fire and the ebbs and flows of hearty conversation. She moved to stand before the hearth once more. There were empty seats scattered about the room, but she was tired of sitting. Her drink had made her a little light-headed, a feeling she enjoyed almost as much as she enjoyed the warmth of the flames.

"Still here?" said a familiar voice.

She looked up to see the dark-haired man standing beside her.

"What's your name?"

He was handsome. She's decided that already many minutes ago, even before she'd sipped her drink. Before she'd wondered if he might be watching her.

"Ardena," she said in a whisper. "I'm from the plain," she added, realising her mistake as she said it—there was no need to tell him something so obvious.

"Mine is Karas, and I've been to your plain," he said.

"Really?" She wondered how she had managed not to notice such a man before, if what he said were true.

"Just passing through on my way to other towns and other plains."

"You're a traveller?"

"That I am."

She could smell the heady musk of his skin, feel the warmth of him, despite the fire, despite the impropriety of such thoughts.

"Perhaps you will travel to the plain again sometime? Perhaps I shall see you then?" It was the rum in the tea talking, she knew, making her far more brazen than a girl ought to be.

"I hope so, Ardena," he said with a smile, and then he was gone, swallowed by the crowd as a new batch of sodden travellers pushed through the doorway and Linsy ran out to take their cloaks.

◇◇

A surprise awaited Dena when she pulled back her eiderdown and prepared for sleep that night. An envelope poked out from beneath the corner of her pillow. She tugged it free, knowing who it must be from before seeing her name on the stiff cream-coloured paper. A letter from Nadira, somehow smuggled to this room without Keony's knowledge, for that girl was no friend to either sister, Dena was sure. As she slit the thick paper with her fingernail, she knew that this letter would bear dark news, and that her sister would have taken a grave risk to write it.

My Dearest Dena

Forgive my haste, but I am desperate. The Adestani court is a terrible place—no place for a daughter, and I feel it is a girl child I carry within me. I will not have her raised by the whip and the knife.

The Autumntide Ball will be held tomorrow night. You must beg Keony to be allowed to attend as a serving girl in the hope of seeing me again. Keony is in love with my husband. She is cruel and will relish the chance to make my sister work. You must bring me a servant's garb and we must escape together. These rubies are for a bribe, should you be discovered.

Dena, do not get caught. These people are unspeakably brutal.

For my daughter's sake,
N

Dena's eyes welled with tears as she looked to the place where the letter had been concealed. She slid her fingers beneath the pillowslip, where they brushed against something hard and cold. Her sister's ruby necklace. She tugged it free and held it up to the light, fighting tears all the way. What would happen to her sister if the jewels were missed? What if she herself were apprehended as the thief?

She stuffed them back beneath the pillow, needing time to think. How would she ever be able to help Nadira escape? Who could she turn to? What could she do?

She sat on the edge of her bed and hung her head. "I'm sorry, dear sister," she whispered as the tears washed down her cheeks. She cried for hours, the sound of her misery masked by the battering of the rain and the lashing of the trees outside her window.

It was not Keony who brought her breakfast tray the next morning, but the silent older servant. Unlike Keony, she knocked before entering the room. Dena sat up as she pulled the heavy curtains open. Outside, the sky was as grey and bleak as ever.

Dena felt for the rubies under her pillow, half expecting them to have vanished during the night, but they were still there.

The woman busied herself setting up Dena's meal.

"I suppose I am to spend another day in Adestan, with the weather being so foul."

The woman looked up from her work, then gestured to indicate she should come down from her bed and eat. Dena smiled and was about to throw back the eiderdown when she saw something that made her blood freeze. A small detail she had somehow missed, no doubt because of the older woman's voluminous lace cuffs, obviously designed to hide her disfigurement. One of her hands was missing. Even from a few feet away, Dena could see that it had been sliced off cleanly at the wrist.

The woman saw the look on Dena's face. She bowed her head in shame, flicked her arm so that the lace fell to cover the stump, then left the room without looking back.

Dena understood what she had not seen before. This servant had been a noblewoman once; as dignified as Nadira and all the other fine ladies of the court. This was why she did not speak. What crime could she have committed to be punished so cruelly?

Dena sat back on the bed, her head reeling, echoing with the words in her sister's note: *the whip and the knife.* She snatched the rubies from their hiding place, clutched them in her fist, drawing them close to her heart. *I'll get you out of here*, she promised. *Somehow.*

After she had washed and dressed, and tucked the rubies safely inside her undergarments, Dena went downstairs in search of Keony. She was not in the kitchen or the hallway. Dena crept stealthily through the house, room after room, well aware that she was overstepping boundaries, but she knew her time was limited to the duration of the storms and the impassibility of the road.

The corridor opened out into a parlour far less grand than the one where she had been received by her sister. A flash of movement caught her eye. Reflections in a mirror. She trod softly, angling her body for a better view of curled hair and an energetic flurry of hands.

Dena stopped still. It was not two ladies talking that she could see, but Keony sitting by herself practising handsign! Dena recognised some of the words from when Nadira had been taught: *man* and *handsome* and *better*. *Marriage* and *deserve* and *plain folk*. Keony smiled as she formed each word, blushing and pouting and lowering her eyes.

You stupid girl, thought Dena, inching closer to the shadows almost by instinct. *As if the master of this house would fall for the likes of you.* And then it struck her—he had fallen for a commoner once, why not believe it might happen again? Keony wasn't half the lady Nadira was, but as a fantasy it made perfect sense. Perhaps Dena could use it to her own advantage?

Dena backed slowly out of the room. She paused for a moment, then re-entered, this time deliberately treading hard to make the floorboards squeak. Keony appeared in the doorway, a dark silhouette radiating caution.

"I've been looking for you," said Dena, lacing her voice with as much meekness as she thought she could get away with. "Bad weather is still keeping me from returning home."

Keony did not reply. Dena continued talking to fill the uncomfortable silence. "If I must be detained, I would like to see my sister again, if I may."

"You may not," said Keony. "Mistress Nadira is far too busy with the Autumntide Ball preparations. We are *all* extremely busy."

Dena cleared her throat. "I do not expect a formal meeting. I only wish to *see* her again before I go. There is no need to trouble a handmaid or a translator. Perhaps if I could—"

"Lady Nadira is not to be disturbed. Autumntide is tomorrow night—do you not know what that means?" Keony took a small step forward, bringing herself into the light where Dena could see her face. "But of course you don't know. How could you? Autumntide is not celebrated amongst the plain folk."

"I have heard of it," whispered Dena, her eyes downcast. "A very grand occasion. Although, of course, I have never seen it."

"No, I am sure you have not," said Keony. "I am to be senior kitchenmistress this year. My role is extremely important."

"Will my sister be promenading with Master Etan?"

"They shall both promenade," said Keony, her eyes shining.

"Then I would like to be there, too. Might not a small servant's role be found for me? I will cause no trouble. I only want to—"

"Out of the question!" said Keony indignantly. "We do not just pull servants off the street for the Autumntide Ball!"

Dena bowed her head in penitence, holding her breath, hoping against all hope. She could feel the weight of Keony's eyes on her, hear her mean little mind ticking like a clock.

"There is one *small* chore you might be suited for," said Keony coldly. "It's a *speaking* role—few of our maids are well suited to the task. When canapés are presented to the lords and ladies in accompaniment to their wine, you may stand beside the tray and describe the contents of each morsel."

When Dena raised her head she saw the cruel smirk on Keony's face. "I would be honoured, if it meant another glimpse of my sister."

"You will be honoured indeed. With any luck you might see Lady Nadira for a moment or two, although don't go expecting too much. You may not speak to her. If you try to, I shall have you whipped."

Dena took a deep breath. "Thank you, Housemistress Keony. You have been so very kind."

Keony sniffed, then pushed past Dena and strode out of the room.

Dena learned quickly that the role of speaking servant was the lowest of the low. She and four other unfortunates were made to memorise list after list of ingredients until they could describe each canape to Keony's satisfaction.

Keony's eyes shone clear and bright as she ordered the servants from task to task. For such events, she apparently outranked the silent servant with the missing hand, a situation no doubt founded in practicality.

Dena did not feel safe with Nadira's rubies in her care, but she knew she could not leave them in her room, so she tucked them inside her brassiere when she changed into her servant's uniform. The shift was brown, drab and neat. In it, she looked the same as all the other serving girls, a fact Nadira would know full well.

When no one was looking, Dena took a second, larger uniform from the cupboard and pulled it on over the first. She felt cumbersome and enormous in the double layers of fabric, but no one gave her so much as a second glance.

Dena had thought the alehouse large, but upon entering the ballroom, her jaw dropped at the immensity of the space. Several thousand people could have been accommodated with room to spare. The walls were adorned with bright frescoes depicting minutely detailed plants and animals and scenes of mountains, rivers and fields. Even the high, curved ceiling was painted bright blue and dotted with stars, held in place by sturdy-yet-delicate columns of wrought iron wreathed in vines.

An orchestra played soothing music on a corner stage designed to resemble a garden gazebo, complete with caged birds and potted palms.

The talkers were made to stand against the wall, their hands folded and eyes downcast until their services were required. Keony was busy with so many details. Too busy to supervise the girls and see that they did not raise their eyes to gawk at the lords and ladies arriving through the arched entrance at the far side of the room.

Dena's eyes darted in search of Nadira. She presumed her sister would be easy to spot, but there were several pregnant women present, each heavily laden with jewels, as indeed were all the guests, men and women alike.

As the space gradually filled, Dena imagined she was observing a garden filled with strutting peacocks, each one prouder and haughtier than the next. The gowns were so exquisite, the jewels so bright, that for a moment she lost herself in the spectacle of it all.

The sound of clapping hands brought her back into the moment. Keony paired each talker with a waiter as he emerged from the kitchen, then sent them out into the crowd to perform their tasks. Dena's waiter swiftly manoeuvred himself to a position on the left of the orchestra, and Dena trotted dutifully beside him, sneaking a look at the faces in the crowd when she could. Once in place, she recited her menu, noting the looks of disdain on the ladies' faces. None sampled the canapés. The air around her was filled with the deep voices of men and the silent fluttering gestures of women's conversation.

On her third foray into the crowd with the waiter, Dena spied not her sister, but Karas, the man from the alehouse. He was dressed in a fine uniform of royal blue and silver. She lowered her eyes at once and began her recitation. When finished, she stole another glance in his direction and discovered he was staring directly at her, a broad smile on his face. He reached forward and sampled a treat from the tray. "Delicious!" he declared. "Make them yourself, did you?"

Dena opened her mouth to answer when a sharp glance from the waiter made her change her mind. Karas reached over and grabbed another. "I could eat the whole damn tray!" he declared to a burst of polite laughter from his friends. The tray cleared quickly and Dena returned to her place against the wall. To her horror, she discovered he had followed her back. "I can get you a tray for yourself if—"

He laughed. "It's not the tray I'm interested in, girl! I remember your face from the alehouse. I took you for a traveller. I had no idea you were a servant in this house!"

Dena could feel her face flush. If Keony caught her speaking with this man, she'd punish her severely. "Please, Sir, I may not speak with the guests. I will get into trouble."

"Undoubtedly," he replied. "Pity. I hate these damn balls. Everyone's so busy watching what they say, minding who they're seen with. There's never anyone interesting to talk to."

He cast his eye around the room as he spoke, a disapproving frown on his face. The kitchen doors burst open again. Dena quickly hurried to the side of the nearest waiter.

She performed her recitation again and again throughout the hours that followed, each time searching for her sister, each time returning to the wall disappointed. She felt so helpless. So hot and uncomfortable in her heavy double uniforms. What if she *did* locate Nadira? What then? Were they to run from the ballroom together out into the enveloping darkness? The cold pressure of rubies against her chest did nothing but reinforce the helplessness she felt.

The one fortunate aspect of the evening was the busyness of Keony. Dena presumed that she would be tied up in the kitchen. When the double doors burst open again, Keony appeared, sweating, clutching a pail and a cloth in her hands.

"A spill near the bay window—one of you clean it up," she barked, her attention already shifted to something else.

Seizing the opportunity, Dena grabbed the pail and made herself scarce. This was the most freedom she had been allowed all night and she intended to use it well.

The spill was found and mopped within minutes. Dena wandered through the crowd pretending to be in search of another. No one was paying her the slightest attention. With her dour uniform, pail and grim expression, she could move as freely as she liked so long as Keony didn't catch her.

Dena slunk amidst the jewels and corsets. Her eyes had finally acclimatised to the sight of such finery and splendour. Now all she wanted was her sister.

Finally she spied Nadira. Dressed in azure velvet, she stood alone, her hands cradling a goblet, no doubt to avoid unwanted attempts at conversation. When their eyes met, Nadira's brow softened with relief. She turned her back and headed for stained glass doors at the far end of the ballroom that led to an outside balcony. Dena waited a moment, then followed, clutching her pail with both hands.

Outside the air was cool and clear, thick with the scent of recent moisture but no rain fell now. Nadira waited for her sister in the shadows. Once she was sure no one was nearby, Dena ran to her, set her pail down and they embraced.

Dena gripped her sister's shoulders. "Nadira, there are so many people. How will we ever get out of this place? I don't think I can go through with it. I'm sorry, but—"

Nadira pulled free of Dena's grip. She stepped forward into a clear shaft of moonlight, then took Dena's hand lightly in her own.

Nadira opened her mouth. She guided Dena's hand to her lips, then gently pushed two of her sister's fingers inside.

Dena gasped in horror. She snatched her fingers back and cradled them against her breast. "You have no tongue!"

Nadira pressed her lips together, her eyes glistening with tears. *The whip and the knife.*

Handsign was no mere affectation. The faint sound of music escaping from the ballroom took on a sinister tone as Dena comprehended the elegant silence of the ladies of the Adestan court. And their reluctance to taste the canapés.

Nadira tugged on Dena's uniform. With the moon so bright, Dena could make out the lines of tension etched around Nadira's eyes. Lines that had not been there a year before.

Together they pulled the spare uniform up over Dena's head. Dena then helped her sister undress, tearing at the lacing of her bodice with her nails. There was nowhere to hide the elaborate gown. They could only wedge it into a dark corner and hope it would not be discovered before they were far away.

As Nadira pulled the servant's uniform over her head, moonlight revealed the whip scars on her back. Dena sucked in her breath. Working as fast as she could, she bound Nadira's intricate hair braids in the dirt-brown scarf. A rough job, but it would have to do.

The uniform was large enough to conceal Nadira's belly. In it, she looked dull and lumpen. As long as she kept her face downcast and no one asked her any questions, the sisters had a chance.

Dena handed her sister the pail. "Head for the servants' staircase. I shall follow behind you. Don't look back."

Nadira nodded. She slipped quietly through the stained glass doors. Dena waited only a few moments before leaving the balcony. So far they had been lucky. Almost too lucky, but she didn't want to dwell on that thought. She could not see Nadira in the crowd and could not chance looking for her, nor directly into the faces of the ballroom guests. The steady pounding of her heartbeat drowned out all other sounds. Even the orchestra became faint and distant, along with the raucous laughter of men and the clink of crystal glasses.

A sudden crashing sound a few feet ahead made her jump. Nadira! She ran forward and found a pool of red wine, glistening like blood sprinkled with splinters of shattered crystal. A man had dropped his glass. He was very drunk and he pointed accusingly at Nadira, whose head was bowed, her shoulders trembling in terror. The man was attempting to admonish her, but his words were jumbled with drink.

"Fetch a mop this instant, you stupid girl," barked Dena. Nadira didn't move. Dena stepped forward, pulled a cloth from the pail and shoved her roughly. "Go now!" she said, and Nadira moved at last, heading for the servant's door as fast as she could.

Dena dropped to her knees to the accompaniment of ugly laughter. She mopped up as much of the spilled wine as the cloth would take, then stood, curtsied roughly, and followed Nadira to the stairs.

She found Nadira cowering behind the door, trembling in terror. Dena looped her arm through her sister's and guided her down the stairs. She stashed the pail and cloth in a cupboard on a landing. "We must take water with us," she told her sister.

The empty downstairs kitchen was illuminated by shafts of silver moonlight. Leaving Nadira by the door, Dena tiptoed to the pantry. Half a loaf of bread and a row of water bottles on thin leather straps sat within easy reach. She slipped the bread into her uniform pocket, selected a bottle and filled it from a pitcher. She turned to leave, only to see a silhouette of a woman blocking the doorway.

Keony! What should she say? What could she possibly say to explain why they were creeping around the kitchen in the dark?

The silhouette stepped forward. It was not Keony, but the servant with the missing hand. The two regarded each other for a moment in silence. The woman looked to the water bottle, then to Nadira, and finally to Dena. And then, to Dena's complete surprise, she stepped aside. Dena quickly gathered her wits, taking her sister by the hand. The woman's eyes shone clear and bright. She would not betray their secret.

As the girls were about to leave, the woman took a knife from a kitchen drawer, offered it to Dena, handle first.

"Thank you," Dena whispered. The woman nodded, her expression impossible to read in the half shadows.

With the knife and bread in her uniform pocket, and the water bottle slung across her shoulder, Dena and Nadira hurried to the servants side entrance that led from the kitchen out to the street, snatching two half-sodden cloaks from the racks as they went. There was no time to think, no time to consider their options— either they made it back to the plain on foot or they would both be brutalised at the hands of the Adestani nobility.

The streets lay silent and deserted. "Where is the gate? I can't get my bearings," said Dena. Nadira wiped her tears with her sleave and pointed. They hurried, conscious of the crisp sound of their shoes on the pavement.

At first the gate guards' hut seemed deserted, but sounds of grunting from within soon let them know that it was not. Dena stopped at the door, uncertain of what to do. A girl emerged from the darkness within. She eyed the sisters cautiously. Nadira stepped forward quickly and placed something into her hands. The girl smiled, revealing two missing front teeth. A prostitute! Dena tried to mask her revulsion, but if she saw it, the girl didn't care. Nadira had given her the jewelled necklace she'd been wearing at the ball. The girl slipped the necklace into her pocket, then led the sisters through the guard's hut and out the other side as the sound of rutting emanated from the back room.

How much of tonight's sequence of events had been planned by Nadira? Had anything been left to chance? The timing of the invitation to coincide with the season of terrible storms, the full moon, the distraction of the ball, the prostitutes in the guards' hut? Without each of these elements, escape would have been impossible, yet here they were, shivering in their thin brown uniforms and damp cloaks, picking their way across the straw-patched road with only a few moonbeams to guide them.

Nadira strode purposefully, a look of grim determination on her face. There was so much Dena wanted to ask her, but all questions would have to wait until they were safe—if, indeed, they would ever be safe again.

The road wound steadily down the hill and, mercifully, it did not rain. Dena prayed rain would follow to wash away their tracks. If they could make it as far as the forest before they were missed, perhaps they stood a chance. She tried to force darker thoughts from her mind. Where were they going? They could not return to the plain— that would be the first place the Adestani would look. For now, it was enough that they kept moving. Enough that the moonlight held steady and true, and the road did not subside beneath them.

Eventually the forest came into view, a dark impenetrable mass of trees. Dena knew it to be crisscrossed with well-worn paths, but they would have no hope of navigating it without daylight. She had to place her hand on Nadira's shoulder to stop her marching head first into the blackness. Nadira seemed not to care if they couldn't see, as if all she wanted was to run from the Adestani.

They had travelled the road for perhaps another hour when Nadira tripped and fell. In hauling her sister to her feet, Dena saw that her shoes were shredded to ribbons. She had not thought to swap Nadira's shoes for suitable footwear. Her ball slippers been delicate: ornamental and useless.

"Why didn't you tell me?" Dena protested, making her sit as she tore strips off her own skirt to bandage her sister's bleeding feet. Nadira didn't utter a sound. She stared at the road before them with glassy eyes, and Dena cursed her own lack of foresight in not stealing sturdy boots from the servants' quarters.

With the first weak rays of dawn came the point where the road cleft in two and the plains lay spread below them like folds of rich cloth. The right-hand path would be the easier way—easier both for the sisters and their pursuers. The left led through the forest, and clung to the hills like fur on a wolf's back.

Nadira stared ahead with eyes that reflected nothing but pink and orange streaks across the sky.

"They will be coming for us soon," Dena whispered.

"I'm afraid that's true," said a deep voice behind them. Dena spun around. Behind them stood Karas, his hands resting on his hips.

Dena stepped in front of her sister, spreading her arms in a futile gesture of protection.

"What do you want?"

"From you? Nothing. I've come to take the lady back home where she belongs."

"She does not belong in Adestan."

"Her husband says otherwise."

"Her husband is a tyrant."

"So I have heard. But he is also my master, and if I do not return his property to him, I shall not remain on his payroll."

"My sister is no one's property!" Dena's eyes filled with tears.

"Was your mother not paid a dowry?" he gestured to Nadira's belly. "Does she not carry his child? These are our laws, girl. If you do not like them, stay away from our city. Stay on the plain eating dirt where you belong."

"They will cut off her hand."

"There are worse punishments."

Nadira made a whimpering sound, a sound more befitting an animal than a human being. She stood and stared out over the cliff, her face still and expressionless. She took a step closer to the edge, the movement dislodging a handful of smaller stones and sending them tumbling downwards.

"Let us go," pleaded Dena. "I will give you Nadira's rubies."

"A thief as well as an abettor!" said Karas. "Girl, you have nothing to bargain with. I have offered you your freedom. Take it and run home to your plain. I will not make the offer again."

Dena slipped her hands into her apron pocket, wrapping her fingers around the kitchen knife's sturdy handle. Karas's eyes followed the movement.

"But I do like rubies," he added. "Better give them over before you go. In return, I'll tell her husband I lost you in the forest."

Nadira took another step closer to the edge of the cliff. Dena positioned the knife so that the blade angled upwards against the thin fabric of her apron pocket.

"If she jumps, I'll be taking you back to Adestan in her place," said Karas. "You're not worth much, but at least the Master will be able to take his revenge."

"Come and get them yourself," whispered Dena.

Karas laughed and shook his head. "I am a bounty hunter by trade. I've been hunting runaway women for years. You cannot possibly win."

As he moved forwards and reached out, Nadira kicked a large stone over the edge. His eyes flicked to the movement and at that moment Dena lunged upwards with the knife, angling the blade to slide under his ribcage and pierce his heart, thrusting with more strength than she knew she possessed. She stepped back suddenly, her hands raised in horror as Karas crumpled to the ground, a look of utter disbelief frozen on his face.

Nadira smiled and stepped away from the cliff. She knelt and began to tug the bounty hunter's boots from his cooling corpse.

When this was done, she moved to do the same with his cloak. Dena helped also, relieving him of several items: a knife, a coin purse, a compass, a water bottle and a pistol. When he was stripped of everything useful, the sisters tipped his body over the edge. A rain of tiny pebbles tumbled in its wake.

"We can't go home to mother," said Dena. "That's the first place your husband will look."

Nadira unlaced the boots and forced her feet inside them. They were too big, but with the bandages, her feet filled them well enough to walk in. She sloughed off her own sodden cloak and slipped the bounty hunter's dry one around her shoulders, hugging the rich blue fabric close against her damp skin.

"Where can we go?" whispered Dena, unnerved by the look of utter stillness on her sister's face. *We have killed a man, robbed him and thrown his body onto the rocks, yet she does not flinch? What happened to my little sister who was once all sweetness and light?*

Nadira stood tall and straight. In the bounty hunter's boots and coat, she looked nothing like the fragile creature Dena had discovered trapped within the walls of Adestan. Nadira pointed to the east, away from the plain and all that Dena had ever found familiar.

"The coast? We must travel to the coast? But there's nothing there but Port Daran and a thousand leagues of ocean."

The sisters looked back the way they had come. In the distance, the cold grey stone of the city wall blended seamlessly with the sky.

Below them, the plains rolled on for miles, a repetition of grey and green vanishing into the mists of early morning.

"And beyond the ocean, Nadira, who knows what? Foreign lands! Places where we don't know their language, nor understand their ways!"

Nadira nodded with certainty, and as the weak rays of dawn blossomed into sunlight, strong and true, Dena saw not her little sister, but the Lady of Adestan she had become, and knew that she was right.

BEYOND THE FARTHEST STONE

A whale had washed up on the sand. A big one too, three times the regular size. Perhaps even four. Hard to say—few of us van hands had ever gotten close to one. Whales were rare on the sandy flats below Grimpiper. Rarer still that they ever crossed the stones. But this one *had* crossed the stones, alright—and a whopper it was, too.

"Gimmee a lookee!" After scooting up the wagonside, Errol made a grab for Laddie's glass. Laddie caught the movement in the corner of his eye. He snatched the glass away at the last moment.

"Come on, you bastard—give us a go!"

I squinted, shielding my eyes against the glare. "You sure it's a whale? Might just be a massive lump of rock."

Laddie sniffed and wiped his nose along his arm. "No fear, this stretch is bare from tower to tower. That thing weren't here last Road trip, that's for sure."

We sat there gawking on Doc's wagon top until Shashi yelled for us to get back to work. The point riders would see to it. Rajiv and Skeet had already broken off to do a recce of the whale with weapons raised. Not that guns or blades would stand for much against a creature forged of living steel and stone.

The van slowed a little but it did not stop. Not with ten wagons hooked up end to end and deliveries due in 'Piper before nightfall. The stench of burning butyl wafted upwards from the wheels. Everyone had seen it now and the air was filled with the smack and clatter of flipping trapdoor lids. Regulars scrambling up top for a look, hanging off the guardrails and jostling disgruntled tourists from their places.

I stole a glance at the Sammaryndans when Laddie wasn't looking. The tall, dark one with curly hair was peering through a silver spyglass. The fancy kind that cost a camel's price. Of course he would own one. They probably all did. Snatches of their excited chatter carried on the wind. If they hoped the van would stop, they were in for disappointment. Caravan master Elias stuck to a strict schedule. Grimpiper's merchants were not to be kept waiting. Not even for curiosities as big as beached stonewhales.

It was said the Heartland had always been deadly; harsh even back when sands were green and fabled cities of glass and silver ruled. Russet earth, hard-baked flats that stretched forever. Lawless, even long before the Ruin. A place where wars were fought and lost. Home to monsters, big and small. Folks with skin like lizards who could turn themselves to stone for camouflage. If you could believe such stupid things—and I sure didn't. The tourists, however, believed anything you cared to tell them. The coast, from where they hailed, was apparently a land of fools.

The Sammaryndans had captured my attention since they joined the van at Bluebottle. The four of them always sat together, whether by the communal fire at night or riding up top in the coolness of late afternoon. They had appalling manners, sniffing contempt at the fly-speck outposts, one cluster of shacks being much like any other. Three lords and one lady, flashing coin and squandering water. Reeking of superiority and contempt. They'd come in search of relics, same as every other coastal traveller. Gruff old Croker didn't mind them perching on his wagon so long as they paid up.

The Sand Road skirting round the Heartland's jagged edges had been forged on coin and kind. Not much of either going down this quarter—why else would our caravan master have sold those Sammaryndans passage? I'd wager he was already sorry. So different from the regulars who joined us for short hops. Brimming with chatter, popping uproad to visit a cousin or down the other way to see an aunt.

Dust didn't cling to Sammaryndans like it did to the rest of us. Their elegant fabrics were trimmed with golden thread, silver beads and semi-precious stones. Bright colours, not the dull old browns the rest of us were stuck with. Arms weighted heavy with bands of gold. Jangling so you could always hear them coming.

If these were merely travelling clothes, what must their finery be like? I pictured elaborate wedding gowns stiff with encrusted rubies. No wonder they never spared a glance for me, with my old brown trousers and well-patched shirts, hair hacked short to save on water. Why would the tall one ever notice me?

I didn't even know his name. He was the worst of them: pompous, arrogant and rude. If he did glance my way it made me nervous. Sometimes I forgot what I was doing or things I'd been going to say. He was an idiot. They were all idiots. They didn't appreciate the danger in these parts. Their kind didn't appreciate anything. They swigged hard liquor and smoked skunkweed with the camel drovers. They seemed to find such stupid things amusing. Not one of them had ever suffered. At least I could hate them all for that.

The girl had come to Doc at last port-of-call with a rash of sand fly bites. I'd been out the back tent mixing pastes, which I did sometimes to help when Doc was busy. She'd always been so kind to me. I checked the girl out through the ripped tarpaulin, her honey-chocolate skin and amber eyes. She spoke her woes with the condescension of a queen. Not that Doc picked up on the nuances. Bites were bites, no different on the arm of a Sammaryndan princess than on some crusty old bone fossicker's arse. I'd been finishing up when Missus P came busting through with a busted arm and her three screaming brats. Doc got on with setting the break, the amber-eyed girl's lip curling with distaste at all the noise. Clutching her bulging coin purse where all could see it.

"Three gold," I told her, out of spite. *Three gold coins*, but she didn't even blink. Doc would have killed me but she was far too busy to notice. Half the doctoring she did, she did for free.

Honey chocolate princess counted coins into my palm, then left before I could even close my fingers.

Doc had been distracted on this trip. She still felt bad about the kids we lost in Transom. The soil down there is tainted. All their vegetables grow funny; peculiar, elongated things like lopped off body parts—and a higher rate of taintedness to match. It wasn't just the soil, said Doc. In Transom Swathe they hung off every word as though she was some kind of holy prophet. Trusted her, even when their children died, figuring if she couldn't save them, no one could.

We'd been welcome, no matter what they thought of Elias and some of the less reputable services plied from his wagons. Others reckoned it was vans like ours that spread sickness up and down the Road. They figured travelling medics as bad news and saved their coins for the next bone-shaking shaman.

Each trip was getting more difficult than the last. The skies beyond the Verge were blooming wilder. The stories too. What had once been campfire bullshit was starting to sound half real.

When it because clear the van would not be stopping, the tall Sammaryndan stood, embroidered sand cloak billowing in the breeze. Easy to figure his intentions. He was going to make his way up front and demand we pull to a standstill. Hold up business a couple of hours just so he and his friends could check out the beached stonewhale.

With arms extended to aid his balance, he picked his way carefully across the wagon tops. One large pothole could send him tumbling, crushed beneath the wagon's hardy wheels. I held my breath.

The wagons shuddered, lurched and jarred, but his footing was secure. He reached the place I sat without a problem, then made a big show of ignoring me.

"You're wasting your time," I said as he edged past. "Elias will never stop the van for you."

The Sammaryndan paused. In one swift and unexpected motion he crouched down to look me directly in the eyes. Gusts of wind nipped playfully at his long dark curls. His golden earring glinted in the light.

"Your caravan master will stop," he said assuredly. "There's not much you people won't do for coin."

"No he won't."

He smiled. "We'll see about that."

For a moment it seemed like he was going to add something else but he thought the better of it, stood and resumed his precarious journey as the wagon jerked him roughly from side to side.

I swallowed my surprise—and the hard lump in my throat. Why was there never a clever answer on my lips? A thousand insults burbled to the surface, but only after he was well out of earshot.

It did not matter. Elias would do me proud. He hated whales— he'd told me so himself.

Three long whistles and a gunshot split the air. Two more point riders left their flank positions and approached the whale, unshouldering their rifles as they went. The great wheels strained and the van began to slow but, again, it did not stop.

Soon the breeze was laced with more than burning butyl. Shouting. Male voices. Three or four. This time it was my turn to put a smug smile on my face—not that anyone else was watching.

The point riders circled the whale, wary of surprises, watching each other's backs. Snipers poised on the wagontops. Insurance.

Nothing happened. The whale remained as dead as dead and the point riders returned to take their stations.

Eventually the tall one made his way back along the wagon tops, squeezing past those seated. Nobody paid him any attention. All eyes were on the returning riders and the whale getting smaller and smaller in the distance.

The tall one had to pass me to rejoin his friends. There was nowhere else to go. He didn't stop, nor glance in my direction. He carried himself like a merchant prince, yet was smart enough to watch where he put his feet. It wasn't just clumsy folk who fell from wagontops. Or got pushed when they pissed the wrong folks off.

The clouds were beginning to streak with orange, shadows lengthening as light leached from the sky. We would soon be upon Grimpiper and the Angels would begin their nightly battles overhead. As the arrogant Sammaryndan took his place, the last of the point riders rejoined the van and the wheels began to gather speed again.

The beautiful girl with the honey-chocolate skin put her arm around the tall one's shoulders, her silhouette elegant against the reddening sky. I bade the beached stonewhale a silent farewell, feeling three gold coins in my shirt pocket. Wondering what I might spend my riches on.

◇◇

By the time we had the trunks unloaded, the line outside Doc's makeshift clinic already stretched halfway along the street. Doc always had an errand waiting. She wrote me a list—which I couldn't read, of course. Made sure I knew which was the *right* apothecary. Doc was only interested in proper medicines. Most sold nothing but charms and juju bones.

A cooling breeze had enveloped the twilight streets. I walked briskly, dodging ragged children playing in slimy gutters. They scrambled to their feet to chase me, shouting 'foreigner!' at the top of their lungs. In between breaths they begged for coins—almost as if they could smell the gold on me. In the backstreets of Grimpiper, every local face is known to every other. To them I was rich, no matter how worn my boots.

The slum had sprawled since my last visit, with families crammed into every available space. A few streets on, the pavement was less cracked. I bought a bag of hot roasted chestnuts from a vendor, happy to risk burnt fingers as I walked. Around the next corner I tossed a couple to a skinny dog who didn't seem to mind the heat at all.

Grimpiper's town square wasn't much. Not compared to the likes of Fallow Heel. I could smell it long before there was anything to see. Bustling with life and light, it seemed all Grimpiper's hoity-toits had crammed themselves into the open space which was bordered by some of the tallest buildings on the Road. One alone stood five storeys high, its balconies strung with coloured lanterns. Well-dressed folks strolled casually arm-in-arm, safe enough in the presence of hired guards. Relic vendors called from darkened doorways, holding their dodgy wares above their heads.

The apothecary was down a crooked alley, then another two backing on to unpaved road. No lanterns here, nor kids, nor guards. Illumination spilled from a row of shopfront windows. All old and patched with mismatched panes of glass. I knew the one I wanted straight away. The most exotic window of them all, hung with an array of twisted things. Desiccated horrors with oversized fangs. Creatures who'd worn their skeletons on the outside, some of them with two heads, others three.

I took Doc's list to the man inside. He shooed me away while he got on with his grinding.

Those three gold coins felt solid in my pocket. More money than I'd see in a year or more. What to buy with it? I hadn't got a clue. Just having three gold coins set my heart to beating fast.

I dawdled along the stretch of windows, fending off harsh glances from proprietors within. The last window on the street was filled with fabric. Bolts in rows, half faded from the sun. Centre front, a plastic mannequin without a head, its torso garbed in the most amazing thing. The dress was old—it had to have been—no seamstresses' hands could ever stitch so fine, yet heat and sun and dust had failed to blemish it. Three gold coins—would they even be enough? Of course they would, only where would I ever wear such a garment?

Three gold coins. Easier to dream of such a treasure than walk around with it burning in my pocket.

When I got back with Doc's supplies, the line stretching down the street was twice as long. She called out thanks without looking up. Doc barely had time for mixing and bottling, nor half the other things that needed doing.

"I'll unpack it for you, if you like."

This time she glanced up and threw me a smile. "Would you, love—that's really awful kind. There's a cot out back. Not very big but you can kip in it while we berth here if it suits."

I lugged the bags out through the swaying beads. Set the stuff out neat so she could find it. Like she said, the cot was small but it sure beat sleeping underneath the wagon.

A tinkling bell heralded the arrival of the next patient. I busied myself with arranging bottles and jars. Wondering which one of them contained spiderbalm. Sooner or later somebody always got bit.

The reassuring pattern of Doc's voice filtered through, punctuated by a chorus of coughs, wheezes and whines. Last year Grimpiper had been struck with sweating flu. It remained to be seen what would be this season's killer.

A delighted squeal echoed all around as I unscrewed a jar and sniffed its murky contents. Livvy Parke, her voice like a rusty door hinge. One of those who never knew when to shut it. Saved up her whole year's aches and pains, then released them on Doc like a torrent of storm water.

I tuned out, stoppering the paste jar tight and picking up another. That tall, dark Sammaryndan and his friends would be out there, wandering the streets. Poking fun at local customs. Coins dripping from their pockets—lucky if they managed not to get robbed or beaten to a pulp in a back alley.

I tuned back in to catch the chatter mid-stream.

"That thing she birthed was way past calling tainted. Had the face of a goat and the back end of a lizard."

"Did it live?"

Doc's voice dripped with genuine curiosity. I listened harder. Just in case it turned out to be true.

"No—thank mercy, it did not."

"What became of the body?"

"Burnt it, of course. Same as always."

Doc expressed no disappointment but I could sense it all the way out back.

"And there've been other signs as well. People vanishing off the streets."

"What signs? What people?"

"Clouds that didn't look like clouds. Storms that come out of nowhere, churning up the Verge without no warning."

I paused and put the paste jar down. It seemed like an age before the woman carried on.

"Emory and Sonnet was the ones what vanished last."

"Ah. But that Emory was always a bit flighty. Maybe he got too close? May be he went uproad chasing whales? He's young, you know. It happens."

The woman gave a dismissive grunt in response to Doc's opinion. I pictured her slapping the air with her ruddy hands.

"He wouldn't have gone on uproad whaling without saying goodbye to his mother."

I smiled. I could almost hear Doc's mind ticking over. Evaluating. Weighing things up.

"And 'sides, it's not just the flighty ones what's taking off. It's good solid folks too—folks with responsibilities."

So it wasn't just me then. Seemed like half the Sand Road might have had enough of the endless dust and heat. Those Sammaryndans hadn't travelled all the way down here for the view. It was relics they were after and they paid a fortune for them. Worthless junk honest folks could make no use of. Town squares from Bluebottle downwards had been crawling with relic merchants the past year or two. Not long ago it had all been grub vendors and palm wine stalls. Far grander profit could be turned from junk than food. Food needed to be watered, raised and cut whereas relics just got pulled up from the sand. Easy money—and who could blame anyone for that?

But some of those relic hunters paid a hefty price, going further and further afield to score their bounty. Way too many got lost to storms, not to mention quicksand, skates and even whales. The Verge was deadly enough on its own, never mind what lay beyond the stones.

Next up, a septic cut in need of cleaning. The patient wasn't much for talking so I stepped up to the tiny window, a rough, square thing hung with a threadbare scrap of cloth. Outside, the lamps were lit and people moved briskly, hurrying home to cosy hearths. The air hung thick with the scents of cooking. Delicious spices so common to this region. Suddenly I was tired when I hadn't been before. Those three gold coins did not belong to me. But I was going to keep them all the same.

I awoke with a start. The beaded curtain swung from side to side, a silhouette blocking the pale light bleeding through. I sat up and brushed the hair out of my eyes. Tugged the ragged curtain to let in light. It was the Sammaryndan girl, hands clasped against her chest. Make up smudged around the eyes, her long hair streaming from it's once-tidy braid. A sand cloak that had barely seen dust or sun. When she stepped up close, I saw that it was torn.

"What do you want?"

"The doctor . . . Is she here?" she said. "Your people always berth in the . . . lower quarter."

My people. We were all the same to her, from caravan master down to lowly van hand.

"Doc's not here. I don't know where she is." Which was partly true, though I've long had my suspicions about her relationship with our gruff old caravan master.

She looked so helpless standing there in the stark room's dimly filtered light. The girl who had everything. Suddenly everything didn't seem to add up to much.

"I've got no one else to turn to. Might not your caravan master help? My father is a wealthy man back home."

It was then I noticed the bareness of her arms. Arms that had jangled with gold not hours before.

"What happened—"

"My father would pay a handsome sum to see us safely home . . . "

I sat up properly, feet planted firmly on the boards. That would be Elias's call, not mine. I had no authority to speak for him.

"Please. No one will help me in this terrible place!"

"I don't even know your name."

"Mirella," she said. "I come from—"

"Sammarynda. Yes, I know."

I paused. This wasn't my job, my problem, nor my responsibility. "Where are the men you were travelling with?"

Her words spewed out in a jumbled mess. "He's an idiot, just like his brother. I couldn't stop him—once he'd seen it, it was all I could do to—"

"Seen what?"

"The whale."

The whale. I swallowed. Suddenly my mouth was very dry. "Who is he? This idiot you mention?"

"Iskandar. My betrothed. His friends are Hanis and Ando. Where Iskandar leads, they follow. Always."

My boots were where I'd thrown them. I pulled them on, checking my knife was in safely in its sheath.

"I fear the worst—only I don't know what it is. But you do, don't you? You know what's inside that horrible thing."

"Inside it? You're telling me they went *inside* the whale?"

She nodded meekly. "For the treasure. The men in the tavern told us . . . "

"By Holy Fatma's blessed skirts! You Sammaryndans are cursed with shit for brains!"

Laddie and Errol would know what to do. But Laddie and Errol weren't here. First night in town, they were always drunk. By time they sobered up it would be too late. "Looks like you're on your own," I told her.

"But my father—"

"Your father is hundreds of miles away. What guarantee have I got that he will pay?"

"My word," she said in a meek voice that trailed away to nothing.

Her word was as useless as the rest of her but the whale . . . that was something else. *Iskandar.* A princely name for such a fool. To have risked his life over bullshit tavern talk. The 'treasure' they spoke of was whale brains and hearts, not gold and precious jewels. Relics spun from tiny cogs and wires. Brains and hearts that were brokered to the fortress cities. Great skill was required to cut them out intact.

"Do you have a horse?"

She nodded, clearly grateful somebody else was taking charge. I grabbed an empty waterskin from the hook and slung one of Doc's field kits across my shoulder.

Mornings were normally noisy occasions filled with the bustle of cooking and eating. Not today. The morning fire wasn't even lit. Had the entire town been drunk last night? Was everybody sleeping through till second tea? Three drovers stood inside the courtyard brushing down their camels. One of them looked up as we emerged.

Mirella hugged her arms against her chest, eyes darting furtively from side to side.

"They don't bite," I assured her. "Not most of them, anyway."

Her bare arms were bruised—plain to see now that we were in the daylight. "Did someone hurt you?"

"No," she snapped. "I'm fine."

A few feet away stood a saddled horse bearing Hallam's colours. Somebody—one of the drovers, most like—had thought to provide it with a bucket of water.

I filled the 'skin from the central pump, noticing that Mirella's ripped dress was the same one she'd been wearing the night before, which suggested she'd not been to sleep at all. No wonder she looked like an old woman.

Hallam's nag was probably hungry but was willing enough to walk so we mounted and slung the waterskin over the pommel.

In daylight, Grimpiper's streets were faring little better than the slums. I expected to see more people out and about, heading for the cactus fields or dune melon plantations.

The sky was clear. No stormsign on the horizon, no peculiar clouds. No vultures circling either—that, at least, was promising. We rode most of the way in silence, eventually encountering her own horse's tracks which stood out fresh and clear. The wind had barely nibbled at their edges.

"He's an idiot, but I love him," she blurted suddenly. "That's why his father sent him out here, you know. To experience the rugged richness of life. To sample its raw beauty."

Raw beauty. Not words I would have chosen to describe the Summersalt district which stretched for miles and was littered with every kind of broken thing. Melted slag, glass and steel, sometimes bricks, occasionally even weathered wood and plastic.

Secreted amongst it all, precious relics. Useless, shiny trinkets sold to Sammaryndan scholars who put them in great museums in glass cases.

"What is that?"

She leant forward in the saddle, shielding her eyes and craning her neck at a line of stones, all different shapes and sizes, undoubtedly placed by human hands.

"The stones mark the boundary between Verge and open Heartland," I explained. "We cross them at our own peril."

The stretch of sand beyond the Verge had an eerie feel to it, despite the not-too-hot-yet warmth of the sun. The subtle hump of low dune crests shimmering in the heat haze. A little farther on, three horses—the purple of their livery bright against the sand and washed out sky—and something else.

A bulbous, semi-circular thing, the bulk of which lay buried below the sand. The stonewhale we had all seen from the van. Mirella's knuckles whitened from her tight grip on the saddle.

She turned to face me, stray gusts of wind messing up her hair. "That's where they went in. I waited as long as I could bear."

"Stay here." I slid to the sand as silently as possible. Hallam's three horses stared back at us, tails switching at flies. Dwarfed by the unwieldy mass of sun-weathered stone.

The hairs on the back of my neck pricked up. I swallowed.

Mirella began to dismount. Instinctively my hand went out to stop her.

Our horse snorted and shook her mane. The other horses glanced back at us, passive and disinterested.

Mirella cupped her hands around her mouth and called "Iskandar!" at the top of her voice. The sound seemed to shimmer in the stillness of the air. When it had faded, she tried again. "Hanis. Ando!"

There was no reply to any name. When she was done with shouting, her eyes came to rest on the whale's stony casing.

I couldn't take my eyes of the thing. The longer I stared at it, the harder it became to tear my gaze away. "Mirella," I whispered, "I'm going inside to check it out."

"The men in the tavern said—"

"I know what those men say. And camel drovers—some days they speak of practically nothing else. Those whale brains fetch a pretty price if you can get past all the old world tricks and traps."

There was a moment of silence before she nodded her agreement. She chewed her nails, her face a sickly hue. Looking so helpless, like a doll and every bit as useless.

I'd scavenged relics before—who hadn't? Climbed down steep ravines in search of missing goats. Weathered sandstorms, flash floods and landslides. I could take care of myself.

"It's bigger than it oughta be. Maybe it's just a shell. Stay with the horses. I won't be long."

She stared at me, bug eyed, as I unhooked the waterskin.

"Be careful."

"I will. I'm always careful."

I took a long draught from the waterskin, then thrust it into her arms. She smiled unconvincingly. The expression of a woman who had already lost far more than she could bear.

What did anyone really know for certain about whales? With every dug up relic came a thousand bullshit stories. Tales of skies once filled with giant metal birds. Ships that could fly through air and under ocean. Shiny clever thinking machines that could answer any question.

Sunlight burned my cheeks as I peered up at its bulbous stony mass. It reminded me a little of the domed flatbread ovens they have in Spearcrosse, only much, much bigger. The size of a rich merchant's house. It might have been an ordinary lump of rock, tempered and weathered across centuries. Only it wasn't.

I walked around it, trying to gauge how much of its bulk lay concealed beneath the sand. Its outer casing gave off a vague animal reek. Laddie had once told me whales were part living and part other things.

On the far side an opening, jagged with loose stones, gaped like the mouth of a dead beast. Tracks led right up to it, then vanished. There was no question the three riders had gone inside.

I approached cautiously, concentrating on detecting the slightest movement. Nothing. No wind. No skittering of sand skinks across the surface of the sand.

"Iskandar!" I called, then waited. "Hanis! Ando! Anybody?"

Anxiety curdled in my stomach. Those three gold coins were pressing heavily against my heart. Mirella's friends were dead for certain, but I knew that when the Doc found out—and she would—I'd be facing down those kind blue eyes, explaining why I didn't even try to save them.

The temperature dropped as I ducked beneath the jutting bricks. Inside, the air smelled musty, like the cloth Doc wrapped around her precious doctoring books. An old smell, tickling my nose, stale and dusty like crumbling paper. Tainted and corrupt. The smell of dead things.

With feet planted firmly on the ground, I waited for my eyes to adjust. The chamber was ovoid, its sides inset with thick black ribs jutting out and curving upwards to meet in a peaked ridge above my head. Mustiness gave way to pungent animal stink. There was no sign of treasure, nor of the three idiots who had come charging across the sand in search of it.

Something like a well sat at the chamber's centre. I edged towards it with cautious steps. The floor was metal, the same sort as the ribs. Old world metal. The kind no one knows how to make any more.

The well's ceramic rim was smashed. Large enough for me to fit through if I was crazy enough to try. Glassy shards littered the floor, crunching beneath my boots.

What to do? As I glanced around in search of options, something caught my eye. A shape embedded between two black ribs. A relic? I edged to the ribs for a closer look, expecting anything but what I found embedded in the wall. Arm bones, thigh bones, a pelvis, a skull; a skeleton's worth, but a skeleton of what? Twisted and contorted beyond recognition, those bones belonged to no animal I had ever seen.

The wall itself was of a dark, clay-like substance. I crouched to examine a spinal column attached to a tail. Definitely tainted: an elongated neck, extra limbs and even horns.

Another skeleton was embedded further along, its surface meshed in a lacy cobweb curtain. Maybe not cobweb—the stuff glistened wetly. I moved on, tripping on something invisible in the gloom. Three things, it turned out: a bag, rope coil and knife. I stopped and stared. No relic hunter would ever abandon his knife.

So many things were said about whales. Most of it rubbish—lies passed from one group of skunkweed addicts to another, none of whom had ever seen one, let alone been inside. But Elias's warning was fixed in my head: *stay away from them, no matter what*. No explanation offered. Generally his word was good enough.

I edged towards the well of shattered ceramic, peered down into thick, soupy black at a sequence of embedded metal rungs. Surely those three idiots hadn't dropped their equipment and charged down there blindly? But if they hadn't, where were they?

My stomach churned as I stared into the darkness. Wait—was that a light? Something weak and flickering. Might have been my eyes playing tricks. Might have been a lot of things. No way was I climbing down those rungs. I would go back out to fresh air, sunlight and Mirella. We'd go back to 'Piper for back up. Proper tools and a posse of men. Everybody had heard a story about someone who'd disturbed a whale. They'd either gotten rich—or gotten hurt. Sometimes both. Whaling was a job for hardened adventurers. Professionals—not idiot amateurs like Iskandar and his Sammaryndans. Or me.

And that's when I saw him. A man embedded in the wall directly across from that first set of bones. One of Iskandar's friends—the man with close-cropped hair—stuck fast in a sticky segment of chamber wall. His face a twisted grimace. Fear, rather than pain. Stuck like a camel trapped in quicksand.

Was he dead? I went to him but kept my distance, not brave enough to touch. The clay-like substance glistened wetly, its sickly sheen reminiscent of raw meat. More like flesh than clay. The heady whiff of decomposition made me gag.

He *was* dead. No need to touch to be sure. I backed away and returned to the fractured rim.

"Iskandar? Is anybody down there?"

My hoarse voice almost sticking in my throat. No response, just my own faint echo and maybe something else. Something like a low, distant moan. I listened for a moment longer, then realised the time had come: either run back to Mirella or climb down.

Blackness beckoned. It was now or never. I tested my weight. The rungs were sturdy. Steady breathing, in and out. Eventually my boots hit something solid.

Light! A palm thatch torch abandoned on the floor, its embers still aglow. As I picked it up and held it high, stone shuddered beneath my feet. I spread my hands to steady my balance. The movement ceased as suddenly as it had begun. Just a tremor, a portent of worse to come. My eyes adjusted quickly to the muddy blend of ember light and shadow.

A second tremor struck, this one dislodging a stream of tiny scorpions amidst the dirt and sand. The floor lurched suddenly, almost throwing me off balance. I dropped to a crouch until the rumblings subsided. A thudding and clanking sounded somewhere within the stonewhale's bowels. The palm thatch caught, spluttered and flickered wildly. That's when I saw the blood. A long wet streak of it, sticky and fresh, trailing all the way along the geometrically patterned floor.

"Iskandar!" My voice came out in a pathetic croak, "Are you in there?"

He had to be—there was nowhere else. Dead too, like the other one? I gripped the torch for comfort as much as light. Flame fingers stretched across the smooth grey curve of the walls. A dark shape at the chamber's farthest end. A massive growth that budded from the floor. At its centre, a clammy face tilting upwards. Iskandar's face. I had never seen anyone so frightened.

"Iskandar! I paused. Did he even know my name? "Mirella brought me. I've come to get you out."

Iskandar didn't answer. With his dark hair sweat-plastered against his scalp, he was barely recognisable, yet I had known him in an instant. Did he realise his friend was dead? And what about the other one? Whose blood had I stepped over?

The floor trembled, accompanied by the squealing grate of stone grinding against stone. The surface was patterned with segments of light and dark, the pattern obscured in patches. I drew a sharp breath when I realised why. Dismembered body parts lay strewn in all directions—an arm closest to me, chunks of unidentifiable flesh elsewhere, most still garbed in scraps of ruined clothing.

"Go back to town," said Iskandar, his voice dry and rasping with fear. "Fetch men and ropes. Go quickly!"

The whale's gentle rumblings shuddered through the soles of my boots.

"There isn't time."

"Fetch them!"

The terror in his voice made my heart beat faster. "The whale is on the move, Iskandar." I squatted, one hand gripping the metal rung for balance.

"Get help!" he shrieked.

I spoke as forcefully as I could manage. "There's no time, Iskandar. You know that. Get up from that chair and come to me. This whole place is deadly."

Iskandar stared at me coldly for a few precious moments, beads of sweat trickling down his forehead. "Can't get up," he croaked. "The chair's latched onto me."

Iskandar was babbling. Completely useless. I was going to have to get us both out.

"Ando stayed in the—"

"Ando is dead, same as the other one. This whale is going to dive. We can make it out—but only if you move!"

Iskandar eyed the floor, then shook his head. "The chair's plugged into my arms."

"What do you mean plugged in? I'm going to throw you the torch."

And I would have, only at that point torchlight revealed something horrible. Iskandar's body was entangled in rope. Or entrails. Or perhaps a combination of the two.

"What the—"

The floor moved again, filling the room with that same screeching grate of stone-on-stone. Iskandar screamed and I abandoned cautious reason. Letting go of the rung, I ran to his side, my boots slapping hard against the tiles. Iskandar flinched.

His face was as pale as the stone beneath him. My heart sank as I understood. The chair had him prisoner, just as he had said. Blue tendrils—I could only describe them as that—curled out from its back and sides to plunge right into his flesh. Blood dripped to the floor in sticky rivulets. Up this close, I could smell it.

"By Holy Fatma . . . " Swiftly I pulled my knife from my boot, dropped the torch and began hacking into the repulsive things. Iskandar screamed, as if it were his own flesh I was slicing. Each cut tendril recoiled with a jerky motion, blue ichor spraying in all directions. I clamped my lips together. Whatever that stuff was, I didn't want any of it inside me.

With his sweat-slicked skin bathed in torchlight, a spark of understanding crossed his features. Iskandar began to fight, tugging the severed blue things from his skin and flinging them as far as he could manage. He hauled himself up, screaming all the while, lurching and swaying like a drunk.

"There's some sort of light in here—we can do without the torch. When I put it out, you can use it to help your balance."

Iskandar nodded. He wiped his clammy palms against his trousers and widened his stance. I hoped he did not notice how much blood he'd lost.

A charcoal stench filled the air as I stamped out the flames. He fumbled as the ground shuddered again, then gripped the end in one hand like a walking stick and let it take much of his weight.

"Come on!"

Iskandar took one careful step and then another. He took a third, then stopped. A piece of bloody silk-wrapped meat lay by his foot. His legs began to buckle.

"Concentrate! There's nothing you can do for him now."

Iskandar leapt across the bloodied chunks that had once comprised his friend.

"Almost there," I said, just as the ground lurched violently, sending Iskandar sprawling forward. I grabbed him. He panicked, scrabbling for my arm with both hands.

"There's no time!" I shrieked.

I gave him a leg-up to the rung. Iskandar vanished into darkness. I hauled myself up after him.

"Don't touch the walls," I shouted at his back. The violent lurching of the whale threw me from side to side. I tried not to look at Ando's embedded form, but even in the dim illumination, I could see he'd sunk deeper into the fleshy walls.

Bright light streamed through the jagged entranceway. We ran towards it, flinging ourselves out through the whale's mouth to safety. It had already skittered several feet across the surface. We scrambled out of its path, turned and watched in utter horror as the thing tilted further forward, then dived suddenly, its entrance gorging quickly with sand. The ground spasmed, then, I swear, it belched. Soon nothing but a ripple of sand remained.

◇◇

We'd limped it halfway back to town when Doc appeared. How

she knew where to search, I'll never guess. Doc always knows. It's kind of like a taint on her. Maybe that's why Elias keeps her close. Errol was with her, carrying her bag and a parasol that had seen much better days. Still good enough to keep the sun at bay. Cast some shade for Doc to do her work.

Mirella and me eased Iskandar onto sand. Doc knelt right there and sewed his punctures up. There was more blood out of him than in—or so it seemed. Mirella started crying like a baby. I tried to shush her but she wouldn't shush. She'd held it in as long as she was able.

It would be a long road back to Sammarynda, especially for travellers not blessed of coin or kin. Hallam took some rough convincing before he'd cough up what they paid out for the horses. Said he oughta keep their bond on account of the nags being left out in full sun. It was Elias's boys that saw him right, I wouldn't wonder.

Our van is heading off again, uproad to Evenslough. The north bound caravanserai is full to bursting. Seems like half Grimpiper's going travelling. With the relic trade expanding, it's no surprise.

I went to look for Mirella in the shade of the old clay fort. The camel drovers say its walls have stood for a thousand years. Nobody remembers who'd built them or why; a low band of mud brick abandoned to the desert. There'd been buildings once but, over time, the sand had claimed them. Nothing remains now but walls, straggly date palms and a well.

It was where folks came to wait for the south bound vans. Mirella and Iskandar were dressed so dull that at first I couldn't find them. Iskandar's bandaged arms were concealed beneath his travelling cloak, his golden earring traded for food and water.

They saw me before I found them. Both got to their feet as I approached. Mirella took my hands between her own. She squeezed as Iskandar glanced off to one side. The once proud Sammaryndan prince too embarrassed to look me in the eye.

"He's doing well," Mirella lied. "Look—you can hardly see the scars."

He didn't show me and I didn't look.

"Stay with the van the whole trip back," I warned. "Don't even piss without an armed escort."

Mirella nodded enthusiastically. Iskandar stared into the far distance. A sea of dunes and more dunes after that. He shifted his weight, a move that made him wince.

"We owe you everything," said Mirella. "But there's one thing I don't understand. Our passage home—who paid for it? Our own wagon. Meals and a sniper on the roof? Such things do not come cheap."

I shrugged with all the nonchalance I could muster. "Some damn fool with a pocket full of gold, I guess." I turned and left before she said another word.

Not sure where I'm heading next. Carillon sounds good. Spearcrosse or Windcap Veer. Elias offered me a job on point, providing I learn to shoot straight as I ride. A decent wage so I'll take him up on that. The van is snaking up to Fallow Heel. And maybe I'll check out that whaling for myself, now that I can rightly call myself a veteran.

The stink of whale gut still lingers in my hair, mixed in with the scent of something else. Something bigger than the Sand Road's length and breadth. Something calling from beyond the farthest stone.

THE BRIDE PRICE

The rococo splendour of the lobby did not faze Padraic, but the thought of selecting his future bride filled him with an unaccustomed nervousness.

"How old did you say they are?" he asked. His companion, Dasan, also unimpressed by the finery of their surroundings, gave a slight shrug as their footsteps echoed loudly through the hall. "Not old enough," he said. "Not yet. We select them early so they may begin their training. Did you not read the brochures? Do you never listen to a word I say?"

Padraic laughed; the small polite sounds of an uncomfortable man. "Of course I listen. I listen to every word. But this place—"

"Terrifies you? Of course it does. It's only natural to feel this way. Brides are an expensive business. Choose poorly and your father will never forgive you."

Padraic fingered the edges of his jewelled collar studs. "I will not choose poorly. Perhaps I will not choose at all. Perhaps I will not meet a girl that I like?"

Dasan laughed. "You won't *like* any of them. You will *love* them all, and furthermore, you will find it impossible to choose a mere *one* to take as wife. But choose you must. Your father is strict and he will be most annoyed if I do not bring you home to New Ceres with a bride arranged."

Padraic dropped his hand to his side. Ahead of them, below a magnificent archway of red and gold striped brick, enormous doors of lacquered oak swung inwards to reveal a petite woman in a red embossed kimono standing with her hands clasped. As she bowed in greeting, Padraic noticed the stillness of her hair. Every blonde strand fixed firmly in its place. "Her hair contains as much lacquer as those doors," he whispered, nudging his friend.

"Shhhhh," replied Dasan. "Madam Lotus, what a delight to see you again. I swear you have not aged a day since my last visit."

Madam Lotus bowed again, deeper this time. The two men stopped a few feet before her. Dasan bowed in return; the slight condescending motion of the exceedingly wealthy. Padraic's bow was deeper, fuelled by uncertainty.

"My Lord's firstborn is in need of a wife," said Dasan. "We have come all the way from New Ceres."

Padraic felt the blood cooling in his veins as Madam Lotus cast her eye upon him. His face was the first point to come under scrutiny; the arch of his brows and the shape of his nose. Next, his shoulders and torso. Madam Lotus took one delicate step forward and then another. She moved around him, examining him as if he were an alabaster sculpture.

"I have many brides to choose from," she said, licking her lips. "But three of my girls in particular will most suit your needs, I think."

"Madam Lotus is never wrong," said Dasan. "You'd do well to follow her advice."

"I will choose my own wife," said Padraic.

"Of course you will." Madam Lotus clapped her hands and a bevy of assistants emerged from the darkness beyond the wooden doors. Without laying a hand on his person, they whisked Padraic swiftly through the doors and out of the lobby. Glancing back, Padraic saw that Dasan had remained behind to talk business with Madam Lotus.

"Aren't you coming with me? What if I make the wrong choice?" he cried, his voice reverberating off the distant walls.

Dasan turned his head. "You will choose well. I have every faith in you, my friend. Every faith!"

◇◇

The heady scents of honeysuckle and passionflower filled his senses as Padraic was blindfolded and led down passages that twisted and turned. His query about the need for a blindfold was met with peals of delicate laughter and still more floral scents; some familiar, some not. When at last the veil was lifted, Padraic found himself in a chamber, its walls thickly padded with elaborate tapestries. The chamber appeared ancient, yet it smelled like a summer garden. The assistants fussed around him, flitting and tittering like birds. In a couple of heartbeats he was seated on a low lounge, his back propped up with cushions plumped and fluffed. His shoes were whisked away, replaced by slippers. Firm hands massaged his shoulders. A tall drink stood by his right hand and beside it a tray of sweetmeats. He began to relax, overcome with drowsiness. *I do not have to choose a wife*, he reminded himself. *I have only to examine the girls on offer.*

"You must not make your choice based on beauty alone."

Padraic sat up with a start. He had felt no additional pressure on the lounge, not noticed the older woman settle herself beside him. Severe in her kimono and immaculate make up, she might have been Madam Lotus's sister.

"They are all lovely, but each possesses individual talents and traits. You should consider your business needs as you make your selection. Ask them questions. Ask them anything you like."

A young girl entered the chamber. Her face lit up with joy when she saw Padraic. As he opened his mouth to speak, another entered the chamber, followed by a third, a fourth, a fifth and a sixth.

Padraic felt his heartbeat race, his throat constrict with imaginary thirst. They were so very young, and yet they held themselves with the grace of mature women. As they nestled at his feet, he felt as if he had known each one for ages. Comfort and familiarity, that was what he felt.

The girls spoke their names in turn: Karis, Toba, Mischi, Jaede, Coral and Roma. Padraic glanced from face to face, searching for anything that might make his decision easier: a blemish or a frown. A sense of falseness or insecurity.

"Questions," said the older woman beside him. "Ask them questions." She had not offered him her own name.

"Where are you from?" Padraic asked none of the girls in particular.

Some sort of signal passed from the older woman to the seated girls so that Karis understood she would be the one to answer.

"I was born on Alpha Neuve, my village so small it does not have a name. My parents were farmers once, but now their lands lie fallow with grain blight. I have eight brothers and sisters and all of them go hungry. Should I be selected for marriage, my bride price will set them up on new, fertile land. No one will starve again."

Karis's eyes shone with held back tears as she told her story. Each of the other girls nodded in sympathy.

"My parents are dead," said Jaede, "killed by a tsunami."

"My sisters and I were raised by my grandmother. Now she is too old to work and we must fend for ourselves. I am the eldest," said Toba.

"Things are not well on the outer rim," said the older woman, intruding into Padraic's absorption so much that he almost scowled at her. "Those who are able flee to New Ceres and the other successful colonies. Those who cannot must manage as best they can."

Padraic listened to more of the girls' stories, nodding with sympathy at the harshness of their lives. The older woman soon steered the conversation in other directions. Directions designed to showcase the girls' wit and charm.

Amidst discussions on the value of poetry, Padraic leaned forward and questioned Karis suddenly. "How does it make you *feel*, to be sold as a wife so that your family may prosper? Would you not come to resent that it was you who paid the price?"

Karis smiled kindly, her lips set firmly with determination. "I would consider myself fortunate indeed to have a husband such as yourself."

When Padraic's meeting with the girls concluded, the older woman escorted him down a wide, marble corridor and into another lounge area very similar to the first. This room was filled with reclining men and attendants, all women, serving refreshments. A haze of pale blue smoke hung above them, scenting the air with the aromatic familiarity of tobacco and herbs.

The lounge beside Dasan sat vacant. Padraic took his place and nodded as an elegant woman in a pale pink kimono served him iced tea in a tall frosted glass.

Dasan smoked, drawing deeply on the nargeelah's elongated stem. Padraic watched the smoke curl and dance within the glass bowl of the apparatus.

"Were you able to choose?" Dasan asked after exhaling an exuberant lungful.

Padraic shook his head.

"It is no matter," said Dasan as he passed the stem to his friend. "Your body will have chosen for you. The selection rooms are designed containing sensitive monitoring apparatus. Your vital signs were recorded as you encountered each girl, your conversation closely assessed. All data will be cross referenced. There is one amongst the many—trust me on that."

Padraic pressed the stem against his lips, then paused. "They were all so lovely. So young, and yet—"

"Not like ordinary New Ceresian girls, is what you are thinking." Dasan laughed. "And indeed they are not. Madam Lotus charges a great deal of money for the skills that she imparts. When you get your bride home, the true value of the purchase will become evident."

Padraic nodded, still holding the stem of the nargeelah without smoking. "They are wives, Dasan, not purchases."

"As you say." Dasan clicked his fingers to summon an attendant. "My friend here would like a massage. He is very tense."

Padraic sat up suddenly, as if waking from a dream, the nargeelah stem in his hand forgotten. "No," he said, "I would not like a massage. I would like to speak with Madam Lotus about my wife."

The attendant led him to another chamber, this one smaller than the others, featuring a single low lounge beside an elaborate floral display. Next to the lounge, Madam Lotus waited and beside her, Karis, holding her hands palms up, one cupped delicately inside the other.

Padraic glared at Madam Lotus. He wanted to yell at her, tell her that he couldn't be expected to make such an important decision under so much pressure. That the time allowed for choosing was not enough. How much time would ever be enough? But Karis's eyes shone with adoration, fixed on his every step as he walked across the chamber floor. Madam Lotus and the attendant left them alone, exiting without a word.

Karis reached for his hand and motioned for him to sit beside her. "I know what you are thinking," she whispered. "That it is too soon to know if you can love me. Too soon to be the judge of a matter of such importance."

She placed his hand between her own. Such tiny palms, he

thought. Such delicate fingers. "But you should know that I feel no such hesitation. My own heart is free of doubt. I knew as soon as I saw you. You are the one, Padraic. You are the one I want."

Padraic cupped her face in his hands, his thumb brushing the soft peach skin of her cheek. He stared into her emerald eyes and knew that she meant every word of it.

"How old are you, Karis?"

She blinked, sending shivers down his spine. "I shall be fifteen standard Earth years old when you return for me. I shall be a woman fully grown, and ready to be your wife.

As he took her in his arms and kissed her, Padraic felt an object being pressed into his hands. He looked down at an ornate porcelain key inlaid with jewels.

"Take this key back to New Ceres with you as a promise of good faith," Karis explained. "When you return, you will exchange it for me."

Padraic nodded. The key was symbolic. A receipt for the down payment on her bride price.

"We will meet again in one year's time," she whispered, and then in a heartbeat, was gone, led away by yet another of the nameless attendants that served as staff in Madam Lotus's world.

When escorted back to the rococo lobby, Padraic was shocked to find Dasan tossing a porcelain key in his palm. A key almost identical to his own. "But you already have a wife," he said.

Dasan brought a finger to his lips as the two of them were escorted back outside the building to where a shuttle waited to return them to their vessel.

Padraic still clutched his key in his hands. Dasan had pocketed his already, his mind moved on to other things.

Padraic waited for the appropriate moment. "But what of your wife? What of Loren?"

"I have grown tired of her," Dasan said at last. "Loren no longer pleases me."

"But what of your children?"

Dasan shrugged. "What of them? My children belong to me. Loren has no legal claim to children sired through surrogates. The eggs come with the wife—one of the advantages of doing business with Madam Lotus. No messy family complications should you change your mind. It's all part of the bride price."

Padraic considered Dasan's words as the older man made a string of business calls and notations in his Planner. He wondered what would become of Loren, but felt too uncomfortable to pose the question.

Instead, Padraic stared out the shuttle's window at the cityscape below, admiring the ordered shapes of civilisation: the straightness of roads and the brilliance of blue pools inlaid like jewels.

"Loren will be taken care of," Dasan admitted at last. "She will be offered an apartment and employment. The company will see to it. Such details are their concern, not mine."

"But she is your wife!"

"No, my friend, she *was*. Business is business. I am a primary executive merchant. I work hard to keep your father rich. I deserve a new wife as reward."

Padraic slipped a hand into his pocket to wrap his fingers around Madam Lotus's jewelled key. Its surface felt smooth and cool against his fingertips. He turned it over and over again, mulling over the uncertainties this day had brought forth. *I will take good care of Karis*, he promised himself. *I will never be like Dasan.*

◇◇

"Why has the ship stopped?"

"Why are we not moving?"

The complaints of business travellers and the chink-chink of dice on tabletops muted the soft music seeping from the walls of the cruiser's first class passenger lounge. The music, designed to pacify nervous travellers, irritated Padraic as much as did the lounge itself. It seemed as though he spent half his life in spaces such as these, luxurious pauses separating where he had been from where his father would have him go next. And always, the inevitable attendants proffering refreshments or whatever other service was required.

As the slender girl in charcoal silk bent forward to place a cocktail by his armrest—a drink he had not asked for—he grabbed her wrist. "What is the problem," he demanded. "Why have we stopped?"

The girl stood still, waiting patiently for Padraic to release her. "The captain apologises for the inconvenience," she said. "A refugee transportation container from the outer colonies is stranded in this sector. We are legally obliged to offer assistance."

Padraic released her as murmurs of "outrageous" and "unbelievable" filled the space along with a series of exasperated sighs.

Dasan pulled his favourite possession from his pocket: an antiquated fob watch believed to be from Earth itself. He flipped its gold case open with his thumb and frowned, then slouched his body into the comfortable recesses of the lounge chair.

Padraic knew that the girl who had been serving drinks would whisk the empty glasses away. When she returned, it would be with a selection of game boards and dice, although the dice would be unnecessary. Men such as Dasan carried their own in their pockets as lucky charms. Dasan's dice were made of ivory; carved from the tusks of long-extinct Earth beasts.

Alongside the game boards would come the nargeelahs; one to be placed strategically amidst each group, the stem to be passed from lip to lip as a gesture of equality and friendship.

Dasan and his companions would get gently stoned and gamble away a few thousand credits to help the time pass.

Padraic stood suddenly, leaving his drink untouched. No one challenged him as he left the lounge and his companions to the rattle and clink of precious ivory and crystal flute.

Padraic did not know where he was headed, nor, indeed, how far it was possible to explore within the confines of the ship. He decided to walk until somebody stopped him. It was not possible to get lost. No matter where he went, eventually there would be a man or a woman in a crisp braided uniform to guide him gently back toward the comfort of his cabin. Just as there always had been his whole life.

Now and then he would dip his fingers into his pocket and touch the key to reassure himself that the events of the past day had been real. He pictured Karis, her wide green eyes shining, and he wondered what became of Madam Lotus's other girls—the ones not selected as wives.

As Padraic left one corridor behind and entered the next, he expected to encounter many travellers like himself and Dasan, but the cruiser's bars and private lounges were empty. The absence of sound disturbed him. He could not even hear his own footfall on the luxuriant carpet. *My world is hermetically sealed*, he told himself. *Every part of it controlled at every point.*

Eventually he reached an elevator. Should I go up or down,

he wondered. Down seemed the more appealing selection so he chose it. Moments later he stepped inside, and in the seconds following his brief descent, the doors parted and Padraic stepped into an empty space. A storage bay of some sort, he presumed. His footsteps echoed loudly on the metal floor as he continued his exploration. As he walked, he began to hear faint muffled sounds from somewhere up ahead.

At the far side of the space he found another elevator, this one only offering the option of down. He entered its battered-looking metal cage, travelled downwards for a few jerky moments. When the doors parted he stepped out into another world.

The smell hit him first; the stench of unwashed flesh, followed abruptly by the sound of children crying amidst a sea of utter disorganisation. Everywhere he looked were people standing, sitting or lying prostrate. Some huddled together in groups, cowering from those others who ran amongst them, knocking bundles of goods to the ground in their wake. The air was thick with chatter, so much so that it was impossible to think. Impossible to breathe in the cloying, human stink.

And yet, Padraic did not turn and call the elevator back. He stood still for a moment to calm himself, blinking imagined smoke from his eyes. As he became accustomed to the smell, he began to notice little things. The people around him were not all of the same race, nor of the same social caste. As he stepped amongst them, moving forward through to whatever gaps became apparent, he noted that while some refugees—for who else could they possibly be—were dressed in tatters, others were garbed not so differently from himself in finely spun, expensive cotton shirts and business slacks. Their shirts were soiled from the rigours of uncomfortable travel, but the quality was evident, as it also was in their mannerisms. The way they carried themselves.

And yet others seemed as if they had never known the safety of home. Women with lank hair and bony arms clutched at filthy, squalling children. Some tried their best to sleep, although Padraic wondered how anyone could ever hope to sleep in such confusion. The sleepers' faces were still as stone. As if, having finally laid their heads down, they would stay that way forever.

Each step took him further from the safety of the elevator, deeper into the struggling human tide until he was sure he could feel its very pulse. No one touched him. No one bothered him, and this only added to his sense of confusion. He was not one of them, even if his cleanliness was the only thing keeping them apart. Why weren't these people hanging off his clothes begging for help?

He walked on amidst the chaos. Abruptly, one voice distinguished itself from all the others. Padraic looked to its source and saw a woman with her hair bound up in a scrap of purple cloth. She moved amongst the mass calling out a single name. The name of a lost child, he presumed, after the swift movements of two boys playing tag attracted her attention.

Her face has seen too much harsh sunlight, he thought. She is probably not as old as she looks. Her gaze fell upon him for a moment, then moved on as she continued her search.

He did not intend to follow her but a jostling in the crowd behind forced him forward, and so forward he continued, listening to the fire in her voice as she cried "Henna! Henna!" over and over.

The woman carried a cloth bag and a red plastic container slung across her back. She trod carefully, and Padraic saw that her boots, though worn, were sturdy and practical in design. Her calves, too, were strong and muscular.

He followed as close as he dared, trying to keep a respectable distance, yet worried about losing her in the crowd. Eventually she ducked below a makeshift awning. When he moved the cloth aside, she was gone.

Unsure of himself, both why he followed her and where he was headed, he paused for a moment to catch his breath, amazed that he could no longer distinguish the dirt of the people around him. His sense of smell had become acclimatised, as had his sense of personal space. He had stopped flinching when others accidentally brushed against him.

Padraic craned his neck in search of the woman, strained his ears to try and catch the sharpness of her voice. Suddenly there it was again, this time behind him.

"Why are you following me?" she demanded as he spun around.

"I'm not," he began.

"You were following me just now," she stated. "What is it you think you want?"

Padraic considered. "Who is Henna?"

"Who are you?" she replied.

"No one of consequence."

"Indeed," she said, making a show of eyeing his fine white shirt and jewelled collar studs. "How unfortunate for you that your captain was obliged to stop and pick up common refugees. How tiresome it must be—"

Padraic had opened his mouth to argue when the sound of another woman's wailing sang out clearly above the bustle and hubbub of the throng.

"Henna!" cried the woman beside him as she ran towards the terrible sound, her quarrel with Padraic dismissed. Padraic followed her instinctively, trying to keep up without tripping over boxes, bags and bundles of well-worn possessions.

The crowd thinned to reveal a woman seated on a mat surrounded by other women. She clutched a bundle to her breast and cried. The most mournful sound Padraic had ever heard. He did not need anyone to explain the scene to him. The bundle was her dead baby.

The women around her made comforting noises but there was nothing they could do.

"The guards will come soon to take the babe away," said a woman's voice. Her again. The woman with the headscarf he had originally followed. "The rules of transportation are very strict. Those who die are to be jettisoned into space. There can be no exceptions."

"Is this Henna? The one you were calling?"

The woman shook her head. "Henna is my daughter. I do not know this woman's name."

"I'm sure the authorities will perform the—"

"These women are of the Urzu faith," the woman explained. "Her dead infant must be washed in clean water and blessed, then wrapped in a clean cotton shroud before burial. The ritual is vital to the passage of the soul. Without it, the babe will walk in limbo."

Padraic studied the crying woman's face. The redness of her eyes, the lines of pain etched by grief.

"Then we must see that it is done."

The woman in the headscarf shook her head. "You rich have no understanding of anything. No knowledge of anything *practical*."

Her eyes scanned the crowd again in search of her daughter. Padraic followed her gaze to where a girl of about twelve years stood clutching a bucket to her chest.

"Henna! Don't run off like that. Stay where I can see you."

Henna looked up at her mother, then returned her gaze to the crying woman with the dead baby.

"This container was never designed to transport so many," explained Henna's mother. "There is not enough water to spare for washing. The red plastic squares everyone carries? They hold our drinking allowance. We are permitted no more than that."

"I have plenty of water. I will go back to my cabin and get some for her," said Padraic.

"That is very kind. But do you really think your friends will let you back down here bearing such a gift? Look around you. These people are exhausted. Most of them are glad to have made it this far. They're not thinking straight. They haven't considered what might be available on the ship that is transporting us the final leg of the journey to New Ceres. Should they consider it, and decide to help themselves, I doubt your people could stop them."

"What is your name?" he asked.

"Alla."

"Alla, my name is Padraic and I am a man of my word. I will bring her water and I will be discreet about it."

Alla smiled sadly. He could tell she didn't believe him.

The murmuring of the crowd lessened as a bearded man in pale blue robes pushed his way to the mat where the bereaved woman and her companions were sitting. One of the companions stood to greet him. Instinctively, the crowd inched back to give them space. Some moved away for additional privacy, but the gaps were soon filled by others keen to watch.

The companion and the bearded man conversed in low whispers. Below them on the mat the woman with the dead baby cried, moving back and forwards in a rocking motion, clutching her child like she would never let go.

"Five hundred cubic centimetres of drinking water each day is our allotment. Barely sufficient to sustain life," said Alla. "We are due no more until tomorrow. There were supposed to be sonic showers set up for us but I haven't seen them. Our evacuation was sudden. Fortuitous. We were allowed to bring only what we could carry. A new life awaits us on New Ceres in every respect."

"I will bring water," said Padraic.

"There isn't time. The guards will know about the death

already," she said, gesturing to surveillance nodes embedded in the low ceiling. "They won't be far away."

Over Alla's shoulder Padraic could see the blue-robed priest, standing, listening with a look of stillness on his face.

The woman's sobbing ebbed. She seemed exhausted, as if she had no more tears to cry. Suddenly another sound separated itself from the general murmuring of the crowd. A young girl's voice, clear and shrill. Once again Padraic craned his neck for a better view.

Alla's daughter, the girl called Henna, moved from person to person, the bucket clasped tightly to her chest. "Just a spoonful for the baby. One spoonful you can spare, no more."

At first there was no reaction. Some shunned her defiantly, others lowered their gaze so as to not have to meet her fierce stare. But most, after a prolonged pause, reached for their precious red plastic container, unscrewed the cap and dribbled a little splash into the bucket. Just a little, but a little from the many would be enough.

Finally, when she had coaxed enough water to make a sloshing sound, Henna took the bucket to the woman with the baby and placed it at her feet.

The priest nodded, understanding, the beginnings of a smile cracking his rugged features.

Padraic smiled too, but Alla did not. "I swear we have only made it this far by Henna's rat cunning," she said. "She's a good-hearted child. Tough, but kind. It's her begging that's kept us fed these past two seasons. There are still some decent city folk who'll throw scraps to a hungry child. But the water's no use without the white cotton. Henna doesn't understand."

As the priest crouched down beside the woman, someone cried out "The guards are coming!"

All but one of the mother's female companions leapt to their feet, linking arms to form a protective circle around the mat. Padraic and Alla were shoved in separate directions as a contingent of uniformed men pushed their way forward, the clanking of their body armour contrasting sharply with the murmuring of the crowd.

Unsure at first of what to do, Padraic took his place in defense of the mat. He studied the red and gold braid of the guards' uniforms, the glossy sheen of the weapons gripped tightly in their gloved hands as they approached.

"This is not necessary," he said calmly. "The mother wants only—"

The nearest of the guards shoved him roughly to one side with the butt of his weapon. Another stepped forward, pushing Padraic to the ground. In that moment, the crowd of refugees surged and Padraic's voice was lost in a sea of angry outcries. Others stepped in to fill the spaces separating the mat and the guards.

Padraic clambered to his feet, gripping his bruised flesh as he heard the sharp click-clack of weapons being armed. Surely they will not fire upon these innocent people, he thought. Surely not. Above, the glassy node of the surveillance system observed impassively.

He searched for Henna and Alla, but all he could see were the heads and shoulders of enraged refugees. Behind him, the atonal chanting of the priest began. Would the ritual words be enough without white cloth for the baby's shroud?

The crowd surged again. As Padraic raised his arms to steady his balance, he noticed the fine white linen weave of his own shirt.

Quickly, he turned his back on the guards. He needed time to think but there was no time. Padraic fought his way to where the mother sat, pulling his shirt over his shoulders as he moved.

"This garment is clean," he shouted to the priest. "I have only worn it this hour past. It is of the finest cotton. Will it suffice?"

The priest glanced up from his ministrations. He did not understand Padraic's tongue, but he looked down to see what he was clutching in his hands. Suddenly he nodded enthusiastically, reaching out to take the shirt.

Padraic stepped back as the priest spread the shirt on the mat. With the bucket beside him, the priest gestured to the mother's companion. The woman gently prised the dead infant from the mother's arms. She passed it to the priest and he stripped it of its swaddling, chanting as he worked.

He held the infant tenderly, scooping handfuls of water from the bucket, anointing each of the babe's tiny limbs in turn as he chanted with a slow, steady rhythm.

With each moment, the anger of the crowd intensified. Padraic clutched his bruised shoulder, expecting every minute to hear gunfire.

But the guards did not fire. Suddenly, in unison, they shouldered their weapons and waited for reinforcements. They stood as still as automatons, eyes staring blankly ahead. The noise of the crowd fell away, layer by layer, until all that could be heard was the priest's chanting.

Finally that sound ceased as well. The circle of women parted and the mother stepped through, her white shrouded baby clasped tightly in her arms. She presented herself to the guards and allowed herself to be led away accompanied by priest and her companion.

It was over. The gentle murmuring of regular conversation returned as people separated into small groups, linking their arms, laughing with relief that matters had not become much worse.

Padraic, still clutching his bruised shoulder, watched Henna stoop to retrieve her empty bucket. It was only then that he noticed a detail he had somehow missed earlier. A detail concealed by the oversized shirt she wore. The child's left arm was missing past the elbow.

"A land mine. When she was five," said Alla who had been watching him the whole time. "She says the missing flesh sometimes pains her, although I don't see how it could."

"I will buy her a new arm," said Padraic, his eyes shining.

"On New Ceres?" Alla shook her head. "Such technology is forbidden, as you well know. She has managed without it these past seven years and she will continue to do so."

"I can make her whole again," he said, placing his hands on Alla's shoulders. "I have great wealth. I can make anything happen."

Alla smiled kindly. "The gift of your shirt was much appreciated. But my daughter does not need your help."

He looked to Henna again just in time to see her duck behind an awning as two uniformed guards approached, these ones with their weapons holstered.

"Sir, we have instructions to escort you back to the first class passenger lounge," said the nearest of them.

"I will find you!" He called back at Alla as the guards marched him back towards the elevators. "I will take care of you both." Alla smiled again as the guards took him away.

◇◇

"You have been gambling, I see," laughed Dasan. "This time, the shirt off your back. You must pay better attention—who knows what you will lose next time."

Not nearly as much as I almost gave away for nothing, Padraic thought, heading for his suite.

"Hey!" Dasan called after him. "I want to know the details. Is it true you went wandering amongst the refugees? I take my eye off you for five minutes . . . "

Back in his suite, Padraic pulled the porcelain key from his pocket. He tossed it in his palm, feeling the weight of it against his skin.

Dasan's face appeared around the corner. His eyes shone from the effects of too much drink. "There are plenty of well-bred hostesses on this ship. You have only to ask—"

"Dasan," Padraic said, "I am not ready for marriage. I have seen nothing, I have been nowhere outside my father's realm. But I will honour the girl who is linked to this key. I will not allow her family to starve on my account."

Dasan smirked. "Is that what she told you? A heart-wrenching tale of poverty and desperation?" He threw back his head and laughed heartily, his body slouching against the door frame. "Those girls are bred for the bride market. Obedient wives, sold before they were even conceived. None of them have ever starved. Why do you think Madam Lotus runs her business so far away from civilised space? Laws are lax. Not everywhere is like New Ceres, my friend."

Padraic's fingers tightened around the porcelain key.

"Put a shirt on," said Dasan. "Then come back up and have a drink."

As Dasan left, Padraic held the key up high. Elaborately engraved, indulgently ornate, it disgusted him, as did everything it represented. He threw it across the room as hard as he could, shattering it into pieces against the far wall.

"Valet—the refugees on board this ship. Where are they to be set down?"

"I'm sorry, sir," replied his room's communications node, "That information is not currently available."

"You will let me know the minute it *is* available," he snapped.

"Certainly sir," replied the valet.

"I will find you, Alla," Padraic said to his mirror reflection. "I will find you both and make you safe." He wondered what his father would say if he caught his son sheltering a refugee woman and her amputee child in his home, but found for the first time in his life he didn't give a damn about what his father thought.

STREET OF THE DEAD

"I'm driving round to Bob's," said Ern. "There's UFOs in his chicken house again."

Maree paused, the socks she was packing dangling limply from one hand. "Dunno why you'd bother—they won't lay again after this. You know what happened last time. I need you to load the trailer."

"Won't be long," he said, pushing his hat firmly in place as he opened the front door. The flyscreen clattered loudly behind him, obliterating Maree's parting words. She knew nothing she said would make any difference, even if he'd heard. She walked through the kitchen and fastened the flyscreen latch properly, still holding the socks.

Outside, the lawn lay brown and parched, the orange trees she'd planted five years earlier listless in the still, dry heat. The sky, as always these past few months, was filled with tiny silver discs that flitted about like insects, forming occasional patterns and swirls against the blue.

"I'm not leaving without Claudie," said Debbie, pouting.

"Well then, you'd better find him, hadn't you?" replied Maree. "He's probably under the house. You know how funny he gets whenever we go away."

"But I've looked there already." Maree's youngest daughter's signature whine was edging its way into her voice. It wasn't her fault. She was tired. They all were.

"Then you'd better look again. We can't come back for him."

"But Mum! What if—?"

"Or maybe try the shed. We have to leave soon. There's nothing I can do about it."

Debbie spun on her heel and darted out the back door, calling the cat's name as she ran. Maree glanced after her.

Supposedly the silver discs weren't dangerous. The voltage they occasionally discharged was slight and didn't hurt, not even as much as an ant bite. But Maree had decided not to tell her daughter about the Brewzynskis' Siamese; how they'd found it dead on their verandah last week with nothing to explain how it died.

Maree didn't trust the UFOs, nor the federal authorities that were making local farming families relocate to a new community development out at Terrapin Flats, so new that it wasn't even marked on any of the maps. The farm had been in Maree's family for three generations. They'd survived droughts, bushfires and the free trade agreement. If their soil were really contaminated, they'd have known about it years ago. Maree wasn't buying it—she suspected the move was connected to the strange little silver discs. What the hell were they? Where had they come from?

Ern got back an hour later.

"Bob says they're bussing the uni kids back down from the city."

Maree's heart jolted at the thought of Karen. She'd been talking about travelling through South America with a friend before the phone lines started playing up. Maree wanted their eldest safe at home.

"Reckon she might know something about all this UFO business? She's doing computers. Must've learned something more about it all up in the city."

Ern grunted his agreement. He headed straight for the fridge and drank deeply from the two-litre container of orange juice in the door. She didn't bother to tell him off for not using a glass. They'd been instructed to leave all foodstuffs behind as well as all white goods. Where they'd be living soon had all amenities built in. Maree didn't like the sound of that. She wanted her own fridge, her own washing machine and dryer, not something generic a faceless government bureaucrat had picked out of a catalogue. She hadn't liked the sound of anything since the UFOs began to swarm.

Maree watched in the rear view mirror as Debbie flicked through the latest issue of *Dolly* magazine. Maree hadn't read a magazine herself since *Women's Weekly* lost the plot and joined the ranks of the worst of them. "My boyfriend is an alien; fashions from other worlds"—she expected a frivolous reaction from teen magazines and tabloids, but the rest of the advertising world had gone insane overnight, too. Fashionable protective clothing, gizmos either to attract the discs or repel them. Articles on how to communicate with alien beings, or acquire protection via psychic angels. Families were being moved off their land, but all the commercial world could do was find new garish ways to make a buck out of the situation.

Maree wanted to reach round the back of her seat and yank the lurid magazine away from her daughter's grip, but she stopped herself, sat back and took deep breaths. Better that Debbie stayed distracted by the magazine instead of thinking too much about poor missing Claudie.

A bright flare of silver on her left dazzled Maree, bringing her back into the moment. It took her a second to comprehend what she was seeing. A small shack entirely covered in silver discs. Ern pulled the vehicle over to the side of the dusty road.

"That army guy told us not to stop," said Maree.

Ern got out, leaving the motor running as he approached the shack. He walked as far as the gate, leaned over it, brought both hands up to shield his eyes from the glare. Once he'd seen enough, he returned to the car, slammed the door shut a little harder than necessary.

"Nailed on," he said, aiming the Toyota and trailer at the road.

"I thought they were too hard. That nothing could penetrate the silver casings?" said Maree, trying for one more look before the car sped out of range.

"Two boys at school did it," said Debbie from the back seat. "Darren Barrister and Michael Broody. They put a saucer in a vice and smashed it with sledgehammers till it bust open. All this liquid dripped out, silver, like thermometer stuff."

Maree flicked her eyes back up to the rear view mirror as Debbie turned a page.

"Reckon I can get a pair of Flak Pantz for my birthday? They're extra thick below the knees, like cricket pads. Just in case the UFOs zap you."

"Deb, those boys shouldn't have been messing with that saucer. Might have been dangerous. Anything could've happened."

"There's nothing in them, Dad. Just that dripping silver stuff. Karen said the government's been cracking them open for months to see inside. When they're new they're really hard but after a few months they get softer and you can smash them open so all the goo leaks out."

"When did Karen ring?"

"She didn't—there's still something wrong with the phones. She emailed. She said Darren and Michael should have left the discs alone."

"She's right," said Ern. "Don't you go messing with those things."

"I wasn't even there!" Debbie cast the magazine aside and pulled her laptop from her backpack. "Karen sent me some pictures from some website. Want to see?"

"Not while we're driving, honey."

Maree focused her attention on the road ahead, somehow comforted by the familiar sound of the Macintosh booting up and the gentle tapping of Debbie's fingers on the keys. The sky was stark blue and mercifully clear of UFOs for the time being. There were fewer of them in the long stretches of sky between towns. Someone on the radio had suggested they were attracted to electricity.

They passed the lifeless carcass of a kangaroo, and then another. Several other mangled furry shapes that could either have been foxes or wombats. Was it just her imagination or was there more roadkill than usual?

The petrol station at Nangatta looked the same as it always had except for the large number of cars parked beside it.

"Can I have a Coke?" said Debbie.

Ern reached into his pocket for coins. "That's the Everinghams' ute," he said to Maree, passing the loose change to Debbie across the back seat. "Told me they weren't gunna relocate, no matter what."

Ern and Debbie got out of the car at the same time. Maree paused to watch her husband stride across the gravel towards the group of men in checked shirts and jeans congregating around the Everinghams' vehicle. A flicker of movement caught her peripheral vision—UFOs milling around the petrol pumps. Glancing up, she saw many more of them hovering in clusters. Just like insects. If they weren't so large and made of metal no one would ever have noticed them.

She followed the arcing silver trail across the sky, back to the ground where a group of girls gathered around the Coke machines. Her own daughter stood at the centre of them, holding her laptop open so everyone could see the screen. Debbie balanced the computer on one palm, swigged Coke from a can with the other. What were they all staring at?

She returned her gaze to Ern. He'd acquired a newspaper and was rolling it on his knee while listening to Alf Everingham speak.

Maree felt the pressure of her bladder. She pushed the car door open just as Ern took a swipe at a low-flying UFO. He hit it square on and sent it shooting sideways. Maree paused, expecting the thing to zap him, but it didn't. The silver disc wobbled for a moment, stabilised its trajectory and flew upwards to join the others of its kind.

Somewhere behind her a dog yelped. She turned to see a border collie leaping enthusiastically into the air, trying to catch a UFO in its jaws. The girls around Debbie's laptop pointed at the dog and laughed. Maree headed for the toilet block.

When she emerged five minutes later the girls were still staring at the screen. Debbie's Coke can lay abandoned on the ground and she balanced the computer with both hands.

"Better go to the loo while we're here—and put that can in the bin," said Maree. "What's so fascinating, anyway?"

Debbie looked up and angled the screen around so Maree could see. The pictures displayed were dark and fuzzy.

"What's it supposed to be?"

"They reckon that's where the saucers come from," said Debbie. "A gap in space where there aren't any stars. They started pouring through one day. Nobody knows why. They just keep coming and coming with no end to them."

Maree leaned in closer, tilting the screen for a better view. She saw an expanse of stars with a dark mass fouling the lower right quarter like a stain.

"Who told you that? Where did you get this picture?"

"Karen emailed it. She reckons this guy at uni hacked a secret government site. Supposed to be a secret only now everybody knows."

Maree examined the image again. "Could be anything. It's probably a fake."

"Karen doesn't reckon. She says Sydney's full of UFOs, covering the streets like autumn leaves. Hey, can I have an ice cream?"

Maree looked across into her teenage daughter's pale blue eyes and freckled skin. "Sure honey, but don't take too long. And don't forget to go to the toilet."

The landscape surrounding Terrapin Flats had changed subtly since the last time they'd been out this way. Maree couldn't immediately say what it was that was different, only that things weren't the same. The army presence was obvious, but that wasn't it.

"Road's new," said Ern, as if reading her thoughts.

She nodded. It had been dirt two years ago. This new one was slick and black, flecked with shards of silver that sparkled in the sunlight.

Maree noted several other vehicles on the road: sedans, utes and four-wheel drives.

"Don't see any coaches," said Ern. "Would've thought there'd be those buses from Sydney by now."

"Karen's probably there already," said Maree. "Probably checked out the house and nabbed the best room for herself."

"Hey—Karen's online!" said Debbie. "Airport's working—they've got wireless out here. Oh. She says she's not coming. Doesn't trust the government. Says we shouldn't go to the new place. Not after they built these roads from—Oh crap, the connection just died."

"What are you talking about?"

"The Internet cut out."

"Maybe you should stop the car, Ern."

"Too late."

Up ahead loomed an army checkpoint. A line of vehicles stretched behind them.

"Put the laptop away, honey," said Maree. Debbie didn't argue.

Ern wound down the window as a young soldier approached.

"Good afternoon, sir. If you and your family'd like to stick to this road for another K, then turn right at the fork. There'll be a sign. Is this all of you?"

"Just the three of us," said Ern.

"Thank you, sir. Have a nice day."

The car passed through the checkpoint and continued along the road.

"Did you notice that soldier's eyes?" said Ern. "Silver irises. Never seen that before."

Over the crest of the hill lay the fork that the soldier had promised. They turned right and soon came upon a row of squat, ugly buildings made from the same sparkling material as the road.

"You don't suppose they're houses," said Maree.

"Warehouses, looks like," said Ern

"Debbie, honey, what did Karen say was wrong with the roads before the Internet cut off?"

Debbie stared at the buildings as they passed. "Only that they're made of crushed-up UFO saucer shells mixed with bitumen. Karen says there's no end to them. The UFOs keep coming and soon the whole world's gunna be covered. When the shells get old, you can crush 'em and mix 'em with stuff. Karen reckons the scientists don't know what else to do."

The road's incline was noticeable. The patch of sky above the traffic stream was dotted with silver discs. Ahead, they could see a town completely constructed from the sparkling black substance, both roads and buildings alike.

"Reminds me of Calle de los Muertos," whispered Maree. She had gone to Mexico with Ange and Tracey straight after they all finished their higher school certificate, well before she'd settled down with Ern. "The pyramids were made of speckled granite. Teotihuacán. It means the street of the dead."

The traffic was bumper to bumper now, moving slowly and steadily, feeding into a long, dark gash in the earth.

"Reckon that's an underground car park?" said Maree.

"I don't like this, Mum," Debbie said. She shrank against the back seat as they neared the gash. The inside was all silvery, the same dead metal hue as the UFOs. "It's kinda like a . . . a great big mouth swallowing up all the cars. Let's go back."

Her voice was squeaky with panic.

"Everything'll be OK," said Ern, tightening his grip on the steering wheel.

"Yep, I know," said Maree, winding up her side window and placing her hand on her husband›s knee. Clouds of silver discs continued to flit and skitter overhead as one by one the cars vanished into darkness.

SAMMARYNDA DEEP

The woman nestled amongst the cushions would have been considered beautiful had her right eye not been torn from its socket. The scarring was brutal, hideous. From the moment Mariyam entered the bar, she had been drawn to the scarred woman and her entourage. As fate would have it, the man she had hoped to meet at the Starfish that afternoon was one of the scarred woman's friends.

"Haptet, at your service," he said, smiling and pressing his lips to the back of her hand.

"My name is Mariyam," she replied. "Behameed said I was to seek you out. He promised you would be my guide, should I ever find myself in Sammarynda."

Haptet's eyes widened. "Behameed! The old dog. He is like a brother to me. Please join my friends. Let me buy you a drink." Haptet could not wipe the smile from his face. "Behameed! It's been years. Is he here with you? I've not seen him on the peninsula for a decade at least."

Mariyam settled herself amongst the cushions and smiled. News, it seemed, did not travel quickly in these parts. The old trawler captain Behameed had been dead five years, but he had said his name was as good as currency along the peninsula. About that, at least, he had not lied.

Alcohol pulsed warm currents through her veins as she surveyed the room while listening to Haptet tell stories of his troubled youth, spent crewing on Behameed's yacht back before the war. Mariyam laughed along with the rest of them—and

85

some of her laughter was genuine. This was not the Behameed she had known. This one seemed like a reckless idiot rather than a hero of Maratista Plain.

The decor of the Starfish echoed its name. Five-pronged motifs, both painted and woven, covered the walls. Above the tables stretched a fishing net laden with desiccated creatures, each one tinted in pastel shades.

Mariyam tried not to stare at the woman with the missing eye, whose name she now knew was Jahira. A difficult task. Jahira was, simultaneously, beautiful and hideous. She'd be used to the whispers and stares, the pity in the faces of strangers. Mariyam turned her attention to the others; handsome, well-groomed men and women whose names she would not need to remember. She noted their familiarity; the brushing of skin against skin, the way they leaned in on each other when they spoke. So much intimacy. She felt a sudden swell of emotion. Her eyes moistened, but she fought the feelings down. These were not her people. This was not her home.

"Tourists everywhere!" exclaimed Haptet as he dragged on his water pipe, causing the coals to flare. Both Jahira and Mariyam watched the smoke dance in the glass chamber as he exhaled. He gestured to a group seated at the far end of the room. "They come only for the jousting season to fill their pockets with baubles and poke their noses where they don't belong."

"But surely you welcome the money *we* tourists bring," said Mariyam, casually feigning hurt as she waved for the waiter's attention. "You may have been born here but you were educated inland, same as me, Haptet. Same as me. Your accent betrays you. Perhaps there's more similarity between us than you'd like to admit?"

A young boy in a white linen smock approached, proffering a drink on a tray. Mariyam took it as the coin Haptet tossed spun and clattered on the shiny metal plate.

"You have caught me out," said Haptet, winking at her slyly, "And now you must tell us—which of the grand inland cities are you from?"

"I was born in Makasa," said Mariyam, "I'll bet you that boy is destined for Allamah University, or any one of a dozen others in the ancient city."

"Perhaps," said Haptet, "or perhaps not. Sammarynda is a port of many choices. If the boy wants to go to Allamah, his father will find a way. But few of our people settle permanently in other cities—did you know that?"

Mariyam didn't, but then there was much she did not know about Sammarynda and its inhabitants. How easily these people had accepted her amongst their number. Haptet was right. She was a tourist, and not a very well-researched one. She had come to Sammarynda to put an end to her nightmares. When she'd left home, nothing else had mattered.

"Why have you come to Sammarynda?" Haptet asked. "What is it you are seeking?"

"Something different," she replied after a considered pause. "Isn't that what all travellers seek?" She looked to Haptet as she spoke, but he had become distracted by another man seated at a table near the door. An inland trader; a Bedouin, dressed in thick desert robes.

As she watched the men talk, Mariyam became aware that Jahira was watching her, staring intently with her one clear eye. Mariyam sipped her drink, a reflex action. Where to look? The damage to the woman's face was so visible, so obvious. Why did she not wear a patch or a veil? Mariyam longed for Haptet to rescue her, but he had become so deeply absorbed in conversation with the desert man that the mouthpiece of his water pipe rested idle between his palms. When she looked again, Jahira returned her stare. Mariyam smiled, a feeble gesture laden with unintentional condescension and sorrow, then she looked away too quickly. Damn, but she couldn't help herself. She studied the patterned fabrics of her companions' garments, waiting for the tide of conversations to envelop her once more.

A soft hand pressed upon her shoulder. Mariyam looked up at Jahira's ruined face as she positioned herself to nestle beside Mariyam on the cushions. Up close, the wound was infinitely worse that it had appeared from a distance.

"Please," Jahira said, "allow me to explain."

Mariyam stared into the empty socket, and then into Jahira's whole eye, which shone as clear and bright as sapphire. Only then did Mariyam notice the heavy make-up the woman wore to enhance the beauty of the one eye she possessed. Her lips were painted, her cheeks rouged, her eyelid rimmed with ebony kohl and dusted with fine gold powder.

Mariyam drained the last of her honey vodka.

"You are Haptet's friend?"

Mariyam nodded, wondering immediately who this woman was to him. A lover? Surely not. A sister, perhaps?

"My missing eye," Jahira said, gesturing to the mass of pink scar tissue, "It is my honour."

"Your what?"

Her lips parted as she prepared to explain, but her words were drowned out by a commotion amongst the camels hobbled together a few feet outside the doorway. Men shouted to each other across the low tables and brightly coloured cushions. Mariyam watched Haptet as he watched the men from the interior leap up and tend to their disgruntled beasts with the same amount of caring and focus you'd expect them to expend upon an injured child.

"We do not speak of these things amongst strangers," Haptet remarked later as he and Mariyam strolled along the bank of an artificially constructed lake. Both moons were out, and the constellation of Kashah the Dog-Headed Warrior sat directly overhead. Mariyam gazed up at it, as if trying to decode its shape and meaning. Haptet studied her face in turn.

"Jahira said her ruined eye was her honour but I don't know what that means," said Mariyam.

Haptet nodded. "Sammaryndan honour is a private matter. Not something we would usually explain to tourists. But as you are a friend of Behameed's . . . " He glanced upwards at Kashah for inspiration. "When one attains true adulthood in Sammarynda, one must render upon oneself an honour. It may be a small thing or a great thing. The choice is entirely one's own."

Haptet stopped walking. He grabbed the fabric at the base of his shirt and pulled it over his head, turning to reveal the naked flesh of his back. A thick scar snaked from his left shoulder blade almost all the way to the base of his spine.

Mariyam stared. "From the war?"

"No," said Haptet, releasing the fabric and turning back to face her. "That scar is my honour. When my time came I asked two friends to hold me down and a third to wield the scythe."

The light of the moons cast a pearly luminescence on his skin. Mariyam frowned. "You *chose* to be scarred? Surely you can't be serious?" And then the truth of his words hit home. Jahira's eye. Mariyam gasped, bringing her fingers to her lips.

"I don't expect you to comprehend our ways," he said, gesturing to the path ahead. "For some, honour may be a scar. For others, it may be a sacrifice. Giving up something of great value. Do not waste your pity on Jahira—she is in no need of it. You may find her honour hideous, but I assure you, the people of this city do not."

They continued their stroll along the lake in silence, soaking up the ambience of the night.

"Mariyam, why have you come to Sammarynda? Is it for the water jousting? The season is just beginning, but you seem so incurious about it. So distracted."

Mariyam looked up at Kashah again, as if seeing the face of the dog clearly for the first time. "Yes," she said, "the jousting. I have come to watch the men fight."

Haptet could hear the half truth in her words.

"There is an island to the north where the women weave the most exquisite cloth. You must buy some to take home with you—it is unlike anything else, I promise."

Mariyam nodded, allowing Jahira to guide her through the morning markets. They did not hurry. No one hurried in this part of the world. Sammaryndans made time for the little things. They were keen listeners, astute observers. Details were valuable: the difference between living and merely existing.

Now Mariyam could see the Sammaryndans' honour everywhere. Scars were popular, although few were as brutal or as visible as Jahira's. She had learned that the peninsula sported a whole caste of medical practitioners whose only work was to inflict damage on healthy individuals as they entered adulthood.

Mariyam picked up a length of cloth and twisted it in her hands. The silver fibres woven throughout it shimmered.

"I have always wanted to visit Makasa," said Jahira as she reached for another bolt of fabric, shooing away the saleswoman with a flick of her hand. "Was that where you became friends with Haptet? In Makasa?"

Mariyam feigned distraction as she scanned the crowd in search of a particular familiar face. A futile exercise, she knew. The man she sought would not be strolling through a marketplace like this. *He* would be preparing himself for the evening's festivities, practicing his balance or his swordsmanship if, indeed, he was here at all. *I should have made this journey ten years ago. Even if I find him now, it's too late.*

Mariyam observed a man with a limp; a girl with a cleft lip; another so thin that her clothes hung off her bony frame like rags. How could she not have noticed any of this when she had first arrived?

"Perhaps there is something else you would like to see?" Jahira had noticed Mariyam's gaze wandering away from the embroidered cloth on the table. "Leatherwork? Jewellery? I'll take you to the silversmith quarter if you think you can stand the noise."

Mariyam smiled. "I'm happy to wander through the market."

Jahira nodded. "Then let us walk this way. I have some purchases to make."

Mariyam felt sunlight bathe her skin as they pushed through the throng of shoppers and hawkers, tourists and tradespeople. Now and then she was shoved or jostled by the compact, hurtling forms of children absorbed in their games of catching and chasing, refusing to let the thickness of the crowd slow them down. The sharp tang of unfamiliar aromas. Spice sellers crouched in doorways beside woven baskets deep with the many-hued ochres of their wares.

Everywhere, images from the ocean: fish carven into doorways, serpents embroidered onto coats, shells painted with precious metals, looped through silver chains on slender necks.

Most fascinating of all were the apothecaries, their windows festooned with the twisted forms of desiccated creatures, the origins of which Mariyam could only guess at. Monstrous amalgamations of fang and bone. Surely such unnatural fusions could not occur in nature? Mariyam placed one hand upon Jahira's shoulder, gesturing with the other at a malformed shape dangling from red string beside a net of dried frogs.

Jahira shrugged. "It is from the Sammarynda Deep. Some of the curiosities thrown up from the crevasse have medicinal properties. Others are fierce poison. Many apothecaries make their living solely from determining which is which."

Mariyam longed to step into the doorway's darkness, to be enveloped by the multi-fanged strangeness within, but Jahira had moved on already, keen to get to the fresh produce section before all the best choices were gone.

Her mind filled entirely with images of scissor teeth and warped bone, Mariyam turned a corner to find a group of black-shrouded women squatting in the shade of a crooked awning, their wares spread before them on a square of faded cloth. Jahira had hurried ahead with her basket. Mariyam glimpsed her through an archway that led to row after row of laden barrows.

The squatting women ignored Mariyam until she crouched before them and pointed a slender finger at the row of glass vials lined along the cloth. Vials containing a substance that glittered and shimmered, even in the shade.

"What are these?" she asked.

The women eyed her coldly, not bothering to mask their contempt. Mariyam asked again, this time in Barter using the accompanying hand signs. Reluctantly the nearest of them answered, but the word she uttered was unintelligible. A name, probably, in a local dialect. Something with no equivalence in any other tongue, certainly not in Mariyam's.

Gently she lifted a vial from the cloth and held it up against the light. Colours coiled and swirled within. Whatever it was, it was beautiful.

A shadow fell across Mariyam's face.

"Tourist junk," said Jahira, looking down on the old women with annoyance. "Let me take you to the artisan quarter if it's trinkets that you really want."

Mariyam rose, brushing sand from her skirt. "But what's inside the vial?"

Jahira paused. "Shavings from Glass Rock. These ancient whores are too old to sell themselves, so they thieve a little of our long-abandoned cultural heritage and peddle that instead."

One of the women said something to Jahira. She snapped back a reply in the same tongue. "What they're selling is illegal. I should report them to the Harbourmaster."

"No—don't do that," said Mariyam. She closed her fingers around the vial and dipped into her purse for a coin. "Is this enough?"

"More than enough," said Jahira. "You shouldn't encourage them."

Mariyam threw the coin down on the cloth, and the faces of all three women erupted into cheery smiles.

"That is more than these hags see in a week, but no matter. Let me take you somewhere you can waste your money on high quality merchandise."

That evening back in the Starfish, Mariyam sat with Jahira, Haptet and their friends gazing out across the ocean, watching reflections of the two moons, Neme and Kryl, spill ripples of gold across the water.

Mariyam felt inside her pocket, rolling the smooth glass beneath her fingertips.

"So," said Haptet, lifting the wine pitcher, "tomorrow the jousting begins. Have you chosen a champion? Have you placed a bet?"

Mariyam shook her head. "Such a strange ritual. What is it for? Why do the men fight each other?"

Beside her sat Jahira. Next to her, another man she did not recognise. The left side of his face was stained with an intricate pattern that ran all the way down his neck to vanish amongst the dark hairs beneath his shirt. His honour or his art, she wondered. Was there any difference between the two?

Jahira leaned against his shoulder as she sipped from a long-stemmed glass.

"The joust was once a political event, but now it is merely a display of athleticism and skill," said a dark-skinned woman dressed alluringly in turquoise and gold. "Sammarynda has been peaceful for years. No one fights any more."

"I shall bet on Orias," Jahira said loudly. "I have won money on his steady stance and deft manoeuvrability three years in a row."

Orias. Mariyam froze at the sound of the name, but only for an instant. No one had noticed. No one had been watching her.

"So typical of you to bet on a prince," said the turquoise woman.

Jahira made broad theatrical motions, feigning indignation at the suggestion. "Orias is no mere prince! Orias is a hero of the war!"

"Nevertheless, a prince he is—and all the ladies bet on him," said Haptet. "And he wins because he is a skilled and masterful warrior. It is almost impossible to make an honest profit as a result."

"A prince indeed?" said Mariyam, afraid of the tremble in her own words as she uttered them. Surprised they did not lodge in her throat and choke her. "I didn't know Sammarynda had a royal family."

"It has dozens of them," Haptet laughed. "But Orias is my friend. I will introduce you. He is like a brother to me. Did you know he fought in the battle of Maratista?"

"Really?" said Mariyam. "He fought? Then I am impressed. I know how few warriors walked away from the battlefield that day."

"You have heard of Maratista?" asked Haptet.

"I have been there."

"To Maratista? Are you serious?"

For a second Haptet and Mariyam locked eyes, but the waiter began to clear the table and the moment was lost amidst the clinking of glasses and the ordering of food.

Fireworks exploded below them on the beach, accompanied by the squeals of children and the barking of dogs.

"Today Jahira spoke of Glass Rock," said Mariyam, raising her voice. "I would like to see it. Will you take me there?"

Haptet nodded, regarding her curiously. "Tomorrow," he said. "I will take you there tomorrow."

From a distance, it seemed to Mariyam that Glass Rock had been inappropriately named. It was not made of glass at all, nor anything that resembled its texture. The mineral—whatever it was—seemed to suck light from the air. It stood out from the surrounding rock formations like a dark stain.

"I want to touch it," said Mariyam.

"No," said Haptet. "Touching is forbidden."

"But old women scrape away fragments to sell."

"Maybe," he replied, "but all the same, it is forbidden—and for very good reasons."

Haptet seemed much darker than when they had first met. Was it because of Jahira's affection towards the tattooed stranger?

Unlikely. These people were comfortable with each other's oblique infidelities. No, it was Glass Rock itself that was setting him ill at ease.

"If I can't touch it or climb upon its surface, may I at least learn its history?" she asked, fingertips brushing the vial of swirling particles concealed within her pocket.

They climbed a little higher along the ridge until they stood directly opposite, the two cliffs separated by a stretch of water. Glass Rock seemed to beckon, drawing their gaze toward it although there was little to see.

"Below Glass Rock lies a crevasse that chasms downwards for miles. No one knows how deep it is. No one has ever touched the bottom."

Mariyam stepped as close to the edge as she dared. The water was crystal-aqua, same as it was all around the Sammaryndan peninsula. But the water directly beneath Glass Rock was as dark as a starless night.

"Our ancestors went to Glass Rock when all hope was lost. They would paint their bodies with a poultice of oils and shavings from the Rock itself, then stand over there, right at the very edge."

"They would throw themselves off? Suicide?"

"They would dive, but not to their deaths—although those who did not enter the water smoothly would sometimes break their backs and drown."

Mariyam stared at the black stain beneath the water.

"The divers entered the Sammarynda Deep. They would swim down into darkness, vanish for a time and then they would return. Changed," said Haptet.

"Changed? In what way?"

Haptet frowned, searching for the right words. "In many ways. It's hard to be specific. No one could predict the form a change might take. Sometimes a diver would emerge with a different face. Other times he or she might appear the same, but no longer be the same inside. Particles from the rock are believed to be an integral part of the process. The old market women who sell the shavings are from a particular bloodline—a tradition that goes back hundreds of years."

Mariyam recalled the twisted carcasses hanging in the apothecaries' windows.

"Touching Glass Rock is against the law," Haptet continued. "No one has stood there for a century."

She stared out across the water, imagining the swift, lithe form of a diver cutting a shimmery arc through the void, before plunging into the abyss.

"Why is it forbidden to dive?" she asked.

Haptet shook his head. "The changes. They were too unnatural. Too swift. Too severe. If we are to change, we must do so slowly, by degrees. The Deep made monsters of us. We were almost destroyed by the power of—whatever it is down there."

Mariyam nodded, unable to take her eyes from the dark patch of water.

Haptet cleared his throat. "Mariyam, yesterday you said you had been to Maratista. May I ask—"

"A long time ago," she said. "Many years. I don't wish to talk about it."

Behind them a horn blared: a drawn-out, mournful sound.

Haptet's face brightened, glad of the interruption. "The festivities will soon begin," he said. "We can get a good view of the boats from here." He led her back the way they had come, then down across another stretch of cliff.

Below, the slender watercraft made a pattern like thatch across the still surface of the harbour. Each was decked in different colours.

"The prince you mentioned last night," said Mariyam. "Which of the colours is he?"

"Prince Orias? His colour is dark blue."

"The colour of the Sammarynda Deep?"

Haptet stopped. He turned to face her. "What a curious thing to say. Nothing is the colour of the Deep. *Nothing at all.* Prince Orias's blue is deep and rich, but it does not devour light!"

Mariyam nodded. "I would like to see the boats up closer. And I would like to meet your prince."

Haptet smiled. "I knew you would. I have arranged it already. You will fall in love with him—I can assure you of that. Every woman does."

"No doubt," she said, masking her bitterness as best she could, leading the way back down the rocky path that wound around the cliff side all the way back down to the beach.

◇◇

Mariyam felt herself gently mesmerised by the relentless swirling of the dancers' multi-layered skirts. The entire population of Sammarynda had come down to the water's edge for the opening of the jousting festival. Several people had explained how the mock battles to be fought in the long boats tomorrow were symbolic of yet another war from a distant time. The survivors of that skirmish had settled this part of the inhospitable coastline and turned their talents toward farming the sea.

To Mariyam, it seemed as if every night in Sammarynda was a celebration of something. Flaming torches cast a warm glow upon the skin of merrymakers as they watched small boys heft long sticks to play at mock jousts on the grass. Youths tattooed with multi-coloured swirls wove in and out between the tables bearing baskets of sugary treats wrapped in twists of coloured paper. These they tossed into the crowd, or pressed into the hands of small children.

"I wish I had learned to dance when I was young," Mariyam shouted to Jahira.

"There is still time," Jahira said. "Why don't you stay here with us for awhile? I know someone who can teach you. Age is not important."

Mariyam sat back in her chair, sipping her drink as a line of pretty little girls in pinks and greens, shells woven into their hair, bangles on their wrists, snaked past the tables, laughing and squealing. No one minded when items were knocked to the floor. No one cared about anything other than their unadulterated, radiating joy.

The long boats were moored a little way offshore, their decks encrusted with paper lanterns. The sky lit up with fireworks, these even bigger and brighter than the ones the night before.

Suddenly a wall of cheering erupted from somewhere to the left of their table. The crowd began to part, foot by foot, and the lanterns increased their luminosity as the men who would perform tomorrow's joust made their way through the cleared space. Each was garbed in fine garments expertly tailored to the contours of their bodies. Decked in their individual colours, each walked tall and strong and proud, aware that they were there to be admired.

"I've been in love with Orias for years," Jahira whispered as she clasped Mariyam's hand between her palms.

Mariyam nodded, the pace of her heartbeat quickening. "Orias" wife must be a very fortunate woman."

Jahira shook her head, smiling sadly. "Orias has never chosen a wife. He does not allow himself love the way we do. It is his honour."

Mariyam gripped Jahira's arm. "What do you mean he doesn't allow himself love?"

Jahira turned to face her, and Mariyam sensed her own fingers tightening their hold. The dark space where Jahira's eye should have been still shocked her, no matter how many times she saw it.

"You know about our honour, Mariyam. Both Haptet and I have explained it to you."

Mariyam shook her head. "Your scars. I understand them. But—"

"Not all scarring is physical," said Jahira. "Orias's scars are in his heart. Apparently there was a woman during the war. They fought together, side by side. They were captured and imprisoned at Fallam Keep. Both suffered greatly in the enemy's hands."

Above them, a firework exploded suddenly, erupting into a magnificent flower, then flickering away into nothingness.

"But they endured, Orias and his lover. They survived, and escaped to fight for vengeance at the battle of Maratista Plain. Orias was a young man then. He had not yet chosen an honour for himself. When the war ended, he realised no mere wound of flesh would ever suffice. Only one thing held meaning for him. The woman he loved so much. So Orias sacrificed her for his honour and returned to Sammarynda. Or so it is said. He does not speak of such things with me."

A field of twinkling roses rained as betrayal stung Mariyam like a scorpion's tail. The pit of her stomach fell away into nothingness. Orias had abandoned her without a word of explanation. Sacrificed her to the mores of a culture she didn't even know existed. *Why didn't you tell me? Rather I had died in the pits of Fallam Keep than endured these years alone, never knowing why you left, never understanding anything of the truth . . .*

Her breath rasped in her throat as her heart beat louder and louder, in syncopation with the footsteps of the approaching men. Orias. *Prince of darkness, Lord of aching and despair.* She could

97

not yet see his face, just his silhouette against the fireworks and the gentle swaying of the gaily painted crowd.

For all these years she had dreamed of one single perfect moment, wondering what she would say to him as they were reunited. But this was no dream, and as the gap between them closed, time slowed and the years that had stood between them unravelled, fading like trails of gunpowder across the burning sky.

All you had to do was tell me. The truth would have freed us both.

Each warrior of the joust strode past, waving at the cheering crowd as confetti swirled and danced on heady currents. Time slowed further until it dripped like honey as Orias took another step directly into her line of vision. He saw her. Their eyes locked. Time paused, and in that eternal fragment, Orias glimpsed her scarred soul laid bare across her face. He learned the true price he had paid for his honour. Orias remembered all of it. Every moment they had ever shared, as clearly as the moments they had not. A shadow passed between them, a cold electric chill that sucked the brightness from the fireworks and made the coloured specks of paper tremble to the ground like dead leaves.

And then it was all over. Mariyam turned her face away and the warriors continued on their heroes' walk. Time resumed its regular rhythms. When she looked back he had gone.

Flecks of sunlight shimmered on the water as the boats positioned themselves to begin. High on the cliff spectators nestled comfortably into wooden chairs, or sprawled on coloured rugs.

The empty chair beside her made Jahira nervous. "Are you sure Mariyam didn't say where she was going? Why travel all the way from Makasa if not to watch the main jousting event?"

Haptet shrugged. "She never even mentioned the festival before I brought it up. It's very strange, but I have the strongest feeling it was never the reason for her coming here."

Jahira craned her neck to search the crowd. "Maybe she has gotten lost. You know her best, Haptet. Is she one who might lose her way in a crowd?"

Haptet shrugged. "I have known her only minutes longer than you. I can only guess at the sort of person she may be."

Jahira stared at him. "Really? You are not old friends? You seemed so familiar!" She glanced across at the others, all of whom shrugged as well.

Haptet shook his head. "I met her for the first time in the Starfish. You were there. She was curious about your eye. Remember?"

"Yes—but I presumed—"

"No," he said. "I did not know her before that day at all—only that she said she was a friend of Behameed's. I'm beginning to wonder if we haven't all presumed too much."

"She came here to find Orias," said Jahira, pulling her cotton wrap tightly across her shoulders, even though it was not cold. "Now that I think about it, I'm certain. Last night at the festival. Didn't you see what happened when they met?"

"Look!"

A gasp rippled suddenly through the crowd, causing all heads to turn at once to the cliffs behind the beach. A lone figure stood atop Glass Rock, her skin shimmering in its sheath of glittering oil. Clearly a she, despite the distance; the curve of her hips well defined against the impenetrable shadow of the rock's obsidian surface. And equally clear was her intention. The woman was preparing to dive the Sammarynda Deep. She stood poised as still as the rock itself, eyes cast downwards, waiting for the perfect moment. Waiting for the crowd to quiet itself.

"Haptet," whispered Jahira, "I think that Mariyam is *she*—the inspiration for Orias's honour. Mariyam is the woman from the war."

Haptet's eyes widened. "But that's astonishing. Where is he now? Out on the water already? Did he board the boats with the others?"

Jahira didn't answer, nor did she turn to discuss the alarming development with her friends. She understood perfectly. The dark current that passed between Mariyam and Orias last night. Anguish that had inflamed the very air around them. They were not strangers. Neither were they friends. Something powerful bound them together, trapped them in each other's vortex, unable to escape. Mariyam had come to Sammarynda to slash those bonds forever. It was she who'd paid the price for Orias's honour. All she wanted now was freedom. "I'm sorry I didn't understand," Jahira whispered. *"I would have chosen the very same way."*

One of the long boats pulled away from the others and headed for the shore. Orias's blue, Jahira noted. Was Mariyam aware of it, so high up there on Glass Rock? If so, she gave no sign.

The murmuring of the crowd intensified as people began to notice the boat, and the single figure in full jousting regalia who leapt from its prow out into the shallows, kicking up clouds of foaming white water as he waded to the sand. Once on land, he raced for the rocks, stripping off jewelled leather as he ran, his pace slowing but not his determination.

Atop Glass Rock, the diver stepped forward to the edge. Was she staring into the abyss below with terror and trepidation? Or was she calmly appraising the future she had chosen for herself? Her stillness did not betray her thoughts. No one would ever know her truth.

The twittering of the crowd intensified as Orias clambered up the rock face, small stones and chunks of earth raining from each foothold. The brown rocks gave way to the cold solidity of Glass Rock's extraordinary mineral composition. Orias kept climbing.

The crowd gasped in unison as the diver raised her arms above her head. *No. Wait for him, you must wait. He has almost reached the top.*

The diver did not wait. She crouched, then pushed her body upwards and outwards, cutting a graceful swathe through the air, then falling like a spear. She broke the surface of the water cleanly, a blade plunging home with a killing thrust. Barely a ripple marked her passage.

As the water's surface smoothed, all heads turned upwards to the rock face. The climber clung to Glass Rock like a spider, inching forwards and upwards, somehow finding handholds where there were none. A tide of sympathy washed over the crowd. He was too late. Too late to stop her but he didn't know it. He could not see that she had dived already.

Finally he hurled himself the last few feet, tumbling in a heap onto the rocky dive platform. He rushed to the edge, peered over to stare at the dark crevasse below the water. His shoulders slumped. His head hung in despair.

The crowd hushed. No one dared whisper now. Every one of them felt his sorrow and his tragedy, whatever the story that lay beneath it all.

Orias turned his back on the ocean. He walked away, then suddenly stopped, spun around and ran towards the edge, flinging himself into the air, assuming the diving position as he fell to the accompaniment of ten thousand screaming onlookers. He did not break the surface cleanly, but the ocean took him, just as it had taken her.

◇◇

The night was still as porcelain, the ocean flat and calm, as if laying in wait for something great to happen. Something that would change the world forever. For Jahira, things had already changed. Things that could never be put right.

While Sammarynda grieved for its drowned prince, Jahira waited for a sign that the legends of their land were true and not just fancy tales made up for tourists. Every evening she climbed the cliff directly opposite Glass Rock, sat cross-legged at its edge and gazed down at the dark patch of water, darker than the night sky itself. Not even Neme and Kryl cast their reflections upon its shadowy smudge.

On the third night of the third week the surface of the water broke. Something emerged, coughing and spluttering, flailing its limbs in panic. Jahira leapt to her feet and ran down to the beach, grateful for the starlight that prevented her from stumbling on loose rocks. Kashah the Dog-Headed Warrior observed as she stripped off her clothes, plunged in and swam to the struggling form, which had begun to shriek and howl in panic. Jahira was a strong swimmer. She managed to haul the struggling one to safety.

As the two of them lay panting on the sand, Jahira realised she had rescued a child. A girl of no more than twelve or thirteen, pale as alabaster, thin as a reed. She wrapped the coughing girl in her coat. She had to get her home quickly. Away from the beach before anyone saw what the Sammarynda Deep had cast out in exchange for the city's most beloved prince and the stranger who had led him to his death.

As they stumbled across the sand, their feet crunched down hard on small shells and fragile bones of twisted sea creatures tossed onto the shore by the dark Sammarynda tide.

The girl could not speak. Terrified guttural sounds issued from the back of her throat. Not a language but Jahira understood it,

SAMMARYNDA DEEP

101

just as she was not surprised by the thin webbing of skin stretched between the child's fingers and toes.

Jahira responded in as soothing a tone as she could manage, promising to protect the child and keep her safe from harm. But the child would not be safe, Jahira knew. The child would never be safe. The citizens of Sammarynda port would hunt her down and kill her without question, just as they would kill the old market crones who had sold Mariyam Glass Rock fragments—if they hadn't done so already. Superstition festered below the surface. It would not take much to return the land to the violence and terror of centuries past.

By the light of Kashah, Jahira understood that her missing eye had never been her honour at all, but merely a cosmetic thing, an act of vanity, performed to draw attention to herself. Her true honour would lie in protecting this child of the Deep: the unholy fusion of Mariyam and Prince Orias, whatever the cost, even if the price required was her own life.

SEVENTEEN

Grandma C was talking about the war again and Emily listened patiently, her hands folded in her lap. Grandma C liked to talk about the London Blitz; how everybody had pulled together to help everybody else. She liked to tell Emily that the world had once been a nicer place. Emily had never seen anywhere nicer than Blaxlands. She wondered if Grandma C could be remembering history right. She'd seen the Blitz on TV. It was all about bombs and broken buildings, everything shattered in black and white. Blaxlands was a vast expanse of woods. Trees and grass and streams. It had its own water tank, power supply and defence system. You couldn't ever bomb Blaxlands. All the Grey Estates were hooked up to a satellite array.

Grandma C started nodding off in her chair. Emily got up off the carpet and patted the wrinkles out of her pinafore dress. She glanced at Billy but he was busy with his colouring books, lying on his stomach, his legs kicking lazily in the air. Billy was content to colour until Grandma C wanted him to do something else. Billy never minded whatever Grandma C wanted him to do. He never took the initiative unless he was paid for it.

Emily rescued the sloping teacup from Grandma C's lap. She took it into the kitchen and placed it on the sink. She wasn't going to rinse it out if the old lady wasn't watching.

"Ping me when she wakes," said Emily.

"'Kay," said Billy, not looking up from his colouring. Maybe he actually likes colouring, Emily thought, although it didn't seem that likely. It didn't matter so long as he pinged her—and she knew he would. They were a team, Emily and Billy, and Grandma C was a pretty decent gig.

The old lady would doze for an hour or two, during which time Emily would be free to explore the grounds of Blaxlands undisturbed. Last month she'd found baby deer down by the stream. The first wild animals she'd ever seen apart from cats and rats and dogs. They were so beautiful. She'd lain in the grass and watched them for ages. It was so nice knowing that they were safe. No one was going to try and eat them. No one was going to shoot them just for fun.

You couldn't hear gunshots at all in Blaxlands, nor sirens, explosions or horns. You could lie in the grass and fall asleep. No one would try to hurt you.

There were no deer today but she found a family of swans on the lake. They headed towards her as she walked across the tiny wooden bridge.

"I'm sorry," she told them, realising she'd forgotten to bring any bread crusts from Grandma C's kitchen. When the birds learned her pockets were empty they moved away, leaving her alone to soak in the glorious sunshine.

She ran across a stretch of freshly mown grass, waved at a family enjoying a picnic. Two little girls in pink taffeta waved back as their mother shook out a red and white checked cloth. She skipped past a groundsman, austere in his prim blue uniform. He ignored her completely. She loved it when that happened. Loved the fact that once you were inside the walls of Blaxlands, uniforms paid you no attention at all.

She was about to explore a row of old buildings when Billy pinged. They looked like they might have been storage sheds, but they would have to wait till next time. Emily turned around and headed briskly back to Grandma C's unit, trying not to feel depressed about how few 'next times' she had left.

Back inside the unit, Billy was showing Grandma C his colouring.

"Have you been playing in the garden?" she asked.

"Yes, Grandma. I saw some swans today."

"Oh! How lovely. Billy's been a good boy, haven't you, Billy?"

Billy blushed and shifted his weight from foot to foot.

"Would you like me to rise out the teacups?" said Emily.

"Oh—would you, dear? That's very kind. You'll make some lucky man a wonderful wife one day, Emily."

Emily caught the barest suggestion of a smirk on Billy's face.

"How about a cookie, Billy?" she said dryly.

"Oh yes, do give him a biscuit. He's been so perfectly behaved today."

Billy was perfectly behaved on every visit, thought Emily as she lifted the cookie jar down from the shelf and held it open for the boy. He grinned at her cartoonishly as he took a few, stuffing the extras into his pockets for later.

Grandma C had sat back down in her rocker again so Emily took a couple as well. The less of her pay she had to waste on food, the better.

An hour later as golden light spilled out over the landscaped parkland below the balcony, Emily and Billy woke up Grandma C and told her it was time for them to leave.

"We don't want to miss our bus," said Billy.

"I do wish you could both stay longer," said Grandma C, her eyes glistening.

Not as much as I do, thought Emily.

Emily sighed as the three of them traded goodbye kisses on the front porch. "See you next month, Grandma," she said, and she hoped very much that she would.

Back at the gate, Sheree and Jai changed out of their Emily and Billy costumes and took advantage of the free showers, even though they'd used them already that morning. Sheree loved the smell of the rose petal soap and the fact that it lingered on her skin for days to come.

"You didn't take anything, did you?" she asked Jai as they waited for the bus. Jai, already wired into his pod, didn't answer, although she knew he could hear her.

"You better not have taken anything," she warned, although she figured that he probably hadn't. There were random body searches on the bus. Edible stuff was OK, but anything else had to have been signed for. Jai wasn't stupid enough to throw in a gig like this one for the sake of a few stolen trinkets. He was probably the sharpest ten-year-old she'd ever known. Sheree thought about him often when she was back in the city, wondered if he had a family or was part of a gang. He couldn't be on his own, surely? He'd never asked her for help. Maybe he did have a family to go home to when he wasn't playing Billy up at Blaxlands.

The bus dropped them off at Central. Jai gave her a cursory wave as he headed off down Broadway, hands thrust deep inside his bomber jacket pockets. Wherever he was going, he didn't seem too worried about it.

Sheree crossed the lights at Chester Street, heading for the pipes where she'd stashed her stuff. The Grandma C gig earned her enough credit for a week in a dorm, but the weather was still mild and the stench wasn't too bad since that flash flood washed all the brown weeds and dead rats out of there. She had a few things hidden: a sleeping bag, some protein bars. The smell kept most of the scavengers away and this wasn't the worst part of town. The pipes were OK, but you had to be careful. You always had to make sure you watched your back.

She couldn't see any fresh tags, colours or other signs of gang activity, but she loitered in the protective shadow of a doorway for a while, just in case. Better to be safe than gangmeat. She reckoned she could live in the pipes until the developers came back, if they ever did. The billboards advertising 'a new kind of executive living' and 'refreshingly different shopping' had been bleaching, tattered in the sunlight for at least a year.

Later, nestled in her mother's tattered old sleeping bag, Sheree watched the laser lights carve advertisements above the city skyline. A thousand birds swooped and tumbled in the pillar of brilliant white shooting upwards from the top of the Stock Exchange tower. Birds, or were they bats? Why were they always drawn towards the light?

She ate the cookies she had filched from Grandma C, chewing slowly to make each one last as long as possible. Seventeen was going to be so tough. She tried not to think about it, but she knew her time was drawing very close. Sheree licked the last of the cookie crumbs from her palms as sirens echoed across the city streets.

◇◇

Billy was amusing himself, making soldiers out of Play Doh Bake. When Grandma C asked, he told her they were soldiers, but they looked more like homies to Emily, right down to the coloured bandanas around their necks and wrists.

"I can't seem to find my jewellery box," said Grandma C, frowning. "The one with the lovely dancing ballerina. I can't find where it's gotten to."

"Can you remember when you saw it last?" asked Emily, feeling a little concerned, although she knew there was no need. Grandma C knew she was always losing things. She'd never accuse Emily and Billy of stealing. Never even think of it.

"Shall I look in your bedroom?"

"Oh yes. Yes, dear, please look."

Emily padded across soft carpet. The bedroom smelled musty, like lavender and old woollen cardigans. Even with the light on it was dim in there.

The bedside table was cluttered with ornaments, as was the dresser but there didn't seem to be a ballerina jewellery box. When she tugged open a drawer, she found it stuffed with stockings, rosette soaps and crochet squares.

"I suppose it must be locked away in storage," said Grandma C. "Be a dear for me, Emily, go see if you can find it."

Grandma C motioned to one of the drawers. Inside it, Emily found an old-fashioned key on an enamel keyring that said Sunshine Coast in bold yellow letters.

"I don't know where my storage is," said Grandma C.

"That's OK," said Emily. "I'll find it."

Billy didn't look up from his Play Doh Bake army as she slipped out of the flat. Emily knew exactly where the lock-ups were. She knew every inch of Blaxlands; from the place where the laundry trucks picked up their loads to the pet cemetery down beside the rose garden. She'd managed to map out the entire grounds, stolen hour by stolen hour over the past two years. Today she wanted to check out what looked from a distance to be a stormwater drain. She had time—she would tell Grandma C she had gotten lost. If Grandma C even asked. With any luck she'd be fast asleep in her rocker by time Emily returned.

She decided to get the jewellery box first. Best to have something legitimate in her hands just in case, although security had never bothered her before.

The storage lock-ups were all in a row, all identical save for the numbers stencilled on the front. Emily looked for the one that matched the number of Grandma C's flat. The lock was stiff and ancient—pre-electronic. She had to throw her shoulder against the door to force it open, then feel along the walls till she found the switch.

When the bulb flickered on, Emily gasped. The storage bay was completely crammed all the way to the ceiling with junk. Antique chairs, a chaise longue, dozens of irregular-looking lamps. An upended mattress, books, magazines, a baby's crib complete with moth-eaten netting. Tennis racquets, ancient lace, a billiard table bearing a load of tightly taped cardboard boxes. Emily squeezed between the spaces, stepping over skis and piles of winter coats. Grandma C's whole life was in this lock-up. Nobody had been in here for years.

Nothing looked remotely like a ballerina jewellery box. Sheree's mother had had a jewellery box too. An old wooden thing, carved and polished with a brass clasp at the front. It was one of the last possessions Sheree had pawned. She'd hated having to part with it.

As she shut the door behind her, Emily noticed that the lock-up walls were double brick. It had been warm inside. Warm and well insulated.

There was nobody about as she made her way across the lawn. She cut across the bridge, past the gazebo and down to the place where she had spotted the stormwater drain the time before last. It was situated quite near to the perimeter wall. The surrounding cement drainage pan was choked with water weeds. It didn't rain so often any more, yet the surrounding soils were damp and swampy. Did the cement drain lead to the outside? She climbed down as close as she could manage without wetting her feet, leaning forward to peer into the tunnel's darkness. Was that a patch of light at the other end? A torch. She would have to bring a torch next time. And boots. She would have to wear boots. There might be gumboots in the lock-up. Suddenly a hundred possibilities flooded through her mind. Everything she'd ever need was in that lock-up. Everything but food and water. A place that no one ever went. A place that was warm and safe.

Back in the unit, Grandma C had forgotten all about the jewellery box. Billy's face was smeared with jam, his cap perched jauntily at an angle—Billy's signature. Billy had an extensive repertoire of well-practised scruffy little boy poses. He grinned through an overstuffed mouthful of pikelets as Emily sat beside him at the table. Grandma C tut-tutted, which was Emily's cue to reach for a serviette and wipe the muck off his face.

She could feel Grandma C's eyes on her skin as she took a pikelet for herself and spread it sparingly with jam and cream. She longed for protein and hot vegetables: red meat and roast potatoes, green beans and brussels sprouts instead of all this sugary stuff.

"A girl's got to watch her figure," said Grandma C sternly, right on cue as Emily bit into the pikelet as daintily as she could manage. "When I was a girl, young ladies used to eat at home *before* they went out calling."

When you were a girl I bet you never lived in a sewer pipe. When you were a girl I bet you didn't sleep with a knife gripped in your hand.

Billy crammed another pikelet into his mouth and Grandma C laughed. "Such a healthy appetite, your adorable little brother. Her eyes glassed over and Emily reached a low hand across the table to snatch another pikelet from the plate.

"What the hell happened to your face?"

"Nothing," said Jai, pushing her hands away. Turning his head so she couldn't get a good look at his eye.

"Looks like you've been in a fight."

"I'm OK," he said, his voice raised. "'S nothing. Just some guys." He pushed the door of the boys' showers open, leaving Sheree alone in the waiting lounge, her heart thumping wildly. Would they let him into Blaxlands today with his face all cut like that? What if they were both turned away? Today was her last chance to get at the stormwater drain. She'd been back to Blaxlands once since her last Emily gig, just to the outside wall during daylight and it had been impossible to get too close. There were uniforms with dogs, and someone might have seen her casing the point where the storm water drain met with the wall.

She showered quickly, running over all the possibilities in her mind. Two more visits left on her card. Two more chances, unless . . . She'd never allowed herself to fantasize about the possibility of contract renewal. Seventeen was pretty much it as far as contract grandchildren went. Unless the old lady was particularly fond of you, but it was so hard to tell with Grandma C. She usually slept through half their visit, and only paid a vague kind of attention through the parts she was awake for. It was as though what she wanted them mostly for was background noise. The ambience of grandchildren with an occasional Hallmark moment thrown in here and there. Sometimes she took photographs. She always had cookies or cupcakes waiting. Always had something for Billy to play with, sitting there cross-legged on the plush woollen carpet.

Sheree sighed with relief when Jai emerged from the shower. His face wasn't too bad once the blood and dirt had been washed off.

"What you gonna tell her?" she asked.

Jai shrugged. "Fell off my bike?"

Sheree shook her head. "It's mostly bruising. What about a car accident?"

"Okay."

The uniform at reception frowned, but Sheree pulled Jai tight against her chest and started explaining all about the accident and how lucky they were that nobody got killed. The uniform knew they weren't really brother and sister, but Sheree went on and on about the crash, hoping in the end that it'd be too much trouble for the uniform to bother deviating from his regular schedule. The gambit worked. He eventually keyed them in and Emily and Billy walked across the grassy expanse to Grandma C's unit block.

"I owe ya one," he said, knowing full well that Emily and Billy were a package deal, and she'd have been knocked back too if he hadn't passed inspection.

Grandma C was devastated at the sight of Billy's face. The morning was lost in a blur of tears and hugs, special treats and righteous indignation. Billy took it all in his stride, and not for the first time Emily noted his enthusiasm for the role. If he played his cards right, Billy might see his contract through another seven years clear. There'd be options for him when Emily turned seventeen.

Grandma C was far too agitated for her regular nap. With all attention on Billy and his terrible ordeal, Emily wandered from room to room, checking out the ancient ornaments that adorned the old lady's shelves. Miniature replica Greek vases. A souvenir ashtray from Ana Capri. A plastic Eiffel tower. A blessed virgin entombed in a vial of holy water from Lourdes. The water had evaporated to the halfway mark, as it had in several snowdomes that had a shelf all to themselves. She wondered if she should offer to top them up from the kitchen tap, but decided she couldn't be bothered. Not today. Not when she had so much else to worry about.

Billy's voice emanated from the lounge, telling the car crash story over again from scratch. Once the tale had been decided upon, he hadn't wavered from the plot. He told it repeatedly with such precision and clarity that Emily herself was beginning to believe it actually happened. She didn't want to think about how the kid's face really got so messed up.

She was about to head to the balcony when something on the table in the spare room caught her eye. Grandma C didn't go in for smart paper. She preferred her magazines in real paper-and-print, yet there was clearly a glossy sitting on that table, activated, with pastel pinks and blues spilling across the page like butterflies.

Emily stepped cautiously into the room. She lifted the edge and dragged it closer. "Please don't be true," she whispered, heart pounding. "Please let it be something else."

But it wasn't something else. It was a brochure featuring smiling, laughing children grouped in twos and threes. Pretty mums with cherub babies cradled in pink bunny rugs. *Perfect Families* said the headline. Emily felt her eyes well up with tears.

There was no fanfare when you reached the end of your contract, Sheree knew that. You just clocked off at the end of the day and some fat prick in a uniform punched a code into his computer.

"Do me a favour," she said to Jai as they dried their hair.

"Sure," he said, nodding as if he'd actually taken time to consider it. Pretending he hadn't noticed how thin and haggard she was looking this month.

"Tell her you want the Play Doh Bake. Tell her you want to make soldiers."

Jai nodded. "Sure, whatever." He paused for a moment. "You're seventeen this week, yeah?"

"Yeah," she said. *Happy birthday to me.* She wanted to tell him about the gang that had commandeered her pipe. How they'd found her sleeping bag and lain in wait, hoping to catch her off guard. It was pure luck that she'd seen their silhouettes and shadows. Pure luck she'd been looking out across the skyline for the bats. They'd chased her but she made it made it to that broken part of the embankment where you could jump down onto the freeway. She caught her breath on the median strip with car horns blaring and drivers shouting abuse. The gang made fisting gestures but they didn't follow. Too many cameras. Too much trouble to be worth it. She'd been sleeping rough ever since. It was going to have to be the stormwater drain or nothing.

Grandma C had baked a cake with strawberry icing and sugar butterflies. Seventeen candles, all of them lit. Emily tuned out as Grandma C droned on about responsibility and challenges and hopes and dreams. Fought back tears as she blew out her candles. She nodded at Billy as she cut the cake.

"Grandma Crowthers, can I make Play Doh Bake soldiers today?"

"Of course you can, my poppet, of course you can."

The three of them ate their cake in silence, then Emily excused herself to visit the bathroom. On the way she slipped into the bedroom and removed the lock-up key from its regular place in the drawer. Back in the lounge room, she surreptitiously pressed impressions of both sides into a chunk of bright blue clay. She managed to turn the oven on and bake the chunk without Grandma C being any the wiser. If Billy worked out what she was doing, he gave no signs of noticing.

She returned the key to its proper place. "Billy, didn't you say you wanted to feed the swans?"

Grandma C smiled at Billy as though expecting his very first words.

"Sure," he said.

Emily grabbed the bag of bread crusts. She took him by the hand and led him out the front door and across the lawn to the little wooden bridge.

"Reckon she's watching?" he asked.

"I reckon she's picking out her new set of grandkids from the fucking brochure is what," said Emily. "Listen, we haven't got much time. Has anyone said anything about your contract?"

Billy shook his head.

"Then I guess you're OK to keep coming. Maybe she's just getting another one to replace me."

Three fat swans made a beeline for the bridge. Emily took a handful of crusts from the bag and scattered them haphazardly across the water.

"I'm sorry you're seventeen," said Billy.

"Yeah," said Emily, "Me too."

Back in the unit, Billy said he wanted to take his soldiers home, so Grandma C signed a chit for them, and for the birthday gift she gave Emily; a pink and gold enamelled bracelet. Sheree had pawned all of Grandma C's other birthday gifts over the years, through necessity rather than choice. Maybe she wouldn't have to sell this one. If things went right, maybe she'd be able to keep it.

When the goodbye hugs and tears were done, Emily and Billy walked back up to the gatehouse in silence. She took a full ten minutes in the shower—the longest time allowed—then studied her own reflection in the mirror as she dried her hair. How hard her stare had gotten over the past few weeks. How bitter the expression on her face. This is gonna work, she told herself. This has got to work.

They showed their chits, the Play Doh and the bracelet to the uniform, then Sheree held out her wrist for scan and deactivation.

"What the fuck?" said Jai as the uniform pulled his wrist down to the scanner too.

"Time's up, buddy," said the uniform, one hand resting handy to the gun on his belt.

"I'm not seventeen, she is!" he screamed.

The uniform shrugged. "Says here both Crowthers contracts checking out permanently. Sorry kid. Nothing I can do about it."

"I told you I saw those brochures," hissed Sheree.

Jai looked crestfallen. It was the first and only time Sheree had ever seen him playing anything but cool.

"You got somewhere to go?" she asked.

He nodded.

"You want me to walk you home?"

He shook his head.

He's just a little boy, she reminded herself. He's only ten years old. Been acting so tough all this time, but he's just a kid inside, same as me.

There was no one else waiting at the bus stop. Jai didn't say anything. He just kept staring at his shoes. If he was crying, he didn't want her to see.

"Jai," whispered Sheree. "Know why I made that Play Doh key impression?

He shook his head dejectedly, his pale face resting between his palms.

"Can you keep a secret? I mean *really* keep it? If I tell you, you can't tell anyone."

Jai shrugged, kicked at the pavement with his shoes.

"I reckon I can get back into Blaxlands through the stormwater drain. The cement's all cracked and busted up with weeds. No one's fixed it for ages. Reckon I could crawl through the mud and stuff and make it back inside." She placed her hand on Jai's. "Reckon I could make a place for myself in the old lady's lock-up. I could get food from the bins at night—they throw away a heap of decent stuff. Reckon I could live there till the old lady dies."

Jai stopped kicking the ground and looked up.

"You could come live with me if you want." Her heart thudded loudly inside her ribcage. "We'd be safe in there for ages."

Jai looked out across the bitumen as the bus approached, the noise of its engine drowning out the thudding in her chest.

"You're gonna live in there?" he said as they braced themselves against the sudden lurch of the vehicle's departure.

"Yeah," she said. "I am."

When they got to Central, Jai thrust his hands deep inside his bomber jacket pocket. He flicked the hair from his face and said "See ya round," and then he slunk away into the descending twilight.

Poor kid, she thought. Poor Billy. Poor Emily—only Emily's gonna do something to help herself.

There were plenty of all night kiosks on the Broadway strip. Places you could get a key made up, no question. She picked a place where no one knew her face, used the money she'd made at Blaxlands to buy herself a pair of sturdy docs and a torch. She could only risk catching a bus back out partway. After that, she'd have to get off and walk, but that was OK, she knew the way.

The night was still and clear, the skies devoid of bats and birds. She wasn't sure if that was a good sign or a bad one as she hung the key around her neck and tucked it inside her shirt.

The bus was half empty. No one gave her a second glance. Sheree walked for an hour along the road, keeping to the shadows of the trees when she had a choice. The walls of Blaxlands loomed like a castle fortress from a movie. She kept her cool, staying away from the electricity poles and the light, ducking under bushes to crouch when a car went past.

She found the place where the drain ended and the wall was cracked. The torch revealed a gap but it wasn't very big. She had to get down on her belly and wriggle like a lizard through the grass. The cement was rough and cold, wet and slimy in other places, but she pushed herself forwards, grabbing handfuls of smelly weeds to haul herself along. She grazed her hands but she didn't care. So long as her key was safe. So long as her torch didn't fail.

After what seemed like hours she made it through, staggering out of the stinking water into a patch of silver moonlight. Blaxlands lay before her like an enchanted kingdom. Sheree fell to her knees and kissed the grass. Already she felt safe. Just a little further to the lock-up and then she'd be able to rest.

At first the key stuck in the lock. He heart jumped, but it was just because the key was new. She forced it and it turned, and then she pushed her way inside, flicking on the switch to find everything just as it had been that day she had searched for the ballerina box.

First thing she did was strip off her sodden clothes and wrap herself in a big warm overcoat. Next she made herself a bed out of blankets and other coats as far away from the door as possible, behind the billiard table and its many boxes.

She forgot all about being hungry. Food could wait till later. Right now she was safe and warm and the happiest she had been in many years. Sheree switched off the light, crawled into her bed and slept for twelve safe hours straight.

It wasn't safe to leave the lock-up any time before darkness fell. She could handle being hungry but thirst was making her feel ill, otherwise she would have spent a second night in there, snug and safe. She crept to one of the garden taps to drink, then filled an old plastic kettle she'd found still in its box, undisturbed, it seemed, since the 1980s. The kitchen bins yielded a wealth of single serve snacks in protective plastic sachets. Not very hearty, but she'd lived on worse before.

Back in the lock-up, she thought about how she might arrange the space. Only the back section away from the door. An upended mattress shielded half the room from view. She would reinforce it, make it into more of a wall. There were bound to be other things in here that she could use. Old clothes, maybe. Books, most likely, too. She'd once liked reading, back before her mother died. Back before everything had got so hard.

The best thing about the lock-up was that she could go to sleep and not have to worry about anyone coming. Tomorrow night, she'd explore the laundry. If she had a nurse's uniform, or a groundsman's blue overalls, perhaps she could move about during the day? No one would notice her at all. She could talk to the swans and look for the deer. She could wave to the picnicking families and they'd wave right back, none the wiser.

Sheree awoke to the scraping of metal. Harsh clanging and a spotlight in her face. She'd been dreaming of flying into the light. First she thought she'd crashed, next she thought she was back in the pipes and a gang had flushed her out. But it was worse than that. Daylight flooded the lock-up as the roller door rattled open.

"No!" she screamed, "This can't be happening. This is my one safe place!"

Uniformed arms pulled her to her feet, cuffed her hands behind her back and dragged her into the harsh sunlight.

She'd had nothing on under her blankets, so they draped one of the coats across her shoulders for modesty's sake. The uniforms marched her to the security wing. They pushed her into a cell and a few hours later a slight woman in a nurse's uniform brought her some clothes to wear. The nurse didn't speak, but her face was etched with sympathy.

"I wasn't trying to steal stuff. I just wanted to be safe," Sheree blurted through the tears. "Must have been cameras in the drain. Must have been watching from the moment I came in," she repeated, over and over.

Later the nurse brought her sandwiches and sat with her while she ate them.

"What are they going to do with me? Are they gonna call the cops?"

"I'm sorry. I don't know," said the nurse. "You don't have anyone, do you?"

Sheree didn't answer. She ate her sandwiches and drank all the water. "Can you ask them for my bracelet back? The one Mrs

Crowthers gave me for my birthday. I didn't steal it. I had a chit for it—you can ask."

The nurse said she would ask, but Sheree never saw her again. Two security uniforms came soon after to take her away. They marched her across the manicured grass, past the little bridge where a white haired lady stood feeding swans, her grandchildren by her side. The lady held the bread bag open and the smallest child, a girl in frilly pink and yellow, grabbed clumsy handfuls and tossed them into the water.

As the swans rushed in to gobble the bread, Sheree thought the old lady looked a bit like Mrs Crowthers, and the boy looked a lot like Billy. It's not him, she told herself. Billy would never have sold me out. It's just another kid on a job. But as the kid, whoever he was, turned to watch, he tugged his cap to one side and smiled, staring indifferently as the uniforms dragged her away.

ALL THE LOVE IN THE WORLD

If only Jon hadn't been the one to find her, rostered on his sentry duty up high above the wire. If only he'd been out the back busting furniture for wood. I could have claimed she was a looter, shot her square between the eyes. Jeannie spoiled everything. Wormed her way into the Crescent, set her sights on kicking me from Jon's bed. Tricking them all with her innocence and sweetness. Fooling every one of them but me.

"Why can't they put her in with Brian and Joyce?"

"No room. They've got grandchildren in there."

And God knows what else. Brian used to be a bus driver, kept his yard so spick and span and a little dog too old to do much yapping. Next door to him was once a childcare centre. Now it was filled with Princes Highway refugees and all the tinned stuff we'd been able to scrounge.

Jon's and my place had four rooms. I put Jeannie out back where the telly used to be. Watched her waving cheerily at Darren and Julie, the nice couple over the side fence. She treated me with deference. Obeyed my rules. Respected my possessions, but we both knew it was only borrowed time. I observed her step-by-step ingratiation into our tight community, checking out one man after another, calculating which of them had what. Darren was handsome and closer to her age, but two little daughters bound him tight to Julie. All roads of logic and opportunity led to Jon, no matter how you did the maths. And besides, he was already smitten.

Jeannie volunteered for extra farming. Said she loved nature and watching things grow. Every spare patch of Crescent soil was put to vegetable production, Al Messina's roses the one exception. They'd been his pride and joy before. No one had the heart to pull them out. He grew his share of carrots where his front lawn used to be. Cabbages down the side passage. Avocado vines along the fence.

We were safe enough. Safe as anyone could be. Our Crescent home was blocked at either end, the creek behind our houses widened, banks fortified with razor wire and sacks of dirty sand. Across the road, a concrete sound barrier protected us from the highway, serving its duty as a battlement wall.

We had enough cans to get by for now. The future would be anybody's guess. Chris Cloakey's swimming pool was permanently half filled with scuzzy water. It rained a lot but we boiled it anyway. Used stormwater drain runoff for washing. It wouldn't take much to poison the lot of us.

Jon had been mine for ten whole months. I thought it was a blessing. That something as wonderful as love could bloom at the end of the world. He'd never have looked at me before the war. He stopped looking at me the day that bitch showed up, all big brown eyes and begging for something to eat.

He played guitar. Beatles and Pixies mixed with songs he wrote himself. We still ran stuff on batteries, clinging to the comfort of that electronic glow. Pointless, noisy shooting games. The real shooting had mostly passed us by.

Weekly meetings were all about our chickens and whether or not to dig up the bitumen road. We voted yes. More soil was needed for potatoes. There was talk of expanding the barricade up into St John's Road. That one got a yes vote too. The streets behind us had lain abandoned for months.

The couple on the corner's yard was still chocked with Christmas decorations. Giant reindeer and snowmen dioramas, shit that never made any sense in baking Australian Decembers. I said they ought to pull them down. That vote went against me. I said we didn't need reminding. They seemed to think it important not to forget.

◇◇

I lost Jon incrementally in stages of politeness. Humour was the first to go—our private little jokes. She ended up with everything: the sex, the love, the laughter. The laughter cut the most because it proved he didn't care. Jon became so formal in my presence. Straight up with necessary exchanges, like ones he had with neighbours either side. Conversations reduced to business transactions. *If I give you this, perhaps you'll give me that.* When I lost Jon I got nothing in exchange. Sympathy from others, not enough to make a stand.

He wrote songs for her. Cooked her special treats. Stole from my hidden stash of chocolate even though I never touched his private stuff. I overheard them whispering in the darkness.

"Jeannie, you brought the light back to my life."

Give me a break, you heartless bastard. Before she got here, you and me were fine. But you've forgotten all of that, just like you always traded up. I bought that he felt guilty he'd survived. Most folks 'round here did. I didn't.

So I endured their hush-hush tones, their giggles and their love. It was the love that killed me—if it had been just sex, I might have borne that well enough. But Jon truly loved her. He'd always been a princess chaser even in the days before. And Jeannie was a princess, albeit a barefoot one in ragged jeans.

People don't ask questions when they want something to be true. I never pondered the coincidences that drew Jon to my side. He never questioned his right to upgrade. Jeannie read the lot of us like books. Sized us up and took the things she wanted. I spared so little thought to all the lives we'd left behind us. All her thoughts were focused on the future.

But then my world ended a second time. Jon got cocky. He got lazy. When summer came around again, he skipped the usual precautions. Got sunburned and stung by insects when all those months before he'd been so careful. We'd both been careful in so many ways. The Crescent had a lot of things but it didn't have a doctor.

Three got sick after forage detail behind the Westfield mall. Each came down with typhoid—at least that's what it looked like. Temperatures soared in the 40s, stayed that way a week. Jeannie fussed and fretted. She soothed Jon's fevered brow, fed him aspirin, left poignant, wilted flowers by his pillow.

As weeks wore on, talk turned to the need for proper treatment. Who knew what horrors lurked beyond our barrier wall? Of course there would be corpses. Dead things that attracted flies. Busted sewer pipes, open latrines. One little insect had been all it took. And this was when our haven came undone. We were all good neighbours. Better than we'd ever been before. But would we risk our lives for one other? The answer, when it came to it, was no. Were there even any doctors out there? Rumour was all we had to go on.

I sat with Jeannie, by his side, watching her mop his sallow brow. Wishing she'd stop play acting the part, if only when we were alone.

"You never told us where you came from. Before," I added. For clarity.

"Sydney," she answered, not looking up. That girl rarely met my gaze.

"After Sydney. There's not much left of the place, or so I'm told."

She shrugged. "I travelled round. Same as everybody, I guess."

I'd painted my own delicious picture of her past. Sleeping her way into temporary shelters, getting cast out when she failed to pull her weight. In Crescent, she was always on hand to do the pretty jobs. I never saw her mucking out the chicken coops, digging toilets or burying the dead.

"He might die, you know."

"Don't be silly. He'll be right. Just needs a little time to sleep it off."

"And what if he's not?" I smirked. I couldn't help it. "Life might get much harder for you then."

I thought she was going to let it go. Pretend she hadn't heard, just like she pretended not to see me often enough. In my mind, I was already planning reclamation of the back room. I'd make it into a sitting area. Sew some cushions, bring out some of my books from under the house.

"I'm carrying his child," she said, so smug as she turned to face me. "Not a damn thing you can do about it, either."

And with her smile, my world disintegrated. Everything I'd come to fear was true.

"Bullshit," I said defensively. "Jon would have told me." But I knew he wouldn't, even if he'd known it to be fact. Maybe he didn't. Maybe it wasn't even true. Once I'd felt such pride in the bond I imagined between us. But there'd been no bond. Just a void so desperate to be filled.

"I'll be needing extra room when the baby comes. I'm thinking you can probably move out back."

And Jon slept on, oblivious, as clueless as the day he'd left my bed. She didn't care whether he lived or died. In a perfect world, he'd be lying awake now, listening to the honest truth unfold. His heart would swell to bursting with regret for me, the good woman he'd so carelessly discarded.

Jeannie sat cross-legged on the carpet. Leant back, stretched her legs out straight before her. Tuned out from my presence once she'd played her trump card. Pink toenails, crystal beads around her ankle, earrings sparkling in a shaft of bitter sunlight.

I watched her, knowing precisely what came next. Funny how these things work. How crazy they seem in the light of day, how wretchedly perverse. I left her with him, to her mopping and his slumber, said nothing when she wasted yet another votive candle set between a chipped glass dolphin ornament and one of Al Messina's precious roses, plucked.

I paced the length of the Crescent and back, watching Darren and Julie's girls raking fallen twigs and branches into piles. The street seemed strangely claustrophobic, houses packed too close together. They hadn't been before garages were tricked out into makeshift homes. Across the road, six caravans were parked permanently in shade. A cloudless sky made no promises of rain it couldn't keep. We'd been lucky with our water so far. I wondered how long our luck was going to last.

I saw two choices, each as clear as day. Let Jon die or fight to save his life. Don't think I didn't dwell on the former. There'd be some small satisfaction in it for all he'd put me through. But I loved him and love's a stubborn thing. How often it has its wicked way with us.

I told Darren and Julie I was going for antibiotics. Asked if they needed anything for the girls. Their neighbourly kindness had included not stating the obvious. Saying nothing when it was clear I'd been usurped.

"Some vitamins," said Julie. "But are you sure it's safe?"

Hell no—I'm sure I'm going to die.

"Head for town," said Darren. "Messina's picked up fresh chatter on the shortwave."

He presented me with a hunting knife, Julie shot me a worried stare, followed by three precious pots of honey. I was touched—

she'd been saving those for better days. And he knew full well he'd probably lose the knife. Good people, as I'd always said. It's not easy hiding two little girls from the world.

Crescent had no rules about leaving. None of us were beholden to the others. We'd thrown in our lot together because it worked. Because we were scared of what the world had become. We'd seen the cities burning before the news cut out, heard tales of roadside massacres, rape and pillage. Of poisoned water and blackened skies, most of it ninety Ks from where we lived. The south coast had its own problems. Its own resources too. Factions formed. Barricades went up.

I'd been amongst the Crescent's first, comprehending the necessity of animals and seed. In our semi-rural landscape, these weren't hard to come by. In all, we hadn't done half bad. We had enough so long as we didn't get complacent.

"If there's any help out there I'll do my best to find it."

That was all the promise I had to offer. A year ago, the streets had still been full of crazy. Guns firing, hoons doing burnouts, crashing cars. We took our stations along the barricade, silent sentinels against the darkness. But our nightmares failed to flesh to substance. Gradually the violence petered out, left us alone with our chickens and our terror.

Yet here I stood, about to leave it all behind. For what—the faded bloom of love? I'd go the back way over the creek to draw the least attention. Tell the lookout I was on the scrounge. All the nearby houses had been picked clean. Brian would presume I knew my stuff. I left him pulling handfuls of privet from the crumbling creek bank. His own yard had been spotless, even back before. Skipper lay snoozing in the shade. That lucky old dog was far too tough for eating.

And where would I be heading? Crown Street Mall as it had once been known. A corralled space for shoppers, free of cars. Fridays had once boasted a local produce market. In the 1800s it had been a cattle track. God knows what was being made of it now. The shortwave reckoned it was hosting a witches' market. Any medicine to be had would come from there.

What did I have to barter with? Honey and a knife. A tube of vegemite and the last of my precious chocolate. Better a pack of witches got those than the one who'd invaded my home.

I went back in for one last look at Jon lying in his fevered sleep. Stared at him so lovingly, Jeannie lost beyond my line of sight. The chiselled contours of his face. Tan skin that never seems to fade. God, how I love him. My heart aches with the weight of it. A burden I've carried across two lifetimes now.

◇◇

I remember how the city used to look before the war. I remember how I never used to look at it at all. Took it for granted, every curbed and guttered inch of it. Cocooned myself in the luxury of ignorance.

We'd been late teens, young and stupid, full of ourselves and naive insight. Five of us had shared that house, a crowded space, more than not, half filled with strangers, nights of wine and candlelit guitar. Pretty girls, dreadlocks and nose rings. Talk of Tibet where the air was clear, the people so humble and wise. Jon occupied a central space. Everything was more fun when he was around. Girls fell for him like dominoes. He'd have them, then move on to other things.

I wanted him, but *all* of him, not just the paltry crumbs on offer. I wanted his mind, his honesty, his trust. I wanted to stand amongst the handful he called friends. Poor Megan, dull and plain. Jon doesn't have female friends, don't you know?

I never fucked him back then, no matter how many times he tried it on. Not that I didn't want to—my God, it was all I wanted. But I'd seen what happened to all the girls who let him in. I wanted him to care for me. He rarely remembered their names.

I left that house after one particularly humiliating night. Didn't see the guy for twenty years. Fell in and out of love a dozen times. Couldn't bring myself to settle down. I often glimpsed him from the corner of my eye. Jon on the ferry, Jon amongst the theatre crowd. Jon asking an old friend how I was doing. Of course, he was never really there. Our old group disintegrated, as such groups are wont to do. Now and then I'd hear a whisper. He's done some acting. He's in a band. Of course he was—anywhere there'd be women to adore him. So many options before the world got scared.

What I didn't expect was to find him staggering down the Princes Highway, in shock, half naked with a fearsome case of burns. Had he been searching for me? I convinced myself he had. Fate or providence or perhaps some Act of God. Nowadays, I don't believe in any of those things. I'm back on the highway leaving my home behind.

I could almost pretend the war had never happened. For all I knew it hadn't—it's not like there was much to see. Radio silence. Television snow. Intermittent Internet for a month or two. Then Al Messina raised some chatter on the shortwave. We learnt about the witches' market and other groups like ours. After the initial exodus from Sydney, not much. The flotilla to New Zealand. Planes flying overhead. I often wonder how many of them made it. We had some trade with other friendlies, then that business with the gangs. Swore you'd never have got me off the Crescent after that. Six months of sporadic gunfire and ceaseless hungry dogs.

I kept my head down, hoed cabbages along the verge. Collected rainfall, boiled it fresh and clean. Thanked God for the fecundity of chickens and the fact we were the first to raid the Westfield ruins.

Truth is, the world has fallen silent. None of us know what's out there any more. Beyond the shortwave, the best we've got is Jeannie's stories. Quite frankly, I don't believe a word. That girl never suffered a day in her life. Never worked either—she's far too smart for that. Her sordid tales run like half remembered movie plots. Teenage novels. Television dreams.

Three roads lead me to the city centre. I pick the least convoluted route. Fewer opportunities for ambush—or so I hope.

I mount the hill that rises up behind the Crescent. So bare and naked with half the houses burnt. I hope the rain has washed away the details. I don't want to know what happened here.

I'm scared for Jon and I'm scared for me. Knife gripped tightly in my hand, eyes scanning left and right for movement. But there's nothing. Where did everybody go? There were people up here not that long ago.

The tar is cracked, strewn with leaves and broken branches. I make a note to tell the others—all this excellent firewood. *When I get back* . . . I put one foot before the other. *When I get back* covers so many things.

Down the dip and up the second hill. I'm too far gone now. Out of safety's reach. Now might be the time for feeling lucky. I'm not falling for it. Too many movie moments crammed inside my mind. My heart sinks when I spot the barricade. It looks abandoned but

I'm going to play it safe. Find another way to join the main road. Dogleg down around the kindergarten, a steep decline to where the station used to be.

I move quickly, no time for indecision. If I stop too long to think I might change my mind. Take fright and run back home to Jon and Jeannie. But how would I ever live with myself if he died?

There's something moving around inside the kindy. I hope its only possums and jog quietly down the hill. The train tracks would be quickest but there's so much room for ambush. No. I'll take my chances on the road.

A row of garbage bins still standing, their plastic wheels choked thick with weeds. A lone ibis prowls the pavement. Keeps its distance. Checks me out.

Ugly white and purple agapantha flowers have claimed these ruined suburbs as their own. Bowing sagely in the breeze acknowledging my predicament.

I hear the rumble, spin around but it's too late. A gang is bearing down upon me. Rollerblades with helmets, weapons raised. I can't outrun them. There's nowhere to hide. I'm stunned like a rodent caught in headlights, the sound of their wheels thunder like a road train.

So I drop to my knees, cover my head, kiss the tar goodbye. The road shakes so hard it might swallow me up. Yet it doesn't. I wait for pain that isn't going to come. They have passed me. They didn't even stop. Skated around my whimpering form, like I was a pothole or a log.

I sit in the road for ages chewing my fingernails. *The world has ended, right? There really was a war?* Because some times I can't be sure, and this is one of them. Skating the post-apocalypse simply never occurred to me.

I wish Jon was here. It'd have made him laugh. But he wasn't laughing, was he? He was dying.

Dusting off my faded jeans, I put the knife back in my hand. Scan first the empty gardens, then the train tracks for . . . whatever. Continue my trek into city central, sticking to the cyclone fence this time. Figuring I'd be able to see anyone approaching from the tracks.

Other people have the same idea. We maintain a respectable distance. I long to ask all the usual questions. Who are you? How well are you surviving? But I don't. I keep on walking, eyes firmly fixed upon the prize.

Some are ragged, others dress like joggers, pre-apocalypse. Shamed, I put my knife away. No one else is wielding weapons, although several walk with staffs. I keep my distance, shun eye contact, yet all the while I'm filled with wonder. Something's going on here. Something strange.

Garbage blows down Keira Street. I try to picture what the shopfronts once contained. They've all been looted, the glass smashed long ago. That fact aside, the structures seem in place. At the end of the street, a paved and shaded plaza. The centre of town as much as it ever was. The stage still stands, once the domain of fashion promotions and teenage beauty pageants. Today it's filled with jamming musicians: guitars, flutes and clarinets. A sax to the side. Two dreadlocked girls with bongo drums. People join or leave as they see fit. The sound they make is surprisingly melodic.

At the foot of the stage little children sit in groups. Children in the open. Unprotected! I stare at them as though they're apparitions. Surely no parent would take such a risk. Am I the only one who understands?

I feel invisible as I move amongst the crowd. And it is a crowd— the largest I've seen for years.

They're garbed in many colours, a hodge-podge of pre-war fashion trends. Some clearly enjoy the art of it. Diamonds over khaki camouflage, suits and swimwear mixed. Definitely something Caribbean going on with hair. And makeup. Too many clown eyes for my liking. Some look like they've been living in pajamas for eons.

Vendors hoist wares up high on sticks. Clothing, paperbacks, tools. Others seem to be selling potions. Pharmaceuticals mixed with other things. Or maybe it's all just lolly water. How am I ever supposed to tell? I need a doctor, a pharmacist, a nurse. None of this lot looks to fit the bill.

"What have you got for typhoid?" I shout up at one of them. Up because he was wearing stilts to make his presence felt.

"Sounds serious," he says as he rummages in coat pockets. Draws something out for me to see. "Take three spoonfuls and call me in the morning." He laughs like an ocker Baron Samedi.

"You've got to be shitting me." The stuff he's selling looks suspiciously like Vegemite. He's not getting my honey or chocolate in trade for that. I push on past. There's plenty more clowns where he came from. Plenty more of everything except what Jon needs.

A blanket spread with children's toys brings me back into the moment. Little plastic action figures from shows no one will ever see again. More traditional items. Plushie animals. Coloured blocks. *Jeannie and his baby.* I keep walking.

Further down the mall I see more serious types of shopping. Bearded men in greatcoats, hunting rifles unconcealed. Smoked meat strung across a doorway. What kind is anybody's guess.

And, inevitably, arguments. Squabbles over details of exchange. But I don't see a single fight. Impressive in itself.

The wafting tempt of ganja. Two scruff-haired teenagers, both stoned. No one has bothered to tell them the world has ended. Like it makes the slightest bit of difference.

And then, finally, a group of women cooking pancakes on a skillet, looking like they might have stepped out from a Sunday bingo hall.

"I need medicine. Real medicine," I tell them, crouching. "Know anyone who can help?"

"Not 'round here," says one of them, dusting sugar. "Feeling poorly are we, love?"

I tell them about Jon and the other two sick neighbours, omitting all mention of Jeannie and other things.

"You want a dispensary," says the one who still sports relatively suburban hair. "Last one left's at Corrimal Surf Club. The bike track's your best bet."

They give me a pancake. That was nice of them. I remember that bike track since back before the war. A haven for muggers and rapists, even then.

When night falls, things begin to change. I realise I'm no longer safe. Daylight was such a civilising factor. I look for the pancake women but they're gone, back to their fortified bingo hall, or wherever. I curse myself for being stupid. For taking my eye off the ball. Would the beach be safe? Would anywhere? All I know is that I can't stay here.

The music has gotten heavier, skaters on battered boards muscle in as people drift off into twilight groups of two and three. This is tribal country and I do not belong. I grip my knife, certain I'll have to use it. Knowing I'll be lost if I even try.

That's when the fear starts working me over. How did everything fall so quickly into ruin? I'd had a life, a man, a home, then *she* walks in and all of it is lost. Suddenly I'm walking down a darkened street with a knife, praying I won't be killed while she lies safe and warm in what used to be my bed. And he lies dying. Not if I can help it. That's the thought that spurs me on my way.

Just you try and take him away from me . . . That's what I'm thinking as I pass a group of three. They eye me with great interest. My scowl seems to put them off. I don't know why—they could take me down in seconds. But they don't so I keep moving. I hear the beach about a block before I see it. The stadium sulks alone in shadow. Without power, it might as well be a rock.

The beach is a fairyland of bonfires and flaming torches. Squeals of laughter, screams of something else, all mixed and mashed together. Behind the fire, the pounding of the waves. I'm not going near it. I can reach the bike track overland.

Abandoned apartment blocks stand guard along the coast road, the cafés looted long ago for foodstuffs. Now and then I pass a solitary traveller. No one makes eye contact. Maybe they're all like me? Cast out from their homes and hearths, fugitives from everything that's sane. Women and men whose tribes no longer want them. Can they smell my fear like I can smell my own?

I spend the night in the ruins of a looted boutique. Torn curtains stained with oil provide a bed. I sleep with the knife. I don't sleep, mostly. Maybe drift for a couple of dreamless hours.

Morning light brings with it inspiration. I can do this thing and be home within a day. I realise I've been selfish. It's about Jon, after all. The man is dying, yet all I think about is me. And Jeannie, of course. That bitch is never out of my mind. I'll bet she never spares a thought for me. She's already scored her trophy, especially if she's really pregnant.

Three people die if you don't make it. Four. I forgot to count myself. So I steal through the urban undergrowth, eyes alert for ambush.

The beach is strewn with bodies. Hard to tell if they're sleeping or if they're dead. Huddled clusters of folks who might be families. It's ages until I get why no one's bothering me. I look fucking dangerous. I have murder in my eyes. Wielding my knife as though I know how to use it. I smile when I realise this is Jeannie's legacy. I don't even look like a woman anymore.

But the old bike track looks dangerous too. Am I any kind of match for it? One little knife against the ruins of civilisation. Doesn't matter. I'm not going back without those drugs.

A stiff breeze rips along the headland, tousling long ribbons of grass. It's beautiful, the view, stretching all the way past three beached cargo ships and out to sea. A thousand countries I'll never get to visit. Nameless strangers speaking in foreign tongues. The brisk sky streaked so innocently with clouds. Like nothing ever happened. Like the world was always this way.

A string of people walking single file. They look harmless so I put my knife away. We nod at each other, pass politely. Women mostly, two small children in the middle.

Will Jon and Jeannie expect me to care for their baby? Am I supposed to be its aunt? A domestic helper. An aging au pair. Not fucking likely, I declare.

I stomp on fallen branches, kick stones out of my way. Space is at a premium on Crescent. No spare rooms, garages or empty caravans. If I throw them out, there's nowhere else to stay. Two days ago, that house had still been mine. My choice to leave has tipped the power balance. When I get home they'll make me take the room out back. I'll bet the bitch has moved my stuff already.

And then, way out to sea, I glimpse something wonderful. A whale spout. No. Wait—two! A big one and a little one. I stop to shield my eyes. Whales had long been choosing to swim this coast, but in all my years down here I'd never seen one. Probably because I'd never stopped to look.

I walk on, steeling myself for the inevitable. *They've become a family. Rules of ownership have changed. What you have to offer is what counts.* I try not to think about Jon and Jeannie. The track is strewn with garbage, picnic tables overturned.

Treetops pulse with the hum of cicadas, brown abandoned husks litter the ground. Weeds already choke their way through fences. Another year or two and this path will be gone.

◇◇

The sight of Corrimal Surf Club is welcome, as is the orderly queue snaking along the sandy path. I claim a sunbleached plastic seat beneath a vague attempt at shade. The woman beside me nurses a broken arm.

"Fell off me roof," she says before I've even asked. She doesn't look too worried. If it had been me, I'd have been in a panicked state. Broken bones, infected gums. Appendicitis. All these things can kill us. Not to mention all those things we haven't thought of.

The guy in charge is clean and that speaks for something. He might have been a doctor once, although he looks a little young. Others mill around the red brick structure—whether they're doctors or nurses too or just people embracing newfound purpose, I can't say.

I turn my chair to face the ocean, surprised to see it packed with bobbing heads. A moment of panic until I get the picture.

"They're surfing!" I announce to the woman with the broken arm.

I might as well have said the sky was blue. Life goes on and life for them is surfing. Always was down Corrimal way. It makes more sense than many things I've seen. I mean, why not surf just because the world has gone? Why not skate or rollerblade? Play guitar or bongo drums. Am I the only one who doesn't get it? Me with that knife pressed so hard against my heart.

Where are the roving bands of cannibals? The *Mad Max* cars and displays of outlandish human cruelty?

"Am I missing something?" I ask the woman. She didn't hear me. Probably just as well.

"I'm Daniel," says the doctor, wiping his hands on his pants before offering to shake mine. "Got a problem?"

"Sure. The world ended—only nobody seems to have noticed," I answer dryly.

He smiles. "Some days it seems like that. Other days . . . " He glances across to an area near the treeline. Once again, it takes awhile for me to get it. Row after row of human-shaped dirt mounds. So people have died here after all.

I tell him of Jon's symptoms: the fever, shits and rash. "Three of them have it," I add, almost an afterthought. Everything's not about Jon, I remind myself. Only, it is. My entire world.

"Might be typhoid fever," says the doctor. "They keeping fluids up? Got some Amoxicillin left, that's all."

When we go inside he rummages through shelving that had likely once held books. The red brick walls feature sporting plaques and trophies, most to do with surfing.

"Nosebleeds?"

I nod.

"Gut ache?"

"That too." *And hey, how about some cyanide to take care of my domestic issues . . .*

"The bus goes back tomorrow. Do you think you could lend a hand?" His voice trails off. Something boring about boxes and shovels.

"The what, excuse me?"

"To leave now means you'd have to walk. But I could really use some help with stocktake."

He's talking about a fucking bus that travels into town along the road!

"Only once a month," he says. "You're lucky you turned up when you did."

And in that instant I have a vision of the future. The bus a hundred years from now, hitched behind two horses, dragged on patched up rubber tires. Making its gentle rounds of a district choked by weeds.

"I can stay," I tell him, fascinated.

Turns out three of them in the surf club had been doctors. Mad keen surfers too which is probably why they stayed. We lie on lounges drinking beer kept chill in tidal pools. Way past expiry date like anyone cares.

Sharon and Brianna, the other two, catch waves until the sun goes down. I tell Daniel everything from both before and after. He nods knowingly when I get to Jeannie. I find myself wishing she'd wound up here with him.

"You did the right thing. What else could you do?"

"He might be dying while I'm lying here drinking your beer."

Doctor Daniel shakes his head. "Unlikely," is his prognosis. "Unless I'm wrong," he adds as afterthought.

All of this is wrong, and I don't know what to make of it. We drink beer long into the twilight. We think we see the whales again just as the sun is setting. A mother and baby cavorting off the rocks. But Daniel's not sure. As he's fond of saying, those whales might turn out to be something else.

◇◇

Brian is on lookout when I make it back to Crescent. "Where the bloody hell have you been," he sings down from the treetop, hunting rifle slung across his back.

"Shopping," I tell him, holding up bright blue boxes of Amoxicillin.

He slaps the air, exaggerated, lets me through.

The Crescent seems much smaller than it was before I left it. Work has begun on pickaxing up the tar. I catch a few hullos as I wander down the road. Strange, as though I'd just popped up to the corner shop for milk. Was it merely two and a bit years past we were doing such mundane things? Only a week since I'd gone out for the drugs? The sound of my own footfall troubles me. I walk like a gunslinger marking out new territory.

What was I expecting? Children running out into the street? Kind-faced mammas with hair tied back in scarves? Is Jon dead or does he live? In a couple of minutes I'm going to know for sure. Those minutes lengthen as I stride across the yard. Slip through the side entrance, heart thumping. I pause in the hallway, relief flushing my skin like heat rash. There's a gentle strumming of guitar out back. A style I'd recognise anytime and any place. Jon once told me he played every day for thirty years. So he wasn't dead of typhoid after all.

I close my eyes. The music's beautiful. He's beautiful, even with the radiation scars. We had our moments. Times when I was the happiest woman alive. Days I wished the dream would never end.

I sneak into the kitchen, glad to find it empty. They're both outback, Darren and Julie too. Jeannie's fussing over one of the children, hoisting her up and down to make her squeal. She throws a pretty smile at Darren. Julie catches it from the corner of her eye. I watch through the window as she calls instructions to her daughters, makes some small excuse to sit beside him. The look upon her face is one I recognise. In the mirror, oh so many times.

Jon strums *Blackbird*. He always played a lot of Beatles. In the horse-drawn world of a hundred years, such songs will belong to no one. I always loved to hear him play. To watch him too—those sinewy brown arms.

I place the Amoxicillin upon the bench. Sneak into the bedroom, surprised to see my things have not been moved. I pack quickly, ears straining for the screen door sliding open but all I hear is Lennon and McCartney.

My rucksack bulges with useful items. Very few keepsakes. Not much left worth keeping. All my favourite t-shirts. Swimmers, sunglasses, blue jeans. The gold heart locket left to me by Grandma.

I don't leave a note.

Outside, wind tears through the treetops, sets the telegraph wires to rippling. Unseen cockatoos screech their discontent. Skipper cocks his leg against a cabbage row as Brian stabs at the furrowed earth with a pitchfork.

"Where're you awf to now then, luv?" he says, resting the pitchfork, gesturing to my pack with his free hand.

"More shopping," I tell him.

We used to have the exact same conversations, only back then he'd been fussing over flowers in his own front yard. Post-apocalypse has slowed his state of mind, but it seems like not much else had changed for him. Brian is already living in the horse drawn future. I bet he misses television, that's all.

"Aww, you bloody women," he says, grinning with ancient crooked teeth.

A cockatoo swoops between us. I shade my eyes against the sun, follow it back to its branch.

"Regards to Joyce," I call out, acknowledge a wave in trade. This time, I walk the length of the Crescent, clamber over the stacked car barricade. Stand for a moment to stare back along the street, then beyond to Mount Keira in the distance. Wind tugs dramatically at my hair. In front of Al Messina's roses, three small girls play cricket. A fourth child sucks its thumb and stares.

The last I ever see of any of them.

DEAD LOW

They were seven all up if you counted the pilot—and Clancy always did. Qamar had the smarts to demand a fee in lieu of a share of the plunder. Smarts enough to get paid regardless. He never went in but he'd always got them out. More than once by the skin of their back teeth. He cut things close but close was good enough for Clancy. She wouldn't have swapped him for all the jewels on Europa.

The Sargasso Drift was not for the faint hearted. Not for greenhorns either. She knew she should have left the kid at base. Konte was excited for all the wrong reasons. Busting out and itching for a fight. Trouble was the last thing Clancy needed. The Sargasso Drift was trouble enough on its own.

"Looks like an elephants' graveyard," said Kyah, picking at her fingernails as Clancy enhanced the view. Before them, a sea of debris meshed with frozen rocks. Shattered hulls slept nestled amongst them, their once shiny surfaces pockmarked by centuries of micro impacts. Booster cylinders, photon drives, modular components battered into new and unrecognisable shapes. All jammed together to form a large amorphous mass, like a cancer or a blood clot. And something else; a substance registering as a brown-grey shadow that looked as though it should have been rock, but wasn't.

"This here's what you call a dead low," Clancy explained. "Everything adrift in this part of the system ends up here sooner or later."

Corvettes, cutters, blockade runners, battle cruisers, satellites, zips and flails, and all the other junk detritus illegally dumped from freighters.

"Elephant?" asked Konte, the kid in battle fatigues so new, the fabric was still stiff and shiny.

"An ancient kind of ship," said Pace. "Freighter. Pre-Empire. Reckon this is where the Horgis generals sent their ships to die."

"No way!" said the kid, his eyes as wide as saucers. He turned to Clancy. "Can't we get in closer?"

"Not until we have to." The grim tone to Clancy's voice gave them all an early warning. All except the kid, of course, this being his first time out. Nobody wanted him along for the ride. Virgin heroes were generally the first to fall, usually dragging some other poor bastard down with them.

"First in, first serve for salvage rights," said Kyah. Her hands were trembling, which meant she was on the juice again. Not good.

"Hon, we're far from being the first. A good many of those shattered hulls belonged to salvage crews."

"Not good ones, though. If they were good, they would never have bought it so easy."

Clancy decided to let it go. Regret was already gnawing at her edges. The lies it had taken to get them all this far. After all, the ship belonged to Pace. His ship, Barbuda's map, but the heartache was hers and hers alone. If she was wrong then none of it was going to matter.

"So what does the scan say?"

DeVere was already on it. "Highly mineralised," he offered.

"Tell me something I don't already know."

"Can't null it out," he added. "Too much interference. Iron's blocking out the good stuff."

"Recalibrate the search coil," Clancy suggested. "Qamar, can you nudge us in closer?"

"I'm picking up life signs. At least I think that's what they are."

Clancy shook her head. "You won't be able to get a clear screen or field. What you're reading is the driftweed. Enough of it to fool anything we've got."

"You telling me that brown shit is alive?"

She shrugged. "Technically speaking, it's classed as war surplus."

"Which war?"

"One of the bad ones."

DeVere was nodding. "I know all about that stuff. Sucks its warmth from out of the UV spectrum. Stinks up an airlock— nothing like it grows back home

"Don't forget poisonous. Remember Six-oh-Six?"

"Station that choked on their own emissions." DeVere nodded grimly. "CO_2 scrubbers choked with weed, caked like plaque around the ventilators. Everyone dead in a couple of hours. Nobody even knew it was there until it killed em."

"Boost the discriminator," said Clancy. "Take us as close as you dare." She stepped back from the control screen and motioned for the kid to follow.

"So you're Padraeus's nephew," she said when they were out of earshot of the others. "When you get back, tell your uncle he owes me big time."

"He told me you had history. He told me lots of things"

A severe glance from Clancy encouraged the kid to change his tune. "I won't let you down. I'll be careful. You'll see—"

"What I don't want to see is any of these expensive professionals on the slab." She stared at him hard enough to knock the glib bravado from his face. "Throw your own life away in a fit of reckless heroism, I really don't give a shit. But I need the others. All of them. Catch my drift?"

He nodded and was silent after that. Good, thought Clancy. His youthful enthusiasm had been ragging on her nerves for hours.

They all said she was crazy but Captain Clancy didn't give a damn. They also said a lot of other things. Called Barbuda a pirate king, a despot and a crazy. Most of what was said of him was lies. There were truths in there, buried deep, as truths so often tend to be. It wasn't her job to sort them out for others. Clancy's brief was to find proof of his death. There were worse things out Sargasso way than dying.

Clancy didn't trust her crew. What she did trust was their greed. Only the greedy ever chanced Sargasso. Barbuda had been greedy. Fortune hunting laced his veins like venom. But there'd been other sides to him. Their time together hadn't all been flame and heartache.

Harker's Binnacle had been the lure—and might still be for all she knew. If anyone had actually found the thing, she'd have heard about it. What it was, now that was an interesting question. Some labelled the Binnacle a quantum impulse drive, others the well of souls. Still others referred to it a crucible spike.

Whatever the fuck it was, she didn't want it. All she wanted was her husband's bones. Just to be certain, certainty being the one true thing money couldn't buy.

"So one of those ships is a treasure barge?"

The kid again. She'd completely forgotten he was standing there waiting for fresh instructions.

"Diamonds the size of your head," she told him. "Treasure from a hundred thousand courts. Centuries of it, smashed against the frozen rocks. Dragged here by the power of Dead Low. The Horgis generals built their palaces from gold bricks. When the war was over, barely a third were recovered."

Konte nodded, his own eyes sparkling like gemstones. "So when do we get to go in there?"

She slapped her comm. "Qamar? What's the story?"

"Suit up, Captain. You're on."

"Now," she told him, "providing you think you're ready."

"I'm ready," said Konte. "I was born ready."

She rolled her eyes. The rest of them were already kitted, places taken inside the airlock chute.

"Docking," said Qamar. "Give it fifteen, then all clear."

"In your hands," she told him, "same as always."

"I'm getting a flicker. Something . . . " DeVere slapped the mobile tracker with the palm of his hand.

"It's the weed. I'm telling ya. Just the weed."

"The signal came from inside, not from outside."

"Weed," said Amaranta. "You're forgetting six-oh-six."

"Grav's still on. Be grateful for small mercies."

"What the F—now it's lit up like a nova cluster." DeVere glanced up quickly, then over his shoulder.

"Ghosts," said Clancy. "Nothing to worry about."

"You seem mighty certain of the fact."

"D'ya think I'd actually be standing here if I wasn't?"

"Quit your bitching," ordered Clancy. "We don't have much time. We get in, get rich, then get out fast as lightning."

They travelled the rest of the corridor in silence, the occasional outburst from the tracker the only sound other than their own heavy breathing and footsteps.

Pace clutched his pulse rifle close to his chest as they cautiously rounded the corner. Nothing was waiting but a wide, open space, its ceiling spilling weak illumination.

Clancy stopped suddenly and removed her helmet. "Cyclers are still ticking," she said, taking a deep breath. "The air is old and stale, that's all. Probably nobody's breathed it for a century."

"What was this ship?"

"Imperial yacht, 44th dynasty," chimed in Konte. "Red and gold were their colours, dated to the time of exodus." He gestured ahead to the farthest wall, which was not a wall at all but a massive tapestry. It featured a crest flanked by a couple of mythological beasts. The lower half was ragged and rotten, stained with something that might have once been blood.

"Something's been making a meal of this wool," offered Kyah, who had gone up close to poke at the thing with her gun.

"Dustbugs and weevils. Rugrust, maybe coppermould."

"Not unless those bugs you said got teeth."

She inserted her rifle through a hole, then ripped. "Something's definitely been chewing on this."

"Hey—that's a historical artefact!" said Konte.

"It's a piece of junk is what it is."

The kid looked crushed.

"Come on," said Clancy. "Don't forget we're on the clock."

"What are we looking for exactly?" said Konte.

"Same as usual," said Pace.

And you can just go right on thinking that, thought Clancy, although she did agree on one important point. If there was treasure here, finding it would keep everybody happy—and distracted, at least for awhile.

The imperial yacht had been splendid once, whatever its provenance. Built in a time when no effort was spared on ridiculous decoration. Slaves had probably constructed the hull as well as upholstering the innards. A brothel, perhaps, or a gambling barge, or maybe something stranger.

"So what about all that gold showing up on the 'scope? I'm not seeing anything but mouldy curtains." Impatience laced

Amaranta's voice. She'd been on this detail before. A different ship, the same old story. Half the leads they tried were always duds, no matter what the scanners had to say.

"Tapestries," said Konte. "They're not curtains, they're—"

"Whatever. Maybe we could strip the core? Might be parts worth salvaging in there."

"No time," said Clancy. "You're forgetting about the weed."

"Right," said Amaranta with much uncertainty.

DeVere cut in. "Something moving on the—"

The thing struck out of nowhere, lightning fast with grasping metal hands. Pace was faster. He let it have a starburst in the chest. Centre of mass. Old school reflexes. This wasn't the first time they'd saved his life and hopefully wouldn't be the last.

The attacker went flying but it didn't fall. Just stood there humming and rattling its shiny bones.

"What the fuck is that?" said DeVere, barely managing to get the words out before it lunged at them a second time.

Clancy drew her blaster and disintegrated its head. What was left of it fell back convulsing on the floor. Pace and Amaranta stood alert for others like it. Pace walked over and gave it a surly kick.

"A soldier I think. Looks like standard issue."

"Not according to this."

DeVere held the tracker for them all to see. "The damn thing's blinking life signs."

"Show me that," said Clancy.

The others stood back to give her room. She glared at the screen, frowned, then dropped to her knees, checking over the twitching apparatus in search of . . . none of them were game to ask.

"It's dead."

It, not he or she.

"No blasting anything else without my say so. There might well be survivors here."

"Survivors of what? The Horgis war was a century ago."

"I said no shooting. Get it?"

They all indicated that they did, DeVere and Amaranta subvocalising private chitchat as they continued down corridors, everyone but the kid dropping well back from Clancy's line of sight. All wondering, not for the first time, what the hell they were really doing here. Clancy's reputation raised occasional red flags. A couple of expunged adventures she shrugged off blithely as 'R&R'.

The kid could barely contain his excitement. The thing still twitched as he recorded it from every angle. "See the legs? They're definitely off a KLAN-DY model but the torso—that's from something else entirely. Not military issue. Never seen one like it. Probably Boehm-Glauss catalogue from—"

"Will you shut the fuck up please?" Clancy stared him down incredulously. "There might be more of them. They might be trying to kill us. Jesus, Padraeus's gonna owe me big time for this."

Room after room after musty room. Most had been stripped bare. Others piled high with what looked like barricades or, ridiculously, part of a hand built maze.

They'd been sticking together since the thing had lurched at them, but all the empty rooms that followed was leading the salvage team to relax its guard.

"I'm getting a signal," said DeVere.

"Gold? Tell me it's gold."

"Yeah, Amma, the tone says you might be right." The blip hiccoughed and he slapped the wristpad with agitation. "I can't get a clean feed. Something in this shithole's blocking the signal."

The commlink crackled, rendering Qamar's voice in jagged spits. "Weed's on the move, boss," he said in a cool, calm voice that betrayed no hint of panic. Another of the reasons Captain Clancy always hired him.

"How long have we got?" she asked.

"Couple hours, maybe. One to be safe. For certain no more than two."

"Keep your eyes open," she said back at him.

"Always do, boss. Always do."

"We split up," said Clancy. "Three teams, three directions. It's the only way."

"Are you fucking crazy?"

"Yes. Why do you ask? Kyah and Pace. Amma and DeVere. Thirty minutes max. Just like old times, yeah?"

They didn't hang around to quibble. If they didn't find the gold in thirty, they'd have nothing to show for the expedition at all. And I'll have no way to pay Qamar, thought Clancy. Not a thought she wanted in her head. Pilots had stranded welching captains on asteroids for less. Hopefully it wouldn't come to that.

Konte stuck close to Clancy, a gesture enforcing his greenhorn status in the others' eyes. Only a newb would consider it safer with her.

He cleared his throat. "That thing back there. You reckon it was really a soldier?"

"Damn straight," she said, her mind on other matters. An absence of life sign readings before the fact being one. The kid was getting on her wick, tailing her like a lovesick pup. One more of many things she didn't need.

"Whatever Padraeus told you about the salvage life, it's bullshit, pure and utter. You think I'm joking? Not a lot of jokes in this line of work."

"I'm not in it for the money."

"Really? That makes it worse. Much worse. What the hell are you looking for out here, then?"

The empty rooms were a worrying thing. Someone had been here before them. But if that was true, where were the tags? The obligatory territory markers of their profession.

Konte cleared his throat. She noticed the way he was gripping his pulse rifle. Far too tight. The damn thing was likely to go off in his hands.

"I was hoping I could ask you something . . . "

"Sure kid—fire away. Only cos you're Padraeus's nephew. Everyone else knows they're not supposed to ask."

Because there was only one thing he could possibly be asking. The same thing everyone always wanted to know.

"Uncle Padraeus said you were hooked up with Captain Barbuda back in the day."

"If by hooked up, you mean he was my husband, yes."

"Your husband?"

"No need to sound so surprised, kid. People get married for lots of damnfool reasons. Even pirate kings."

That shut him up for a while, just like she knew it would. They always shut up when she used the H word. It made their relationship sound almost respectable as, of course, it had been. One of the better choices she'd ever made. If only fate's black hand hadn't intervened.

Another corridor and another room, both filled with an absence of treasure. DeVere was still slapping the scanner to kingdom come, which could only mean the weed was getting closer. Time was ticking, seconds dragging into minutes. Their first hour couldn't be very far off from up.

Konte crept a little closer. "So how exactly did he die?"

"Captain Barbuda? He didn't."

Silence followed, just like it always did. "But the funeral was broadcast on the wire, pictures beamed to fifty million screens. Yeah, there was a funeral. Doesn't mean Barbuda was in the coffin."

She realised she'd been ranting out loud when the kid let out an embarrassed "Oh."

"No one ever proved nothing," she continued. "The corpse inside that coffin wasn't his. And wouldn't you have thought I could have told the difference? Those DNA scrapes were fake. They can fake anything, kid. Nothing is proof of anything. They can do whatever the fuck they like . . . "

He stared at her, lips pressed together, gun clamped tight against his chest.

"No need to panic, kid. I know what they say about me."

"They?"

"Everybody, pretty much—including your blessed uncle Padraeus. They think I'm crazy, combing the Sargasso Drift for clues. Signing up every hot shot get-rich-quick jockey with stars in their eyes and meteors in their heads."

"I don't think you're crazy." The kid smiled weakly, shooting her the kind of smile that should have been reserved for younger women.

"You will, eventually, kid. Trust me. You will."

The next turn brought something completely unexpected. A solid wall reaching almost ceiling height made of cobbled together bits of junk. Antique furniture, hydraulic jacks, gutted consoles, other items of doubtful and dubious provenance.

Clancy slapped her comm to life. "Pace, are you getting this? Looks much like a barricade to me."

"Man, that's crazy stuff. Watch your arse," he added, his voice crackling with interference.

"Barricade against what?" said Konte, his arms resting passively on his gun.

"Stay alert!" she barked. "Keep your finger on the trigger."

It was hard to tell in the dim light, but she thought she saw his face flush with embarrassment. Not that she could see much through the visor. "And stay behind me. Last thing I need is you getting shot and Padraeus screaming blue bloody vengeance on my tail."

He clutched his rifle and nodded vigorously.

"Talk to me, Qamar. Anything moving around in here I oughta know about?"

"Nothing, boss. Just three teams on foot exactly where you all should be. Sargasso Drift's another matter. That weed is definitely on the move. I've cranked the dampers but the heat's still bleeding. Pretty sure it's what attracts it. I might have over-estimated—"

Crackle and hiss cut the last of his words in two. Clancy held her breath until his voice returned.

"—ty-five minutes, maybe. Whatever you're doing, you'd better make it snappy."

"Y'all hear that?" Clancy shouted into the ether.

Each responded with their regular comeback.

"Come on, then. You heard the man. Never argue with a pilot, I say. I'd feel a lot safer if the damn internal sensors weren't all on the fritz. Hey—what the—"

The kid's lower lip hung open. "The thing lit up. Just for a second. Lights all over the place. Now it's blank."

"Interference, like DeVere said. Something to do with the Drift itself. A Dead Low, just as Barbuda called it. Don't worry about it, kid. There's nothing here."

He looked uncertain. Almost as uncertain as Clancy felt. Forty-five minutes, and they'd yet to find anything at all aside from a mess of rotting tapestries, a broken robot and a sheer wall of useless bits of junk.

"So kid, that history lesson you were handing out back there. What were you calling it—an exodus?"

"Uh huh," he said.

"Ships like this one?"

"Oh no—it's far too small. This looks to have been a pleasure cruiser. Some rich family's private yacht. You wouldn't get far in a ship like this, especially with a rebellion on your tail."

They passed the barricade wall without incident, guns raised just in case. Behind it, the blasted remains of another one. Beyond the rubble, yet another corridor, this one opening out into a larger space. And a larger barricade, solid, made entirely of metal.

Something caught Konte's attention. He approached the wall before Clancy had time to stop him.

"If I'm not mistaken, that's a genuine antique! Third dynasty—"

His words choked off as a mechanical arm lunged out of the mess of compacted steel and grabbed him by the throat.

Clancy moved like lightning. There was no time to think. Within a second she'd whipped an imploder from her utility belt, primed it and slapped it to the place where the arm met the wall. The kid struggled for air, wide-eyed and useless. She slapped his visor shut just in time. When the pulse 'verbed, he was thrown backwards, metal fingers still clutched around his windpipe. Clancy grabbed the severed arm and hurled it across the room. The kid was still too shocked to do more than blink.

The comm crackled to life as one by one the others reported in. "What's going on there?"

"Sensors showed an energy discharge—either of you down?"

"Relax, everybody. We're okay. One of those barricades got a little friendly is all."

She signed off without further explanation. That could come later. Right now they were almost out of time.

"Get up," she said, offering her hand.

He took it, lips jabbering, no sound coming out. The arm remained where she had cast it, twitching feverishly from side to side.

She opened the comm again. "Where are you at, Pace?"

"Some sort of treasure room. Gold like you've never . . . Clance, you really oughta see—"

"Make it snappy. I want us all out of here sooner. Qamar's estimation of that weed veered most likely to the hopeful side."

◇◇

She only took her eyes off the kid for a second. Maybe two. Certainly no more than that. When next she looked, he was grappling with something nasty.

"Don't touch it!" she screamed. "Step right back!"

Too late. The thing was already in his hands, dangling limply by its whip-thin tail. "War surplus," he said, letting go. As if he handled such things every day.

The thing hit the deck with a satisfactory thud. "Synthetic, mostly, which is why the screens don't read them as life signs. We'd best be getting out of here," he added.

The kid had changed. Suddenly there didn't seem to be much kid left in him.

Clancy's heart was thudding wildly. Loud enough to drown the ringing in her ears. "I have to check something out," she told him. "Won't take a minute. You head back to the airlock."

He stared at her, his eyes betraying nothing of the kid she had been mollycoddling not even an hour previous. "So it is true what they say about you. You're no treasure hunter. You think he's still alive out here."

Clancy eyed him coldly. "Your point being . . . "

"Not my point. Uncle Padraeus's. Barbuda owes him money."

She snorted. "An unlikely story, but even if he did, it's not my problem." She shot an uneasy glance at their surroundings. "Go back to the airlock. No one's asking you to wait . . . "

Konte raised his pulse rifle. She ducked out of instinct as he let off three succinct blasts above her head. "Rats," he said before she had time to ask. "Lots of them."

And he got them all, which was mighty impressive for someone who was supposed to be a newb.

"You're no nephew of Padraeus's" she said. "None of that clan's ever been able to shoot straight."

Something staggered in the smoke-filled corridor. Something far too large to be a rat.

"Hold your fire!" Clancy screamed.

She didn't need to. Konte had seen it too, not to mention heard the noise it made. A high-pitch howl that was anything but human. In the blasting light, it looked to be a small, thin girl, shielding her eyes from the harsh illumination. Or a boy, perhaps. The arm was covering the face. Konte gripped his rifle tight as Clancy fought her way through the smoke and glare.

"Stay on point. There might be more of those rats!"

He shouldered the weapon, but mercifully the rat attack was over.

Clancy took small, carefully measured steps, wary not to make any sudden movements.

"Hey there. We're not going to hurt you."

The child looked human enough close up—and more of a *she* than he, to Clancy's eye. Not that it mattered. What could a child of any kind be doing here on a derelict ship?

"My name's Clancy," she said in a gentle whisper. "Hey little thing, what's yours?"

The child didn't answer. She froze, one arm still covering her face. The light leached all the colour from her hair, which cascaded down her back in a filthy, matted tangle.

When she'd gotten as close as she dared, Clancy dropped into a crouch and placed her blaster on the ground beside the child.

"Careful," said Konte.

"She's just a little girl."

"How?" said Konte. "How can that possibly be what she is?"

Clancy had to think about that one. "I don't know, kid. I don't know." She reached out gently, fingers grasping at the air that lay between them. "Take my hand," she whispered. "Go on—I won't bite you."

Smoke plumed and coiled through the air between them. Konte stepped in closer, his shadow falling across the captain's own.

"Cap'n Clancy—look. That brooch pinned to her chest."

"What's that?" Clancy's voice had lost its customary hardness. The child had her utterly distracted.

"It's the imperial crest of Horgis. Like on the tapestry up front."

"So? What if it is?" She crept in closer, inch by inch. "Hey, look at me. You don't have to be afraid. Are you all alone on this great big ship?"

She glanced back over her shoulder suddenly. "For fuck's sake, will you get that bloody light out of her eyes. She's just a kid. She's just—"

Qamar's generally crisp, clear voice had an edge of panic to it when he cut through on the comm. "Can't hold back the weed much longer. Can't get through to the others either—too much interference. What's going on in there?"

Clancy lunged, quick as a cobra, grabbing the girl by the wrist. The child screamed, a hideous sound like an animal fighting for its life. Clancy tightened her grip, dragging the wriggling harpy to her feet. "There isn't time for this shit," she spat. "If we don't get out of here, we're dead." The kid's shrill terror was soon masked by blaster fire.

"More rats," explained Konte, knocking them out of the air as they launched themselves. One of them thudded hard against Clancy's shoulder. She let out an involuntary wail of disgust before yanking the child free of their range.

"Not just rats!" he added, his voice drowned out by blanket fire.

Things were coming at them from all directions. *Things* was the only word that came to Clancy's mind. Mechanical assemblages hotwired to hunks of meat. Body parts enmeshed with camshafts and poppet valves. Magnetos and coil wires and battery boxes. Things she'd never seen before. Things she hoped she'd never see again.

All the while, the girl screamed her lungs out. Clancy dragged her forward with one hand while firing rounds indiscriminately with the other. The monstrosities kept coming even after they'd been blown to pieces. The pieces kept attacking, the mecha pushing the meat ever onwards.

They ran through rooms and corridors, Clancy screaming at Qamar for directions, a feat he managed, despite the interference and the noise.

"Where the fuck are the others?"

"Right ahead of you, boss. Right, then right again."

The sight they came upon was not a pretty one. The corridor was strewn with what the auction houses comically referred to as pirate treasure. Crap that collectors fought and died for. Imperial knick-knacks. Plates and spoons and goblets, tiaras, coins and crowns. Useless junk pressed from gold and platinum. Centerpiece to the gaudy opulence, a corpse stripped to the bone, white ivory glistening amidst remains of entrails. Beside it, DeVere, half-eaten, all screaming. Clancy put a bullet through his skull.

"It's almost on you," screamed Qamar.

"We're done," spat Clancy. "Get us the holy fuck out of here."

The girl was still emitting hideous, subhuman sounds. Both Clancy and the kid had ceased to hear them.

Konte stared at DeVere's steaming remains, even as the machine/ flesh things came crawling after them. That's when she noticed Kyah and Pace pressed up hard against the airlock, still and silent.

"Open the hatch!"

"I'm on it, boss. I'm on it."

Minutes later, all five were safely on the right side of the airlock. Another minute, back out in space. Clear, cold space, entirely devoid of animated meat puppets.

"Qamar, you're worth every buck I've yet to pay you," whispered Clancy.

◇◇

The kid was more upset than Clancy had ever seen him.

"You shouldn't have put a bullet in DeVere. He might have stood half a chance of surviving."

"I had my fucking hands full," she screamed back, brandishing the child like some sort of excuse. "And anyway, he'd have done the same for me. At least, I hope he would."

Konte shook his head. His whole body was shaking. Aftershocks from the horror they'd left behind. Only then did they notice the girl had fallen silent.

"It's all over, baby. It's all over," whispered Clancy.

"Close the can, I'm busting us clear," barked Qamar through the comm, his voice as reassuring as any mother's. "Hang on tight."

They could see the weed advancing on the viewscreen, spilling like an obscene lava flow. A stain encasing the places they'd just been, mobile lichen welding itself to metal.

"It's alive," stated Konte.

"So. What if it is? That fact doesn't fill me with obligation."

As if on cue, both of them turned their attention to the child.

"It's okay, honey, we're out of danger now. I told you everything would be alright."

The girl fell into a foetal position the minute Clancy let go of her wrist. Clancy dropped into a squat beside her, gently grabbed her spindly wrists and pulled them away from her face.

"Mother of Jesus—what—"

She jumped back as if she'd been bitten by a snake. "Her face. There's something wrong with her fucking face."

Konte knelt down, one hand on his gun. The other brushed greasy hair from the child's eyes. "What the . . . "

Neither of them said anything. They just knelt and stared. Eventually the child moved of her own accord. Only the child wasn't a child at all. Small as one, most likely from decades of malnourishment. The person who crouched before them was old. Ancient as the imperial court itself.

Her withered face was like a sun-dried apple, her hair a river of spiderweb.

"Mother of . . . "

Qamar's voice cut across the tension like a laser. "We're clear," he said. "Damn foul stuff can't touch us now."

Silence. Neither Clancy nor Konte had words left in them.

"Hello? Is everyone okay?"

Clancy swallowed the lump stuck in her throat. "Just get us the flaming fuck out of here Qamar."

The 'girl' they had unwittingly rescued had apparently been born Princess Arinakah Horgis. Konte knew where to find that kind of data. DNA checks made sure there was no doubt.

"Might still be a bounty on her?" said Kyah.

"No. Leave her alone."

Something in Clancy's voice tone warned them off, filled in the words she wasn't up to saying. Princess Arinakah sucked on a water bottle. If she'd ever been capable of speech, that time was long past. According to all the data they'd configured, she was something like ninety standard years old. She'd been living on that ship since she was six when the Dead Low had claimed the ship. Sucked it into the Sargasso eddy. Nobody knew she was there. Nobody aside from surplus war machinery.

"But how did she survive?"

"I don't know, kid. She just did."

"And those things with the meat-and-gear extensions?"

Clancy shrugged. "Who can say for sure? Self-repairing bodyguards. Perhaps even the life-extended remains of her own relatives? All we know is she managed to stay alive."

In the next compartment, Kyah and Pace were bickering over spoils, a fact that made Clancy want to blast the both of them out the nearest airlock. Trash and trinkets. Junk in anybody's era or language. Nothing compared to . . . see, that, she figured was the problem here. What to do with a ninety-year-old princess who couldn't even speak a human language?

"I should probably blast her out an airlock too," said Clancy, thinking out loud.

"But you won't," said Konte.

"No. I won't at that. She is gonna be yours and Padraeus's problem. Payback for sending you to spy on me."

She expected the kid to argue, but instead he solemnly nodded as Qamar set about the task of steering them home.

Clancy turned her back on the lot of them. Another day, another dollar as the saying went, despite both days and dollars being obsolete. No matter, she reassured herself. No matter. She'd scored enough loot to keep the *Ebeneezer* flying. Enough to keep Barbuda in her sights. He was still out there, which meant she was still looking. And Harker's Binnacle, there was always that.

ARCTICA

The child's shriek pierced the stillness of the ice. He fell, but quickly scrambled to his feet as his pursuers, two uniformed men swathed in furs, closed in on him. The men moved clumsily in their protective garb, but their clubs were raised, their knives long and sharp.

Amadina watched from the deck of the *Cotillion*, angling her body away from the inevitable conclusion about to play itself out on the ice. The dark rim of rocks was too far away. The child would never make it to safety. He would end up a crimson smear on the white like so many others before him.

She turned her face, pulled the blanket tight as the hunter's club found its mark. Glaciers huddled still and silent along the horizon, oblivious to all acts of human atrocity. Amadina hugged her shoulders against the cold, turned back to watch the hunters drag a dozen small corpses into a heap on the ice floe.

"They were checked for the marks, Miss. All of them."

She turned to see a young man dressed in the uniform of the San Sebastienne Coast Guard. He was clean shaven, unlike most of his fellow seamen.

"Indeed. And were the children checked for marks before or after they were clubbed to death?"

The young man cleared his throat, averted his eyes from her icy stare.

"Before," he answered. "By the book with refugees—always. We do what must be done. There's not a one amongst us who relishes the tasks we are required to perform out here in the wastelands of Arctica."

"Killing is killing," she said coldly.

"It is *culling*, not killing, and we cull only those who are marked. Forgive me, Miss, but you know it can be no other way."

It was a small motion but she caught it; the way his eyes flickered to her wrists for an instant before looking back up at her face.

Amadina exhaled sharply. "You'll be wanting to check me then, I suppose. Captain Saris has already—"

The young man's face flushed crimson. "Please, Miss, I meant no offence"

"None taken," she replied, sloughing the blanket from her shoulders. She bent her right elbow, unbuttoned her sleeve, pushed the fabric away, holding up her pale wrist for him to inspect.

"Its all right Miss, I don't need—"

"I assure you it's no trouble," she replied dryly, repeating the process with her other arm. "I'd rather not run the risk of being mistakenly clubbed to death by an over zealous officer of the San Sebastienne Coast Guard."

He gathered her wrists gently in his hands, tracing her delicate veins with his thumbs.

"Lieutenant-Commander Orlandis Jake, at your service, Miss," he said softly. "I never had any doubt that you were one of us." He gave her hands a gentle squeeze. "I'm sorry we couldn't provide you with more suitable attire."

"My name is Amadina Sande," she replied, pulling her hands free as a gout of yellow flame erupted below them on the ice. Three charcoal silhouettes heaved dark bundles onto the burning pyre as Amadina rebuttoned the sleeves of the oversized men's shirt the Purser had provided along with flannel undergarments and a pair of dungarees.

"This clothing is adequate, if inappropriate, thank you."

"You have been most fortunate, Miss Sande. If the *Cotillion* hadn't been patrolling nearby you would surely have died on the ice. Shipwreck survivors don't last long in these waters. If the ship hadn't chanced by on special assignment—"

Amadina smiled. "It seems we have different definitions of fortune. Everything I own, save for my precious specimen case, is now at the bottom of the Arctica sea. All my larger botanic samples, my textbooks and my notes. Two years' work, Lieutenant-Commander. All of it gone."

"But what are two years' notes compared with a human life, Miss Sande?"

"What indeed?" she replied.

The cabin they assigned her was small but clean, eight feet long and twelve feet wide. One third of it was occupied by a bedstead, the rest with furniture such as a chest with two drawers and two shelves which also held a pitcher and a washbasin, a looking glass and a commode. She did not mind the cramped quarters as they afforded her privacy, separating her from most of the crew who slept in the forward house.

She locked the door and laid her specimen case out on the bedstead. It contained explosives, not enough to sink the *Cotillion*, but enough to damage the cannon if she could just get close enough to lay the charges unseen. Failing that, her plan was to sabotage the firing mechanism. She had no idea how the cannon worked, but she had observed that the Master-at-Arms was extremely protective of a small wooden case that he kept under lock and key, much as she guarded her specimen case against inquiring eyes.

Amadina spent the remainder of the morning alone in her room checking over her equipment, considering her options. An ensign brought her a small meal of cold beef and ship's biscuit at noon. Her first task, she reasoned, was to get herself into a position of trust, so that she could stroll the deck unsupervised.

She tried to rest, her mind racing with the events of the past thirty-six hours. Until now, the refugees had done nothing to defend themselves against ongoing slaughter, nothing to fight back against the law enforcement of San Sebastienne. For ten years she and Tobias had tried to hide their people and protect them in secret. Amadina couldn't sleep, couldn't even close her eyes without images of carnage and desolation exploding across her mind. She tried not to picture Tobias and the many ways in which he might have died. Best not to think of the ones who didn't make it. *The future is for the living*, she reminded herself. *Only the strongest survive.*

Loud voices in the corridor aroused her curiosity. Amadina pushed her door open a crack. The sailors were speaking in a foreign tongue—the rough language spoken only by the native inhabitants of the Arctica coastline. Clearly something of great interest was taking place on deck, so she locked her door and followed the men up the narrow companionway.

The sky erupted above the ship in a mess of swollen purple. Neon flashes shuddered beneath wisps of cirrus. A peculiar phenomena known as the Luminance. Amadina could see patterns in the lightning, but could not interpret them. For this task Captain Saris had employed a woman from one of the fishing villages that huddled among rocky inlets of the coast.

Amadina went to stand beside Orlandis, watched the Captain struggling to unfurl his charts in the wind. The Luminance Reader seemed oblivious to the fierce weather. She pulled her shawl tightly around her shoulders and concentrated on the sky before them. Amadina, herself chilled to the bone, noted the precise manner in which the Reader held her head. Small movements signalled changes in barometric pressure. When she finally spoke her dialect was unfamiliar: different again to the language of the sailors.

"What's she saying?" Amadina whispered to Orlandis, resisting the urge to rub some warmth into her shoulders. He pressed a finger to his lips and whispered back. "There's a new fissure opening in the sky. The Reader will help us locate its point of origin before it tears in full." He nodded toward the prow of the *Cotillion*. "That's what the cannon is for—to seal the fissures before they fully form."

Amadina eyed the cannon: three tonnes of polished bronze containing within it the power of the sun. She glanced sideways to check that the Captain was busy conferring with his Reader. Casually, Amadina strolled across the deck and approached the cannon's sturdy base. She stretched her palm upward to touch its shiny surface.

"Be careful, Miss," said Orlandis, following close behind. "That's a very expensive piece of equipment. Imported, all the way from Marakiss. Don't find that kind of technology in San Sebastienne."

"How strange. Is it true that it fires bolts of concentrated sunlight?" She rested her hand on the metal, then withdrew it quickly. "But it's so terribly cold."

"I'm afraid I'm not at liberty to discuss—"

"Step away from the cannon," said Captain Saris. "Lieutenant-Commander, what is that woman doing above deck? I want her with the rest of the off-watch crew below."

Amadina rubbed warmth back into her hand.

"I'm curious, Captain Saris, how ever does one repair a tear in the sky with concentrated sunlight?"

The Captain stared at her harshly, ignored her question, turned back to his business with the Reader. As if on cue the colours of the Luminance began to bleed from yellow-purples to deep red. The Reader began chattering excitedly in her foreign tongue. Amadina wanted to stay and observe the proceedings but she allowed Lieutenant-Commander Orlandis to put his arm around her shoulder and escort her back down the companionway.

The Saloon was large, its centrepiece a thirty-foot table with chairs on either side of it, all bolted to the floor. A skylight was positioned overhead, from which hung an ornate glass lantern, a barometer and two casters well furnished with decanters, bottles and glasses.

"Miss, I must apologise for Captain Saris' behaviour. He is a man under many pressures, and sometimes the social niceties escape him."

"Why do you hunt the people with the marks?" Amadina asked, as she and the Lieutenant-Commander sat down opposite each other at the nearest end of the long table.

Orlandis held his glass steady as an ensign hurried over to fill it three quarters full with wine.

Amadina held her own glass out for the boy to fill. The blanket slipped from her shoulders to the floor.

"Surely mere children can do no harm, marked or otherwise?" she said. "Why not simply abandon them on the ice if you wish them to perish? Let the elements take their course?"

Orlandis sipped his wine, sucked the residue from his teeth. He leaned toward her, reaching around the table's end to pick up the blanket but she was quicker, retrieving it herself and folding it neatly across her knees with a deft hand.

"Miss, I was wondering. How much do you understand of the refugee problem?"

She shook her head. "Very little I'm afraid. There is talk of people falling through great fissures in the sky. All I know of it for certain is that those who bear the marks are shown no mercy."

Orlandis shook his head. "Miss Sande, if only you would consider our position. These are dangerous places and dangerous times. The law is written with good reason and we must obey it."

Amadina nodded, as if considering. "But who are the marked ones and where do they hail from?" She sipped. "Surely not from the sky as people say?"

"I'm afraid that's classified information, Miss, I'm not at liberty to confirm or deny anything." He lowered his voice. "Truth is, I don't rightly know, only that they present a significant threat."

"What kind of threat?"

Orlandis sipped his wine. "A *significant* one. But it's nothing for you to worry about. Why don't you make yourself comfortable? We'll be another two weeks amidst the floes before we return to San Sebastienne."

He motioned for the ensign to top up Amadina's glass. She could feel the weight of his eyes upon her, smell the tangy sweat upon his skin.

"I am very tired," she said, pulling her glass close to her chest. "Perhaps we can continue this discussion in the morning?"

"As you wish, Miss Sande," he said, smiling, downing the remainder of his wine in one gulp.

◇◇

Amadina awoke at four bells to the sound of trampling overhead. Something she had quickly become accustomed to—the men getting ready to swab the decks with sand and water, a task they performed before breakfast without fail.

Orlandis had provided her with a calico wrapper to cover her inappropriate attire. Apparently it had been left behind by a previous lady traveller. What sort of woman might such a traveller have been? Amadina thanked her anonymous benefactor. She felt much less conspicuous with her dungarees hidden from plain sight.

The jaws of the boom squeaked loudly as she stepped upon the deck. The first thing she noticed was the subtle shift in the quality of the light. The embers of sunrise had long since faded, and yet the horizon before them shone with an intense illumination. Not the colours of nature at all, but the colours of heartache, loneliness and desire. It turned Amadina's stomach to see them now, to behold this terrible rip in the atmosphere above the water, hanging suspended like a storm cloud. And yet she could not take her eyes off it. The rip held mesmeric qualities. Sailors feared it as a form of lorelei, overpowering their senses with terrible beauty. It called to them, dragged them down and under. A wound in the sky, a ragged gash connecting this place with another. It was said that you could stand at the edge and behold eternity, see your past and your future combined in a moment of simultaneous clarity. No Luminance Reader was comfortable standing directly beneath it. It was also said that at certain astrological junctions, the rip in the sky rained down human flesh.

Amadina strolled the quarterdeck, her arm linked through that of Orlandis. She had flirted coyly with him since her "rescue" from the ice, always with the suggestion of something more to come, yet never quite delivering on the promise. His affectations and his eagerness repulsed her, but the Lieutenant-Commander was her best chance of survival, both aboard the *Cotillion* and, later, back in San Sebastienne, if that was truly where the ship was headed. How fortunate she had been to have made it this far without discovery. But one could not rely on the vagaries of fortune forever.

She was careful to pay scant attention to the cannon, nor to appear too knowledgeable about Arctica, its Luminance phenomena and sky fissures. In their strolls around the various decks, Amadina fussed about frivolous things: the filigree work on railings and doorways, carven images of water serpentes decorating the cabin doors.

How utterly adorable! How perfectly exquisite!

Her aim was to make herself innocuous to Captain Saris and the more quick-witted of his crew. They must believe her a shipwrecked gentlewoman wishing desperately to return home. Nothing more.

The Luminance Readers were the most fascinating of all. Small sinewy women with wind-toughened faces and ice-hardened hearts, they had carved out a niche market for themselves, guiding ships to their destinations through the treacherous ice floes. No one understood how they were able to interpret the bruise-coloured fluctuations of the Luminance, nor sense when a new patch of sky was about to tear—or when it wasn't. The ice floes of Arctica were littered with rotting hulls and splintered masts, evidence of those captains too cheap or too foolish to employ these strangely gifted women.

It became clear to Amadina that it was not the Lieutenant-Commander, but the Master-at-Arms on whom she would have to focus if she wanted to disable the cannon. Not an easy task to accomplish. The Master-at-Arms was a dark and brooding man called Clay, not a ladies' man like her pet Lieutenant-Commander Orlandis. Twice she had tried to corner Clay alone and twice he had made it clear that he favoured weapons maintenance over female company. In preparation for the third attempt she strapped a delicate bone-handled pistol to her lower calf. If he wasn't attracted by her face, her figure or her wit then perhaps antique weaponry would do the trick?

By her estimation she had only one more day until the *Cotillion* would position itself directly below the newly-forming fissure identified by the Reader. She had to find a way to stop the cannon from sealing the opening forever.

Amadina followed Clay onto the poop deck in the early moments of sunrise. She lingered by the lifeboats, watching him polish the cannon with a scrap of oily rag. Two sailors swabbed the length of deck between them. Neither paid any attention to her or the Master-at-Arms.

This time Clay had brought his small wooden case on deck. As Amadina deduced, it contained a mechanism essential to the operation of the cannon. A lens perhaps, or a key—some method of calibration or ignition. She crept closer, but he had his back to her, making it impossible to see what he was doing. Closer still, she was startled by the sound of footsteps. The hatch flew open and two figures emerged from below. Amadina ducked between the lifeboats, watched as the Luminance Reader and her companion crossed the poop deck and lit hand-rolled cigarettes. Snatches of their chatter wafted on the wind. Unfamiliar words that made Amadina feel suddenly out of her depth. What if she had estimated wrongly? Was she all out of time? How close to the fissure did they need to be in order to seal it?

Sounds of life stirred from below decks: the clatter of pots and pans in the galley, thuds and thumps that signified activity. The Readers had their backs turned. Amadina strode from her hiding place, crossed the deck to the prow where the Master-at-Arms was crouched over his work. The contents of the small wooden case were laid out on the deck spread across a piece of fine black velvet cloth.

He grunted as soon as he saw her, climbing to his feet and drawing a pistol from his belt. Amadina smiled coyly, tried to look as though she was interested in him rather than the equipment.

"Such a glorious sunrise," she said. "I never tire of them. Do you?"

"Cap'n Saris ordered you to stay below," he growled, balancing the weight of the pistol in his hand. "Now get!"

Amadina pouted. "I only want to know how the big gun works. Won't you show me?"

She had been right about the lenses. None of the other instruments laid out on the cloth were even vaguely familiar. Clay stepped forward, blocking her view of his work. He cocked his gun, aimed the barrel at her heart.

"You might've fooled the others but you ain't foolin' me. Now get yerself away from things that don't concern you."

Amadina raised her hands in a gesture of defeat. The Reader and her companion stared as she turned and walked away. Did the Master-at-Arms know something or was this just his way with all strangers?

She found herself a quiet section by the rail, stared glumly out across the waves at the solid white mass of glaciers lacing the horizon. The emerald sea lay dark and still, occasional flickers of movement catching her eye. Flying fish skipped across the glassy surface, quick ribbons of pink and blue, gone before she could get a good look at them.

The bustle of the day began in earnest as she leant upon the rail. Two sailors appeared beside her, pulled cigarettes from their pockets, offered her one. She accepted, allowed the nearest man to light the tip. The pungent scent of burning seaweed bloomed.

The sea was everything in these parts. They ate from it, smoked from it, fashioned tools from its weeds and creatures, braided sea hemp that formed the *Cotillion's* rigging and sails. All of their remedies came from the sea, as well as their legends. Sea life was the flavour of salt, the colour of sky, the texture of scales.

One sailor grunted at the other, pointed out across the water to what could only have been the ridged back of a serpente diving and ploughing through the waves not fifty feet from the ship.

She had never quite believed the tales of serpentes, whales and merfolk told so frequently in the taverns of San Sebastienne. Now that she'd experienced this strange and beautiful landscape for herself, Amadina found herself able to believe in a great many unbelievable things.

The fissure in the sky widened visibly as they neared it. Its colours swirled and metamorphosed with a rhythm and pulse understood by nobody but the Readers. Amadina noted that the deeper hues were always accompanied by storm clouds, roiling cumulus masses that seemed to dog the ship.

Finally the *Cotillion* paused beneath a spectral bloom so vivid and intense, it hurt her eyes. The Captain positioned the ship as close as the Reader would permit. All around them, packed ice: a narrow channel the only passage through. In a few hours it would squeeze shut and, if they were not careful, they would be trapped.

The crew of the *Cotillion* had grown more restless each day as the ship began angling itself to position below the fissure. Many of them wore talismen around their necks, crude stone representations of Teya, a water goddess from the old religion that still flourished in Arctica's outlying settlements.

How long would the ship sit here before the cannon was to be fired? She could not risk drawing attention to herself by asking. All she could do was watch and wait. The entire morning was endured in a state of anxious anticipation, spying on the Captain and the Master-At-Arms, the ship's bell striking every half hour to mark the passage of the day. Orlandis was nowhere to be seen. The Captain spent the hours after noon in conference with his senior officers. Amadina watched the sails being set, sailors climbing dexterously up and down the rigging. By nightfall, the ship was once more on the move.

◇◇

She awoke in the early hours with the sense that something was wrong. It took her a moment to realise what. The ship was still. How long had it been so? Had the cannon been fired while she slept?

She dressed hurriedly, checked the explosives packed so tightly into her specimen case, grasped its handle firmly and pushed her way up on deck through the throng of milling sailors.

"What's going on?" she asked, her heart thumping wildly in her chest. Purple lightning flared above amidst a boiling mass of cloud. The *Cotillion* had reached the crux point below the fissure, but the cannon had not yet been fired.

She cursed. The weapon would be too well guarded now, she would never get close enough to it to blow it up.

She fought her way to the starboard railing. Above the ship the sky writhed and pulsed with eerie incandescence, but it was not the light show above that caught her attention. Figures ran across the packed ice below. It took her a moment to realise that they were not sailors, but refugees. Attacking the ship this time, not running from it.

Gunfire sounded, almost inaudible above the commotion. Gripping her specimen case tightly with both hands, she pushed her way forward toward the prow.

When she slipped and fell it was Orlandis who dragged her to her feet.

"Get back below deck!" he screamed, trying to push her in the opposite direction. She twisted her wrist from his grasp and pulled away.

The cannon pointed directly upwards. It looked different. The Master-at-Arms had attached an unfamiliar device to the barrel. A focusing mechanism for the light, perhaps. Captain Saris stood beside him accompanied by a contingent of his guard.

She felt a hand on her shoulder.

"Miss Sande, it is not safe. The ship is under attack. I suggest—"

Amadina lifted her wrapper, withdrew the pistol from her garter. Squeezed her way through the crowd, lugging her case with one hand, Orlandis shouting, following close behind.

When she was as near the cannon as she could get she swung around suddenly, pressed the barrel against Orlandis's temple. "Disarm that cannon, Lieutenant-Commander, or I will blow your head off."

She doubted that either the Captain or the Master-at-Arms would value Orlandis's life ahead of their precious cannon, but she had run out of time and options.

Orlandis raised his hands and she prodded him forward with the gun.

"I am a crack shot, Lieutenant-Commander," she lied.

The air filled with metallic clanging. Grappling hooks slammed against the railings. More gunshots, shouting, occasional shrieks of pain. Carrion gulls dipped and soared overhead, oblivious to the roiling Luminance above. They could smell the approach of death, even through the cordite and the lightning.

She pushed Orlandis forward until he stood beside the cannon.

His face wore an incredulous look as she placed the specimen case at her feet. Saw that the Captain also had a gun pressed hard against his temple, held by a man wrapped well in leathers and furs.

"Tobias!" she exclaimed.

Tobias motioned to her specimen case. Another fur-clad man stepped forward and bent to retrieve it. Amadina exhaled, unaware that she had been holding her breath. It was over. Tobias was alive, and she did not have to face the problem of disabling the cannon on her own.

"Who in Teya's name are you?" bellowed Captain Saris.

"She's one of *them*," replied the Master-at-Arms. "Told you you should have left her on the ice."

Orlandis shook his head. "But she can't be. She has no marks—I checked."

Amadina eyed him cautiously. "None that you can see. Some of us are luckier than others."

The man in furs pulled the specimen case open.

"No need to use the bomb," she said. "The cannon is useless without its lenses—smash them and there will be no risk of damage to this vessel.

"No," bellowed the Master-at-Arms. He struggled wildly as Amadina ripped the keys from his belt and unlocked the section of the cannon where she had observed the lenses to be stored.

"Wait," said Tobias. "This ship could be a powerful asset with its cannon intact. A weapon against our oppressors. We could fight them ship to ship."

The men in furs now outnumbered the sailors. They had won the fight before it had even begun. The Cotillion was safe in rebel hands.

"Miss Sande."

She turned to look upon the whitened face of Lieutenant-Commander Orlandis.

"Who are you people?" he asked, his voice wavering. At that moment that she realised how much she pitied him and his officially sanctioned, soft-bellied San Sebastienne crew.

"You've never even asked that question before, have you?" she said dryly. "Yet you are quite prepared to hunt and murder us in cold blood."

"Refugees," he said coldly. "Enemies of the State."

Amadina smiled sadly and shook her head. "Enemies of *whose* State, Orlandis? Have you ever given thought to what the word *refugee* actually means? For all you know I could be your great, great grandchild. Would you be in such a hurry to kill me then?"

Orlandis frowned, confused by her words.

"Don't strain yourself trying to comprehend my meaning, dear fellow. I shall explain it all quite clearly." She tightened the grip on her pistol as she spoke. "We *refugees* think we may be from your own future—the future you are forging with your hatred and your violence—but we cannot be sure if there are one or many futures attached to this cold, forsaken place."

Amadina stopped to catch her breath, aware that Orlandis was hearing her words, yet failing to take them in.

"We dive through the fissures when they open," she continued. "Many of us die in the attempt, but we do it all the same. You cannot imagine what it's like where we come from, Lieutenant-Commander Orlandis. No hell in your religion compares with the world we call our home. If you could experience it for just one minute, you'd understand why those of us who have the chance throw our own children through the fissures. Most will perish. Those that do survive the journey are betrayed by their birthmarks. They are the marks of slavery, Lieutenant Commander. We come here seeking sanctuary, yet we are hunted down and culled by you like animals."

Captain Saris shook his head. "I don't believe you. And even if I did, surely our world cannot sustain inhabitants from its own *future* as well as its present. In all probability you have caused the very cataclysm that has afflicted your own time."

"We did not cause this evil," Amadina spat. "We have come here to save the future. We have come to save us all."

Amadina turned her attention from Orlandis to the Captain. "Life is life, Captain Saris," she said. "You cannot blame us for fighting for it."

Tobias tightened his grip on the boarding pike. "The ship is ours now, Dina. Lets pitch these bastards into the sea."

"No," replied Amadina coolly, her eyes on Orlandis once more. "Let's not. Set them down on the ice with a week's provisions."

"But they're murderers," he growled. "Women and children—"

"And for all we know they're our great grandparents too. We will not become the creatures we despise. Not if I have any say in it."

"We won't last a week out here without shelter," said Captain Saris. "Might as well shoot us where we stand."

"We shall inform the Coastguard of your predicament when we reach the nearest port," said Amadina, nodding at the Luminance Reader and her companion huddling by the rails. "I'll bet those two know exactly where they are. They'll guide you home to safety for a price."

The Reader took the cigarette from her mouth and spat on the deck. Amadina smiled. "You'll make it," she said. "And now we have a chance to make it too."

"Great Teya— Master-at-Arms . . . Clay—what the hell are you doing with the cannon!"

Amadina turned in time to see Clay break free of his bonds and wrench control of the cannon from Tobias' men. "Get him away from there," she shrieked, her voice tossed on the icy wind and lost in the maelstrom of fresh fighting that erupted across the deck. The crew were greatly outnumbered, but the sight of the Master-at-Arms in control of his precious cannon filled the sailors with renewed vigour and spirit.

The Master-at-Arms seemed crazed. With the strength of several men, he elbowed and bashed aside all attempts to constrain him. Amadina held her breath. He wasn't just fighting wildly—he knew what he was doing. His thick but nimble fingers grabbed items from his lens case that had been strewn across the deck. These he affixed to the canon's focusing mechanism. A fur-clad man grabbed him from behind. Clay roared and swung around, smashing his attacker's spine against the brass body of the gun. The man groaned and sank to his knees, as Clay kicked his assailant aside.

The barrel lowered as Clay moved behind it. He heaved his burly shoulders against the brass until it swung to face the dark mass of refugee fighters still swarming across the ice.

"I'll send you back to Hell," he shouted as a nausea-inducing hum disturbed the air. Amadina clamped her hands against her ears but the awful sound continued to penetrate. She could hear nothing else, despite the roar of battle. It took her a moment to realise that she was shrieking. Her mouth hung open as Tobias launched himself at Clay just as the cannon let off a bolt of light. Amadina's arms fell to her sides. She couldn't see what the beam had done but she could hear it. A few moments later the wind brought with it the pungent scent of charred flesh.

Tobias and Clay continued to grapple, locked in a violent embrace, evenly matched in size and strength. Amadina, sick to her stomach, ran to the cannon, her arms outstretched. Protecting her palms against frostburn with her sleeves, she pushed against the barrel with all her strength. When it didn't budge, she threw her shoulder hard against it, catching a glimpse of the carnage on the ice below. She had expected blood, but there was none to be seen, just melted slurry and the charred, still shapes of fallen men. Sailors gave chase to wounded survivors through the filthy ice.

She shoved her weight against the barrel, again and again, trying desperately to force its aim away from the survivors. She had succeeded in budging it a couple of inches when another body slammed against her side. Orlandis, bruised and bloodied from the battle on the deck.

"Help me," she screamed, "before it's too late."

He was weak, but between them they managed to swivel the weapon and aim it out across the water where it could do no further harm.

Tobias—where was he? No longer struggling with Clay on the deck. Her eyes searched the crowd. There he was, a knife protruding from his upper arm. The Master-at-Arms was nowhere to be seen.

"The Luminance!" cried a voice from the crowd. The roiling purple blemish loomed directly above the ship. Ruddy bolts of lightning stabbed the clouds. The air hung heavy with the stench of sulphur. Amadina's stomach heaved. The smell triggered a memory from the day of her own passage, tumbling through the electric void, landing in Arctica's freezing waters and into the safety of waiting nets cast by Tobias and his crew who dragged the handful of lucky survivors to safety. The beam from the cannon was intended to seal the rip connecting this world and its future. Damning her own people to their unendurable present.

"Nets," she shouted to Orlandis. "We must have nets. Are there any on board this vessel?"

He did not have a chance to answer. A sailor in a bloodstained uniform seized him and hurled him to one side. Amadina heard the unmistakable sound of a gun being cocked. Clay, so close she could smell his foetid breath. His gun pointed directly at her heart.

"Say your prayers, little lady. If you're the prayin' kind, which I sorely doubt."

Sailors swarmed across the deck, bruised and battle-bloodied, but very much in control of the *Cotillion* once more. Several gathered around Amadina and the cannon, clearly under orders to return the weapon to its original position.

Amadina stood her ground. "Men like you destroyed the world," she said. "You'll see. And your own children will end up paying the price."

"Careful with that thing," Clay barked, momentarily distracted by the sailors' rough handling of his precious cannon. "It's a delicate piece of equipment. Very dangerous."

Two sailors bearing the cannon's bulk slipped on the bloodied deck. The cannon lurched. A third sailor rushed to help. Amadina took her chance, throwing herself away from the weapon, dropping to all fours and crawling through the throng of bodies and the freezing sludge of blood and dirty ice coating the deck. The third sailor raised the butt of his rifle. Clay bellowed as the sailor, an impostor, smashed it into the fixed lens again and again until the gun was half buried in the contraption's innards. Shards of glass scattered on the wind.

"By Teya's mercy, what have you done!" The Master-at-Arms tucked his pistol into his waistband, hurled himself forward to pummel the impostor with balled fists.

The cannon shuddered. A humming sound began, barely audible at first, but increasing in volume slowly, building to an excruciating crescendo. Amadina could hear it clearly from the far side of the crowded deck where she slumped, exhausted, against the rail. Something was wrong with the device. Where was Tobias? Had he been killed? Must she again suffer the agony of not knowing?

She had to get off the ship, even though death awaited her on the ice below without shelter or provisions.

A dark shape hit the deck before her with a sickly thud. She stared at it stupidly until another fell, and then another. The third had landed face upwards, its neck at an impossible angle.

Amadina scrambled to her feet, hauling herself up using the railing as support. She tilted her face skywards. The Luminance, fully opened now, was spitting bolts of lightning and disgorging bodies.

"The cannon's going to blow—all hands abandon ship!" cried a familiar voice, almost inaudible over the sickly hum of the cannon. Tobias? She searched for him amongst the crowd. Sailors and fur-clad refugees alike stopped fighting and started fleeing the *Cotillion*, dodging falling bodies as they thudded to the deck. Some tossed ropes over the side, others scrambled down rope ladders. Still others threw themselves overboard, preferring to chance drowning or broken bones over the cannon's inevitable explosion. Amadina looked to the ice and then the cannon. It vibrated wildly, glowing with unearthly light. The Master-at-Arms stood beside it, transfixed, mesmerised by the weapon's incredible power.

She stared at the icy blackness beyond the ship. Could she bring herself to do it? Cast herself upon the mercy of the Arctica Sea one more time?

Movement in her peripheral vision. A lifeboat lowering over the side with a pulley, swinging precariously as the two figures seated within gripped the rollicks trying to steady it. The Luminance Reader and her silent companion. With her ears still ringing from the cannon's hum, Amadina gathered her bloodied wrapper and ran toward the boat, taking a flying leap over the side and landing squarely within it. The women shrieked as the ropes gave way and the boat plummeted downwards. The splash of the landing was obliterated by the sound of the cannon exploding.

Amadina curled into a ball in the bottom of the lifeboat, as small as she could make herself as she prepared to die. Icy water licked at her skin through her clothes, but it was water from the bottom of the boat, not the sea itself. The hull had remained intact and she was not injured by the blast. She tried to will herself to sit up, but terror and fatigue held her still. She could hear the whimpering of the women beside her as the boat jerked violently from side to side but it did not overbalance and after a time it too was still, and all she could hear was the thudding of her own heart.

The world around them had fallen silent, no shouts of terror, no cries of agony as might be expected in an explosion's aftermath. All she could hear was the ocean. Was everybody else dead?

Eventually curiosity overran fear and she uncoiled herself from the lifeboat's protective depths.

The ship's hull had been shattered by the force of the exploding cannon. She watched breathlessly as a blood-smeared section of the deck slipped soundlessly beneath the surface.

Hanging above the splinter-strewn water was a sight for which she had no words. The women beside her in the lifeboat clung to each other, also speechless. The Luminance was gone, as if ripped from the sky by a giant hand. Beyond it, the *fabric* of sky itself, inset with the all-too-familiar depths of Hell. A scorched and ruined cityscape shimmering under blistering sun. Her homeland, just as she remembered it.

Shapes moved through the smouldering silhouettes of buildings. Large, streamlined contraptions the size of whales, but with legs and other appendages, small heads and glowing mantis eyes.

"Dear God in Heaven, what have we done?" Amadina whispered, her knuckles clenched white against the side of the boat. Surely she was hallucinating, an after-effect of the explosion, but the chill of the air against her damp skin told her otherwise. All she could do was stare in horror as one of the war machines approached the ripped sky's edge. It swivelled its targeting sensors out at her across the water, antennae twitching as the warm air met the cold. She opened her mouth in a silent scream as the metal beast aimed through the tear in the sky and fired.

THE ALABASTER CHILD

The whole time we'd beat him, Chaedy had leered at me as if he knew some goddamn awful secret. Just another sly dog relic dealer, same as all the others. I still don't know how he got out of that cage.

He was old enough to be my grandfather—not that I'd ever had one. Him and his kind had picked the Verge bone clean, yet somehow good stuff was still getting scrounged. Relics worth big coin in Sammarynda. Broke Highway was the pot o'gold, he'd confessed through shattered teeth. Eventually. It took us half the night.

I hated the filthy smirk upon his face and the fact that none of us could smack it off him. He seemed amused that Dartmoor was sending *me*. Laughed himself sick over it. I took the job anyway— why wouldn't I? Us stateless types can't afford to be too picky.

Three weeks on and I'd had to kill a stranger. My knife remained embedded in his chest. I knelt beside his lifeless form, groped blindly for the handle. Warm, sticky blood ran down my hand as I raised the blade at the sound of approaching footsteps.

He'd lunged at me unexpectedly, his weapon drawn and ready. Not the first to try it on when he saw I was a girl. Won't be the last one either but I'm tougher than I look. Harder too. The road sure takes it out of you.

A woman's face ghosted from a flicker of torchlight. She stepped towards the fallen man, paused a moment, kicked him hard. Then once more in the ribs for good measure.

"Serves him right," she said smugly. "Deserved everything he got, and anyway, who's going to speak for him out here?"

She didn't give my knife a second glance. "Did he get you, love? Did he hurt you very bad?"

"He came out of nowhere," I explained. I didn't—"

"Ah, don't sweat it any. You did his wives back home a favour. But whatever are you doing on Broke Highway all alone?"

Looking for something, of course—aren't we all? According to Chaedy, that artifact had come from some place near here. A curious relic of brass and shiny silver. A *special* place, he'd called it—said I'd know it when I saw it. But he'd have said anything at that point of proceedings. So far I'd seen nothing of value. Just a lonely desert highway strewn with ruins of a thousand lifetimes past.

"Come sit by the fire, then. You'll catch your very death." The woman gave the corpse a final kick. "Get that warm robe out from under him. Won't be needing it where that bastard's gone."

Not in the mood for arguing, I tugged the robe free while the woman held the torchlight firm and steady.

"Name's Ennah," she said. "Got business in Brokehart. Obviously." She indicated her swollen belly with the hand not holding the torch.

"You're pregnant?"

"Aren't you?"

I shook my head.

"Thought that was why he was after you. Oh well. His mistake."

His mistake, alright. I hadn't meant to kill him. I hadn't meant to do so many things, amongst them following Chaedy's cryptic hints to the arse end of the world.

Ennah led me back through darkness to a campfire where two young women huddled close. Both looked up when we approached but neither spoke.

"That one's Lahela, the other one's called Ruth. Ruth, fix the lass here some beans. What did you say your name was?"

"Gehenna Diel." I told the truth. There didn't seem to be much point to lying.

"Fix Miz Diel here old Shithead's share. He landed on the sharp end of her blade."

Ruth scrambled to her knees and filled a bowl from the blackened cooking pot. She passed it over, admiration glowing on her filth-streaked face. Neither girl seemed troubled by news of *Shithead's* death.

"By Grace, it's good to have someone to talk to," Ennah said. "Shithead didn't like us signing. Treated us like cattle to market he did."

Lahela looked to be no older than Ruth, fourteen, maybe fifteen. Both were pregnant. I wondered if they were sisters. They seemed so terribly young and vulnerable. Like they'd already seen far more of life than was good for them.

"Neither of you can speak?"

Both shook their heads, their faces flush with something resembling shame.

"They've been fixed," said Ennah.

"Fixed? What is 'fixed?'"

"Show her."

Ruth sat forward on her haunches. She took my hand, opened her own mouth and placed the tip of my index finger inside. I reeled back in disgust at the thing I touched. The stump of a tongue, crudely cauterized. The girl lowered her eyes.

"Who did this to you?"

Ennah shrugged. "Their own people quiet them, I guess."

Quiet them? No matter how far I travelled, cruelty never seemed too far behind. Some days I was glad I remembered nothing of my own childhood. Other times that empty gap of years was all I thought about. "Why are you going to Brokehart?" My beans, uneaten, sat beside me on the ground.

"Only two reasons anyone bothers with that town. The Manor House or the Tide."

I'd never heard of either but I didn't want to tell them that. The three looked harmless but out here in the Badlands, things were rarely exactly what they seemed.

"I'll take his papers, pay the brokerage fee," said Ennah. "Wrap my face and cover up with his cloak. No one'll be the wiser. If they are, I'll pay 'em off. It's not like I got anywhere else to go."

She shot me a look that said I didn't understand. She was right. I didn't.

"And what about them?"

Ennah shrugged. "They birth at the Manor House. At least they'll be fed and warm for a time, then paid when they deliver. They got papers. Forged, but good enough. They'll be all right once we're through the gate."

The girls seemed unconcerned to hear their futures plotted out by others. Both were captivated by the fire, watching yellow and orange flames dance along the burning thornbush twigs.

"We're going to have to bury him," said Ennah thoughtfully. Otherwise dogs'll be bothering us all night."

That got the girls' attention. They scampered off into the darkness, making strange sounds in their throats that I later recognised as tongueless laughter. When they eventually dragged it to the fire, the naked corpse was missing genitals and a face. Rocks had evidently been used to perform the mutilations.

The four of us dug a shallow grave with hands and knives. When the burying was done, Lahela retrieved the dead man's possessions: boots, his coin purse and a shirt.

I eyed the shirt distastefully.

"Have you seen yourself?" said Ennah.

Even in the low light of the fire, I could see my own was filthy, ingrained with dirt, dried blood and who knew what else. The boots were mine if I wanted them. The coins we split four ways.

Once the excitement was over, Lahela and Ruth curled together by the fire. Dogs howled hungrily in the distance. At least I hoped they were dogs.

"You from 'round here?" Ennah asked.

I shook my head. My origins were uncertain. I didn't even know how old I was but she didn't need to know that. Most folks guessed me somewhere around thirty.

"Broke Highway sees a lot of travellers. They come to Brokehart for Tide harvest thinking to strike it rich. Mind you watch your back *and* your front. Nobody in Brokehart can be trusted."

"I'll mind," I assured her. "I'm not here for any harvest."

"Sure you are," she smiled. "One way or another, that's what everybody comes for.

No wall protected Brokehart from the savagery of the desert. No gate or bridge, just scattered stones and a lopsided canvas awning propped on ancient poles. Underneath, a fat man dozed, nestled comfortably amidst a stack of faded mats. His desk was a packing crate inscribed with heat-etched symbols. Upon it huddled a thick pile of brittle papers, weighted against occasional breezes with a rock.

"You must give him a coin and tell him a name," Ennah whispered.

"What coin? What name?"

"Doesn't matter."

The fat man raised a bushy eyebrow. He swigged from a glass bottle as the four of us approached.

Her face and body wrapped up tight against prying eyes, Ennah thrust a wad of papers at him impatiently.

"Family business?" he inquired, eyeing Ruth and Lahela with casual interest. He rifled through the topmost pages before directing a sideways glance at me.

Ennah tossed a pouch of hammered silver down. He picked it up, gauged the weight then pocketed it with a swift, well-practiced motion.

In exchange for my own coin I received a clumsy disc of clay stamped with what looked to be a number. Once that was done he waved us though.

Out of earshot, Ennah shrugged. "Some days you gotta fight for it. Some days no one cares. Luck's on your side today, Gehenna Diel. Hope she stays with you. You're gonna need her when the Tide comes in. No one leaves this cursed town 'til it does."

"Tell me more about this Tide."

Too late. Ennah was already distracted by the cluster of women in loose-fitting shifts gathered before the black gates dead ahead.

"Sorry friend, but it's the end of the line. Ask anyone about the Tide. It's what they're here for."

Ennah unwrapped her face and affixed a cosmetic smile. I did my best to appear disinterested as women converged on the three of them, patting their bellies as if they were long lost family members, which, for all I knew, they might have been.

The walls of the Manor House were high and topped with fearsome shards of broken glass. Beyond its black-lacquered railings, well-muscled guards patrolled. There was even a garden, a patterned scattering of succulents. At its centre, a pillar upon which sat a statue. An alabaster child, its arms outstretched in search of comfort. Something I suspected there'd be little of in the whitewashed buildings behind.

Offering coin for babes seemed harsh, yet perhaps no more so that the lives Lahela and Ruth could have offered children on their own. Ennah's, I sensed, was a different story, but she hadn't chosen to share it and I'd decided not to ask.

Now and then young women, sometimes pregnant, sometimes not, would cross the well-manicured courtyard bearing baskets of laundry. The guards ignored them and, eventually, I did, too. There were no children, babes or otherwise. The buildings beyond the metal gates were silent.

Brokehart's main street extended in a sullen strip edged with rows of dilapidated shopfronts. Most were made of mud bricks, the occasional extravagant porch of sun-warped wood. Discord radiated, a sense of menace lurking just below the surface.

The street was wide enough to take four wagons side by side. Five if they were the coastal type rather than the all-terrain vehicles of the interior. Further along, the buildings became much grander, the tallest of them topped with domes and spires. Everything in Brokehart was old as time and covered in a clingy film of dust.

Brokehart's transient inhabitants were a mix of races: dark skin, light skin, faces inked and plain. Some wore clothing faded from former opulence. Others appeared to have stitched themselves into sacking.

I went for a casual promenade—an unwise move that drew too much attention. Only hawkers and traders walked the street. Women with hair bound tight in scarves balanced baskets of bread on their hips, selling miserly strips of it to the hungry. Water sellers, too, bulging 'skins slung across bent backs. The Tide was the only topic of conversation amongst the thin-shouldered men and women whispering in whatever scraps of shade the dilapidated awnings offered.

At the far end of the street stood a whitewashed building with smooth oval windows. Scantily clad girls and pretty boys slouched on benches through the glassless frames, fanning themselves against the morning's heat. I turned my back on the brothel. Nothing in Brokehart resonated like Chaedy threatened it would. There was nothing to do but to wait for the mysterious Tide. A wait I hoped would not be a long one.

A spot at a verandah's edge offered paltry shade but conversation was lively. I sat, cross-legged, my back against the crumbling mud brick wall. Here, prospectors with more hope in their hearts than meat on their bones traded enthusiastic stories of other times and other Tides. I strained my ears, gleaning as much detail as I could.

"The '57 was the one. Whole family's fortune grew from that tiny globe. Weren't no bigger than a baby's fist."

"What the jeepers was it?"

"Never did find out. Something from the old time. The damn thing glowed when you set it down on stone."

"I don't believe it. I been 'specting this stretch for a decade. Dug out metal aplenty but never nothing worth big money."

"You gotta know where to look, Cleve. Gotta dig down deep, not just go pecking away at the surface like a chicken."

Laughter erupted amongst the red-faced folks.

"Depends where you're set to digging, don't it? All depends on luck o' the Tide. Isn't nothing clever about it. Just plain ol' luck is all."

Cleve snorted. "They don't tell us all they know. Can't tell me they don't got inklings of what's in there and what ain't."

"They don't know any more than ordinary folks, Cleve. You've done all right. Don't know what you're whining on about."

I waited until hunger made my stomach growl before breaking out my meagre rations. How long would we sit here baking in the sun waiting for something to happen? A few hours at most, I'd thought, but by mid afternoon nothing had changed. People seemed to take things in their stride.

"Will the Tide come in today?" I eventually asked one of the women.

She laughed. "Your first Tide is it, dear? You gotta have patience. Tide comes when Tide comes. Nothing anyone can do about it."

I nodded, wishing I'd held my tongue. The oppressive heat was making me drowsy, sending me to think of other places, other things.

As shadows lengthened and the last dregs of sunlight filtered from the sky, the lines began to break up a little. Some folks apparently had places to go. Others would be sleeping where they sat. Small fires sprang up, with enterprising peddlers hauling carts of dried dung up and down mainstreet. Some, like the woman before me, had supplies of their own. When her fire was going, she, Cleve and the others nudged over to make room for me. I tried not to appear as grateful as I felt.

When they asked for my story, I made one up: how a savage storm had torn me from my caravan. Each had sympathy to spare, a storm tale of their own, and dried meat and figs which they shared without hesitation. Stories, it seemed, ran thicker here than blood. Every one of them had lost a friend or a loved one to the Badlands' unpredictable turbulence.

"This will be my last Tide, for certain," the woman, whose name was Shereet, explained. "I'm getting too old to be digging up a Tidefront. Oughta be home before a hearth fire, grandchildren settling on my knees."

"You don't got any grandchildren," sniffed Cleve.

"Might do. How would you know? Nobody knows what goes on in Sammarynda. Could have ten of 'em by now!"

My ears pricked up, alerted by the name. Long had I ached to visit the coastal cities.

"My Lara went to Sammarynda. Least that's where she said she was heading. Got berth on a 'van heading thataway." She gestured vaguely into the distant darkness. "The 'van come back next season without her. Camel drivers said she made it to the sea, if you can trust what those old dogs have to say."

"I haven't seen any wagons. Nor camels."

Cleve laughed. "That's 'cos the Tide ain't come yet, stupid girl. There's never nothing to see before Tidefall."

"Shush you," said Shereet, glaring at Cleve till he bowed his head to stare at the fire's consolatory embers. "She's new here and she don't know the truth of it—weren't you listening? Didn't you hear about how she got lost from all her kin?"

Shereet leaned in closer and patted me on the hand. "My Lara's about your age, give or take. Wherever she is, I hope someone's feeding her up and sharing their fire. Tide'll come in tomorrow, or a day after. When it does, this dump will come to life. There'll be kites in the air, camels on the road and you can find someone to take you wherever you want, providing you got coin. What matters most is what you scavenge. You're young and quick and nimble with your hands. Not old and slow like me."

"You'll be lucky to find your own arse out there tomorrow," said Cleve, sniggering.

"Will you shut up, you old fool!" said Shereet. "Whose figs you think you're gnawing on right now? Should've left you back in

Arrowfell where I found you, camels or no camels."

"She's so green she don't even got a sack!" said Cleve. He pointed at my humble swag. "That bedroll's no good. What's she gonna fit in that?"

Shereet angled her body, allowing a little more firelight to spill upon me. "No sack? Mercy, he's right! You'd better buy yourself one tomorrow. Got any coin?"

"A little."

Shereet paused to think. "Cleve, give her one of yours."

Cleve sat bolt upright. "What did you just say?"

"You heard me. Give her one of your spares. You always bring too many. You can give her one."

"She ain't your daughter, Sher. Not your business to be looking out for her."

Shereet gazed at me thoughtfully. "No, she ain't my Lara. But all the same, you'll give her a sack, and a sup of wine. Two if she really needs it. And you'll quit your complaining or I swear you'll be out there on your own tomorrow, scratching the sand alone with no one to watch your back."

Cleve turned his face away in disgust. But a few hours later he untied a roll of coarse hessian from his pack and tossed it my way, and the wineskin was passed into my hands. When I settled down to sleep that night, the last thing I noticed before drifting off was that Shereet had moved, and was now lying next to Cleve, his arm draped protectively across her stomach.

The first warm streaks of dawn brought Tidesign, a pale shimmer ghosting the horizon, soon to become a seething borealis.

You'll know what you're looking for when you see it. Take me at my word, Gehenna Diel.

Old Chaedy had been mighty sure of himself. I understood why when I caught sight of the raw blue wall of power, with its roiling clouds and stabbing forks of lightning. The blooming Tide held the whole town to ransom. Pots boiled over, prospectors stopped their bickering mid-feud.

The longer I stared at it, the harder it was to wrench my gaze away. Tidescent filled my nostrils, flooding my mouth with a sharp, metallic tang. Bolts of errant lightning lanced the sand, hardening to fangs of smoky glass.

A brace of camel riders came from nowhere, each with a band of bright blue cloth around their arm. They bore weapons, guns and knives. Brokehart prospectors were made to work in a single line that stretched across the sand, evenly spaced. Clay discs issued at the gate determined order. When whistles blew, we began to forage. Those camel riders kept us all in line.

The line advanced at a snail's pace. Tidestorm hung heavy above us, like a richly curdled curtain. I could sense the weight of it, felt the sand beneath my boots shudder each time lightning struck the ground.

We combed the churned-up sand for relics, items spewed forth from the peculiar turbulence. I copied the others—picked up things and shoved them in my sack. Bits of metal dating from the old time. Cogs and discs and coloured twists of wire. I found a brass spoon, a plastic comb and some polished wood. The tip of a spear, hammered from some sort of silver alloy, obviously of worth. A resin disc, bright, clean and flat. Was everything the Tide brought in so beautiful?

Above, the Tidestorm boiled and spat silvery bolts. Gusts of erratic wind blew my headwrap loose, sending my hair into a wind-whipped frenzy. Forcing myself to look away, I focused my attention downwards, scanning for irregularities. Signs that hinted treasure lay below.

My sack was a fifth full before I encountered something I didn't want to touch. A dead animal, half burned. Nothing I'd ever seen before. Like a rat only much larger, with vicious claws and elongated teeth. Whatever it was, it hadn't been dead long. Perhaps the lightning had killed it?

Not far away, two boys with rough blue tattooed swirls on their faces froze suddenly, eyes cupped to peer into the haze. Something shiny jutted from the sand ahead. I could see it, too. Without a word, they broke the line and ran for it. One tugged it free, shouting loudly to his friends, waving his prize above his head. The second boy whooped for joy, leaping and punching the air with his fist. The boys fought a mock battle for possession of the metal, shoving each other violently to the sand. A third boy scolded harshly, gesturing madly at the forage line. Reminding them where they were supposed to be.

Distracted by the boys, I might have missed it altogether had my boot not struck something hard. Shimmering and smooth, a wheel with smaller wheels inset. Expertly crafted. Nothing from our time. My heart raced. Without doubt, a companion piece to Chaedy's precious artifact. I slipped the machine-thing casually into Cleve's sack, glancing furtively around to see if anyone had noticed.

A clap of thunder sounded. One of the boys leapt suddenly, running past me, hurtling towards the thick of the Tidestorm, howling like a wild beast. Had he lost his mind?

The camel riders were soon upon him. One of them swung a lasso. The rope easily found its mark. The boy toppled. He struggled valiantly, shouting obscenities, harsh sounds muted by the breeze. The grim-faced camel rider raised his gun then shot him like a dog.

Nobody stopped what they were doing. Nobody said a thing. The boy was left where he had fallen, prospectors stepping over him as if he were a branch.

From this point on were slender pickings. No breaks were called for rest. Folks did not share idle conversation. The forage line went on, no matter what. Back towards the town, I glimpsed small children scrabbling in the sands already passed. Now and then one would spot a treasure. Shouting with glee, they'd run back to the safety of the buildings, delivering the precious item to an adult. The camel riders ignored them. Apparently once the line had swept the sand, the forage became a free for all.

Further on I found another of the dead, rat-like creatures. I passed it over but the family beside me did not. A skinny daughter snatched it up and stowed it within her sack, despite its head being horribly bloodied and crushed.

Suddenly I felt sorry for the lot of them. There was no generosity out here. Life was harsh. Every mouthful must be fought for, even a dead rat too precious to be ignored.

Hours passed with little to distinguish each one from the next. Occasionally a cry of excitement would issue from up or down the line. A rich find inspiring hope in some, envy in others. Such cries solicited nothing but scowls of contempt from the family sweating in the sun beside me.

At other times, singing would commence. Mournful, repetitive dirges that served to keep up the rhythm of stepping, bending and digging. I did not join in and wouldn't have, even if I'd known the words. The body of the slaughtered boy lay baking in the sun. Would no one come to claim it? Not while the Tide harvest ran, apparently.

Finally, the light began to fade and foragers broke formation to head back to town in small clusters. I joined them with an aching back and a growling belly. My sack was heavy, my mind focused on the precious relic within. Chaedy and his riddles be damned— the only question left was why Dartmoor's raiders hadn't yet taken Brokehart and its precious Tide by force.

"There you are!" said a familiar voice as I trudged across the sand. "We was worried for you when that boy got done. Saw you staring with yer mouth hanging open. Doesn't pay to mind nobody else's business, girl. Didn't I tell you? Didn't nobody tell you?'

I threw up my hands in protest, but I couldn't stop Shereet's clumsy embrace.

"They murdered him."

Shereet shook her head. "Those Badlanders know how it goes. If they're stupid enough to step out of line, it's their own doing."

I was too tired to argue. Shereet hooked her arm through mine and dragged me back to where Cleve and two others stood waiting. Between them they had amassed several sackloads of goods. My own haul was pitiful by comparison.

"There's always a rush for tallying, but I say it's best to wait. Come eat with us. We can go for tallying together."

The Brokehart we returned to was completely different to the town we'd left. The place had literally come to life. Drab verandahs were hung with coloured banners advertising food and drink and other wares. The air was thickly scented with the smell of roasting meat. Laughter too as friends slapped each other on the back, congratulating themselves on fortunes made.

Children scampered underfoot. Music blared behind saloon doors and the lineup at the whorehouse stretched halfway down the street. Other lines snaked in and out of doorways. "Tally rooms," said Shereet, "But we don't want to be bothering with those just yet."

Individual campfires glowed up and down the length of mainstreet and it was to one of these that Shereet and the others headed. I followed obediently, enticed by the delicious smells. I didn't care if it was camel, rabbit or giant rat. Shereet directed me to a square of scrappy matting. I sat, nursing my sack of curiosities. Shereet shoved the others along and squeezed in beside me. Each campfire sported a couple of men standing watchfully over the others, ancient rifles cocked and at the ready.

"Got enough to see you by?" asked Shereet.

I shrugged. "I don't know what anything's worth. I don't even know what half this stuff is *for*."

Shereet laughed. "No matter what it's for, so long as someone's willing to pay for it." She shouted across the fire. "Hurry up with that meat, some of us are dying of hunger back here."

My belly growled in agreement. Shereet laughed again. She leant in closer, pulling her sand cloak tight across her shoulders. "You look like you're from the coast. Things is different there. Things stay the same, season to season, year to year. But here in the Badlands, things is always changing. Every day is different from the next. Few things stay certain other than pain, death and the Tide. Head yourself back to the coast tomorrow. Hang around this town too long . . . " She scowled and shook her head. "Most likely you'll wind up somebody's dinner, be they beast or man."

I accepted a skewer of glistening meat, tearing into it quickly, lest it turn out to be a mirage and vanish into nothing before my eyes.

"My Lara was smart," Shereet continued. "She got out when she could. I laughed at her. Told her she had airs and graces, but she proved me wrong 'cos she never came back to this stinking place."

Shereet chewed hungrily, juice dribbling down her chin. I wanted to ask about her daughter, how she knew so much about her when they'd had no contact for years. But I knew better. Sometimes believing was better than knowing. Who wouldn't want their child to have found a better life than Brokehart had to offer?

Two skins were passed, one of water, a smaller one of wine. I drank from both while listening to the banter. I felt at home beside Shereet, as though I'd known her years. Someday I'd go searching for my mother. Find out why she'd had to give me up.

"Show us what you scored, then," she said, wiping her hands clean on the hem of her skirt.

I hesitated before revealing the relic with the tiny wheels, each one set so tight inside the other.

"That'll be worth a pretty penny," said a long-faced, ginger-stubbled man. The others nodded silently in agreement.

The wine was flushing my bones with warmth. I leant in closer to whisper conspiratorially. "Don't s'pose any of you ever met a man called Chaedy?"

Beards were stroked, heads were shook. "Can't say rightly that I did," said Cleve, his forehead creasing into frown.

"Who owns this town? Who stops the gangs from claiming it as their own? That Tideline seems an orderly kind of business."

"A boy was killed today, just like you said," whispered Shereet. "Nothing much that's orderly 'round here."

The fireside had fallen silent. The weight of a dozen pairs of eyes bore down on me.

I'd said the wrong thing and did my best to deflect it with a shrug. Before too long harmless chatter started up again. More wine and meat was passed from hand to hand.

Shereet stared at me for a very long time, the firelight lending her features an unusual harshness. "There's nothing to be knowing in Brokehart, child. Can't say I didn't do my best to warn you."

She tightened her grip on my hand then let it go.

"More wine?" Cleve offered brightly.

I said yes.

"Get some sleep," was the last advice Shereet had to offer. "You never know what troubles tomorrow will bring."

I drew my sandcloak close against my skin then curled around my sack of treasures feeling more comfortable and contented that I had in a good many years.

The cold woke me. I smelled old ash and wondered where I was. Ice and cramp had set in to my joints. My head ached abominably. When I eventually mustered the balance to sit upright, I found myself alone beside the fire's dregs. Where were Shereet, Cleve and the others? Why did my head hurt so much? Silence hung in a deathly pall across the street. My stomach roiled and then I panicked, realising that my waterskin and my sandcloak were gone. I staggered to my feet, clutching at my belly. No, the 'skin was still there beside me, half covered in sand as though someone had tried to disguise it. But the sandcloak was definitely missing, as was my sack of treasures.

As I stumbled along mainstreet, I tried to piece together the previous evening's events. So many small details—the wine skin passing to my hands, Shereet insisting I should go back to the coast. Had I drunk so much? Surely no more than a few mouthfuls to be polite. The drink had made me sleepy and then there was nothing after that.

I staggered to the nearest building and slumped my back against it, fighting the urge to be sick with all my strength. Doubling over, I waited until the wave of cramps eased up. Beads of cold sweat collected on my forehead. I wiped them away with my fist. *Had I been poisoned? Had anyone else drunk from that second smaller wineskin?*

The few people who were about moved slowly. Campfires smouldered, releasing thin grey wisps of smoke.

Mainstreet was drained of all the evening's vitality and colour. Broken bottles littered the ground. Bodies too, some of them in pools of blood. There had been brawls the night before, the easy camaraderie of wealth turning ugly with nothing more to fuel it than a spilled drink or a misinterpreted glance.

No. It could not be true. Shereet would not have robbed me. Shereet had been so kind. Another cramp wracked me and this time I could not hold it in. Falling onto my hands and knees, I vomited, shuddering violently until the deed was done. I sat back on my haunches as relief spread through my body, breathing in great greedy gulps of air.

Searching would be pointless. Shereet and Cleve would be long gone on wagon trains bound for larger towns, departed at dawn with nothing but scuffed ground and camel dung to mark their berths. Soon, even the dung would be scavenged by those ill-fated enough to be left behind.

I walked to the end of the street, staring past the edge of the farthermost building at the Tide's ragged remains. A dull smudge of deep azure was all that was left of it. A few sandcombers, children mostly, sacks dragging limply along behind them.

I turned my back on it and walked dejectedly through town. There were people about but none would meet my eye. Was it always this way when the Tide had passed? Everyone gone but those that gambling, greed and violence had got the better of?

My own carelessness and stupidity were to blame for my predicament. Mulling over the events of the past two days, I found myself at a standstill outside the building Ennah had called the Manor House.

I had paid so little attention to it the day I arrived. Now that everything else had been stripped away, the house might be the only chance I had.

The big black gates were firmly locked, with armed guards patrolling the courtyard beyond. Large men in dark garb with rifles slung across their shoulders, they eyed me suspiciously, but neither did any more than that. I posed no threat on the far side of the gate. Each patrolled their section of yard, now and then glancing aggressively through the bars into the street beyond.

Around the back, iron gates merged into brick. In all, the barrier enclosed three multi-storey structures, one of them with massive wooden doors. There was no way in or out of the place, save through the front gates.

Peering through the bars, I could see someone moving about in the rear courtyard. A pregnant woman in a white ankle-length shift.

"Ennah?"

The woman turned. It was not Ennah. She eyed me distastefully before disappearing through a darkened arch. No guards were posted in the rear courtyard. They probably didn't need them.

I wandered back up front again, slow footed, heavy hearted. In the centre of the cactus garden, the alabaster child regarded me with empty eyes, its outstretched arms reaching past me to the Tideline's fast degrading stain. Something about it made me feel uneasy.

So engrossed was I in my own pathetic misery, I almost missed what happened next: first the opening of the farthest building's massive wooden doors. Wagons! Four of them, the horseless kind, with mighty wheels of inch-thick butyl, treads designed to transverse all but the thinnest sand.

Next, a line of stick-thin waifs, boys and girls in shirts and pants the colour of stained parchment. One by one they climbed aboard the wagons, none of them stopping to give a glance behind.

I stared at them hard. So hard I forgot to breathe. *Chaedy, you godforsaken bastard.*

It was not the Tideline he had wanted me to see, but this. The alabaster statue of the child. That child had once been *me*. In the courtyard, others like me. Orphans sold into the trade—whatever fancy name they had for it. Orphans by intent, not accident.

I held no memories before the age of five. Few I'd call on willingly before adulthood. Was this where the emptiness began, right here behind these shiny metal gates? I gripped them tight, pressed my face against cold black. Found myself thrown back suddenly when they groaned and shuddered open.

Little memories, cold and hard as stone. Songs and dances learned by rote. Other lessons known as *tricks of trade.* They all came flooding back in a relentless, sickening wave. Images that would stay with me forever.

I'd kill Chaedy when next I saw him. Not clean and easy either, no sharp blade through the heart.

As the wagons thundered down mainstreet, only one of the children met my gaze. A little thing with big brown eyes, her hair cropped close, uneven. She didn't smile or try to wave, just stared without expression. I raised my open arms to her in parody of the alabaster child, hoping to god she couldn't read my thoughts.

HOLLYWOOD ROADKILL

We were lucky to find her. Lu was dirty but she wasn't sick. Skinny but not malnourished, a rarity since the new lanes got added and fresh produce became a half-remembered dream. As if living Roadside wasn't already tough enough.

I'd been looking for someone like Lu for a long time. She needed training, or course; who didn't, but if my team pooled its resources I figured we could get her cleaned up enough to have a real shot at success. Shira had the legals covered, Derek still had memories of med school and Jase? Jase was muscle. When we got across, I'd take care of the press. We could have done with a style consultant, but style was a little thin on the asphalt this side of the Road. No, We didn't need style, we were going to play the kidnapped waif card—provided the codes I'd bought were good. That was why I needed Derek. Lu was going to have to get hit. It had to look messy or else we'd never get our sixty seconds, let alone our hour in court. The trick was gonna be roughing her up without doing any real damage. No marks on her face—just a little blood and a few scratches for sympathy. Maybe crack a couple of ribs for effect. There were tricks to bouncing off a hood and rolling out of harm's way. Derek was training her up for it. He'd gotten girls across the road before, he said.

Lovely Lu: Tallulah as I had re-badged her, was gonna be our ticket out of here. Our job was to get her across the road. Hers would be to get me through the city gates. The others too, if they could keep up. There'd be casualties. We weren't all gonna make it.

It didn't do to care too much. Getting too attached to your running mates could be fatal.

◇◇

It's Friday night and I find myself staring across the faceless grey expanse of Road, past the fires and occasional gunfire of the median strip. Up into the brilliant flood of neon, laser, crystal and chrome that makes up Hollywood City. I think maybe I was born there amidst the shiny turrets and spires. I have memories of manicured lawns and children laughing. Children dressed identically in little plaid-print uniforms. Children with neat-combed hair and ruddy cheeks. Not the scrawny vagabonds that slink across the darkness here, squeezing between tarpaulins and the shacks, fighting each other in the mud for scraps of garbage. Roadside, if you're still a child at eight years old you might as well be dead, especially if you're slow on your feet, too weak to scavenge or too ugly to sell yourself. Most Roadsiders grew up somewhere else and backwashed here on a rising tide of filth. Hollywood city rubbish barges hover overhead, pausing to dump waste on us from the sky.

But me, I'm from Hollywood City. I just know it's the truth and one day I'm going back there, straight across the Road. Tomorrow is gonna be that day.

Tallulah's asleep now, drowsy from the extra food. The rest of us are buzzing on meth. Just enough to mask the hunger and keep us on the wire. There's no lights at all this side of the Road. Nothing to tell you what's coming or going but the whine of servos and the rumble and growl of engines. Jase says he can feel the big wheels trembling through the asphalt. I believe him. Jase doesn't talk much but when he does, it's always about stuff he can feel. He's big, Jase, big and solid despite the relentless gnawing hunger. Reckon he was built that way, although he's got the same chip extraction scar as the rest of us. When his skin gets cut, he bleeds, but he heals up fast. I wonder what he was, and what he did to wind up Roadside.

And Lu—I wonder about her too because she hasn't got the chip scar on her neck. No scar, yet she can't have been born here. She looks too damn good for that. No, she's from somewhere else— beyond the spires of Hollywood city, perhaps. Makes me wonder what else there might be out there. Maybe tomorrow I'll find out.

◇◇

Derek says it's time. I expect Shira to argue, but she just nods and stares across the Road to the city lights, all neon rainbow-jewelled and winking coyly at us as if to say *come and get it baby—it's all yours*.

Shira knows she was a lawyer in the way-back-when. She didn't lose everything when she lost her chip. Stuff you learned yourself before they chip you, you get to keep all that. Some city folks still raise their kids old fashioned. I would too now, if I had kids, knowing what I know. I've watched too many Roadside wash-ups tumble out of the garbage chute with shit in their pants, incapable of speech because their folks all chipped their babies instead of teaching.

I go to wake Tallulah. Her face is framed with soft brown curls. I wish I could leave her sleeping peaceful as an angel but it's time to do it—and if we don't go now we never will. Jase says this is the quietest time. Fewer road trains and overlands. Less chance of getting hit. Automatic trucks run on sonar rails. They don't need light for sight like people do.

We've told no one we're going but a small crowd has gathered. No one strong enough to mount a challenge or try and steal Tallulah for themselves.

This kid's standing a few feet away with his scabby mouth hanging open. Like he can't believe we're gonna make a run for it. I look away. Part of me doesn't believe it either—or want to remember the set of circumstances that brought me to this point. And there's another part of me, deep down and dark, trying to force its way up to the surface. The part that wants to throw myself under the first set of metre-wide treadlinks. Half the folks at Roadside check out that way, eventually. So much quicker than starvation or disease. No shame in it either. The Roadside folks always make the sign, pretend like the runner was trying to make the median strip at least. No shame in it at all, but me—I take another snort of meth and focus on those gleaming neon spires.

Tallulah's eyes glisten with crystal-meth tears. Jase stands by the asphalt listening, his head cocked to one side. I take a final look over my shoulder at the slum I've called my home. The shack I built from scrap with my bare hands. The shack I traded for a batch of numbers. If the 'Roach has ripped me off I'll be running back just to punch retribution into his face. Which one of us is more desperate? I'm betting that it's me.

I clasp Tallulah's hand in my own, smile as reassuringly as I can manage, and then suddenly Derek says, "Run for it," and so the five of us run.

I think I hear a cheer go up behind us, but I can't be sure. Might be the wind in my ears or heart palpitations, but it sounds like cheering, and there we are, all five of us running forward into night. Striding with purpose because we have some place to go.

Minutes in, the thundering screech of a road train shakes the blackness up ahead. Jase stops so we all stop, still and nervous like rabbits. We can't see it but we feel the blast of hot air as it hurtles *en route* to its programmed destination.

I grip Tallulah's hand tighter, trying to reassure her that we know what we're doing. Trying to remind myself what I'm doing here. The Road is cut deep into the earth. Too deep to see the city lights. We can see each other bathed in the tepid yellow haze of torchpins clipped to our belts. We're taking a risk with that. The 'pins make us easy targets. But somehow I doubt the trucks and trains are programmed to scout for runners. What are we to them but roadkill? Bigger than rabbits, smaller than bears—and even rogue bears are too small to mess up the front of those titanium bullbars.

Jase gives the word and then we're running again. Faster this time, by some unspoken consensus. Vehicles on either side of us, but Jase keeps running and so we do too. I need more meth but I'm not stopping for it. Nothing's gonna stop me till we reach the median strip.

Examining the outline of Jase's broad back in the smudge of available light, I realise something I should have guessed before. He's military issue, plain as day. More machine than human, whether he bleeds like us or not. I wonder why he got discarded, what he did to piss them off, but then suddenly my ears are filled with the screech of metal. The acrid stink of chemistry. I don't know what it was that missed us, but it was damn close. The heat of its engines brushed my cheek as it hurtled past into night. Tallulah stumbles. She can tell how close we came to getting splattered. I grip her hand tighter. Too tight, I know, and I pull her forward towards the bobbing firefly glows of the others' pin lights.

She's barely keeping up, and I think she's crying. Maybe she's too buzzed to get the tears out properly, or maybe she just doesn't want me to know.

Fires burn up ahead on the median strip. We're so close. I get excited, relax my grip on Tallulah's hand, then give it a little squeeze. She squeezes back. She's still with me. She still believes we can do this thing. We don't run straight toward the fires—I drilled the other four on this before we left, but I didn't tell them why. We veer to the right and run alongside the median strip wall for a kilometre. I let go of Tallulah's hand and push her in front of me. We're safe from traffic in single file so long as we stick to the wall.

I'm thinking about the meth foil in my pocket when suddenly Jase stops. He uncoils the line from across his back, steps out onto the road and starts to swing the grappling claw around and around. When it gathers enough momentum, he lets it fly. We wait, straining our ears for traffic sounds, nervous at how far out on the dark road Jase is standing. The claw clatters against rock and falls. Jase reels it in and tries again. This time it catches. He tugs twice to make sure it'll hold, then moves towards the protection of the wall.

Jase goes up first, then Derek. I send Tallulah up next, then Shira, then me.

The wall is a pastiche of cement and brick, easy enough to climb once I'm off the ground.

They're all crouched waiting for me at the top, but I don't see them. All I see is Hollywood City blazing like a nebula. I have to blink, my eyes water from the overload. So close. The most beautiful thing I've ever seen. I want it, more than anything. It was my home, I know it was, and it'll be my home again.

Hollywood light pollution means we can navigate the median strip. It also means that others can see us—and there are others here. Renegades like us, outward bound, half a road away from liberty.

Tallulah sinks to her knees and I realise it's time to eat. Crossing the Road burned up all our calories. Derek shares out what we have. It isn't much, and once again we give Tallulah most of it. Nobody complains. She's our ticket to freedom. Without her we're homeless now as well as helpless.

A few mouthfuls makes us all feel a whole lot better. Shira hands me her canteen and we share the last few sips of dirty water.

We watch as Derek takes Tallulah to one side and runs her through her routine once again.

"My name is Tallulah. I was kidnapped from my apartment," she recites with a trembling voice.

"Blink now, widen your eyes. Innocent and hurt," he says, "that's it . . . that's the *sense* we're going for . . . the *vibe* . . . "

"You've got to help me. My parents don't know where I am. It was Ganglanders took me. I saw their leader's face. I think I've seen him on TV . . . "

"Good, Lu darlin', that's very good," says Derek. "Don't give up on the blinking now. Gotta keep those wide brown eyes clean and clear. We need them to believe you."

I fix my eyes on Tallulah's silhouette, cool black against the blazing lights of Hollywood. So beautiful, both of them—the city and the girl.

"You know she's gonna have to get hit," whispers Shira. "And even if she doesn't, once inside the city, you'll never see her again."

"I'm not in love," I tell her—and I mean it. There's no place in my heart for love after six long years Roadside. And there's something else I don't tell Shira. This is not my first attempt to cross the Road. I've run before—twice, and I've got scars to show for both times, inside and out. I don't tell the others. I don't want them to know how bad our chances really are.

But this time is different because this time I've got a plan. A *modus operandi* and a slim strip of numbers in my wristband that means they've got to open the gate. Got to check out Tallulah's story, no matter how bogus it sounds. Got to patch her up after her accident and pay off her "friends". Once the media drones have fixed on her, even half a chance'll be enough.

I snort another pinch of meth and offer some to Shira. It's dirty stuff but it bucks me up like a punch in the face. My precious city blurs for a moment till I wipe away the tears with the back of my hand.

"We're moving out," I say and the others scramble to their feet and prep for action.

I haven't told them about the spiders—or whatever those multi-limbed things are that patrol the median strip walls. No point in freaking out my team. They know to run from anything that moves. If we're trapped by one of those things, running won't make any difference.

The median strip is maybe half a K wide, thicker in places, thinner in others. The surface is uneven so we have to watch our feet. There's nothing grows on the 'strip at all—no regular garbage deposits like we get back Roadside. Nothing to eat except for rats and runners.

Jase goes ahead scouting for fissures. A deep one could lead us straight to the far side of the 'Strip and to an easy climb down onto the Road. I keep Tallulah in my sights but she's moving as well as the rest of us. Derek must have dusted her up again.

We run in silence, breathing deep and slow. Hoping we're far enough away from the fire to pass unnoticed. But I can't shake the feeling that we're being watched. There's no evidence of anything. Just a sensation in my gut. The ones that live on the Median Strip, they're barely human any more. Caught between the coming and the going, living and dying. Ran out across the road, too terrified to make it back. Or there's those who got thrown back from the city gates. Maybe that's what the spiders are for—to keep the runners in, not out.

I'm sure we're being watched, but we run on regardless. Jase leads us to a section of far wall where the cement is ragged and torn. Rusted metal beams protrude like ribs. Easy enough to climb down without grappling claws.

Only ten lanes remain between us and Hollywood City. A shudder of exhilaration wracks my body. This is the farthest I've ever made it. First time, I never even made it up the side of the 'Strip. Second time . . . I trace my index finger down the length of the burn scar on my thigh. I don't want to remember. This time is the only one that matters. This time I'm going all the way.

Derek goes down first, followed by Shira, who grips Lu tightly by the elbow to make sure she doesn't fall. I'm about to follow when I hear a noise behind me. Something that sounds like metal sliding through soft flesh. I turn in time to see Jase fall, a sharpened spike protruding from his chest. Blood pours from the wound. Jase's mouth opens. His eyes widen and I know that he's taking in the bright lights of Hollywood City with his dying sight. Something yanks him backwards. I don't wait to find out what. All I do is pray he's really dead as I scramble down the jagged concrete fissure for my life.

At the bottom, the others see that Jase is not behind me. They don't ask. All of us turn our faces to the Road and make the sign. We all know the risks, and it's not over yet. There'll be time for grieving on the other side.

This stretch of Road will be easier than the first because this time we have light. Ten lanes illuminated by Hollywood City lights.

We move in single file parallel to the wall, trying to gain a bit of distance from the place where we lost our Jase. We know we have to run soon, just in case whatever took him's still hungry.

Seems like there's more traffic here than on the other side, but maybe that's just because we can see it. Road trains: massive tanks of chromium and grey, barrelling through the night, stopping for no one. Mixed among them, occasional ancient rattlers of rust and grime, ploughing forwards at maximum throttle until the day they shake themselves to pieces.

I've got that feeling of being watched again. The traffic flow increases every hour closer to dawn.

It's now or never. "Run!" I shout to the others. And we run.

Derek and Shira have Lu between them. It was supposed to have been Derek and Jase, but Shira knows what has to be done.

Soon comes the hardest part of all. We'll take our lovely Tallulah and bounce her off the hood of an oncoming car. Something small—a private vehicle. Once we have a drone recording, she'll say her spiel and blink her big brown eyes. The drone will suck up the of code I'll feed it—code for persons on the official "missing" list. Unnamed, uncertain, yet we'll have to be checked out. They'll open the barrier field for missing persons, especially one whose bloodstained face has been broadcast citywide. Whoever's car she bounces off is going to want the problem fixed. They're gonna want us inside the city, far away from freelance TV eyes.

There's nobody guarding the city gates. No need for human guards since the barrier field went up.

I spy the burnt-out shell of a vehicle. My heart lurches. If there's been a smash here recently then no one's gonna give a fuck about our Lu. But when I step closer, I realise the wreck is old, its interior thick with damp moss. Things must be very different here. Back Roadside, the moss would have been eaten long ago.

Derek's briefing Lu again. I can see that she's terrified beneath the mask of meth. I scan the skies for drones—wouldn't do to get ourselves recorded before we're set.

We're just about ready when Shira speaks my name. We're not alone. There's a figure watching us from the shadow's edge. I think it's a man, but when he steps forward into the light I can't be certain.

Man or not, he wears articulated armour hammered from scrap steel, decorated with blood and bones. He stinks of oil and rust and war, even from ten paces off. Bone Man is not alone, but his companions skulk in the shadows waiting for his word.

Shira and Derek shove Lu between them as they draw their knives and prepare to fight for her life. We are no match for these urban warriors crouching beneath the city gate. They will kill us for our meat, throw our bones and gristle to the traffic stream. Hell knows what they'll do to Tallulah. If it comes to that I'll kill her myself.

Precious moments trickle past. As my eyes adjust to the arrhythmic pulsing and flickering of city lights, I count the figures shrouded in the darkness. More than a match for us. We are dead. And yet the slaughter does not begin. Why is this?

"So," the person of blood and bone before me says at last, "How youse planning to get inside?"

I won't tell him. I may have to die, but I don't have to die for him.

"You got a plan," the figure states. "Them that makes it this far always do."

Suddenly there's a high-pitched squeal. Above us a media drone slingshots into view. I can hear the whirr and chitter of its servos, the steady hum of its all-weather 'tronics. I don't look up. Neither does Bone Man. He unholsters his weapon, aims above my head and fires before I have time to flinch. Tiny flecks of burning metal score my cheek as the drone disintegrates.

"I'm betting you got gate codes," says Bone Man. "Give them over and I maybe let you go."

Go where, I think, wishing to hell I had a gun in place of the pathetic blade taped to my ankle.

We can't standoff here forever, I'm thinking. Any moment there'll be another drone, or worse.

"The codes are in his wristband," says a gentle voice. My heart breaks.

"Nice work Lu," said Bone man. In one swift movement his tribe surrounds us. Lu pats us down for ordnance. I expect her to avoid eye contact, but when it's my turn she stares straight at me, eyes as cold as glass.

"Strip off your clothes," she says. "All of you."

As I shed my filthy rags, I realise the thing that's killing me most is that I don't remember anything good about my life. All I know in detail is six years Roadside and some vaguely coloured, half-remembered images from childhood. Little plaid uniforms and soft green grass. Laughter fades, and that's it.

Now I'm naked save for the sickly neon shine coming off the gate. Shira's weeping. Of all of us, she was the one who stood the best chance. Derek's face betrays no emotion. I think he died a long time ago. But me, I was living, kicking and screaming for a chance right up until this final moment.

They're going to have to hack my wristband. I'm not telling them anything. A gust of wind brushes my face, a stray current belched from a passing rig. In a second I'm up and running towards the Road, running as fast as my legs can carry me. All I see is the dazzle of oncoming headlights—the blazing fires of evermore. Time slows, tyres screech and darkness pulls me tight into its breast.

SCARP

We were combing along the beach as usual when the first of the birds were sighted. Not much to see, just three silver specks so high as to barely matter. Jesse had his father's spyglass but most eyes were squinting at the ships. Birds were only birds, after all, even birds glinting silver in the sun.

"I saw lights on the ship last night," said May. "So did Garet."

A few kids nodded in sage agreement. Others made half-hearted shushing sounds. We'd all seen the lights, of course we had, only it didn't do to talk about such things. Not in earshot of Grampa and his Council cronies. For that you could cop a belting. May was only five years old. Too young to know anything about anything. You could already see she'd be a pretty girl. Good-looking like her brother Garet.

"Addie, do people live on the ships?" she asked, then again when I didn't answer quick enough.

"Of course they don't. How could they? There's no food. No fresh water."

Two old hulks sat rusting just offshore, listing at ever-increasing angles. Hulks that had once been mighty freighters, or so the stories told. Freighters that went from port to port, picking up cargo and setting it down again. Their captains brown-skinned men in turbans, others blond, broad-shouldered, bearded types who swore a lot and drank themselves to sleep.

Those cargo holds were filled with rotting treasure. Magical machines that sang and spoke. Lavish garments and lotions for your hair. Whole cars carried in their bellies.

Thrule's last car had carked it ten years back. A stinking, rattling contraption that made noise enough to wake the dead. Grampa said the fuel was killing it. Petrol made from corn pulp was no good.

May was still squinting hard across the water.

"You can't even stand up straight on deck," I explained. "Lights are just lights. Like the ones beyond the Scarp."

That didn't help. Mysterious lights beyond the Scarp troubled all of us. Great searing beams like forks of lightning hammered into spikes. Stabbing the sky and staining it sickly yellow.

The Scarp stretched across the back of the horizon. Rocky cliffs and ocean marked its start and ending points. *Escarpment* was what the Council called it, but it had always been Scarp to us. Steep tree-covered slopes led up its sides—dense, thick and impenetrable, except for tracts felled and terraced for farming. Some sections were nothing but sheer cliff drop. Five watchtowers spaced sentinel along the ridge, harsh silhouettes against the sky.

May sniffed and turned her attention upwards to the birds.

I watched Garet drag his laden salvage sack across wet sand. "Whatcha got?" I asked him but he only shook his head. Celeste hadn't shown yet. Whatever he'd found, he was saving it to impress her.

I pocketed some keyhole shells and sugar limpets but my heart wasn't really in it. The lights on the freighter had been bothering me, too. Like somebody was watching us. Hopefully Grampa hadn't seen them. Anything new set the mean old man on edge. He was hard enough to cope with when he wasn't stalking the promenade, rifle slung where everyone could see it.

I'd been counting off days until his next watchtower duty, a job that took him scarptop for a week. Sometimes two, depending on how much hooch went with him—and rented scrubber girls if you believed what people said. Life was better for everyone with him up there. Better for me and Marina most of all.

Garet leapt up suddenly and called out to Celeste, smiling and dropping the sack so he could wave with both arms.

Celeste came mincing up the beach in one of her floral print skirts. You'd have thought a storytale princess had descended from the sky, what with all the fuss Garet made of her. For certain she'd put on that skirt to impress him. Most of us saved our best for festivals and name days but not Celeste. Celeste always saved her best for Garet.

I hurried to join the cluster of kids poking at slabs of washed-up wood. Stubborn flecks of sky-blue paint still clung to its weathered sides. The tide was creeping inwards, pushing bits of plastic stuck amongst the seaweed. The younger kids would pick it out and sort it into brightly coloured piles. I wasn't in the mood for treasures. I'd only joined the morning's comb to get myself out of the house.

Later I'd go back up there when Marina was good and busy and Grampa at Excelsior Hall or, even better, halfway up the Scarp. Shielding my eyes, I searched for his favoured path, hoping for telltale glints off his rifle barrel.

Thick and lush and full of secrets, the Scarp never looked the same way twice. Some days, with the sun full on it, the treetops almost glowed. Other times great clouds of mist simmered from damp bark and earth. No decent folk lived past the settlement line. Not since the Council shot the last of the *malingerers,* as they liked to call them. And rightly so, Grampa told me, although I'd never been able to see what was right about any of it.

A flash of silver did catch my eye, embedded in a faded wash of blue. Those birds again, still three of them, still circling above in search of a place to land.

Peals of laughter laced the breeze, catching everyone's attention. Garet and Celeste, running full pelt along the beach.

"You are so full of it," shouted Garet, showering Celeste with a handful of sand. She squealed with glee, wrists held high to protect her face, long hair splayed like glorious strands of seaweed.

"You're just chicken," she called out to him. "Chickenshit, the lot of ya!"

Celeste threw a glance in my direction, caught me staring. Smirked.

"I've been further up the Scarp than most," said Garet. "Only Jesse's been higher. Seen tracks and trails that aren't even supposed to be there."

"Only got your word for it though, don't we?" She scooped up sand and aimed it at his face.

Garet ducked. "There's plenty of trails. Trails aren't the problem. You know what is—a bullet in your head." He shaped his hand like a pistol, pressed the barrel against his temple.

"Can't help it if *Addie's* Mum's old man's batshit crazy," said Celeste.

Garet nodded enthusiastically, then aimed his hand pistol at her. Celeste squealed and tore away along the sand.

He followed. Such was the way of things. I might have been used to their constant flirting but that didn't mean I had to like it.

I turned my attention to the Scarp, still hoping for evidence of Grampa's leaving. Paths ran through Scarp undergrowth like tangled strands of hair. Most led nowhere. The ones that did lay under the steely gaze of the watchtowers, where ancient machine guns pointed outwards, defending the valley from invasion. Invasion by who or what was a question never answered, although it got asked often enough.

Nothing out there to be bothering with—the only words Grampa ever offered on the subject, mumbled through mouthfuls of overcooked beans and mash. Marina's face had filled in the gaps. *Don't go asking stuff that will annoy him.* And mostly I didn't. No one wanted to be the one to bring on the blinding bouts of rage the old man seemed to think were natural as weather. It was hard enough to see a resemblance between the three of us. Not surprising. A fierce, scraggly beard hid most of his face and hers sagged in perpetual disappointment.

That spyglass of Jesse's father's had recently revealed fresh curiosities as it was passed from hand to hand atop the silos. A row of burnt treetops high upon the Scarp. Burnt recently—the damage had not been evident a month before.

"Fire from lightning!"

"Don't be stupid. Lightning never strikes that far up the Scarp."

"'Cept it did though, didn't it. Right there in plain view."

"Might have been a fire from something else."

Only it couldn't have been, because if fire started, someone would have seen it. Nothing unusual went unnoticed. Not for longer than an hour or two at most.

So what did lie up there beyond the rocky rim? We all had theories, naturally. Some more ridiculous than others. Most popular was the treasure caves. Looted spoils from before the cities fell. Thrones of solid gold. A vast library tunnelled deep into scarprock, containing every book that was ever written. Diamond tiaras. Medicines that could cure everything from whooping cough to blue-ringed octopus.

I reckoned on a far simpler explanation. The Council didn't want to share their turf. They were kings of Thrule, plain and simple. They held the lookout towers just like they held the guns.

People lived up there, I knew that for a fact. Scrubbers and scroungers surviving beyond the Council's grasp. Not just malingerers. Folks who held to different ways of thinking. Kids darting bare-arsed through the undergrowth like rabbits. Breaking into stores and stealing food.

I thought of those dirty, naked children whenever gunshots echoed through the trees. *Target practice. Wild venison.* A wealth of excuses the Councilmen could muster. The Scarp was the boundary. The shield. The great divide. We lived in its bounty and its shadow. I'd seen the view from atop the Seacliff bridge. As close to scarptop as I'd ever get.

Celeste should not have been urging kids to run the Scarp at her behest. The danger was real. Not just guns—the Scarp was always shedding random boulders. Some reckoned that's what smashed each end off the Seacliff bridge way back.

The kids on the beach were still shoving and jostling, trying to snatch Jesse's father's spyglass from each other when May screamed.

It was a bird of some sort, the strange thing hanging in the sky above our heads, but a bird like no one had ever seen before. A bird that seemed to have a human face. May screamed again as another one swooped. Garet snatched her up and hugged her close.

The birds or not-birds were dancing on the air, all three darting and diving at the beach. The air was thick with a chorus of squealing, some of it terror, much of it sheer, unabashed excitement.

Kids fanned out in all directions, running for their lives until comprehending simultaneously that none of us were actually in danger.

Enormous birds with silver skins and human faces. I'd never seen anything like them. No one had. Light dazzled off their broad wingspans as they swooped with elegance and grace. Now and then it looked like one might land but at the very last instant the bird would change its mind.

Kids chased shadows up and down the beach, laughing and shrieking with delight. I stood, tide lapping at my ankles. Too entranced to move, lest the illusion shatter. This was bigger than the lights beyond the Scarp. Life in Thrule would never be the same.

And then, a sickening crack split the air. One of the birds jolted sharply, then spiralled to the sand like a stone. Some of the kids ran on, oblivious. Others stopped and stared forlornly at the fallen thing, not certain what to do.

The other two birds made a hasty retreat, great wings pulsing with panic.

I was running before I'd even worked out why. Crack after crack. Sounds that should never be heard down on the beach. Rifle shots belonged in the distance, high above the treeline and the rocks. The realm of Councillors, their hooch and their old-time rifles.

I sank to the sand beside the fallen bird. Children formed a ring around it, puffing and panting, standing close but not too close. They wanted to be part of it, whatever was going on. The bird was dying. It lay at an uncomfortable angle, its chest heaving and falling erratically.

One of the smaller ones began to cry. I shushed her—once one started, they'd all be at it. The bird was frightened enough as things were.

The silver skin coating the bird's limbs faded at the neckline. Beyond, the skin was pink and the face was that of a girl. Older than me but not by much. Eighteen, or maybe nineteen. Her brow was furrowed, her features marked with pain. Pink lips parted but no sound came out.

The Old Man strode across the sand towards us, precious rifle balanced in the crook of his arm. Flanked by two of the Cheesewright brothers. Swearing men who liked to boss us all around, smelling of hooch and sweat when you got too close.

"Away with ya," Grampa shouted. "Scoot."

Kids scattered like seagulls. I stayed put. Not the only one— Garet stood a few paces back, his focus entirely upon the bird girl's pain-etched face.

"Out of my way," barked Grampa.

"She's hurt."

"Mind your own business, girl."

I felt the quaver in my own voice. He'd hit me if I didn't move. Kick me if I wasn't quick enough.

"You shot her! What did you have to do that for?"

"I told you to shut your mouth!" He raised his hand and brought it down hard against my cheek.

Nobody said anything. Nobody ever did. The blow stung but I held my ground. "It's a girl. Can't you see that? Not an animal. Not a *malingerer.*"

The old man growled and shoved me roughly to one side. Bird girl was now obscured by the backs of Grampa and Council men, more of whom were approaching, bearing a stretcher between them.

Bird girl was soon hoisted upon it, her pink lips parting to emit a whimper. The mighty silver wings had folded in on themselves, impossible as such a thing might be.

No need to follow. There was only one place the Council men would go. Excelsior Hall, an austere sandstone building that was probably the oldest standing structure in Thrule. Only ever used for important functions like when rich people married each other or the annual harvest ball. Occasionally it got used for other things and this was obviously going to be one of those times. The doors would shut and no one would be let in.

Little kids trailed after the stretcher, bobbing and craning for glimpses of the bird girl. A fleck of silver in the blue above. A flyer circling high where bullets could not reach. The second one seemed to have vanished completely. No, there it was, away in the distance heading for the Seacliff bridge, the remains of which straddled the north end of the beach beyond the rocks.

I shielded my eyes as the nearest flyer dived and made a pass along the row of beachfront houses. Low enough to be hit if anyone was aiming. Fortunately the Council had its mind on other matters. The flyer arced back on powerful wings then headed for the bridge to join the other.

They'd be safe up there for the meantime. Not for long. Nobody marked by the men of Excelsior Hall stayed safe for long.

"She's so beautiful," said a voice behind me. Garet. Still carrying May, he wasn't looking at either of us, but at the furrows of sand scuffed by the stretcher bearers.

The downed flyer had been beautiful indeed. Unblemished skin and high cheekbones sharply defined even through the twisted grimace of pain. Trust Garet to have noticed.

"The other two will be safe up there on the bridge," I said. "Nobody ever climbs it."

Which wasn't true and we both knew it. Climbing the ragged edge of the Seacliff bridge was a rite of passage for most of Thrule's bored youth. I'd done it once. So had Garet. A section of its railing was festooned with ancient rusting locks, the names or initials of lovers carved upon them. Locked forever, their keys cast into the ocean far below. Nobody had made locks like that for a very long time. Nobody remembered how. Today's young lovers tied shell mementoes to the rail with plaited string.

"They won't fly off without her," said Garet, staring wistfully at the Scarp's thick green shadows.

For once, I had to agree with him.

Shipwreck Rock was the place we called our own: a tumbled pile of massive boulders that'd had once sat at the top of the escarpment. According to faded photos on the schoolhouse wall, an old stone jetty used to jut out from its end, long ago, before the wars and the nameless people who had started them. Great summer storms had swept the stones away. Most days kids sat on the jetty's shattered nub, swinging their legs and dangling fishing lines.

Not today. Today we gathered, hands thrust deep in pockets, shoulders hunched against the brisk sea breeze. Celeste stood on the lowest of the boulders, which put her a length and a half above everyone else. Gripping the mossy stone with her bare toes. Offshore winds were known for their unpredictability.

"We need to know what's up there. We need to see it for ourselves—how long since anyone tried to run the Scarp for real?"

A murmuring rippled through the crowd. When someone disappeared, it was widely presumed the Scarp was where they'd gone. Unless there was a body to prove otherwise.

"It's now or never. While everyone's distracted. We'll never get a better chance than this." Celeste stood casually, her weight all on one hip, thumbs hooked through the belt loops of her shorts. Only there was nothing casual about what she was asking. This wasn't the first time we'd tried to run the Scarp on mass. We and our parents before us when they'd been young and dumb and bored enough to try. Picturing Marina hacking through the undergrowth, hauling herself up and over rocks using creepers and vines, was difficult. An image so out of character it refused to sit comfortably in my head.

"They can't watch all of us all the time. Especially not since they'll be watching *her*."

Her. The bird girl with silver skin who'd fallen from the sky. Not fallen—been shot down. That detail made all the difference.

"What are they gonna do to her?" asked one of the younger kids.

Celeste shrugged. "Find out where she's come from, I suppose."

"We know where she's come from," I said coldly, pushing my way to the front. Nodding at the looming mass of green. Nobody looked. Everybody knew where I meant. "The Council maintains the lands beyond the Scarp are uninhabited. The flyers prove they're wrong—what else might they be wrong about?"

"Which is why we have to get up there and check it for ourselves," said Celeste to a chorus of general agreement.

"No, we don't," said Garet. "There's a better way. We front up at the Hall and demand to see the bird girl."

"If we all go, at the very least they'll have to tell us something." I raised my voice to cut across the dissenting murmurs. The crowd wasn't with me—or Garet. It was with Celeste, as usual.

Celeste made shushing motions with her hands. Waiting to speak until everyone was listening. "The Council are all down here. All congregating in Excelsior Hall. Two days they've been shut in there, yakking away at their meeting. Ringing that damn bell for food and drink. And beer. Nobody's doing any work. Nobody is manning the watchtowers."

"You can't be sure of that!" I said.

"Neither can you. But face it—it stands to reason. I say we run the Scarp while we've got half a chance."

Garet stepped up and raised his voice. "Brody and Damon and Drew—anyone seen those guys lately?"

There was a pause while they all thought about it, then a shuffling and searching amongst some of the younger kids.

"Emmy—when did you last see your dad?"

Ten-year-old Emmy started chewing on her finger when she realised all eyes were upon her. Her face was streaked with snot and grime. Not like her folks to let her out in that condition.

"Two days? Three days?" Garet asked.

She stared at him, blank-eyed, then shrugged.

"That doesn't mean anything," said Celeste. "Drew's probably in Excelsior with the rest of them."

"But the Council would never leave the towers unguarded! Especially not now, after this. That's my point. Now's more dangerous than ever. We need to keep a check on what's going on."

But Celeste wasn't listening and neither was anyone else. "I say we run. All of us at once. All who's got the balls for it, that is." That last remark was meant for Garet. He grinned.

"Remember what happened last Scarp run?" I stepped up close so only she and the older ones could hear me. Some things were better said out of earshot of the littlies. "Couple of years back. Three kids killed in a landslide—so they said. Not even their parents got to see the bodies.

Mention of the landslide brought a nervous hush.

"I want to see what's scarptop as much as anyone, but there's no point to running—not while we've got knowledgeable visitors right here. People that know what's out there 'cos they've seen it for themselves."

"So says you," said Celeste coolly. "You don't know what they've seen. You don't know any more than the rest of us."

The word *visitors* confused the issue. Murmuring started up again, the littlies getting bored of being cut out of the conversation.

"Mama says they're silver demons," shouted someone from the back.

"That's a load of crap and you well know it." Then I did what I should have done as soon as I'd got to Shipwreck Rock. Climbed up on the boulder beside Celeste and cleared my throat. "We have to get that girl out of Excelsior," I told them. "Once she's free she can answer all our questions."

Celeste placed her hands on her hips, her gaze focused on the Scarp's looming bulk. "Hey, check it out," she said suddenly, pointing. The pale sky above the Scarp was crisscrossed with searing beams. Nothing we hadn't all seen before. "Something's happening up there for real. Now's our chance! The northern track—all that shooting we heard before was up the southern section."

"Northern track's not much more than rabbit trails," called out somebody unseen.

"It's wide enough. Let's get prepped. We'll take lanterns. There's safety in numbers. They can't shoot all of us."

With that, Celeste hopped down to the sand, her long brown legs carrying her off into the palm thicket, with most of the older kids following on her heels. The ones that didn't lingered uncomfortably, looking ashamed of their caution.

"She's gonna get them killed," said Garet.

I turned to face him, not bothering to conceal my surprise. He had stayed. Since when did he not trip at Celeste's heels like a puppy?

"You don't have to say it," he said. "I know what you're thinking. You don't have to worry either. None of them are serious. They'll give up running long before the halfway point. The quarterway, most like. Celeste just likes to see how far they'll go."

"For her?"

He nodded. "Yeah. For her. Always."

That made me smile. So he did get it after all. I studied the faded freckles on his cheeks. Thick eyelashes much longer than anyone else's.

"I bet I can get into Excelsior Hall," I said. "Find out if the bird girl's still alive."

Garet nodded, his gaze shifting to the place where Celeste and the other kids had vanished.

Excelsior Hall had its stock of secrets, as did the grizzled brace of Councillors who had made the place their own. It hadn't always been the way, apparently. Twenty years back the word 'council' had been taken to mean a collective made up of members elected from the whole community. Elected! As if the Old Man would let some common palm-fibre thresher have a say in anything important.

The Hall's thick, white walls spoke of decades of solemn use. Some said it had once been a church, others thought the survivors had used it to store their precious grain. All agreed it was the oldest building standing. Nothing butted up against it. The surrounding fence was kept in good repair. Nobody got in or out without a reason. My mother Marina was one of the few who did.

She baked for them and delivered food. Mornings, usually, unless something special was going on. Which it had been now for three days straight. Accordingly, Marina rarely left her kitchen except to drop off the baskets morning and afternoon, with barely enough time left over to exchange harsh whispers with the Hall's other regular cooks and washerwomen.

"Where the hell have you been, Adelaide? I've been run off my feet for days. Whenever I need something, you piss off down the beach with all the others."

"Have you seen the silver bird girl, Mum? Everybody's talking about her."

Marina thrust a basket into my hands. "Go see what fruit is left on the branches. They're going through pie like there's no tomorrow."

Her upper lip and cheek were streaked with flour. The scarf around her hair was barely doing its job. Greasy strands hung down around her ears. "Get moving—I haven't got all day!"

But you have got all day, I mumbled to myself. All day every day, the same. There were still some apricots the birds had missed. Not ripe enough but they would have to do.

"Is the bird girl's skin made of silver like everyone says?"

Marina rolled a fat slab of dough across the table. "Everybody would do well to find a better topic of conversation."

"But surely Grampa—"

Marina paused to straighten up and push a clump of stringy hair behind her ear. "You know full well your Grampa never talks to me about anything. She's just an ordinary girl, apparently. Nothing you want to be fussing about."

"She fell out of the sky, Mum. There's not much ordinary about that!"

My head was full of questions but then the flyscreen banged open and Mrs Maniero backed in, sausage arms wrapped around a basket of laundry. I bolted before she set me the task of folding it.

On the fourth day the weather took a turn, grey skies reinforced by a chill wind blowing in across the ocean. The Scarp had a dank and dingy cast to it. Feathery mist sloughed off its steamy canopy.

A guard detail was posted at the foot of the Seacliff bridge. All other eyes remained on Excelsior Hall. No one was doing much of anything, especially since Doc Tatum had been spotted striding up the length of Hargreave Drive, her long red hair pinned up in a serious bun. Whispers travelled quickly that the bird girl was injured or sick or possibly even dead. The doc went in and came out again an hour later, after which nobody was any the wiser about anything.

There'd been no more sightings of the flyers on the bridge. Speculation raged amongst beachcombing crews. Perhaps the two of them had flown off under cover of darkness? Somehow I doubted it. They'd never leave their wounded comrade, not unless the bird girl was dead and I was pretty certain that could not be the case. Else why would the The Council still be holed up in Excelsior day and night?

The push to run the Scarp had all been talk. The kids were combing the beach next morning, same as every other. Had they tried and lost their nerve in the fading light and blackberry infested scrub?

Celeste was nowhere to be seen—which was fine by me until I realised Garet was missing, too. That didn't mean they were together but it hurt just thinking they might be.

"My brother says they're putting the bird girl to the torture," suggested Rianne, one of Celeste's regular retinue. She looked a bit lost without the older girl's protection. She'd know for sure if Celeste and Garet had hooked up.

"Don't be stupid," I told her. Not because I'd put torture past the old men, no, not for a minute, but because if there'd been screams or cries, Marina and her kitchen friends would be bitching all about it while they worked. No, it was the silence that had Excelsior Hall on edge. Whatever secrets she carried with her, that bird girl was keeping them close.

Was Celeste going to make her move or wasn't she? Or had *her move* been nothing more than a careful plan to capture Garet's heart? Opposites attract, like the saying goes. His heart as easy to manipulate as dough.

I stayed away from the beach and all its gossip. Focused on the place that really mattered: Excelsior Hall. My chance would come, with Marina up and back three times a day.

Let the others chase Celeste through the undergrowth and get shot up if they didn't watch their backs. The bird girl with silver skin had all the answers. Getting to her was the one thing worth the risk.

When a chance came, I took it, tying a threadbare scarf around my hair. Up close, I barely resembled Marina but which of those old bastards ever looked at the women who kept them fed and watered? I'd stood deliveries for Marina lots of times. Just never to Excelsior Hall. As I lugged the heavy basket with both hands, a strip of excuses tumbled through my head.

No guards were posted in the yard. Probably didn't need them—the second-storey windows seemed designed with defence in mind. For certain I was being watched, so it was important to show not the slightest hesitation.

The basket was way too heavy for one. With sudden fear, I rationalised the reason Marina abandoned it on the kitchen floor—she'd probably gone for help from the sour-faced bitch who lived next door. Which would put her only minutes behind. I hurried, resisting the urge to check over my shoulder.

The door loomed, large and dark and hard. The decision as to whether to knock, call out or flee was taken from me. The big wooden door creaked open a foot, then another as I lugged the basket inside.

I'd been right about one thing. The man who let me in examined my basket, not my face. I worked out where the kitchen was by following well-worn patches in the carpet.

A pimply-faced teen sat at the kitchen table's farthest end, peeling potatoes into a metal bucket. The face I knew but not the name. Scrubber trash from the farthest southern edge where families lived in shacks with packed dirt floors. Kids nobody forced to go to school because there wasn't any point to them learning anything.

The basket was too heavy to swing up on the table. Better to leave it on the floor than to ask the south-edge scrubber for help. Any minute now the ample kitchen space would fill with men. Any minute now . . . only a minute passed and then another, with me still standing there in almost silence. Nothing but the scraping of the blade against potato, an occasional furtive glance in my direction.

The man who had let me in was not waiting when I slipped back out into the hallway. Muffled voices echoed from upstairs. Lots of them. My footsteps seemed loud and obvious on the floorboards but still nobody came. The hallway fed into a massive space, too large to rightly be called a room. A high ceiling featured pressed lead in floral patterns. White and stained with paint peeling at one end. Three large windows hung with heavy drapes. A mighty table occupied the farthest end. Something shiny lay upon it. Silverware. Plates and cutlery of the kind you'd expect to find in a place like this, only on second glance, they weren't what I first supposed.

Something long and flat and bright. The bird girl's silver skin. My stomach lurched at the implication. Surely not even The Council would do a thing so gruesome. My mouth filled with bile but I had to look. If I left without knowing, I'd never forgive myself. So I crept closer to the table, ignoring the creak of wood beneath my soles, at all times expecting the cocking of a rifle, a hand on my shoulder, a cuff across the head. Muffled voices no longer filtered from upstairs. There was nothing to hear but the beating of my heart.

The silver thing stretched across the table was a flying suit still holding the shape of its wearer. A garment, not skin as I'd first feared.

My hand reached out but I was startled by mens' voices—near and harsh. Footsteps thumping down the stairs. No matter what happened, I must not get caught. There was no time to think. I wriggled in behind the nearest clump of drapes. Made myself as small as possible, face pressed into velvet that smelled of dust.

Heavy footsteps rattled floorboards. My heart pounded loudly, almost drowning them out. Garbled, unintelligible words. They had found me. They'd tell Grampa and he would . . .

The footsteps thundered out into the yard. Suspicious silence flooded the oversized room. Suffocating on the choking velvet, I turned my head and stole a gulp of air.

Out through the window, seven men headed for the Scarp, rifles clutched in meaty hands. Something was happening. Something big. Must be to have drawn them out so quickly.

The bird girl was dead . . . *but what if she wasn't?* What if they had her locked up somewhere like those rotgut hooch pedlars Drew busted out by the southern rocks?

I slid out from the velvet's dusty embrace. A dark rectangle. The cellar door, open wide. It hadn't been before. I would have noticed the cracked and painted doorway leading to wooden stairs.

Charcoal gloom beckoned. I wasn't going down there. Nor would I risk creeping up the main staircase. No way. I'd get off home while the way was clear. Back to explain my excuses to Marina. And I would have, only a sound wafted upwards from the cellar. A mournful wail that did not sound entirely human.

I didn't just hear it, I *felt it*, too, in a way that's hard to describe. It tugged at my innards, like longing or heartache. Fear kept me rooted to the spot.

A snatch of clattering from the direction of the kitchen. Cooking pots knocked over by that idiot boy, perhaps. Brisk footsteps and an angry female scold. The doorway. Still there. Still beckoning.

I would take a look. Just a quick one. Just from the top of the stairs. I would not go down because that would be crazy. Whatever there was to see could be seen from there.

The old steps creaked as they took my weight. Below, the cellar flooded with chalky light, revealing a wall of stacked crates and racked wine. Beside it, a prisoner's cell with iron bars and a bench. The bird girl stood in a stained brown shift, watching as I crept down the stairs.

The chair where a guard was supposed to sit was empty. Bird girl made a flurried motion with her hands. I stopped, glanced back the way I'd come.

She moaned, a less mournful sound than I'd heard before, this time more uncomfortable than anguished.

"I'm not supposed to be here," I whispered. The bird girl was not supposed to be here either. Jail cells were for criminals, not visitors.

She reached her hands out through the bars. I didn't mean to walk towards her. I knew better. Every step was dangerous, taking me deeper and deeper into trouble. *Grampa and his bullying ways, Marina and her tired resignation. Celeste and her retinue, Garet who never had time for me at all.*

Bird girl stopped reaching as I stepped up close, our faces separated by iron and muddy light.

"My name's Addie. Adelaide."

She answered, but not with words. The sounds she made were more like song than sentence.

The cell door was secured with a rusty padlock bigger than my fist. A bucket sat at the foot of the bench. Nothing more—not even a blanket or a cup of water.

"Did they hurt you? Did they rough you up?"

Bird girl's eyes were wide and bright, her skin so smooth and flawless. She reached her hand through the bars again and this time I took it. Her skin was warm, not cold like I expected. She squeezed my hands and I squeezed back.

"I have to go."

She understood. Slowly she unfurled her fingers and withdrew her hand.

"I'll tell my mother you're here. She'll make sure they feed you."

Bird girl nodded and smiled.

I walked back up the stairs, paused at the top to check for people. Crept back into the kitchen, saw my basket had been unloaded. A stout woman stood at the sink with her back turned. The scrubber boy was peeling more potatoes. He gawked at me but didn't speak. Perhaps he was retarded. I scooped up my basket and went back the way I'd come, walking purposefully to the big table, folding the silver flying suit up small as it would go, then stuffing it into the bottom of the basket. The striped and faded tea towel I placed on top did little to conceal it. I kept on striding all the way out the front door, along the path and back through the main gate. Three blocks from Excelsior Hall, I stopped to consider what I'd done. *Stolen the flying suit. Snatched it from right under their noses.* The girl in the cellar had made me do it. I didn't know how, only that it was true.

◇◇

Marina met me a block up from the house, her face all ruddy from exertion. "I know you're up to something. What have you done with the pies and bread? All my hard work—"

"Delivered it," I said smugly, holding the basket to one side so she couldn't easily peer at its contents.

"What—to the Hall? Don Barrowman let you in?"

"Sure," I said, quickly changing the subject. "What was all the shouting about? Is something going on?"

"Some kind of commotion up on the Scarp. Nothing to do with me—or you. Some kids, I think. It's always kids these days . . . "

A gunshot sounded, closely followed by another.

"They're shooting at them! Grampa and his drunken Council mates!"

"Don't you speak about your Grampa like that! Those kids know better. They ought to stay down in the valley where it's safe. Those silver flying people brought nothing but bad luck with them."

"Safe? Nobody's safe with those Council bullies shooting anything they don't like the look of." My face felt flushed. "Don't you see what those flyers mean? There are *other people* living out beyond the Scarp. Not just flickering lights on scuppered wrecks—people like us and who knows what else besides?"

"People like us, heh?" Marina snorted. "Silver skinned demons with wings sprouting out of their backs? I don't think so." She leaned in closer, the lines on her face enhanced by the bitterness of her voice. "There's nothing out beyond the Scarp. The world's dead, Adelaide. We're all that's left of it. Us and the rubbish washed up along the beach."

Not wanting to hear more, I dodged around Marina and headed for one of the paths that led to the water, the clumsy basket banging against my side. Marina yelled after me, wanting her basket back. I hurried on, pretending not to hear.

Bird girl's flying suit had to be returned to her kin. Her name was on the tip of my tongue. Jane . . . Jade . . . Jay . . . Had she told me her name? I couldn't remember. *An open door. Steps leading downwards into darkness. Iron bars and an empty chair. A girl.*

My stomach felt unsettled, like I'd eaten something rotten. I took the path that didn't get used so much because it was overgrown and half forgotten.

The Seacliff bridge was guarded, as expected. Not by Councillors, but by their younger kin, all armed with guns they probably didn't know how to shoot.

The flying suit wasn't heavy but it was utterly conspicuous. The only way I'd get it up the bridge was tied across my body like a sash, thus leaving both hands free—a necessity I'd learned first time I climbed.

The nearest of the men with guns was someone I knew by name. Benjamin Cheesewright, one of three blacksmith brothers. Quick with his hands, even quicker on his feet.

Sweat began to bead across my brow and a sour taste flooded my mouth. The chipped cement pylon next along had better footholds than the nearer, but would I even reach it if I dared?

First time I'd climbed had been a dare. Three of us had gone up together and together we'd been invincible. We never considered we might not make it. Today was different. Today I was truly on my own. Today . . .

"Addie?"

The sound of my own name startled me, so much so that I dropped the basket. It rolled on its side and the silver suit spilled out. I hurried to stuff it back under the cloth.

"Addie, are you OK?"

I glanced up at scuffed thongs, brown trousers, a ripped t-shirt covered in grass stains.

"Go away, Garet. Can't you see I'm busy?"

"What have you got—"

"Nothing! Piss off."

The sour taste in my mouth intensified. The bridge was bigger than I remembered. More imposing, its concrete pocked and crumbled.

The silver fabric refracted light in all directions. No way would it pass unnoticed. No way, whatsoever. Suddenly my plan started unravelling at the seams. Occasional distant rifle pops suggested the Scarp was still flush with Celeste's thrill-seeking idiots. Nightfall wasn't long away. If I set off now I'd be stuck up there after dark.

But I had to try.

Garet placed his hand upon my arm. "Addie, what are you doing?"

I brushed it aside. "Climbing Seacliff—what does it look like?"

"Are you crazy? Council's put a guard on it. Look—one of the cheesehead boys and I'll bet he isn't alone."

I peered through the foliage to where he pointed, even though I'd already seen. Each of the pylons had a man guarding its base.

"I gotta get the flying suit back to the others."

"Why, Addie—who says you gotta?"

That taste in my mouth was getting stronger. "Get out of my way, Garet. Why don't you run back to your girlfriend?"

"Celeste is not my girlfriend."

"Bet you wish she was."

Garet paused to consider his answer. "Sometimes."

"So you followed her up the Scarp like all the others."

He looked uncomfortable. "It's not what you think.'

"You are entirely predictable," I said. "If she told you to jump of Seacliff bridge, I bet you'd do it."

"That's not—"

"Garet, get out of my way. I have to climb the bridge and you can't stop me."

I tugged the suit from the basket and tied it across my body. It moved like liquid, not like fabric. The central section was peppered with solid lumps.

"Benjamin Cheesewright will shoot you down."

"As if you give a shit."

That made him angry, yet he didn't come back with anything. Just stood there staring at me, his brow all ridged and furrowed. "She's done something to you. That bird girl has addled your brains."

"She's trapped, Garet. She needs to get out of that cell."

His eyes widened. "You've seen her? You've been inside Excelsior?"

"Yeah, and now I've got a job to do."

I could do it. Climb the pylon, dodge the bullets, return the flying suit to where it belonged.

Garet stepped closer—so close I could smell the tang of his sweat, and then, of all the unexpected things, he kissed me.

I hesitated for a moment. Just a moment, then kissed him back. His lips were soft, his cheeks and chin rough with stubble. I could have stayed there for a thousand years but instead I pulled free and stepped back.

"What do you think you're doing?"

He looked sheepish. "Trying to stop you. You're not yourself. The Addie I know wouldn't go charging up Seacliff on a suicide mission."

"You don't know me. You don't know anything about me. All you care about is that stupid bitch Celeste."

"That's not true . . . " His voice trailed off because we both knew it was.

"I can't help it, Addie. She's . . . it's just the way I feel."

"And I can't help it either. I've got a job to do."

"Like you keep saying, over and over, like somebody else stuffed that thought inside your head."

I didn't say anything. My face must have said it for me because all of a sudden he raised his hands. "OK, I get it, so let me help you. You need a diversion. Give me half an hour."

"The light's going, Garet—"

"OK then, twenty minutes. Promise me you won't do anything until I get back."

"Then you'll let me climb?"

"I promise."

Twenty minutes was nothing. Enough time to gather my thoughts, observe the Cheesehead brother as he ambled mindlessly around his pylon, rolling one cigarette after another, flicking the butts into the sandy dirt.

First time I climbed had been early morning, the sun's first rays bleeding gently across the sea, warming my face, my heart and my resolve. I had been fourteen. Three years later, everything was different.

The sound of men shouting drowned out my thoughts. I snuck a peek through the weeping bottlebrush. Unbelievably, someone had begun to climb the farthest pylon. Scooting up the crumbling concrete like a possum. Someone who looked a lot like Garet.

That wasn't all. Small dark shapes spilled across the sand but I didn't have time for them. I bolted, my full attention on the nearest pylon while the guard was running away across the sand. Garet was helping me. No way would I waste my chance.

The entire bridge lay in the shadow of the Scarp. I grazed my knuckles feeling for footholds and then I was away, my climb a mix of speed and terrified caution. So far, so good. No one had aimed at me and fired. Higher up, I could identify the small shapes on the sand. Children. Little ones May's age and close. Clever Garet. No one would dare to shoot us now. Not even one of those Cheesehead boys. Tiny witnesses held a lot of sway in Thrule.

Those tiny witnesses began to cry, as if on cue. Clever Garet. Clever May. Together they made a hell of a team.

I climbed some more, then paused to catch my breath. Spread below, sea the colour of damp coal dust. Above it, a flat band of insipid sky set with banks of lumpen cloud.

I climbed on, shrugging off the voices: shouts and threats, the details lost beneath the blanket of my breath. Would they shoot anyway, with the kids all standing there? Would they?

The harder I climbed, the more I started thinking about the Scarp itself. Most specifically, the lights beyond its rim. Lights we had taken for granted all our lives now took on a grand importance. Days had passed before the merest suggestion that the lights and the flyers might be linked. Might be? Of course they were. Both came from beyond the Scarp.

Those lights changed form and colour all the time. Sunrise and late afternoons they were at their strongest, blasting the insipid skyline with pinks and yellows. Sometimes green, too, which all agreed was anything but natural. Green like vomit, green like the weathered flakes chipping off the row of painted weatherboard cottages down along the rough end of the beach. Green like grass stains that wouldn't come out no matter how hard you scrubbed.

Sweat dried cold against my skin. The silvery fabric weighed heavier than when I'd started. Footholds were fewer and less evenly spaced. I couldn't see Garet. Not that that meant anything. He might be climbing the far side. He might have reached the top already. *Or have fallen to his death.*

I grazed my knees and elbows scrambling up the last few feet. I didn't look down until I reached the top.

There was no sign of Garet. Just a bracing breeze, much cooler than expected once I'd unburdened myself of the silver suit. Lights winked on one by one along the beach, a sight more beautiful than expected. From the broken bridge, Thrule looked civilised. Welcoming. Safe. Three things I no longer felt were true.

It appeared I was alone at first. Nothing to see but tumbled chunks of concrete fringed with rusted wire jutting out like ribs. Had they flown off home, the other two? Back to wherever it was they came from? Not that I could blame them, what with Grampa and his cronies blasting anything that moved. Shooting their own just for daring to run the Scarp.

But then, a flash of silver. Two figures, flyers without wings. I held up the suit but they didn't come closer, so I laid it down upon the rock-strewn concrete, then backed away.

Both were girls, willowy and lithe, one a little taller than the other. They crept up, tentative, like rabbits. I backed off further, wanting to speak but worried I might scare them.

The taller girl picked up the suit, then shook it. It moved like liquid in her hands. The strangest thing. I couldn't take my eyes off it, the way it dripped and swirled, then suddenly it was bigger than before and standing by itself. An empty shell.

I swallowed drily as the girls approached, desperate to scream and run for cover, only there was no cover. The ground was a long way down.

"Your friend is in Excelsior Hall. They're guarding her but she looks OK."

The taller girl spoke back. My heart sank as words washed over me. Not one of them was even vaguely familiar.

"I don't understand," I answered. "If you come to the Hall, perhaps they'll let her go?"

Which was a stupid thing to say. Excelsior Hall was the very last place they ought to visit. That's presuming they even made it that far without some damn fool Councillor shooting them in the head.

The shorter one spoke with words more like singing than speaking. Not that it mattered. Her song was utterly incomprehensible.

I was pondering what next to say when the taller girl lunged forward and grabbed my wrist. A lightning motion, so quick I barely saw it. Barely felt it either, despite the girl's grip being iron strong.

What happened next was hard to understand. Light-headedness and then a touch of nausea. My mouth opened and a string of words came out. Not my words even though I spoke them. Words I couldn't even understand. Both bird girls listened in stony silence.

And then it was over, my wrist released. I rubbed it even though I wasn't injured. Something had changed. My head hurt a little, a tingling sensation that was fading fast. The girls' expressions had darkened perceptibly as, incrementally, had the sky.

The taller girl started whispering like she was talking to herself. Only she wasn't. Her words were being soaked up by the suit. The shorter girl beckoned. The suit didn't look so menacing with sunlight no longer glinting off it. It looked like . . .

The short girl gave me a gentle nudge.

"Oh no," I said, backing away. "Not in a million years."

Next thing I knew, it was all around me. Liquid silver flowed, encasing my limbs. There wasn't even time to struggle. Terror dissolved into wonder. Suddenly I knew things, such as the other girls' names. The taller one was Shell, the shorter Alik. The girl in the cell at Excelsior Hall, Jaea. Shell and Alik were preparing to leave. They wanted me to go with them. "But I don't know how to fly this crazy thing!"

Shell sniffed the wind, then took a running jump, wings unfolding with lightning speed as she was enveloped by the updraft. Alik turned, smiled, spread her wings, then did the same. They flew: climbed, dipped, then circled, calling out to me in their lilting, high-pitched voices. *Step off the bridge. The suit will carry you.* It knew what to do. If it didn't, I'd plummet to my death. My heart hammered relentlessly, defiant to the last. My head rebelling against the rest of me. Already I'd seen too much to return to my old life. Thrule was too small, the lights beyond the Scarp too bright.

The second I was ready, the suit unfurled its wings and I took a running jump—held my breath—and then I was flying. The suit took over, spreading my arms, nudging my body this way and that.

Evening continued its gradual descent. Down on the beach, kids ran along the foamy sand, lanterns glowing in the township windows, the dark pull of the sea. Shell stuck close to me while Alik scouted. The Scarp loomed darkly like a cloud.

Far below, atop a massive boulder, a group of kids jumped up and down and waved. Scarp runners. Were they crazy? Out in the open where Council men could find them? I craned my neck to see if one was Celeste, but they couldn't hold my attention long. We swooped down low to gather speed then climbed towards the Scarp's rocky crest. At long last I would learn what lay beyond the boundary. The secret the Council didn't want us to see. The sight they would willingly shoot their own children to protect.

Alik led and I followed, zooming past one of the watchtowers. Finding it unmanned, just as I thought. Climbing higher and higher, cold wind searing my cheeks. Far beyond the towers, the rocks and the singed treeline. I had expected trees and more trees, or perhaps acres of dense, scrubby ground, parched and sunbaked into uselessness. Overgrown roads and the rusted skeletons of cars. Burnt out buildings. Not this. Anything but this.

Beyond the Scarp lay a cratered wasteland. A sight that literally took my breath away. The ground was charcoal ash and cinders. Nothing lived there. Nothing grew. Machines chugged through the sticky dirt. Contraptions like cars with mismatched limbs taking pot shots at each other with beams of light. I wanted to linger, absorbing the horror of it all but the suit's wings swept me higher up to safety. Up beyond the rage of those machine things and their beams, which was just as well—I couldn't steer for gawking.

The Council had been justified. There was nothing left. Nothing that wouldn't harm the good folk of Thrule. No libraries or treasure houses. Not even any ruins. Just ash and dirt and beams of burning light.

I could not go back—I knew that now. The bird people had swapped me for one of their own. Tricked me into leaving home behind. Jaea had been sacrificed—she would die alone in the cellar of Excelsior Hall. I felt for her but there was nothing I could do.

The suit would fly whether I was awake or sleeping, but I was far too wired to do anything but stare at the pocked and desolate nightmare. As darkness settled, I began to spot small fires. Could people survive in such a terrible place? Apparently.

And then, what seemed like hours later, a pulsing, glittering jewel embedded in a mountain's coaly tar. A city, fifty times the size of Thrule. Millions of winking lights like the ones on the listing freighters. *Have you been watching us all these years, perched on the decks of those drowning tubs, waiting for the time when we were ready?*

The freighters made me think of the beach, sand combing, little May and all the others. People I would never see again. The taste of Garet faded from my lips. *Garet had kissed me.* Tears welled and I didn't fight them. He kissed me and all I cared about was climbing the stupid pylon. Right then I hated Jaea more than anyone. Hated what she'd made me do for them. The price I'd paid for rescuing her suit and would keep on paying for whatever remained of my life.

Tears streamed but the chill air claimed them. I felt the suit adjusting, preparing itself to land. The city lights grew brighter, more powerful, more real. A platform jutted like a poking tongue. One by one the mountain swallowed us whole.

THE SLEEPING AND THE DEAD

It is, in most respects, an unremarkable morning, when a malfunctioning mechanical bull jerks its way into Truckstop's goat compound. *Gengis must be stoned again*, thinks Doctor Anna. *Old war machines don't usually get this close.* The thing is bucking and kicking in all directions, metal rivets glinting in the sun. Her spirits lift considerably at the diversion.

Abandoning her Stoli and cactus juice martini, she climbs down from her balcony, brandishing the cricket bat she sleeps with just for luck. Best to smash its tiny mechanical brain before the nuns catch wind of it and freak.

Those nuns freak at everything. Everything is a sign, from shooting stars to cloud formations—on days the desert's cursed enough for clouds.

The bull is nothing but a humble all-terrain load-bearing unit, wandering blind until its battery depletes. Might somebody be using it for decoy? If they are, they're being mighty slow about it.

Time was when she'd have used the thing for target practice. Not today. She's not up for wasting bullets, so she smacks the bat down hard upon its hub casing. It shudders to a standstill, quivers, indecisive in the heat. The air chokes with radioactive dust.

A dozen scrawny Nubian goats watch her sullenly from the sidelines. Beyond them, a cluster of hopeful mothers camp beside the wire. She swears at the goats. The mangy buggers will eat anything; even chipped ceramic shards of clapped-out war machines.

Swinging the bat so the goats don't get ideas, she peers up at the lookout tower. Gengis waves. No doubt he's been watching the whole performance, but when she responds, he signals back in their private code, the sign that means *there's something interesting out there*. She gestures to the goats and the smashed-up bull, but he signals back again. More urgent. Same message.

Fuck the goats then, this must be important. Takes a lot for Gengis to give a damn.

She runs to the tower, discards the bat and climbs the spindly rungs hand over fist. Tries not to get too excited. It's probably nothing, but all the same, she feels her heartbeat quicken.

Gengis is standing when she reaches the top, hash pipe abandoned on his sagging canvas chair. His eyes are wide and blue—the only lively feature in his craggy, toothless face. "Reckon some of them stories must be true."

"What stories?" Anna snatches the telescope from his arthritic fingers. No need to ask him where to point the thing. A metallic gleam in the middle distance. There it is again.

She raises the scope and adjusts the lens, the battered bronze casing warm between her palms.

"Fuck me," she says, and she means it.

In the lens, three men stagger across the baking flats, scrawny and sunburned, but men they are, with ragged vestiges of youth clinging to their tortured frames. Still men enough to potentially be of use, not like old Gengis here, withered and wasted twist of wire that he is.

"Sister Daisy's not getting her mitts on these ones," she mutters underneath her breath.

"Reckon they dug 'emselfs up from their graves?" says Gengis.

When Anna finally lowers the scope, he's sucking on the hash pipe, cheeks hollowed.

"Now why'd you go and say a thing like that?"

"Legions of the Underworld," he croaks through plumes of blue.

"I told you not to smoke that shit near me."

Gengis shrugs, settles back into his canvas chair, legs creaking beneath his feather weight. Angles an inch more into the shade of the battered beach umbrella poised above.

Anna's already climbing down the tower, revolver tucked into the back of her pants. In her excitement, she's forgotten all about her cricket bat.

Venus peers weakly through the glare, wasting her grace on the endless, dusty plain. In the distance, storm clouds sully the horizon. Vast, voluminous boiling things, cauldrons of corrosive isotopes and acid flashback. If it rains today, they'll be in trouble. Rainy season isn't due for weeks. Anna keeps an eye on them anyway, seasons being what they are. High on the list of events no longer to be trusted.

It's Doctor Anna's lucky day. The nuns are in the ossuary chanting at their skulls. They'll sniff the men out soon enough, but not before she's had a chance to claim them. She takes up a position near the goats, doing her best to feign protracted nonchalance. *Thomas won't be one of them. Darling Thomas is long dead.*

It takes another hour for the men to cross the sand. Once they see the goats, nothing will stop them. She stands, revolver at the ready, but she doesn't want to shoot. Not yet. Not before she's heard their stories. Finds out where they've been hiding all these years.

They were soldiers once, judging by the khaki rags still clinging to the ropey sinew of their limbs. *Not just the green*, thinks Anna, when she's close enough to be sure the three aren't apparitions after all. They carry themselves like enlisted men. Broken, beaten, battered, yet still possessed of a military mindset. She'd known it once. Even married it for a time.

The nearest one stares her down with sunken eyes. His torso features a hideous scar. For a moment, it looks like he might drop to his knees and cry. She can't assess their ages through the grime and deprivation—anywhere from twenty-five to fifty.

Anna glances back up at the tower, makes the sign for water, clear, so Gengis sees. He takes his sweet, stoned time descending, ambling across the hard-packed sand, water skin slapping hard against his thigh.

He tosses the 'skin across the stretch of sand between them. The men fall upon it like starving dogs, which they are, Anna reminds herself, regardless of apparent human forms. They shove, claw and elbow, but somehow each one gets to drink. That done, they fall back on the sand, exhausted.

Mere moments earlier she'd been sure they'd kill the goats. Has their strength given out, or do they see her as a benefactor? Someone who'll offer food and shelter?

"Delirious," says Gengis, his face deadpan as always. "The sunstroke's on 'em. Surprised they ain't sunblind."

"But where are they *from?*"

"Hell," says Gengis. "Like I already told ya."

She cajoles the three of them into the clinic's waiting room with the promise of cold corn mush. They eat with their fingers, shovelling food in great greasy gulps like there's no tomorrow. So far as these men know, there isn't. Best to eat up while the eating's good. Doctor Anna watches them at it, enjoying the greedy glistening of their fingers. The sounds they make are almost sexual.

She wants to talk, but the food has made them docile. *Damn!* She should have made them sing for their supper.

Soon they're snoring loud enough to wake the dead. Anna watches them twitch for an hour or two, the unsteady rise and falling of their chests. Coughing and wheezing, farting in their slumber. Perhaps they've travelled further than the hopeful mothers? Not so much *come here* as *escaped from somewhere else.* Finally safe enough to snatch some fitful sleep. She pities them. They don't know the truth. How much safer they'd have been in the crow-pecked wilderness.

She shuts the door and goes outside to brood, leaving them dead to the world. Twelve good hours and they'll be right to talk. Her mind's already clocking possibilities. They've come from *somewhere*, which means *somewhere* exists. A place with men and law and ammunition. There's a half-life to their current harmlessness; they'll be crazy when they wake. Anna knows she must be on her guard.

She has plans for the three of them, plans she doesn't yet fully understand herself. They raise intriguing possibilities for the clinic. If their seed is fresh, there'll be no more need for frozen embryos. But where have they come from? Those ragged military uniforms have piqued her interest. There are no bases within miles of this place. Just the bulls, clanking and creaking, shitting spent ammunition casing across the blasted wasteland.

Scant breaths of tepid wind bear snatches of the nun's familiar banter from the ossuary. Drumming and chanting. Singing—if you could call it that. *An eighth year, a great year,* so they've been claiming for weeks now. Cosmologically auspicious, astronomically advantageous; the planting cycle, the birthing circle, on and on and on, like a hammering headache.

She watches nuns dancing in the dust, spinning and twirling as if the stuff's not killing them. Necromaidens. Fallout wraiths. Praising absent gods for their blisters as well as their dreams. Like her, they have no formal training. Their cult has grown organically, exponentially as the years have dragged. Anna became conscious of the neatness of the skulls long before glimpsing the girls' demented Tinkerbell antics around the gritty edges of Truckstop's barbed perimeter. She might have dismissed the girls as ghosts—the barren landscape groans beneath the breathless, phantom weight of them, but no, the nuns are solid. As solid as forty-five kilos of half-starved girl can get.

The men sleep on, oblivious to the danger. Anna chews her fingernail, revolver on her knee. *You're too late. The world's already dead.* That's what she wants to scream at them all, the hopeful mothers and the mindless irritating nuns. *Go home, all of you. Crawl back into the dust.* But somehow, somehow, she never seems to say it. Not to the huddled masses, anyhow. She whispers to the corpses on the days she gets it wrong. When she botches an insemination or gets bored halfway through. When she wanders outside for a precious cigarette. But mostly, she keeps her feelings to herself, saving them for the windstorms or the open road or tomorrow and the thousand years of nothing left to come.

◇◇

The fertility clinic stands proud and lonely, ringed by clumps of withered palms. International style, with its *brise-soleil* screens of patterned concrete blocks. A monument to forgotten vintage modernism, harnessing the desert's stark vistas and light. The awnings are long gone, blasted to shreds by the elements.

Doctor Anna's work is in the basement. She loves the dark recesses of the earth. What coolant still exists is piped down to the lab. When the pumps fail, that'll be the end of it.

All her work will have been for nothing. It's all for nothing anyway. There's not much left to save.

The clinic's generator is on its last legs. Do frozen embryos have souls? The hopeful mothers think so, dragging their weary bones to Truckstop across a hundred miles of heat and dust.

Women worship at her feet. The walking dead whose wombs still pulse with blood. They leave stones in place of flowers, as nothing grows. Lingering just long enough to ensure the baby sticks, then they leave to make the epic journey home.

Some of them have walked so far just to die upon her doorstep. Others she will kill herself—the ones who can't be saved. Still others arrive already pregnant, hosts to multi-limbed monstrosities. They're the ones she tosses to the nuns. Doctor Anna has no time to spare for monsters. She's not sure what the nuns want with them either. Do they dance and sing and sacrifice them on altars? They can't possibly want more skulls.

Days like these, in the pauses between moments, Anna thinks of Thomas and the world the way it was. Time and indifference have colluded to corrode detail. She fears imagination might be filling in the gaps. Anna remembers shopping malls: vast, glorious, inviting. Celestial music softly piped and a thousand different types of bread. Landscapes littered with useless things.

She hates the functionality of the present. Every tool exactly in its place. Nothing ever gets lost. The past is a phantasmagoria of single-use syringes and sweet, nutrient-free foods in shiny wrappers, make-up, swimsuits, and manicures for dogs. Pets you didn't have to eat when times got tough. Or rather, tougher. Things haven't been merely tough for years.

When she pictures Thomas, he's always smiling. Handsome, forever twenty-one. Always with his shirt off. That's not wishful thinking on her part—he was like that. Half-naked, a glossy sheen to his taut, tanned hide. The kind of guy who could fix motorbikes and cars. Animal musk mixed with engine-oil cologne. Signed up because he wanted to jump out of planes, not because he had it in for Arabs.

Army boys were her type back then. These days anything with a hard cock will do. Not so easy to come by. She prefers them with hair, but the atmosphere decides. She likes tattoos inked before the fall. Everything from hot rods to baby feet. Jesus, naked ladies, dragons.

When Anna takes the three men breakfast, they trade their names through the window bars. The leader gives his as Rocco. The scarred one is Jimenez, the other, Skunk. Food has knocked the crazy from their eyes. A scrub and clean clothes might render them halfway human.

A line of nuns snake past their holding cell, balancing baskets on their heads, white sheet robes flapping listlessly in the heat. Wide awake now, the men scrutinise the girls with military precision, eyes shining. When they glance back at Anna, everything has changed. She can smell the lust in them, feel them straining to focus on the salvation of corn-mush porridge and gritty bread.

The nuns keep a wary distance, as if an invisible barrier holds them back. In their eyes, men destroyed the world and conspire still to pollute what little there is left of it. Their death cult or life cult, depending on your perspective, is a wholly female affair. Men are only good for certain things. They're nasty about it too, with their shivs of sharpened human femur. The nuns keep well clear of Gengis, though. Gengis belongs to Anna. She's told them he's some kind of golem, hacked from living stone and sand. He looks as weatherworn as time itself, face crisscrossed with scars like Martian canals. Sunken eyes like tar pits. No, as far as they're concerned, Doctor Anna can have that one.

The nuns go back about their business, ignoring the men as if they were rocks or goats, blessed as they are with short attention spans.

"You think they're pretty?" asks Anna, her voice laced with artificial innocence. "You think those girls are sweet?"

"Girls is girls." Rocco shrugs. "Looks like plenty to go around."

"Looks can be deceiving."

Rocco smiles, squinting from the sunlight in his eyes. "That old man in the tower's no threat."

"You got that right," says Anna. "Gengis hasn't killed a man in years. But those girls have skull power on their side. You are only three. Sure you want to mess with odds like that?"

He's not listening. Men never listen.

When the nuns have gone, the three lay back, sated, clutching at their groaning stomachs. Anna asks a few distracting questions in her best clinician's voice. Obvious questions. One thing about Armageddon, it cuts through all the need for small talk.

"So where the Hell have you come from?"

Rocco looks at her slyly, weighing her up. Calculating how much he can score in exchange for information. "You run this place all by yourself?"

Anna doesn't answer.

When they realise silence isn't going to get them anything, the men start speaking of a realm below where the light is weak and feeble. Of cold cement inset with crumbling cracks. Of a man who is part demon-lord, part major.

"What's his name?" asks Anna, suddenly interested.

"He goes by many . . . Master, Daddy, Jesus . . . "

The three men joke between themselves, private signals she can't understand. Not the funny kind of jokes—none of them are laughing.

"He was God and we were his lieutenants."

"Yeah," says Skunk, and they're silent after that.

Eventually, the men want to know when she's going to let them out. She needs to put some thought into that one, so she climbs back up the watchtower to see what Sirius has to say about it. Her Dog Star confidante, invisible now, in the sunlight, but shining every night to give her comfort.

Anna watches storm clouds boil along the far horizon. If there's any sign of movement, bells will peal. She's not worried. You don't survive this long out here by chance. Lately though, she's been seeing ghosts. Nothing strange in that—the desert claims them all in its good time. But these are not *her* phantoms. She didn't summon them; deprivation didn't drag them screaming from her psyche. These windborne apparitions linger like imprints, remnants of better places, better days. She's sure they're real in their own way, and that it's the prescience of storms that brings them on.

How long has it been since she bathed or changed her clothes? She probably stinks, and it shames her to acknowledge she only cares because three men have come. There's a splinter in her palm from when she bashed the bull to death. Radioactive dust, she reminds herself.

She kicks her ragged threads into a corner, empties a pitcher into a large tin basin, stands in it and soaps. The liquid is soon rust-coloured. Old blood, she thinks. Old ways.

Anna dresses before her mirror, puts on jewellery. Every piece she owns. A sapphire pendant to match *his* eyes. Earrings. Forty bangles of the finest Mexican silver.

The clinic endures, which is more than can be said for the city of her birth. She's hazy about those details, too. Where she's lived, the places she spent her youth. She must have had a childhood, yet she can't remember one. Not a single warm and fuzzy moment.

Truckstop's provenance, too, is dim and distant. It once sported a pretentious name, some kind of exclusive resort. Deluxe cosmetic tourism. She smiles at the resonance of elegant ladies reclining on crisp, white linen sheets awaiting surgeons to tailor vaginas to match their lips. In the future, nothing is white and bony shoulders are nothing to be proud of.

The nuns like anything smooth and shiny. Crap that glitters. Cellophane or gold, they see no difference. Lately, they've taken to drawing Anna's sign, the eight-point star, which is set above the clinic archway. The dumb fucks think it's holy. Anna knows it's just some corporation logo from before, but she claimed it as her own the day she saw how much it mattered.

The nuns consider her some kind of angel. She's not even a qualified doctor, but hasn't the heart to admit it. She managed to get her head around insemination tech, that's all. Knows how to hold core temperatures steady, knock them out and bring them back alive. Doctor Kamali chose her for her steady hand. Everyone was drunk back then, still living out of cans. The cans ran out long before the booze and hope.

Kamali checked out with the last of the morphine. Couldn't bear the shame of bringing babies into being. What's the fucking point? she screamed, even when sleeping—especially when sleeping. But there had been a point back then, and Anna took it.

The nuns collate their scriptures from a myriad of ancient sources: celebrity cookbooks, women's magazines. That glossy paper made it right through Armageddon, barely blackened by the pyres of burning Bibles. Doctor Kamali rolled cigarettes from the pages of *Revelation*, her faith commensurate with her dwindling tobacco stash. When she died, they made a nest of her old library, plugging cracks in the brickwork with paper pulp.

The only thing that shits Anna more than women is men. Men brought about the end, but they didn't stick around to see it through. Their busted war machinery still litters the landscape, churning dust till the batteries expire. But the men themselves? Where did they go? Anna never did work that one out. To war, she guessed, but which war? How many were there? Was anyone victorious?

Anna had been powerful once—that much she could be sure of. Real power, not this pitiful masquerade. And she'd loved him— Thomas—whoever he might have been. The man with the lion tattoo.

◇◇

She's lingering at her own reflection when commotion snaps her back into the moment. Ugly laughter. Sound carried swiftly through dead air. "Daisy!"

The nuns have deceived her with feigned disinterest. What had she been thinking? As if they wouldn't want three men for themselves.

Anna hurries down the stairs, sandals slapping hard on weathered slate. "Idiots," she spits. "Never should have . . . too hard to protect."

By the time she makes it to the front, the waiting room's surrounded. Nuns occupy every spare inch of balcony, packing in tightly, craning their glass-shaved heads for a better view through the office window's bars. She pushes through the dirty linen mass of them, glad of her own broad shoulders and impatience.

Inside, Rocco has Daisy backed against a wall. Her sheet is torn. The girl bunches ripped fabric against her breast, eyelids lowered demurely in submission.

Rocco's laughter resonates. A deep thing, assured and utterly revolting.

"Step away quickly and you won't get hurt," says Anna calmly.

"I'm thinking that one's fine just where she is."

"I'm not talking to Daisy," says Anna. "Step away, Rocco, while you still have a chance."

He's not listening and neither are his friends. The other two hang back. Silence bloats to fill the space, stifling and oppressive. Beyond the window, placid faces gawp.

"What you've got here is paradise," says Rocco, picking at flecks of grit between his teeth. "A whole town made of nought but little girls."

"Different from the girls you've known," warns Anna.

"Thing is," says Rocco, "we ain't known so many."

"Are there no women in your bunker?"

Skunk's face cracks into a smile. "There's women. Old and skank and butt ugly as all fuck. Which is what he keeps 'em for, natch."

"Incentives," cuts in Jimenez. "Rewards sometimes. If you're really lucky."

"Ain't been so lucky in a long time," says Skunk.

Jimenez's features cloud. That scar on his chest looks anything but lucky.

Seems like it should be Rocco's turn to speak, but his eyes are fixed on Daisy.

"Been dreaming all about her," he whispers.

There's no point warning him to be careful what he dreams of. Rocco is long gone, his mind his weakest aspect. He's fixed on little Daisy with such beady calculation. One move and he'll be on top of her. The other two will do whatever Rocco does. Dogs will always follow bigger dogs.

All three shift their gaze around to Anna. Seeing her as if for the very first time. Most likely true. Yesterday the men had been half-crazed with thirst, half-blind with sun and terror and exhaustion. Anna feels the pressure of their eyes, senses the spell of her authority evaporate.

It's Daisy who makes the next move, as Anna knew she would. She smiles, performs a little pirouette, takes Rocco by the hand, her prayer wheel of human ivory abandoned on the floor.

"Don't be an idiot," says Anna.

Rocco tips an imaginary hat, allows the girl to lead him to the door. The mass of nuns part to let them through.

Still Jimenez and Skunk pause, weighing up their options. Long enough for Anna to make a move of her own. She steps up to block their way with her body. Holds her palm up like an old time traffic cop.

"What the fuck?"

"Why are you here?" she asks them bluntly. "What have you come looking for?"

"Home," says Jimenez.

"Yeah," says Skunk.

"Home," Jimenez says again, like he feels the need to reinforce it.

"Nothing grows here," Anna says, stepping closer. "Even ghosts can't permanently imprint."

Jimenez shrugs. "Those girls don't look like ghosts." It's then that he sees it. He gestures at Anna's eight-point star tattoo, visible since she changed from shirt to singlet.

Skunk has seen it too and is clearly shaken. Both of them stare, wide-eyed. They've forgotten all about Rocco and lovely Daisy.

"Where did you get *that*?"

"Why—what does it mean to you?" She angles her arm so they can get a better look.

Jimenez swallows dryly. All she sees is terror in its purest form.

"Venus," mumbles Skunk in a low whisper.

"The star?"

"The lady."

A look from Jimenez confirms he's said too much. The men have lost their derring-do, dumbstruck by a symbol.

"There's a lady in the bunker?" Anna thinks she'll have to starve the data from them, or beat it, maybe. Whichever way is quicker. "It's just a star," she says and they both cringe.

A piercing shriek from outside sets her teeth on edge. The anguished cry is barely human, gender indeterminate. The nuns take it as their cue to leave, padding softly across the faded linoleum floor.

"I warned him," says Anna. "I warned you all."

Taking advantage of their confusion, she steps back, slamming the door in both their faces.

The trapped men hammer on the sturdy wood with balled fists, yelling out obscenities. Anna's prepared to be a little patient. It's not the first time her clinic has served as a jail. Eventually their arms will tire and they'll try their luck with the barred window.

Somewhere across the sun-baked sand, cruel laughter resonates. The men are hammering so hard that at first they don't make sense of what they're hearing. Rocco screaming, a symphony of pain.

"Tell me more of Venus and the star," Anna shouts through the door, but the men are far too filled with rage to hear her. Their hammering continues, as does Rocco's agony. The latter eventually overpowers the former.

"There's nothing that can be done to save him," Anna cautions. "I can't stop the things those sisters do."

Eventually the pounding stops.

"What are they doing to him?" calls Jimenez, his voice unsteady.

"Practising their religion. *Performing* it. Those girls aren't much in need of practice."

"Which religion?"

"The one that suits their mood. Forget about it. Your friend is dead. There's nothing you can do."

Another scream and the hammering starts up again.

"Whatever," she says, wandering back around to the kitchen to get a drink.

When she returns in half an hour, the men have fallen silent.

"Tell me about the Major," she says, lowering herself to sit cross-legged on the porch.

Occasional screams of torment still echo across the landscape.

"I'm sorry," says Anna. "Really I am." Then she asks again about the Major. "Does he wear a mark like mine?"

Jimenez and Skunk aren't talking. Both are far too horrified for words.

"But he's an ordinary man?" she asks them. "Like you?"

No answer. Not so ordinary then. They don't trust her. They're never going to trust her. They think Rocco's misfortune is her fault. She keeps on at them with questions, but the screaming doesn't stop. The men clam up, concentration shot to Hell.

She leaves them be. She'll come back and let them out tomorrow. There's a trail of red leading to the ossuary façade, but she ignores it. Such details have long ceased to be her business.

She walks the camp perimeter, binoculars dangling, useless, half-hoping to spot another bull. This time she's up for target practice. Blowing the damn thing's head off would improve her mood. But there's nothing past the line of passive, waiting mothers. Nothing but endless sand and sunlight.

Let the storms come and boil away tomorrow. At least that way she won't have to care.

Just past sunrise, the two men still stand defiant. The resonance of Rocco's screams hangs about them like an all-enveloping fog. She's brought a jug of water and two enamel mugs. Holds them high so they can see them through the bars.

"Where the fuck is Rocco?" asks Jimenez through the window.

"Describe the Major and maybe I'll let you out. Take you to him too, if you behave yourselves."

She takes their silence as a yes, pours, then passes each man a mug. They snatch them and quaff gratefully, gulping without spilling anything.

She holds the jug ready in anticipation. "The Major," she reminds them with a waning smile.

"White guy. Maybe forty. Maybe fifty."

"Blond hair, bright blue eyes. Tattoo."

They stare at her eight-point star while they're talking, still mesmerised by its apparent significance.

"Like this?" she asks, baring her bicep for closer inspection.

Jimenez shakes his head. "Nothing holy, Ma'am. He's got a lion."

A lion.

She almost drops the jug. "What kind of lion?"

"Big."

"Where?"

"On his back."

"Holding a flag in its paw?"

They don't answer quickly enough, so she screams: "Is the fucking thing holding a pennant?"

Skunk nods almost imperceptibly.

It's holding a fucking pennant. She stands there, jug gripped tightly, her mind elsewhere. *The lion changes everything.*

Questions chitter through her brain like locusts. Why did she never search for Thomas below the earth? Bewitched by a glamour, the sleight-of-hand of solid rock. Rock can be blasted. Caves can be created. She pictures swarms of men tunnelling through honeycomb like ants, each new chamber comforting and womb-like.

When she's ready, she goes to speak with Sirius. It's not his time yet, but she always knows he's there.

The would-be mothers watch from beneath their ratty awnings. Some days it's their silence that bothers her the most. They think she should be planting babies in her clinic. Making half an effort to save the future from the past. But she can't think straight since the men walked into camp. She hates the way they've turned things upside down.

"There's something I'm forgetting," she tells her Dog Star friend. "Some big secret I'm supposed to know."

The threat of storms has abated. One less problem she has to care about. A lick of breeze against her neck, teasing of coolness yet to come. Perhaps she should kill the men? Put them out of their misery. Forget the shiny illusions they have to offer. The women, too, the queue of hopeful mothers. She could end their suffering so cleanly.

She hears the splintering of wood, comprehends its great significance, yet cannot bring herself to care. The lion lives. He lives. *He lives,* over and over and over in her mind. That lion tattoo is the sign she's been waiting for, a thousand tiny candles flickering in her head. The message from Thomas, a purpose after all these wasted years. Truckstop wasn't the end but the beginning! The kick-off point for a glorious new season.

The skin beneath her own tattoo tingles—the dove on her back, not the eight-point star on her arm. She recalls a Hong Kong backstreet. Crowded, the stink of fish. The lion and the dove. They'd been inked together, side by side as the smoke-choked night filled with stars. Rockets, too. Brilliant fireworks as they kissed beneath the needle's burning repetition.

That was the night they felt no pain. No, the pain would come later, tiresome decades of it, or had it been longer? Who could say? Who bothers counting years when time itself is at a standstill? Only those crazy nuns with their great skull abacus and the ivory hourglass and the blanched bronze sundial, its symbols as worn and faded as history itself.

The nuns. She snaps herself back into the moment, hurries to the makeshift prison to find a splintered door. The stupid men have kicked the damn thing down. Back out on the sand, the nuns are circling poor Skunk and Jimenez like jackals, sniffing their stink, ever vigilant, ever hopeful.

"Where's Rocco?" spits Jimenez, defiant, despite the terror in his eyes.

"I warned him," offers Anna by way of an apology. "Why don't we go and visit him together?"

Reluctantly the nuns fall back. Daisy is with them. They'll do whatever Daisy says. Anna suspects her own safe days are numbered.

What's left of Rocco's corpse has been hammered haphazardly to a cross. The shape is incidental; Anna doubts these girls have heard of Jesus. Jimenez and Skunk stop dead, speechless, even with the nuns too close for comfort.

The girls have spread his innards on a rattan mat, lungs and liver separate. The liver may be the seat of the soul, but poor Rocco's speaks of little but misfortune. Perhaps they ripped it too eagerly from its housing? Between life's fading and the immanence of death sit those precious moments where truths are told. Rocco screamed for hours, but in the end, his passing came as swift as starfall.

A wall of turbulence obscures the horizon, broiling acid clouds spitting caustic phlegm upon the silicon sea.

Jimenez steps forward, fists clenching and unclenching. Anna gestures to the lookout tower where Gengis trains a high-powered rifle on him.

"Tomorrow," says Daisy, interrupting. "Dawn of the eighth year begins tomorrow."

Then, abandoning Rocco's shredded frame to the vultures, Daisy and her entourage hurry to consult the ossuary's great skull mothers, arms overflowing with sticky male entrails.

"You sure about this?" Anna asks the men, eyes squinting in the ochre afternoon glare. "A lion with a pennant. No chance you could be mistaken?"

"What the fuck is the matter with you? Those bitches tore our buddy limb from limb!"

"No mistake," says Skunk, staring straight at her. Anna notes the milky cast of his eyes. Both of them have it. Whatever bullshit they might or might not be sprouting, they've definitely done time away from light. She's amazed they can see at all, what with the glare and the sun-bleached forever. That they saw enough to get as far as Truckstop.

"More water." Skunk holds out his cup.

Anna isn't listening. She's thinking about Daisy's dawning eighth great year, a date of auspice and serendipity. A year when time itself will be tested, debts collected, promises made now answered for.

Not that Anna gives a damn if an occasional throat gets slit in a show of penance. A splash of red looks pretty on the washed-out rocks. But whatever the fuck year they'd thought it'd been, it's *her* year now, goddamn it. Year of the lion and the dove. Reunited like they'd never been apart.

"Take me to your Major and his lion tattoo."

The men pale visibly as the words escape her lips.

"Not in a month of Sundays," says Jimenez. "Not if it was the end of the world."

"The world died thirty years ago, taking all your Sundays with it," she says. "Nothing left here but ghosts and undead friends."

Jimenez shakes his head. "You don't know what you're asking. You don't know."

"I'm asking you to take me as far as the Underworld gates," says Anna. "After that, I don't care where you go."

"Wouldn't even if I knew they way," says Skunk, defiant to the last.

But she knows she'll knock it out of him. A day or longer, maybe three. It doesn't matter. Only the lion matters. "Take me to the Underworld, or I'll throw you to the nuns."

No answer. She isn't expecting one. Perhaps the men no longer care, for what's left for them to care about? Walk another hundred miles or get crucified outside the ossuary? If the nuns are what remain of civilisation, barbarism doesn't bear thinking about. Better to die in the shade by their own hands.

But their hands are trembling far too hard to hold a blade, even if they had a blade to speak of. So they stand in the sun, feeling their bones bleach and fade beneath their meat.

An hour later when Anna calls their names, they haven't moved.

"Come inside," she whispers gently. "Eat and rest. Forget about your friend."

This time they do as she commands, walking like the condemned men they are, eating a final meal, then sleeping the sleep of the dead.

◇◇

There's a giant ghost serpent only Anna can see. She feels it shift beneath the sands, tunnelling through the hard-packed silica fines. Other times it coasts above the surface, moody and bucolic, its rainbow sheath refracting shards of sky and sunset. Colours faded before the rise of man. The thing is blind. It flicks its tail in shiftless grace. Soaks up sun. Heat is the one thing it can never get enough of.

Despite its flimsy corporality, she stays indoors on the days the serpent moves. The would-be mothers have no sense of it. They cross its shadow, pass oblivious through its discontented flesh.

The nuns can't see it either, but they know it's there. They merely wait, charting plans for its massive, elongated skull. A figurehead for their beloved ossuary. It has to die eventually. Everything does.

But today the great ghost serpent sleeps. The men and Anna await the rise of Sirius, the only sigil Anna ever trusts, before setting off on their journey. The others don't yet know of her intimacy with the Dog Star, the dialogue continually running in the substrata of her mind.

The men freeze when they see the bed sheet retinue waiting patiently beyond barbed wire barricades. Seven scrawny nuns, Daisy chief amongst them, flanked by two hardy red-eyed Nubian goats.

Jimenez throws a backward glance at the clinic's cold white walls. "You never said nothing about them nuns coming too."

Anna shrugged. "You reckon I'd know how to stop them?"

Daisy has the raptures upon her, eyes fluttering upwards in her tiny shaven head. Her sisters pay no more attention to the men than to the goats. Each clasps a skull and, apparently, the skulls are speaking.

"They've forgotten Rocco," Anna whispers. "Short attention spans. You don't have anything more to fear. For now."

A gleam of metal catches their attention. Gengis stands guard atop the watchtower's skeletal frame. Utterly motionless against the skyline, as if carved from the very dirt itself.

"What's his story?" mumbles Skunk.

Anna stares beyond the tower, far out across the insipid, pallid blue. She sees old Gengis as the envoy of Sirius, star stuff moulded human, but she'd never tell him that. Soldier of fortune, Armageddon escapee. Last man standing when the dust finally settled. All those things and several more besides. Or is he something else entirely? So deeply tanned, his race long rendered indeterminable.

But he doesn't quit and he doesn't whine and he can hold that rifle steady in a howling tempest. His needs are simple, his problems very few.

"He keeps us safe," is her eventual answer.

Skunk doesn't bother asking safe from what. Perhaps coming to comprehend the pointlessness of questions, he turns his back on Gengis and starts walking.

The slender line of hopeful mothers raise shrouded faces as Anna's expedition strides past. They've learned better than to stand and make a fuss. The ones who've made it this far understand the need for waiting. They sit passively as all their future hopes march north into the desert.

Anna knows they'll be sitting there when she returns. And if she doesn't? Will they die there in their straggly encampments, sunburned faces wrapped against the wind? What will happen when storms inevitably set in?

Not her problem. Very little is, these days. Her own destiny has taken a turn for the better. Finally, there seems a point to all she's seen and done. The clinic has been a holding pattern, sanctuary from the ravages of time. Perhaps she's finally ready to rejoin the world?

Will Thomas remember her? Of course he will. True love is all the Earth has left. Their separation has been a test. An endurance, or perhaps some harsh initiation rite?

Thomas will be a man now, not the smiling youth embedded in her memory. Half-forgotten, yet never quite let go. They were meant to be together beyond fire and flame.

They walk for hours, sunlight dazzling their eyes. Three nuns up front, four bringing up the rear. Anna's doctor's bag weighs heavy, but she's brought it for good reason. She pats its scuffed black leather for reassurance.

"I don't trust 'em sneaking along behind us," grumbles Skunk.

"Their singing shits me," adds Jimenez.

Anna hasn't heard the singing, she's so wrapped up in her private thoughts. But she hears it now, so gentle, bittersweet. Mournful, hopeful, all mixed into one.

The air before her shimmers with the faintest trace of ghosts. Battle scenes. Cars and tanks. People running, screaming through the flames. Rubble raining as buildings crumble. The usual sort of thing. She's long stopped wondering where the pictures come from. Resonance or residue, aftershock . . . afterbirth. All roads led to death, no matter how you look at it.

Sister Daisy is slung with reliquary beads carved from a polished human femur, threaded on string plucked from ancient carpets. Scrimshandering has become the holiest vocation. Many fine clinic scalpels have been liberated for the cause, high art being far worthier than surgery. Anna never argues. She leaves Daisy to her business. Daisy might be crazy, but she's smarter than the rest. All Anna has to do is wait. Time will deliver. All will return to the dust from which it came. She throws a parting glance to the ossuary, a gleaming monument to the end of days. The end of time itself, for past the end of days, who's counting? Does time still flow when all the clocks are broken?

Once some swanky kind of bar, all sandstone, chrome and glass bricks, that ossuary became as good a place as any to store the dead. A sturdy tower of gleaming skulls and bones, if somewhat scoured by relentless desert dust. That dust clings to everything: skin, stone and soul. On a bad day the air swirls thick with it. On a good day . . . *but ah*, thinks Anna, *there are no good days anymore.*

Venus sits sullen in the powdery dawn sky, offering little commentary, as is her way. All today's ghosts are from the cities. Sleepwalking, listless in the tide. They chatter to the void, hooked up to the electronic whisper, muttering mantras under faded breath.

Anna recalls metropoli, those vast and shining jewels. Sheer towers, wind blasted corridors, massive fingers of chromium and glass. Once she walked amongst them, invisible in the slipstream, relishing her anonymity. Banked-up cars from here to doomsday. Gridlocked regularity, spores on crusted macadam. She can smell the gasoline stench, the acrid belching choke of it. The image fades, soaked up by the sand. Patina on retina, industrial residue.

It had been the end of days, although they hadn't known it then. Always autumn, whenever she thinks back on it. Cool breezes, gusts of wind stirring up the leaves. She suspects the seasons past of trickery. There are no changes anymore, only baking heat by daylight. Freezing chill at night when the sun fades.

But some things she is certain of, the startling turquoise of Thomas's eyes, the gleaming smile, the cocksure tilting of his head. Young love so strong you know you're both immortal. Powerful enough to transcend death itself. Only it doesn't. Transcend anything. Thomas shipped out the night the fire rained, all their pointless promises forgotten. *I'll find you,* he told her, although he never did. But he looked for her. She knows for sure he tried.

She's brooding on this issue as she puts one foot before the next, lulled by repetitive patterns of her fellow travellers' footfall.

She stares at the dust-baked earth, trusting the nuns to watch the skies and the horizon and all the nothing lying in between. They like to watch with their sharp little eyes, minds alive for signs and portents. Now and then they pause to evaluate the significance of details all but invisible to Anna and the men: the twist of a skeletal sparrow's spinal column, burnished shards cracked off a rogue bull's metal casing.

The men stick close to Anna, as if understanding they'll never feel safe in this life again. Understanding the world as they knew it is long gone.

All portents aside, Anna continues to see ghosts, knows that they're imprints more than signs. Moments imprisoned by the heat and glare, doomed to eternal repetition and playback. Right now, she sees an army march across argent sands, foreign colours streaming from spear tips. Their breastplates, once golden, are hammered and stained. Lost in time as well as destination. Above their helmets, a plane plummets, earthbound. When it crashes, the sand trembles from impact, yet there is no plane, just as there are no marching soldiers.

Other times, through tears, she sees naked children frolicking with dogs. Their dusky skin repels the glare, teeth as white as reliquary ivory. They're not real. They've never been real. These are island babies, scrabbling for coconuts and shells. They smile at her through a thousand summers. No one told them the world has ceased to be.

The visions become more corporeal, more intense. She feigns indifference, but the mantle's getting thinner.

"Tell me about the Major," she asks the men who trudge beside her. Did they see the plane? She's too afraid to ask.

"Fucking crazy," Jimenez offers after a time.

"Who isn't after what we've all lived through?" She hates the way her voice sounds, the way she speaks like one of them.

"There's crazy and there's crazy," Jimenez says.

Anna can see he won't elaborate unless she forces him. He doesn't want to be the one who calls it. There's no way to dress up words like *psychopath*, but he surely will, if it will keep him alive.

The singing stops, sudden silence jarring. The men freeze in their tracks like startled rabbits.

Anna brings a finger to her lips, mouthing a soundless *shhhh*. Unnecessary. All know something's wrong.

They drop to a crouch, no need for instruction, all but the nuns. They sniff the air like dogs.

If it's a storm come early, they're done for. Nowhere to run and hide. The sand a few feet ahead erupts. The scent of burning ozone, the air alive with sparks.

"Rogue bull," says Anna, climbing to her feet.

The nuns are already onto it, swinging rifles from their shoulders, fanning out in three precise directions.

"It's just a bull," says Anna to the soldiers. "Good target practice—those things can't aim for shit."

But the men don't get up immediately. Jimenez's got the shakes. Skunk crouches, eyes flitting side to side.

"Suit yourselves." Anna moves forward for a better view. She's seen this show a hundred times, but it's not like there's much else to look at.

It's just an old SUGV, 30mm Mk 44 chain gun quadruped. Waterproof and shockproof, but miles away from nunproof. The bull calibrates its sights on Daisy but it isn't quick enough. By the time it's done, the girl has ducked away. The thing is on its last legs, all pretence at stealth corroded. That it can still shoot is miraculous.

The nuns duck and weave their way around it, freezing whenever it gains one in its sights. Then all of a sudden they let fly with rocks. They squeal with glee when they score a strike. It doesn't take long for the bull to fall. The tired old thing collapses on its side, twitches in the sand, battered and undignified.

Though it has never truly lived, it dies a creature's death.

"Fucked up little witches," Skunk mumbles.

Anna's mind drifts as each rock strikes home. The shimmering heat reflects off the sand. Through the gloaming wash, she flashes back to younger days and Thomas, who's vaulting over spike-capped palace walls.

She'd been bathing with her slaves in a marble pool strewn with rose and lilac petals. First the gasps, then the stifled giggles of the waterbearers. Olive branches trembled as Thomas thudded heels first into soft grass.

The three slaves stared aghast at this forbidden male intrusion. But it soon became clear that Anna did not mind. She stepped from her bath, rivulets trailing down her soft brown skin. When she ran to him, the slave girls closed their eyes, turned their faces from the couple's wild abandonment. What they couldn't see they couldn't be forced to tell.

Stray dust particles in her eye make Anna blink. What the Hell memory was that supposed to be? Women's quarters? Slaves balancing amphorae? But it had been Thomas, clear as day. Not her usual flavour of fantasy—she'd never been the slave girl type—but new environments brought new feelings, she supposes. Something in the northern dust or the way the sky has changed.

She can see so much further than she used to.

Seven days pass before they see more clouds, a boiling bank of thunder smothering the horizon, end to end. The goats bleat, nervous. They can smell the air's deceitful chemistry. That night the moon is at its thinnest, bled out by the tainted pallor of dusk.

The nuns drive their skull sticks deep into the ground.

"Which way?" asks Anna.

The men remain tight-lipped. They know, of course. She knows they know. Their steps have been slowing, more hesitant, more wary.

"Why do you want to go below?" asks Jimenez in an uncharacteristic surge of bravado. Perhaps he knows his time is near, his days are marked and numbered.

"You wouldn't understand," says Anna.

"The fuck I wouldn't. I've been there. Twenty stinking years beneath the earth. Darkness like you couldn't even dream."

They've been through this routine so many times by now.

"But that's where *he* lives, so that's where I must go."

So simple, when she says what's on her mind.

"Major Thomas?"

"My Lionheart."

Jimenez scratches at the sand lice in his hair. "That Major never had a heart to speak of."

"Oh, but that's where you're wrong," she coos. "You don't know him. Nobody knows him like I do."

"Like you did," chimes in Skunk. "Like you did. Maybe. And maybe he was sane before the fall. Maybe I could picture that if

I had a gun to my head. But twenty years in darkness sucks the kindness from a man. The man you loved is barely human now."

"You don't know anything about the man I love!"

She's angry now, and the men shift their weights uneasily from foot to foot, eyes on those twitchy, deadly little nuns with their sharpened skull sticks and human femur shivs. The goats keep whimpering and whining in the heat. They can smell the wrongness. They know something bad is about to happen.

Then Daisy starts to make a racket, jibbering and jabbering in tongues, pointing to something tall and glinting. So slim and distant, they all might have missed it.

"Ruins!" exclaims Anna. The men's downcast eyes confirm she's right. They know which way, and now she knows it, too.

Recognition unfolds as they approach. Not much left of the busted-up brick wall: a crumbling tower with a sand-scored plastic sign. The symbol, once familiar. A logo of some kind. She knows she used to know what it was for, but it's gone now, as with the accompanying words and whatever significance they once held. She doesn't care; the words aren't important.

They make the ruined place their camp, skull sticks staking out a perimeter. A fire is struck, bitter lizards roasted upon twigs. A pockmarked canteen passes from hand to hand, metallic-tasting water shared in meagre gulps.

The men sense the futility of their futures; stare at their battered, dusty shoes. The moon is nothing but a sliver now, a frown against the angry carbon sky. When the nuns start singing, Anna wanders off alone.

The stars are bright, but there's not much light to see by. Doesn't matter, she's not going far. She just wants to be alone to talk to her faithful Dog Star friend.

The air's still warm and heady from the day. Something cloying about it, too. Something familiar. It takes her a while to recognise the scent: wildflowers, deep and sweet and true. It's her memory, of course, playing tricks. Nothing has grown out here for years. A handful of scrabbly cactus plants perhaps, desiccated thorns and tumbleweeds.

But wildflowers? Surely she must be dreaming. "What of it?" she says to Sirius. He's bright tonight, watching over her as always. When the moon is insubstantial, she needs him most.

Another scent beneath the heady sweetness. She frowns as she does her best to recall its name. Something . . . living. Something earthy. A flock of black-faced sheep, of all things!

Then suddenly she's on the shaded mountainside. Young with skinny legs and ropy braids. And he's there, too, staring at her sun-bronzed skin. She can smell the musk of him at fifty paces.

They fuck under a shady cedar. He smells of sheep but she doesn't give a damn. Afterwards, she combs stray leaves from her hair with fingers splayed. He lays still, abdomen glistening with sweat.

"You're mine," she tells him. "You must never love another."

He laughs. "Twenty girls from town say you're too late."

She cradles his head in her lap and strokes his hair, aware of the power beneath her fingertips. With the slightest pressure she could end his life. But she doesn't. She loves him as silly village girls are wont to do.

"I can make you mine forever. I can make you do whatever I want."

"If you say so," he says, drifting into a sated slumber.

And he did sleep, too, for a thousand years. Or so it seems to Anna, out here beneath the stars tonight. The memory is confusing. It isn't hers. It can't be. But it feels so real, as real as anything else.

Truth is, she's been waiting here so long she'd almost forgotten him completely. Thomas, her lover, her friend. Her soulmate, if survivors still wore their souls. His absence left a cavern in her heart, but soon it shall be refilled.

The nuns have stopped their singing and the night is cool and still. The gate she seeks cannot be far away.

"I want to remember more of him," she tells Sirius. "I want to see him just the way he was."

And then suddenly she's angry, although she's not sure why. The years she's wasted out here in the dust. The broken-down clinic, seeding all those salted wombs. What the Hell did she think she was trying to prove? She was never about healing. The women who walked to her were doomed. So why did she keep planting all those years?

Sirius winks through the stratosphere. Beneath, a meteoroid burns hollow, trails to nothing.

"I was waiting. Waiting for him."

She turns and hurries back to camp, almost tripping over stones in her haste. She wakes the soldiers and they do not thank her for it.

"He gave you something to bring to me," she says. "I want it."

Asleep not long, their minds are fogged with exhaustion.

"Who?" says Jimenez, blinking grit from his eyes.

"Thomas, you idiot. He must have given you something."

"Lady, we escaped," said Skunk. "Lucky to get this far at all."

"Dug our way up. Bribed our way out to the surface." Jimenez cuts himself off sharply—perhaps he thinks the now-silent nuns are listening.

"But you found me so easily!" Anna says. "He must have told you where I was. Offered guidance."

Her tone suggests she's past the halfway point of reason.

"Maybe it's not him?" Skunk offers. "Maybe he's not your guy?"

She can't even hear him, that's how far she's flipped.

"Can't be a coincidence," she mumbles over and over. "Hardly a chance thing—what would be the odds?"

She finds herself a private space, lies back to study constellations. They changed their names the day the Earth caught fire. Banished are the old guard: the bull of Heaven, the goat-fish, the great one. Tonight she sees shapes close to her heart: the lion, the lovers, the dove. The Dog Star, winking conspiratorially, approves of all her visions. In the background, the periodic bleating of goats and soldiers bickering in low whispers is punctuated by the howling of distant wild dogs. She tracks lonely satellites through the early hours, deaf and dumb, doomed to circle silently forever. She drifts to sleep, a smile upon her face. Imagines Thomas's arms around her own.

The morning light is weak and chill. Tracks bleeding off to the east reveal a tale. Skunk has run off in the early hours. Took a canteen, blanket and a knife.

A nun crouches near his scuffed sand tracks, leans on her skull pole for support. Her name is Wattle and yes, she saw the soldier leave.

"Why didn't you try and stop him?" Anna screams.

Wattle shrugs. "The boy is marked for death."

"Says who?"

"Says Madame de Bethune!" She shakes her stick and the skull swings round to face them.

Anna stares into the skull's cavernous depths.

"Madame says he shall be feeding crows by noontide."

"Not a lot of tide 'round here in case you haven't noticed." But Anna leaves it there. Wattle will not be moved. She lives for that skull on its whittled branch. She'd die for it if she thought it was what the skull wanted.

Meanwhile, Jimenez stews in disbelief. "You ain't even gonna hunt him?" he whines.

"What for when I have you?" She points north. "Is this the way?"

The soldier's sullen shrug indicates she's guessed it right. She's seen a subtle twist of macadam through her spyglass. Up closer, they notice how cracked and warped it has become, boiled and blistered from excessive heat. Further beyond, a stiff shale ridge, gnarled like a crocodile's back.

"Over there," whines Jimenez. "Sure as fuck, you don't need me."

"We need each other," Anna insists.

The walk takes longer than expected. Hours longer under ruthless sun. Too hot for singing. Even the nuns drag their feet, skull sticks trailing swishes in the sand.

Anna's excitement increases incrementally. She half expects a five-point flange of sleek jet fighters to burst out over the ridge in salutation. Fact is, she can see them if she really wants to. Clear as she can see the sand and sky.

As they get closer, Jimenez begins to crack. "I'm not going back down there. You said to the gate. That's the gate ahead. He'll kill me for running out on him. Plenty of men get hooked up for less."

"But you're the messenger!" Anna offers brightly. "I barely remembered anything before you came. Thomas will reward you. Promote you. Shower you with gifts. He'll love you, soldier boy, for bringing home his girl."

But Jimenez is crying as the rock ridge looms ahead. Anna frowns, expecting something grander. An archway, perhaps? Something akin to the ossuary's antique splendour. At the very least, an orifice leading down into the earth's cool recesses.

She's been hoping he'll be there to greet her. Waiting with his handsome, rugged smile. Older, of course. A little gray around the temples. Wiser, too. More worldly than before.

Jimenez keeps blubbering.

"Shut up," Anna snaps.

"Not going back," he whimpers.

"You're going where I say you're going."

She's not really listening. All she's thinking about is that missing doorway as he mewls and blubbers like a baby.

It happens swiftly, no time for contemplation. In a second, Jimenez is leaping. Wattle collapses in a heap upon the ground, her precious Madame de Bethune rolling free of its shaft.

Jimenez manages to liberate her knife. He slits his own throat before anyone can stop him. Does a decent job of it too. Wattle sprawls beneath his bulk, open-mouthed, recipient of warm baptismal blood. His eyes have whited over. He's dead, but he's still kneeling.

Anna's furious she didn't see this coming.

Wattle crawls away on bleeding knees, leaving the soldier's frame to slump all the way to the ground.

The others merely stare in silence. A pause before the prayers. Such deep commitment guarantees no going back. How dull their gaze is. How estranged from living women they have become. Standing there as silent as their skulls, as useless as the mountain ridge before them.

Jimenez's corpse twitches as the last of his fluid drains.

"Thomas would have blessed you." Anna whispers into his ear. She sits with him to catch her breath while the nuns set up a campsite, milking goats and baking damper as they brew a billy full of bitter thornbrush tea.

Anna sees the soldier's suicide for what it is—a sign. Thomas isn't waiting by the gate to let her in. Things might be tougher than they seem, but that's okay. Decades in the sun have taught her patience.

The soldiers regarded him as some kind of warrior king, a pharaoh of the lands beneath the dirt. Even the kindest pharaohs could have cold-stone hearts. To go down there love-blind might be foolish.

She walks off on her own to think. The skyline streaks burnt umber, and for a while it seems there'll be no moon at all. But the moon is there eventually, not far from faithful Sirius.

"What must I take with me?" she asks.

But she knows the answer already. Knew it days before they set out on foot. She brought it with her in her doctor's bag.

Insurance.

It's not that she doesn't trust beloved Thomas, but his minions— who can say? Best be on the safe side. Best make sure she's covered.

The nuns are boiling porridge. Smells like seeds and grass and clay. Tastes like it, too, but it quells the bellyache. After eating will come time for prayer. A few solid hours of pantomime, interpretive dance and religious mumbo jumbo. That's when she needs to act. They think she's holy; she takes great pains not to disappoint them.

The skulls look wise and ancient in the flickering firelight, watching sagely from atop their sharpened sticks. Daisy and her nuns insist the skulls aren't silent. They whisper secrets from the future and the past. Give names to keep track of potential prophecy. Some are helpful, others downright liars. It matters little in any case—the stupid bitches do whatever their hollow-headed bony masters tell them. Drink the stormwater, it's perfectly safe. Dance naked in it while you're at it, don't worry that the acid strips your flesh.

Anna ducks behind a rock, applies the *Essential Oils Sheep Placenta Collagen Mask, with grape juice and green tea extract.* Something scrounged from the back of the clinic's storeroom. She hums a little tune, rocking back and forth as she waits for the stuff to harden.

Apparently such things were commonplace in the world before. Who today would waste a rich sheep's placenta on anything so frivolous as skin? The clammy cling of it reminds her of better days.

Taking care to ensure her tattoo is exposed—both of them, the eight-point star and the dove—she joins the nuns at their fire. They all gasp and make the sign. Beneath the mask, every word Anna speaks is prophecy.

She's known for some time that words themselves don't matter. It's all about the ceremony. The ritual. Gestures and incantations. Flourishes and exaggerations. Nuns gape, open-mouthed as she pulls the pneumatic hypodermic from her coat folds.

"What's your name, little sister?" she asks each one in turn. Firelight has rendered them identical. Mindless creatures of the swarm, like fish or bees—not that she's seen either of those in years. Daisy and Wattle. Hibiscus, Dandelion, Flax, Eithne and Anemone.

"Sting of scorpion, fang of snake." She hisses and spits, making claws of her hands.

Then she's on her feet, dancing between them, kissing cheeks and tugging arms. She jabs each one and they barely notice, hollering witchy nonsense as she reloads.

When the deed is done, Anna slinks into the shadows, peels the sheep's placenta from her face. She'll cast the mask into the fire when the others sleep. She won't sleep—tomorrow is too near. She'll spend the night with Sirius in darkness.

With the tepid dawn comes something new. The pressure of unseen eyes. One pair or a hundred—Anna can't be sure. She can smell it, too, the scent of unwashed flesh. The nuns are busy ministering to their skulls. Their needs come first even when there might be danger—and when is there ever no danger in this world?

The ridge juts defiantly in the sharpening morning light. Less of a crocodile's back this morning, more an impassable wall.

Out in the open they're vulnerable. Exposed. But it's too late— the eyes have already seen them. Is the doorway hidden, embedded in the living rock? Is it somewhere else entirely? Was Jimenez lying all along?

No, his blood is the truest certification. Not that there's much left of it; the sand is scuffed, the red stain but a memory. Something must have crept up in the night. Sucked the iron from the silicon granules. Took the body, too.

Her reverie is broken by the sounding of a gong. Dull reverberations of wood upon metal shattering the air's sullen quiet. She's been expecting this—an invitation, or something like it. A grand pronouncement signalling connection between two worlds.

She takes her time in getting up, brushes sand and grit from her garment's folds. Allows each beat to guide her to its source.

Her shoulders slump when she sees it's only Daisy, hammering on steel with a gnarled tree stump. Throwing her whole weight behind each blow, the resultant sound much deeper and louder than it ought to have been.

Could this steel slab be a door? It has no handle, window slit, nor hinge. When Daisy glimpses Anna, she stops to catch her breath. Starts again as Anna checks its welds. Knobs and rivets infest its farthest edges like hardy boils.

Not a door. A seal. To keep us out or something else inside?

Daisy eventually tires of her exertions. Anna stands lost in private reverie as the last reverberation melts away to silence.

No army of demons burst forth from the ground. The sky does not darken, the wind does not howl. The desert behind her is as still as it has ever been. The ridge remains an oppressive, threatening weight.

She turns to see nuns scurrying like ants, each bearing items essential to their acceptance of the new situation. In moments they have transformed the giant metal plate into a shrine. Somehow they've found flowers in this dead and dreary wasteland. Tiny mean-looking things reminiscent of the nuns themselves. A shrine is always their first response, followed closely by requisite prayers, chants, dances and incantations. They'll strut their stuff until exhaustion claims them, but the door will stay firmly shut. It has been fused to the living rock for a reason. They don't care. Reason has long been the least of their concerns.

Anna's heart sits like a stone. Has she come so far to let mere steel obstruct her? It seems there'd been a time when anything was possible. When the mere sound of her voice could bring a mountain crashing down.

Was she ever a goddess or a princess or a high priestess? It hardly seems to matter now the world is drowned in dust. The water poisoned, clouds so thin and still. The men all limp, the women crazy. Anna doesn't know why she's come here. If she ever had a plan, it's lost to time.

"Let me in or so help me, I'll raise the dead!" She pummels the steel with balled fists, shrieks insults into the tepid wind. Her words evaporate unheeded. Languid whispers tossed from breath to breath.

She leaves the sisters to their silly games, returns to the embers to sketch circles in the sand. The skulls stare down at her in a non-committal fashion. Past death, small details become so irrelevant.

Sudden movement catches her attention. Dandelion scampering along the rock face like a nimble goat. Perhaps the girl has heard a noise. Not far beyond where Anna sits, the hobbled Nubians bleat in nervous bursts. Whatever it is, they've heard it too; or perhaps they can sense or smell a foreign presence.

Moments later, Dandelion's stealthy investigation is backed up by both Wattle and Hibiscus brandishing bone shivs. Anna settles back comfortably to watch. She likes it when the nuns turns into huntresses; the gleam in their eyes at the promise of fresh meat. How much better they are this way; an army swarming like crabs across the rocks to take a city.

Anna's picked her favourite. Wattle would be hitting puberty right about now if she could bleed. Why these children were burdened with such hopeful post-apocalypse monikers, she can't imagine. Anna vaguely recalls a Dawn, a Melody and a Sunshine going back a couple of years. There was even a Rainbow, a buck-toothed horror who'd had the good grace to die of dysentery.

Wattle somehow manages svelte rather than bone-grating skank. She's got a spring in her step and a swivel in her hips. Yes, there are hips, somehow, occasionally visible beneath those dust-encrusted hotel sheets the nuns appropriate as robes.

She's a catwalk model, an MTV rapper. Doctor Anna remembers those things and is occasionally grateful for small mercies. All that tempest of clamour and noise. Apocalypse couldn't have rained down soon enough.

She doesn't stay watching by the embers for long. The cries tell her they've found something of interest. Anna goes to join them, picking over the sharp rocks, wishing she had a little more light to see by.

The girls have found a secret cave. A tunnel sloping downwards. Footprints not their own. A few discarded items. Evidence of occupation. Recent or not—that's the tricky question. Daisy and Wattle light torches bound with pitch. Flax is frightened, wants to go back for her skulls. She and Daisy argue. Not in English. They're jabbering prayer talk but Anna's heard it all before.

"It's a hidden tunnel," she explains. "Passage to the Underworld!"

Flax doesn't care. She breaks from the rest of them, hurries across the rocky waste to the safety of hearth, skull and goat. But she doesn't get far. Something whistles through the air, fells her swiftly, her pale skin and robe splattered red. The sky is spitting rocks. The others sprint for the tunnel mouth and its meagre shelter. Rocks rain down on them, sharp-edged, well aimed. By the time they reach the tunnel, all are bleeding. All but Anna. Miraculously, she has escaped without a single scratch. She would wonder about it but there's no time. The injured nuns are cut and terrified, separated from their skulls, left with nothing but strings of reliquary bones to protect them.

Their babbling continues, punctuated by unbridled shrieks of terror. Soon, a competing noise strikes each one silent. Outside on the sand, something is being slaughtered. Might be the goats, but the terrible gurgling sounds could equally belong to poor little Flax.

Terror keeps them pinned within the comparative safety of the overhanging rock. In time, their attackers begin to show themselves. Black shadows enveloped in the stench of blood. Silhouettes stark against the brightening skyline. Matted hair, bodies wrapped in skins. *Wildmen*, thinks Anna. Her next few words must be chosen carefully.

"We're here for Major Thomas," she tells the one who stands a little ahead of the others. Taller. More sure of himself. The silhouettes step up into the torchlight, blood-soaked bundles slung across their broad shoulders. They carry meat, hopefully the flesh of goats. Their lips and mouths are stained with red, their eyes unfathomably white.

"Do you speak?" she asks, her voice too soft. Too gentle.

The big man looks like he's emerged from the dawn of time. A place where words such as *reason* or *truce* do not exist.

"The road is closed," the wildman says. "Best be off before he gets wind of it."

To her great astonishment, he speaks with a cultured English accent. The sort that used to grace late night talk shows; dimly lit faux lounge rooms with guests in comfy chairs.

"Major Thomas is my husband," says Anna, most determined. "He sent three messengers across the sands to find me."

A throaty muttering escapes from the rest of them, silenced swiftly with a twitch of the headman's hand.

Somehow Anna understands it is the number three that speaks truth for her rather than the unsubtle lie of *husband*.

"I see no messengers," he says, angling his head from left to right. "They died protecting me."

Not entirely a lie, not exactly the truth. Either way, the headman's next response is silence. She tries to assess how many stand behind him without appearing to be counting. Feels the silence corroding her resolve.

"You want to be remembered as the man who kept the Major from his wife?"

The headman smirks. Memory is not high on his agenda. But it's the only thing that matters to her—that and the chance to put the pieces back together.

"You'll take me to the Major or you'll get out of my way."

He's not buying it. She pictures his foul-smelling soldiers raising spears against the skyline. Feels the soft scattering of sand grains blown against her skin.

Where is Thomas? How can this be happening?

The nuns stand, pale-faced, shoulders slumping, eyes trained on the gritty dirt. They make no sound, afraid the slightest noise will draw attention. Hell, it seems, has caught up with them at last.

Then suddenly rough hands appear from nowhere, stripping their burdens: shoulder bags, weapons, tools. The nuns shriek in agony when the men lay hands upon their reliquary bones. Anemone faints, weakened from blood loss.

The headman gestures. Anna looks. Behind her, the tunnel beckons, a dark gash in the ridge's granite spine.

Anna turns her back on the fallen girl. There's nothing she can do for her. For once, the remaining sisters take her lead.

One of the wildmen tugs on Anna's shirt. As he points a grubby finger at her earrings, Anna realises that *he* is actually female. Small breasts apparent beneath the tunic fashioned from scraps of stinking hide.

"Here you go, honey," Anna says, unhooking a silver hoop from each ear. "You need all the pretty you can get."

She expects a blow in trade for the insult, but the wildwoman smiles, revealing jagged teeth. She's still smiling as she stabs the blunt post of each hoop through her earlobes without flinching.

◇◇

The road to Hell is paved with flaming torches. Not enough of the damn things, though, so they trip and slide through that first hour. The passage smells of damp and dank. Slippery lichen covers everything; it's even in the air. Anna feels like she's breathing in great globs of it. The nuns whisper softly as they stumble over loose rocks. The earth is open, swallowing them whole.

The passage twists and turns around bends and corners. Anna misses all the little things she's come to trust. Stinging sand and the biting cold of twilight. Her beloved Sirius and the context of the sun. Is it days they've been walking, or merely hours? No day nor night nor gradients in between.

Will she ever see the light again? She daydreams of it—funeral pyres, orange ochre flames licking Armageddon sunsets. Evenings nestled on the clinic porch with its glorious clear view across the way. High magnification binoculars trained on the ossuary façade. Tasteless art, obscene art, a hundred thousand lovingly polished skulls, display racks packed tight with the damn things, solid as a dry-stone wall. Each one cherished, special, loved.

Not much love going on down here. The wildmen reek like rotting carcasses but, mercifully, don't speak, nor push and shove. All they have to do is keep on moving, which is fine by Anna. Down below to Thomas is where she wants to go.

The passage eventually widens into a cavern filled with others. She thought the wildmen stunk until they met this lot. The reek of shit and unwashed flesh is overpowering. It fills the space entirely, every crevice, every crack.

The new ones are much thinner than the wildmen. Dirtier, too, if such a thing is possible. She thinks they might be children, or runts, or outcasts. Whoever they are, they're blocking the passage downwards.

"We belong to Major Thomas," Anna says. She doesn't trust their wildmen escorts to speak for them or cut a deal on their behalf. Everyone must hear his name just so they understand. *Fuck with me, you're fucking with the boss.*

A toll, it seems, is required of them. Anna removes her silver bangles, casts a glance at her pathetic, disappointing nuns. The journey underground has stripped them of their substance. Not to mention other things: Flax and Anemone and poor old Madame de Bethune. Without their skulls, the girls have nothing. Reduced to little more than frightened children, hungry, hurt and helpless.

All their prayers have turned to babble. They stink of urine and abject, blinding terror.

The tunnel people wrench the bones from round the nuns' necks. Their clothing, too, what little there remains. When they pull off Anna's shirt, a gasp is heard, echoing off the hollow cavern walls. The wildmen escort backs away.

Anna's so angry at being stripped after volunteering her own silver, it takes a moment to work out what's going on. The star tattoo! Eight dull points stained deep into her flesh. Why does everything come back to that damn thing?

They've obviously seen it before, and it scares them half to death.

"I'm the queen of Heaven," she growls like a rabid dog. "Don't you people know who you're dealing with?"

The runts are standing well back now, so she figures they know something. They let her keep her bra and underpants. They're keen to give her a wide berth from this point forward.

The naked nuns whimper. Anna holds her head up high as they're ushered forward into claustrophobic darkness.

When she glances back, the nuns have disappeared without a trace, as if they've never been. She experiences a sudden, unexpected surge of affection for them, stupid and pointless and useless as they were. Anger begins to boil beneath her skin. *How dare they take my nuns away and treat me like a dog! Do they not know who I am?*

Who *is* she, exactly? For a second she almost remembers something important, but as another moment passes, the thought evaporates.

She is made to walk until she's sure she can walk no more. Then, in a blinding stumble, all of a sudden she is there, the Underworld spread out before her like unravelled cloth, a gaping cavern blasted from solid rock. New stench overpowers the cloy of shit and lichen. She knows the stink of stale human defeat. A cocktail of diesel, grease and abject misery. Stretching high above her head, the walls are slick with slimy phosphorescence.

Anna knows this is the Hell of Bosch and Dante and St Theresa of Avila and Fatima and St Faustina. Whitfield's Eternity of Hell's Torments, that world of agony and pains. A place scoured by the baying of the hounds of death, where time destroys all life and wakes the sleeping.

Inferno spreads below her feet, microcosms of suffering and oppression. The groan and squeal of great machines, scalds of steam, bitter sweat, stale air, all tainted with despair and hopelessness. Stink, reek, fug, stain. Nightmare distilled to its bare-boned essence.

Below her, workers toil in gangs, chipping away at the walls with picks and mallets. Gnawing their way through solid rock, widening the Hell pit slowly, inch by inch. The cavern seems to stretch for miles. Anna can't even see the end of it. But this place holds the man she knew and loved. He has need of her and so she has come to him, all but naked into the vile and stinking earth. This fearsome vista is testament to his need. She knows now she is late by several decades. She should have sought him out when the world caught fire instead of brooding in her desert of bleaching bones.

She is not alone. A blue-clad welcoming committee of three tosses her crumpled clothing into a heap at her feet.

"What have you done with my girls?" she asks, snatching up her garments. The heat is stifling, but she puts her things back on.

These three—all men—look like Rocco, Jimenez and Skunk. Practically indistinguishable, if she didn't know for sure those men were dead. They don't answer her question and she smiles to herself, smug and sure. *Idiots, like men everywhere. They'll all get what's coming to them.*

They lead her down a bank of rough-hewn stairs. Hell looks even worse up close than from above. These are not men toiling before her in chains; these are living skeletons wrapped in perished hide. Scraps of khaki speak of who they used to be. The three who'd come to her across the sand had been princes by comparison. The elite. Officer class, not worker drones. Men who had once been trusted.

And as for the women—oh, the women! Ancient sour drudges every one. She felt their hatred and ill-use, scar tissue fused with sinew to the bone. Anna hopes her little nuns are safely dead; their tiny minds are too ill-equipped for the horrors of this place.

◇◇

How long has it been since Anna danced? Rhythmic movement fell by the wayside, lost like all those other things she once swore she could never live without. Decades endured without the beat of a drum, the strum of a chord or the haunting seduction of a flute. The nuns danced, performances without accompaniment, but their movements were never the stuff of life.

Yet she hears life now in the hammering of stone. Repetition like the heartbeat of a slumbering machine beast. Singing too, if you could call such mournful lamentation song.

A soldier leads her forward. She stops, presses a finger to her lips. "Shhh."

The soldier pauses, glances upwards, taps his foot. He moves forward but she does not. The one behind her shoves.

"Shhh," she says again, louder this time. "I'm listening."

The heartbeat's regularity intrigues her, as does the sombre annotation of the singing. The men are willing themselves to death as they chisel further through the mantle of the earth. All the while the beast sleeps on, regardless. Oblivious to their endless suffering.

"It's beautiful," she says.

When the soldier behind her gives her one more shove, she turns on him, spinning quickly to reach and pull the shiny dagger from his belt. She ends his life with one quick thrust. Eyes fluttering, he crumples to the rock. The other two step back to give her room. She grips the knife, warm blood oozing over white-clenched fingers.

A low wall separates the path from the pit below where the ragged men toil. She vaults over the side, landing squarely on both feet, still clutching the knife as she regains her balance. The toilers shuffle to give her room. They stare intently. *An unfamiliar woman is amongst them. A woman wielding a bloodied knife.*

She moves between them, falling into rhythm, hips swaying gently to the beat. They don't touch her, not yet, but she can feel lust boiling like a tide beneath their skins. One touch means death. Not from Anna—at most she could take out two or three before the mass crushes down on top of her. No, death is commanded from above. The rocky platform high above their heads.

The heartbeat continues, syncopating with her own. She slips between them, lets the knife fall to the ground. Each man stiffens, becomes a soldier in her presence, willing to thrust his life into her hands. She splays her fingers, holds them out on either side, fingertips brushing ragged khaki like anemone fronds. Carnality soaks through her skin like radiation. Hush falls across them, dark as shadow. A final shudder as the sleeping beast falls silent. No chipping, no hammering, no excavating.

She sees this army as the men they might have been. Long stone shadows playing tricks upon her eyes. Broad shoulders, straight backs, imaginary rifles at the ready. As she lays her hands upon pallid flesh, eyes roll back in silent climax. She infuses each orgasm through her pores, each tiny death a strengthening of her core.

A new sound. Drumming. The music of war. Feet on concrete, palms slapped hard against taut thighs. She dances for them, a montage of lust, sweat and seed, hips gyrating, belly rounded, breasts that heave and swell. Her own skin glistening slick with perspiration. Building to her own epiphanic climax, when at last they are graced with *his* presence; the lone figure high above on the rocky platform looking down.

She has played out the reunion scene in her head a thousand times. All the clichés patience has made accessible: running along a moonlit beach, fields of gently swaying grasses. Atop a mountain sheltered from wind and rain. The light is always perfect, the temperature mild. Sometimes there's music, sometimes her own joyful laughter, like the playful peal of little silver bells.

Stinking underground caverns packed tight with the living dead was never on the cards. But the setting doesn't matter. Nothing else matters when love is true and strong. Not the ravages of time, nor the cruelties of truth—small things so insubstantial in the face of passion and divinity. When you love so deeply and completely, flames cannot be diminished. Nothing can hold you back from destiny.

When Anna's dance is finished she sets her sights on the rocky platform. Stairs hewn into the living stone, flimsy without rails. She's guessing few invites are issued to Thomas' lair.

Nobody stops her. Nobody dares. The figure stands on the platform, watches for awhile. She doesn't return the favour, all attention focused on the climb.

Though she wills it not to, Anna's pulse begins to race. Flushed with the power of her dance, she's blushing at private memories, love and lust intertwined. A lot can change in twenty years—or is it more like thirty? Time-wise, the fires of damnation haven't left her much to work with. She knows she should be bracing herself for impact and potential disappointment. He's still a man, no matter what this place has made of him. No matter what he thinks he's made of himself.

She's almost at the top before she notices the hooks. Fearsome twists of rusted steel, spaced evenly, suspended from the cavern's roof. For meat, she imagines. A few more paces and she's figured out the truth. The *meat* stuck on the farthest hook is living. Agony has forced all sound from the man's grossly pierced torso. He flips and twitches like a worm tormented by ants.

Jimenez's scar. No wonder the poor devil chose to bleed himself into the sand.

When she reaches the top, a guard of honour pauses to salute. She nods her acceptance of the situation, that she's graduated from *prisoner* to some kind of *guest*. She pauses in the entranceway, takes a deep breath, blinks.

What if it isn't him?

What if it's someone else?

What if?

She turns, takes one final look down into the cold hard cavern filled with desperate men, cowering from the light like it might burn them. What do they think they're waiting for down there? Forests and fields and streams to reclaim the land? The future holds promise of no such luxury. It takes love to recreate the world. Love and light and peace.

And with that thought, she steps across the threshold.

It's dim. Even dimmer than outside. Takes a moment for her eyesight to adjust. When it does, by the light of half a dozen lamps, Anna beholds what is probably the last fat man left upon the Earth. He's wearing jeans, a shoulder holster and one of those blue wife-beater singlets once so popular amongst the tradesman castes. Behind a heavy wooden desk, a wall of crates is stacked high to the ceiling. Mostly liquor and canned pineapple labelled *Guangdong Eat Strong Food Industrial Co., Ltd*, wherever the fuck that used to be. To the left, a low red velvet divan. Upon it lounge two skanky whores, both well over forty, dressed in lingerie that, just like them, has most definitely seen better days.

She'd have known him anywhere, even though his piercing sapphire eyes had dulled. Even though his face had aged and she couldn't see his back. The lion tattoo would be in place, she didn't need to see it to know it.

"Hey Tom," she says, half smiling. Teasing. "How the fucking Hell have you been?"

The man cocks his head, squinting in the dim green luminescence.

"Anna," she prompts him. "Anna Ishtar."

The name feels strange coming off her tongue. Back at Truckstop, nobody bothered much with surnames. She'd been plain Doctor Anna for so long.

The skanks on the couch hurl daggers with their eyes. He's still staring with his mouth half-hanging open.

"We met at Glastonbury," she says, not bothering to mask her irritation. "Dancing before the Pyramid stage. Remember?"

She can literally see him strain to conjure images. The stone circle. A hundred and fifty thousand screaming fans.

"You moved to Edinburgh," she extrapolates. "I followed. And then we had that stupid, crazy fight."

He nods. One thing he can comprehend, clearly. A woman following him somewhere. The rest he seems unsure of and, quite frankly, so is she. Did she come to this country to escape him? What about all those years of tiny, insignificant moments, each one threaded together with the dedication of her longing. The hope that there's somehow been a point to all of it.

"Thomas, it's Anna—your Anna. Don't you remember? The Earth was green and you told me you loved me!"

There's a pregnant pause as he almost sees her. Tries to blink the bleakness from his eyes. Reaches out as if to remember . . . something, then it's gone. He doesn't know her. She's going to have to show him the dove tattoo. She undoes her top button—a slow burlesque performance. Knowing that his women are watching, she pops another one, pretending to fumble. Playing out the tease. She shucks the shirt and turns so he can see her back. She already knows what's going to happen and how much she hates him for it.

"Venus!" he whispers. "Almighty goddess of my heart."

For a long, sweet moment she indulges the illusion that he might actually mean her. But as she turns to glimpse the light of madness in his eyes, she understands it's not about her at all. Nor had it been the dove tattoo. He doesn't even remember the dove. It's the other one, that damned eight-point star. He's been forewarned about it. His eyes are glazed and he's babbling like the nuns. All this rubbish about his regal lady love which, quite clearly, isn't her or the two old broads on the divan.

No, he's talking about her rival. The one that steals the space she's supposed to own.

"Who the fuck is Venus?" she asks. "The one who's sucked up all the fondness in your heart?" He doesn't mean the star. The star is in the Heavens, not cowering in a pain-filled bunker underground.

He barks at the skanks and they scamper from his sight. So does the rest of the soldier guard that snapped at Anna's heels all the way up the stone staircase.

"I been waiting my whole life for you," he says.

Oh Thomas. My Lionheart.

He doesn't take his eyes off her as he walks to a wooden chest beside the divan. He bends, rummages inside, pulls out something shimmery and white, throws it for her to catch. A nightdress or an underslip—whatever the difference might once have been. The cleanest garment she's touched in years. She slips it on, kicks her filthy trousers off. He's still staring like he's never seen a woman dress before.

He's holding a thick ribbon of blood-red satin. Coils it firmly around his palm, eyes locked with hers. She knows something's wrong, but she can't bear to move. Not now, she tells her psyche. *Not when all my dreams are coming true.*

He moves. She thinks he's going to kiss her, but in one swift movement he binds her wrists. Tight and strong. He's done this before. Then he's pushing her ahead of him out onto the rocky platform. A cheer goes up from the crowd below, thousands of starving salivating men all chanting *Major! Major! Major!* like they mean it.

He raises his arms in a victory salute. The crowd shouts louder, more hysterical, more severe.

"Venus walks amongst us!"

She stands there in the underslip, dishevelled hair, wrists bound. Numb on the inside, because this man hasn't got the first fucking clue who she is.

"My name is Anna," she says.

He doesn't hear her.

"Venus!" he hollers and everybody screams.

"Major! Major! Major!"

Anna can hear chanting, too, but not the words they're speaking. The sounds she hears are from an ancient time. One name uttered over and over and over.

Ishtar . . . Ishtar . . . Ishtar . . .

Her name.

And then Major Thomas makes calming motions with his hands. Everybody's shushing, waiting for what comes next. Will he let her speak? Or will he make some kind of statement in her supposed honour?

Thomas speaks. "As one great man once said to another, success is going from failure to failure *without* any loss of enthusiasm. I know that I must fight for the mytho-political paradox. Inside the wire, we're faced with a choice: either accept the presemioticist paradigm of reality or conclude that the task of the modern soldier is deconstruction, given that a regime change is the equivalent of a surgical strike."

Anna blinks. The cavern has fallen as silent as the grave. The men below are sucking this crap up like a sponge.

"Ask not that the journey be easy, ask instead that the Mother of All Bombs be worth it. Reality forms part of the fatal flaw of narrativity. If I do not believe I can do a thing, I definitely can't. So, I choose to believe, then act in accordance, regardless of potential collateral damage."

As the crowd goes wild with whooping and hollering, she stares at him sideways. "What the fuck are you talking about?"

He can't hear her. He can't hear anything but the stamping and shrieking and repeating of his own "Major! Major! Major!" bouncing off the slimy cavern walls. What's left of his soul is a vacant space. Just a shell. She could rattle of magic memories to him for hours and he'd remember some of them, yes, he probably would. But for him, they'd been mere chance encounters. Places they went. Stuff they used to do. Like he'd done stuff and been places with a hundred other girls. Back when the world was lousy with supple, sweet young flesh.

"What have you done with my friends?" she asks him coyly. The nuns had become her very dearest the minute they'd been taken away.

He doesn't answer, but she notes the unmistakable outline of his cock hardening in his pants. How many minutes will be wasted like this in pointless reverie? The audience has fallen to stamping and clapping. No rhythm to it this time. No heartbeat.

He makes his victory sign again. "I answered the call," he tells the air.

Dear gods, is that a swagger in his stance?

"What call might that have been?" she asks so innocently.

Which imaginary government does he think he's serving? Which hallucinatory flag hangs limply in the cavern's flaccid air?

For a moment he almost smiles, almost remembers, almost seems like a reasonable human being, after all. But then, like everything else she ever cared for, that spark of light is gone and she's on her own, stumbling through the ruins of his incomprehension.

"Reality may be used to reinforce class divisions unless it has gone to Blackwater. If dialectic materialism holds, we have to choose between constructivism and decapitation strike discourse!"

She smiles at him sweetly.

He nods and returns the favour. "Knew you'd see things my way, darlin'."

"Yes, Thomas, of course you did."

Anna lunges suddenly and shoves him off the platform. The crowd goes wild once more as he flails and tumbles. When he splats on the stone they leap upon him, tearing him limb from limb with hands and teeth. As chaos erupts, she makes a break for the narrow staircase, hands still bound before her like a slave.

Ragged wide-eyed soldiers leap out of her path. Spread below, the vista of Hell is just as it ought to be: a belching, bleeding catastrophe of pain.

Halfway down, she glances up to check her options.

Memories return in silvery shadowplay, gradually overwriting the last few decades' harm and lies. Anna Ishtar has been stuck fast like a luckless bug in amber. Sleepwalking, locked in soulless repetition.

The staircase flattens to a passage, winds its way along the crumbling rock face. Below, a sea of blood-red angry eyes. One by one their owners grasp their tools, gawp up at her, a chorus of gnashing teeth and salivation. Such a familiar feeling to it, this passing-by parade. She knows she's been this way before, strutted her stuff before endless adoring admirers. Worshippers bowed on bended knees. Songs of praise back then, not heavy breathing. Her ankles had been ringed with bells, her hair braided thick with garlands.

It's the star tattoo protecting her—they choke when they catch sight of it. Trace a pointed symbol in the air. A ward against whatever. One simple talisman protecting her from a thousand harms. *A mighty powerful queen you've got, this Venus, whoever she might be.*

Anna Ishtar can't quite picture her, but she knows enough to hate. The bitch that stole her place in Thomas's heart. Drove him crazy with unfathomable desires.

The pathway leads her ever downwards, further, deep as death into the earth, then along a wide ledge built for heavy traffic. Rail tracks embedded in the living rock. Overhead, power cables dangle in silvery impotence. Then, all of a sudden, the space above her widens. Anna freezes at first sight of the queen.

She's beautiful, just as Thomas promised. Slim and chic and glowing like the dawn. Five hundred feet of gleaming chrome rocket; of course his Venus would turn out to be a big steel phallus. The world might have died, but not that much has changed. And there, etched on the rocket casing, an unmistakable eight-point star. Exactly the same as hers, down to the shading.

Oh Venus, lovely Venus, so beautiful, yet flawed. Cock teaser, wallflower, debutante, *Decameron*, everything they've ever wanted all rolled into one. Whoever brought her here must have had a real good sense of humour, for, with no opening above her head, the beast remains stillborn. Can't be launched, no matter what they do. She stands, abandoned like a naked store window mannequin in an age when stores and windows have long past.

Major Thomas's Venus is a dud. No machinery to arm her. The fool thought blood and poetry would be enough. There's no way out, but it doesn't matter. She won't be going anywhere. But they will.

She clambers up the gantry base, amazed that no one tries to stop her. Hooking her arms through tarnished wire, she has a better view. She can see things Thomas died never knowing about. Something's wrong. Around her, men foam at the mouth; his workers drop like flies, they have a plague upon them. *That stuff's a lot more potent than I realised.*

The air stinks more than it did when she first got there. A sour reek, far worse than unbathed flesh. Now it's Ishtar's turn to say a prayer, small words of thanks to her lovely, lovely nuns who carried tiny passengers within their blood. *Just a little pre-war special, something we girls cooked up through the night. En route* to death, they'd served her well. Done what she required of them.

But the nuns aren't all dead. Three survive, shackled to the rocket's portal. Daisy, Wattle and Anemone, pale ghosts of who they used to be. The fight's gone out of them and the singing and the light. Ill-gotten, ill-used, robes stained with blood and vomit, yet somehow they still stand.

Men push and shove each other as panic takes a hold below. Anger, too. Each man turns upon his brother, no holds barred. They fight with tools, with knives, with claws. Their cries infuse, meld to form the howling of a single beast.

She's wondering why no one's shooting at her. Shots are being fired, but nothing seems to hit. Ancient weapons, lousy aims. Reluctance to fire a bullet at their Venus? Whatever. Not her problem. Good riddance to the masses. Not one amongst them is worth the trouble of saving.

Not a one.

And then, in a blinding flash it all comes flooding back. All she was. All she had ever been. The first one. The holy one. Monarch of a billion mothers, holy lover faded beneath artificial suns. Discarded by the animals who'd once named her sacred. Lulled into a false sense of humanity, tricked into delusions of humility and servitude.

The monsters had fired upon her stillborn army, murdered her babies as they emerged still-dripping from the sea. Ever growing, yet they set the flames upon them, an expression of human unity unparalleled.

You came together to kill my children and, in the process, killed yourselves. You burnt the Earth, scorched air, boiled water. Sent your soldiers scurrying for shelter. And here they are, decades later, burrowing like mutant cockroaches chewing their filthy way to freedom, bellies lined with gravel, minds completely shot. And all for what? Can you even recall reasons? Hatred of all I had to offer, despair at that which I could not?

She's given them everything they'd ever asked for. Sex and death and death and sex. Life and lust. Liberty and loss. Still not enough. Nothing was ever enough.

Suddenly, she's sick of the sight of them all. Poor dead Thomas. His men. All men. All history. Mankind itself and all the violence it has wrought. She can see no further point to any of it.

Daisy chews the blood red bindings from Ishtar's wrists. Once freed, the goddess hugs the three remaining nuns against her breast, quietens their whimpering with her steady beating heart. *Poor little girls, so ragged and so broken. Look what this filthy world has done to you.*

Goddess Ishtar turns her back upon the crowd. She holds her palms up high, feels them glow with white-cold fire. Flames of creation and destruction. Places each hand against the rocket's metal skin.

"I told you I was the queen of Heaven. You dumb fucks really should have listened."

◇◇

The end of the Age of Pisces. The dawn of a new age. Yeah, another one, though there hardly seems a point to it. She's clocked time on various calendars, worn costumes as various gods: Egyptian, Babylonian, Mayan, Hijri. A couple of other favourites. Time ended with the last of the cities, so who cares about the date? Who's counting?

Ishtar stands until the dust has settled, waits for the sky to dare to show its face. Where is Sirius? Her Dog Star, her best friend?

"It's not polite to keep a lady waiting!"

But she waits.

The Dog Star emerges when he's good and ready. Bright as ever, winking through the storm.

"My, didn't you make a mess of things," he tuts.

"Shut the fuck up. It's my world."

"That it is. That it is. So what you going to do with it now it's broken?"

Ishtar shrugs. She's still rattling with righteous indignation and outrage. *All her love, yet Thomas spat it right back in her face . . .*

It takes awhile to notice all the other stars are missing. Even Orion, the true shepherd, the Dog Star's loyal friend. There's only her and Sirius, just like in olden times.

"To death and rebirth!" he toasts, raising an imaginary glass.

"Indeed," she answers, staring sadly out across scorched dirt.

Just the two of them now and for all the years to come. She's not quite sure what happened down in Thomas's Underworld. An explosion, sure, but it's not like the world hasn't seen plenty of those. She and Sirius argue about it incessantly, back and forth, back and forth. Soon she's lost track of continents as well as time. Without stars, it's difficult to navigate. Difficult to hold a thought. More difficult to care.

"So you reckon that fat guy was your boyfriend way back when?"

"Kind of. Yeah, I think so. Maybe. Perhaps he was my husband. Or my brother. Or my son."

She's brooding, so Sirius lets her think on it for a moment before he goes on. "But you waited thirty years to find the truth?"

"Happens to the best of us." She nods.

The weathered sentinel of Gengis still stands guard in his tower, keeping watch on the weary horizon. Turns out he was made of stone, after all.

They walk a decade or two in contemplative silence. Miasma settles down on them like fog. Storms have swept the landscape barren, torn up anything that looked like grass. Even ghosts are fading from the world. She misses them much more than she misses people. Baby Nubian goats, she misses most.

"I liked their ears and their funny little bleats," she tells him, just to break the ever-awkward quiet.

"Can't quite see the attraction myself," he replies.

Storms rage fierce as dragon's breath, tearing great chunks of crust from pole to pole. Fissures belch and fart sulphurous magma. Stepping between hot glaze, she barely feels it.

"Sirius, do you think I might be dead?"

He would have shrugged if he'd had shoulders. "Hard to say. Not much to compare life with now, is there?"

"No," she agrees. "There isn't."

"You could always give them another chance."

"What for? The fuckers don't deserve it."

Over time, their talk turns to other things, not just endless looping feedback of the past. As Thomas and her pride consign themselves to the substrata of mnemonic sediment, small black flowers start to push up through the cracks. Such hardy things, these little petals, sucking moisture from the bone-dry air. Shooting tendrils across the parched terrain, probing ever-gently for foothold.

"Would you look at that!" says Sirius.

"Shhhh," she says. "I'm listening."

"Listening to what—" he starts, but stops midstream. He can hear it, too, the gentle trickling of water. Dribbles glistening over granite, piss-weak spittle gathering in pools. "I told you life would find a way," he says after a time.

"Liar. No you didn't."

"It always does."

She's going to argue further, but instead she holds her breath as one by one the stars fire up again.

AFTERWORD

Beloved childhood friends assure me I've been writing since the early days, yet the ambition of being "a writer" is more recent. "*Writer*" only stretches across twenty years or so. Possibly longer, if I'm being honest, but what's the point of honesty for someone who's chosen a life of making stuff up?

For many, writing's not a living but a lifestyle, a landscape of interlaced communities, exhilarating potentials and shared dreams.The older I get, the deeper I sink into the narratives, no longer content to splash casually in their shallows. Reading and writing have become inseparable actions: Ouroboros swallowing its tail. You can't have one without the other—or, at least, I can't. The more I read, the more I want to write.

My writing was significantly influenced during the six years I spent working for The Spinney Press researching content for a series of books on health and social justice topics. Research that took me way outside my comfort zone, then abandoned me there.

The stories in this collection are dark, much darker than me. I'm no horror writer, yet horror insinuates itself onto the page.The horror of cruelty, abandonment and waste.The relentless search for identity that resonates throughout existence. How to matter in a noisy, overcrowded world. How to stand for something, or indeed stand up at all?

I don't choose my themes. They seek me out and manifest themselves.

A Lady of Adestan

I'd been reading about the ancient practice of foot binding in China: the elegance of upper class purposefully inflicted disability. Nothing in fantasy literature is as remotely unbelievable as what has been done—and continues to be done—to real-life women in the name of honour, respectability and beauty.

Beyond the Farthest Stone

I'm always fascinated by the industries that spring up around new technologies—or in this case, old technologies that have developed semi-sentience and purpose. Set in the far future landscape of my novel-in-progress, *Blue Lotus*.

The Bride Price

Exploring concepts of the ultimate trophy wife: delicate, beautiful, disposable. The boredom that ensues when the super-rich have nothing left to purchase but each other. True value manifests in unexpected places.

Hollywood Roadkill

Making literal the great divide separating those who matter from those who don't. One of those rare stories that slipped out of my head fully formed. All I had to do was transcribe it, which I did in the early morning before work across a week.

Sammarynda Deep

Beauty and sadness intertwined—a story about the high price of secrets.

Seventeen

A prominent editor once rejected this story, stating that he did not believe in its SFnal conceit: the renting of pretend grandchildren by the wealthy elderly. Nothing SF about it—the renting of friends and other necessary relatives is a booming business in Japan. Google it if you don't believe me.

All the Love in the World

On the south coast of NSW surfing happens no matter the weather—and would likely continue right through the end of days.

Cannibalistic savagery is such a banal post-apocalypse default. *Surfin' the apocalypse*—that's more like it! My selfish protagonist welcomed the fall because it brought her the man she thought she wanted. This story details her awakening.

DEAD LOW

Because every SF collection needs a space pirate story.

ARCTICA

This one started off at Clarion and with any luck it'll finish as a novel one of these days. Inspired by two Duran Duran songs: "My Antarctica" and "Finest Hour" (don't judge me).

THE ALABASTER CHILD

A SF western written for Conrad Williams's PS Publications anthology *Gutshot*. The lone traveller in search of a prize who ends up finding herself. Honestly, I don't know why more people don't write SF westerns.

STREET OF THE DEAD

A portrait of outback country people living outside the loop. The loop, in this instance, is alien and frightening.

SCARP

I used to work in a pretty seaside town nestled beneath a looming escarpment that looked different from day to day, sometimes even hour to hour. After rain, steam would rise off the dense forest canopy, making it feel like Conan Doyle's lost world. One early evening, I glanced up and beheld an amazing lightshow bleeding upwards from beyond the blend of treeline and stark brown rock. It seriously looked like a UFO had landed beyond the rim. By the time I was home I'd come up with the whole story. No UFOs, but a small enclave of people tucked away from the rest of the world, the elders enforcing one basic rule: nobody needs to see what's left out there—which means, of course, that every kid really wants to know.

THE SLEEPING & THE DEAD

My post-apocalyptic Ishtar is so jaded she's forgotten she's a god. She enters an underworld bunker in search of . . . well, anything, really. There's not much left of the world. I wrote this one when my father was in hospital following a serious assault. A time of great distress for my family and the pain really bleeds through to the page. Not sure I'll ever write another one like it. Not sure I'd ever want to.

CAT SPARKS
WOLLONGONG, APRIL 2013

ACKNOWLEDGEMENTS

"A Lady of Adestan" © Cat Sparks 2007. First published in
   Orb # 7, ed. Sarah Endacott.
"Beyond the Farthest Stone" © Cat Sparks 2013. Appears here
   for the first time.
"The Bride Price" © Cat Sparks 2007. First published in *New
   Ceres* #2, ed. Alisa Krasnostein, Twelfth Planet Press.
"Street of the Dead" © Cat Sparks 2006. First published in
   Cosmos #9, June, ed. Damien Broderick.
"Sammarynda Deep" © Cat Sparks 2008. First published
   in *Paper Cities: An Anthology of Urban Fantasy*, ed.
   Ekaterina Sedia, Senses Five Press.
"Seventeen" © Cat Sparks 2009. First published in *Masques*,
   ed. Gillian Polack, Canberra Speculative Fiction Guild.
"All the Love in the World" © Cat Sparks 2010. First
   published in *Sprawl*, ed. Alisa Krasnostein, Twelfth Planet
   Press.
"Dead Low" © Cat Sparks 2011. First published in *Midnight
   Echo* #6, eds. David Conyers, David Kernot and Jason
   Fischer, The Australian Horror Writers Association.
"Arctica" © Cat Sparks 2007. First published in *Fantastic
   Wonder Stories*, ed. Russell B. Farr, Ticonderoga
   Publications.
"The Alabaster Child" © Cat Sparks 2011. First published
   in *Gutshot: Weird West Tales*, ed. Conrad Williams, PS
   Publishing.
"Hollywood Roadkill" © Cat Sparks 2007. First published in
   On Spec, #69, The Copper Pig Publishing Society.
"Scarp" © Cat Sparks 2013. Appears here for the first time.
"The Sleeping & The Dead" © Cat Sparks 2011. First
   published in *Ishtar*, ed. Amanda Pillar, Morrigan Books.

AVAILABLE FROM TICONDEROGA PUBLICATIONS

THANK YOU

THANK YOU

The publisher would sincerely like to thank:

Elizabeth Grzyb, Cat Sparks, Sean Williams, Kim Wilkins,
Kate Forsyth, Jonathan Strahan, Peter McNamara, Ellen
Datlow, Grant Stone, Jeremy G. Byrne, Garth Nix, David Cake,
Simon Oxwell, Grant Watson, Sue Manning, Steven Utley,
Bill Congreve, Jack Dann, Jenny Blackford, Simon Brown,
Stephen Dedman, Sara Douglass, Felicity Dowker, Terry
Dowling, Jason Fischer, Lisa L. Hannett, Pete Kempshall,
Ian McHugh, Angela Rega, Angela Slatter, Lucy Sussex,
Kaaron Warren, the Mt Lawley Mafia, the Nedlands Yakuza,
Amanda Pillar, Shane Jiraiya Cummings, Angela Challis, Talie
Helene, Donna Maree Hanson, Kate Williams, Kathryn Linge,
Andrew Williams, Al Chan, Alisa and Tehani, Mel & Phil, Brian
Clarke, Jennifer Sudbury, Paul Przytula, Kelly Parker, Hayley
Lane, Georgina Walpole, everyone we've missed . . .

. . . and you.

IN MEMORY OF
Eve Johnson (1945–2011)
Sara Douglass (1957–2011)
Steven Utley (1948–2013)